A TIMELESS CARESS

Kristine looked up into Sean's eyes, those startling blue eyes, and stopped struggling to break free of his hold. It was an unconscious response. Her body just refused to move. It is his touch, she thought frantically. He had touched her for the first time. Breathing in deeply, she tried to ignore the manner in which his black-Irish hair fell over his forehead, the astonishing way his eyes reflected the same laughter that she had heard coming from his mouth. But in truth, she knew it was his smile that had stopped her dead. It was genuine . . . and it was the very first time she had seen it directed toward her. What was even harder to admit was that the closeness of his body was arousing very unpredictable emotions in her own. From somewhere deep in her subconscious, she heard a small voice telling her that the situation was dangerous, that somehow she had lost control of the encounter. Her conscious mind shouted at her to ignore everything and concentrate on how well his white cotton shirt defined the muscles of his arms and chest, how his smile slowly left his mouth, how his beautiful eyes lost the laughter and became darker, almost haunted, hungry. . . .

TIME-KEPT PROMISES

CONSTANCE O'DAY-FLANNERY

ZEBRA BOOKS
KENSINGTON PUBLISHING CORP.

DEDICATION

FOR MY SISTER, VIRGINIA . . . who found the mirror and sent it up North. That birthday present was the inspiration for this book. Thanks, Ginny, for your love and support.

ACKNOWLEDGMENTS

LINDA CAJIO—for not letting me panic

JOHN SANDELL—for introducing me to a laser printer and patiently answering my frantic phone calls

TOM MULLEN—for making me laugh every week during the second half of the book

BILL, KRISTEN, RYAN, AND MUFFIN—for sticking with me through it all. I'll miss you, Muff. . . .

And

MEGGIE—for taking away the tears.

Thanks, Bretton, you were right.

Chapter One

If there was one thing she'd learned, it was that fame was fleeting. It's allure was like the shimmer of gossamer. Holding on to it was just as fragile; it was, to her way of thinking, as futile as trying to capture the wind. . . .

"I'm telling you—cut your hair! Look what it did for Madonna. Upon occasion, she actually looks decent!"

Forcing a smile, Kristine Gavin ignored the statement and checked with her sound man as they prepared to film the live remote. Holding her microphone level with her chest, she said in a natural voice, "Did you get that, Bobby? How's the audio?"

Through the receiver in her ear, she heard, *"We've got it, Kris. Don't listen to her . . . and don't ever cut that hair."*

Inwardly laughing, Kris turned her back to the tall, willowy blonde she was about to interview for the six o'clock news. "We're going live in two minutes. First I'll do a short intro to the movie and then . . ."

Lynda Nolan stared down at the smaller woman, and flicked back the wisp of bangs from her forehead. "You know, you shouldn't be wearing flat shoes. You need height. And that skirt! Honey, it's down to your ankles. Even at your end of the business, you should know that minis are back. Gaultier, Boone, Valentino . . . they're all showing them this year. Even Bob Mackie, and you know how romantic he can be."

Wincing, Kris tried to smile and regain control of the conversation. Time was running out. "Your dress is lovely, Lynda. Now, after I do the piece about the movie, I'll introduce you and we can—"

"I want you to show my legs."

Kris could only blink in confusion. "I beg your pardon?"

Lynda Nolan lifted the hem of her black strapless mini. "I said I want you to show my legs. I want you to mention them."

Kris looked down at the long expanse of flesh. "Look, Lynda. I have an interview to do. Let's try and make it semi-intelligent, all right? I only have three minutes to get everything in."

"Listen to me," Nolan stated in a low menacing voice. "I was only twenty-two years old when that sonofabitch trucker ran into me. I went through two operations to get rid of the scar, and I want everyone to see that my legs are better than be-

10

fore. You talk about the legs or I get the hell out of here. Damn, I've got to do three more of these things before the premiere tonight."

"Forty-five seconds, Kris. What's happening out there?"

Immediately, Kris turned away from the starlet and whispered a muffled expletive into the microphone. "I don't believe this! Nolan wants us to film her damn legs. How the hell am I supposed to do this shot, when she's trying to hype her latest poster?"

A different male voice came through the earphone. *"She does have great legs, kiddo. My son's got that poster up over his bed. And you've got thirty seconds to get set up."*

Hearing her boss's voice coming from back at the station's control room, Kris let out another unladylike expression, then glared at her crew who had overheard the conversation and were attempting to swallow their laughter. Plugged into one another, they were like family and they treated Kris as if she were their younger sister. In actuality, she was older than most of them, a fact she tried not to think about too often.

Taking a deep breath, she stood next to Lynda Nolan and forced a grin. "Okay, you've got it. We'll do the legs."

Seeing the pleased expression on the taller women's face, Kris looked directly into the camera as she listened to Bobby counting off the time in her ear. This is it, she thought dismally . . . show

11

business.

Plastering a smile on her face, Kris picked up her cue and began to speak. "We're here at the Midtown Eric Theatre for the Philadelphia premiere of *Beneath a Rainbow,* that long-awaited film starring Lynda Nolan."

She instinctively knew when the lens retracted to include both women in the shot. Holding the microphone between them, she looked up at the sweet, innocent face that drove millions of adolescent boys into adult fantasies. "Lynda, you're already famous for that swimsuit layout in *Sports Illustrated,* now you've made the crossover into films. How does it feel to be tagged Hollywood's Greatest Legs?"

Lynda Nolan feigned distress, as if the question was one she was tired of answering. "Actually, Kris, it's a bit of an embarrassment. That's why I chose this particular film. It gave me the opportunity to show that I'm more than just 'legs'. It was a very emotional experience getting into the character of this Appalachian woman . . . and I'm afraid the length of my legs have nothing to do with growth of the character."

Kris could feel the heat of anger rising from her throat. She'd been set up. Determined not to get flustered, she smiled up at Lynda. "And how did you get into character? The film takes place in the early seventies. Did you do a great deal of research?"

Lynda looked uncomfortable, as if unsure

12

where this was leading. "Well, yes. As a matter of fact when we were on location, I talked to many families who were losing their tobacco farms because of the shortage of smokers in this country."

Kris had to bite the inside of her cheek not to smile. "Then, you would say this film deals with a socially significant issue?"

"Yes . . . No! What I mean is, this is the story of a woman's rise from poverty. How she overcame obstacles to become famous."

"As you did," Kris politely interrupted. "Overcoming your tragic accident to continue your career."

More comfortable, Lynda smiled and nodded as the camera panned down her legs. She spoke for a full two minutes about her reconstructive surgery in a Catholic hospital, revealed that she was so bored she had a friend smuggle in a nun's habit. Her voice was full of innocence as she retold the story of a famous male movie star finding her nude beneath it.

Outwardly, Kris smiled in all the right places; inwardly, she cringed. How could she have let this happen? As the entertainment reporter of a local affiliate, she'd done these interviews a hundred times. She was no longer impressed by celebrities and she knew her heart was no longer in this work. She was becoming restless. It was time to move on.

Listening to Bobby's whisper — "Fifteen seconds left" — Kris wrapped up the piece while the camera pulled back for a full body shot of the statuesque blonde.

"Lynda Nolan . . . playing a part she knows too well. *Beneath a Rainbow* premiering tonight in Philadelphia. For Channel Seven, this is Kristine Gavin. . . ."

Kris watched as Nolan was surrounded by her entourage and whisked back out of the deserted theater lobby to her next interview. In her ear, she heard Irv Handleman's short comment, "Nice little bit of fluff."

"It was a piece of garbage," Kris muttered more to herself than her superior.

"You're right," the voice replied. "Get back to the station. We have to talk."

Her shoulders slumped in resignation as she yanked the earpiece away from her hair. She looked at her waiting crew and shrugged.

"I think we just blew it, guys," she pronounced.

Irv Handleman watched as Kris dropped her purse on the rug and slumped into a leather chair. His expression didn't change, although his brain reminded him that he was twenty years older than she was . . . and he was married. Happily. Yet every time she walked into his office, Kris Gavin brought memories of his younger days — days when vitality meant more than getting through twenty-four hours without his ulcer acting up. She always did this to him, this tiny slip of a woman

14

with her shock of strawberry blond curls, wide expressive brown eyes, and a body that, at five foot two, could be mistaken for a teenager's. Combine these with Kris's sharp intelligence and you have one fascinating woman, he thought, not for the first time.

"Nolan was right about one thing," he said as he watched her studying the carpeting. "You should wear heels. And those damn hems of yours make you look like a kid playing grownup." Picking up a thick hoagie, he brought his dinner to his mouth.

Kris's head popped up, but she swallowed back a scathing reply. Instead, she grinned affectionately at the man. "Listen, Irving, give me the A.M. talk show and I'll wear anything you want. As long as you send me around the tri-state area, running after every celebrity that pokes their head in, I'll wear shoes that are comfortable. Do you have any idea how much pressure per square inch high heels put on the feet?"

Leaning across the desk, she broke off a piece of roll and popped the bread into her mouth.

"Hey!" Irv moved the sandwich beyond her reach. "Get your own dinner."

"That, Mr. Handleman," Kris said, pointing to the fat hoagie, "is going to put you right back into the hospital." She smiled sweetly at his glaring expression. "And if you eat it, I'll tell Peg."

He always knew he'd regret that Kris and his wife had become fast friends. "You do that, and

15

I'll assign you Lynda Nolan's premiere party tonight."

Kris sat back in the chair and scowled at her boss. "Be careful. If you force me to spend the evening with that woman, I swear I'll drown you in your own Maalox."

Irv laughed and pushed the sandwich to the side of his desk. "It's a deal. Now . . . let's get down to business. Lois Payton called again. She still wants to do that feature—"

"Forget it."

"Why are you so damn touchy about your family's wealth? She probably wouldn't even bring it up."

Kris issued an unladylike snort. "Wake up there, Irv. Don't you read the Sunday magazine? That woman is lethal with a word processor. Whenever she interviews a woman, especially another successful woman, her teeth show and her claws come out."

"She isn't that bad."

"She said Margaret Bailey's mouth looked like an opened box of Chiclets. What the hell does that have to do with interviewing the best-selling female author in this country?"

Seeing it was hopeless, Irv shook his head. "Okay, forget Payton for now. Let's talk about your spot on the six o'clock."

Kris sighed audibly and held up her hand. "You don't have to tell me again. It blew it. I let her walk away with the interview."

He shook his head. "Like I said the first time: it was a nice piece of fluff. Nolan got in the bit about her legs and you gave the viewers what they wanted."

"It's not what I want, Irv."

"I know."

"What about my piece on the Warrior Gang?" She sat up straighter. "Why can't I take the crew down to North Philly? My connections tell me Romero will go for the interview."

"Jim's going to run it on the six o'clock next week. I want you to turn over the rest of your notes."

"What!" Kris shot out of the chair and stared at her friend. "I don't believe you're doing this to me! Why?"

Irv tried to calm her by motioning with his hands. "Sit back down and we'll discuss this."

"Why bother?" she demanded, pushing her hair away from her face. "You've already made the decision."

"Look, Kris, to switch you from entertainment to hard news overnight just won't wash with the viewer. They expect to see you shoving a mike into Mel Gibson's face, not interviewing a member of a street gang. I'm sorry," he said, taking a deep breath. "Sit down. Believe it or not, there is a bright side to this conversation."

Kris shot him a doubting look, but something about his face made her sit back in her chair.

"Anne Jennings talked to me this morning. It's

17

no secret that she's pregnant. What she said is that she doesn't know how much longer she can continue . . . morning sickness."

Kris remained absolutely still. Anne Jennings was the host of "The Morning Forum" and Kris knew from talking to her that motherhood at age thirty-six meant far more than the morning talk show ever could. Approaching her own thirtieth birthday, Kris also knew she didn't want to remain entertainment reporter the rest of her life. "Who makes the final decision?" she asked tightly. "Larry?"

Irv nodded. "Your name was brought up as one of several candidates for the spot, but the last word is his."

Thinking of the station manager, she said, "He barely speaks to me."

Irv smiled. "But he watches everything we put on the air . . . including you. You're good, Kris. And you can think on your feet. That attribute alone could put you ahead of the others he's considering."

She was dying to ask who else was up for the job, but professionalism held her back. Instead, she stood up and smiled. "I could have gotten those kids to talk about the street life," she said, a hint of sadness in her voice. "They won't open up to Jim in his Brooks Brothers suit."

The older man nodded. "It was a business decision, Kris."

She stared at him for a very long time, again

noticing the receding hairline, the deepening lines around his eyes. He looked tired. Smiling, she picked up his hoagie and walked to where she had dropped her purse. Just before she reached the door, Kris turned back. "I like Peg. And for some reason, she likes you. I'm taking this hoagie because of my friend, Mrs. Handleman, your devoted wife who carefully plans your diet." She bit the other end of the sandwich. "Not because I'm hungry," she mumbled through the spiciness of ham, salami, and cheeses.

Unconsciously, Irv rubbed his stomach. "I think I might just hate you for this," he declared like a thwarted child. "What does my wife ever see in you?"

Grinning, she shrugged while showing an exaggerated appreciation of the sandwich. "Mmm . . . I think Peg's drawn to my kind nature."

"She's never seen you this cruel."

Kris laughed. "It must be this business. Turns a person into a monster."

Irv leaned his elbows on his desk and smiled back at her. "Speaking of this business . . . you might want to dress for the job you're after. You do have legs, don't you?"

Kris made a childish face and looked down to her pastel cotton skirt. "I believe they're under there somewhere, but I don't think Lynda Nolan has anything to be worried about."

Sighing, Irv studied the ceiling of his office.

19

"Jeff has that poster from *Beneath a Rainbow.* She's in purple hot pants from the seventies. . . ."

"You're a dirty old man."

"Yeah, I know, but those legs go on forever." Kris leaned against the frame of the door. "Wasn't it Bette Davis who said, 'In my day, hot pants were something women had, not wore?' " She turned away from his office while listening to his laughter.

No more than three feet into the hall, she circled back and walked up to his desk. Keeping the hoagie out of his reach, she quickly leaned down and kissed his temple. "Thanks."

"What for?" he asked, a trace of embarrassment creeping into his voice. "Letting you steal my dinner?"

Kris gazed down at him, and smiled. If only she had met him before he met Peg. Her mind shook off the ridiculous thought. It was only because she was so fond of him, so comfortable in his presence. She knew he felt the same, despite his sometimes stern attitude. She also knew he was the one who had brought up her name in connection with the talk show. He was a good friend, and she loved him.

"That's right, Mr. Handleman," she said slowly. "Thanks for the hoagie."

A half-hour later, as she entered her townhouse, Kris finally let loose a loud, agonizing burp.

Shuddering at the sound, she hurried into the kitchen. It was that damn hoagie. If only Irv could see her, she thought, grabbing the container of Alka-Seltzer and quickly dropping two tablets into a glass of water. He'd feel thoroughly vindicated. She downed the glassful in one breath, then glanced around her newly decorated home as another burp crept up her throat. Wincing, she swore she'd never touch another hoagie in her life. She didn't care if they were as much a part of Philadelphia as soft pretzels. She'd move to New York City first.

Walking through her home, she casually dropped her purse onto a chair in the living room and headed for her bedroom. She was right, she thought, to have changed the decor from the coldness of art deco to a more traditional warmth. Kicking off her shoes in front of the closet, Kris dryly reminded herself that at thirty years of age, she needed all the warmth she could find.

"Not thirty," she said aloud. "Not yet."

No one answered. There was no one in the empty house to tease her about turning thirty in four days, no one to wrap their arms around her and assure her that it didn't matter. She lived alone, without even an animal to greet her when she walked in the door. Her life hadn't turned out as she'd imagined. She had always thought that by thirty she would be married, have at least one child, and know what she wanted out of life. It was a hell of a thing to approach this momentous birthday and not be sure of what you wanted to be when you grew up.

As she unbuttoned her blouse, she walked up to the cheval mirror that stood in a corner of her bedroom. Looking at her reflection, she made a childish face. They think I'm eccentric down at the station, she thought while throwing her blouse onto the bed. A character who keeps her hemline and heels low to the ground. Cute. That was the way Jim Baynes once described her on the six o'clock, right before they cut away to her spot. Cute. She hated the word. It reminded her of a teenager, someone who hadn't reached maturity in mind or body.

Turning back to the mirror, she studied herself for a few moments before slowly lifting the hem of her skirt. Yes, there they were . . . legs. Lynda Nolan could breathe a sigh of relief, for they were no threat to her. They weren't bad. She wished they were a few inches longer, but the thought didn't keep her awake nights. Just regular old legs. If anyone but Irv had made that remark to her, she would have asked when was the last time a man had to show off his gams to get a job, but she knew Irv was in her corner and he was constantly harping about dressing for the job you want, not the one you have.

Sighing, she let the skirt fall back into place and lifted her fingers to her hair. She thought of the mass of curls that fell below her shoulders as a separate entity, having a life and mind of its own. She'd fought with it in the sixties, ironed it in the seventies, and finally let it have its way in the eighties. As much as she hated to admit it, maybe Lynda Nolan was right. Maybe it was time for something different.

Before she changed her mind, Kris hurried into the bathroom and rummaged through the drawer below the black vanity. Like the lead in a horror movie, she pounced upon the scissors and held them before the mirror while releasing a nervous laugh.

"Here goes nothing," she mocked, and pulled her hair out to one side. With swift determination, she sliced off three inches of strawberry blond curls. Without that weight, her hair sprang up to her shoulders. Kris clutched the severed strands in her fist and stared at her reflection. Well, it's certainly different, she dismally admitted, dropping the hair into the sink. Now what? Knowing she'd just done something foolish, she calmly placed the scissors on the vanity and walked into her living room where she picked up the phone and dialed.

Seconds later, she heard the low seductive voice of her dearest friend and neighbor. "Hello, this is Danielle Rowe. I'm sorry I can't answer the phone right now, but if you leave your name and number . . ."

Kris impatiently tapped her toes against her mauve carpeting while waiting for the message on the tape to end. As soon as she heard the beep, she said, "Listen, Ms. Rowe, I know you're monitoring this so pick up the phone. I have an emergency here."

Immediately, she heard an even louder beep. "Kris! What's wrong?"

Smiling, Kris nestled the receiver between her ear and shoulder. "Why do you do that? Why can't you just answer your phone when you're there, like normal people?"

Danni's voice rose three octaves. "What the hell is wrong? Is there an emergency, or not?"

"I cut my hair."

"You *what?*"

"You heard me. I can't believe I did it."

"Are you telling me you did it yourself? You didn't have it professionally done?"

Kris grinned wryly. "It was a spur of the moment decision. One I should have thought through a little more. The problem right now is that I look like I was caught in a fan. Will you come over here and help me out of this?"

Danni's voice was almost a whine. "I can't cut hair! And besides, I want to be here just in case Brian—"

"He's not going to call, Danni," Kris said gently. "Instead of watching the telephone, why don't you come over here and cut my hair? I'll order some Chinese food," she added as a bribe.

After a long silence, Kris heard, "Mandarin, Szechuan, or Cantonese?"

She laughed. "Lychee Chicken? Sweet and Sour

Shrimp? Moo Goo Gai Pan? You name it; I'll call it in."

"All of the above."

"You must be depressed." Kris held out her shortened hair to again survey the damage.

"Look, do you want my help, or not?" Danni demanded. "You didn't say anything about auditioning for Letterman. Allow me my depression."

Kris stopped herself from reminding her friend that she'd been depressed for over a month, ever since Brian had ended their two-year relationship. Knowing Danni had a right to her misery, she said, "You got it. See you in ten minutes?"

"Make it fifteen. I want to change the message on my machine."

Shaking her head, Kris disconnected and called the Chinese restaurant.

"I'm telling you, it'll look fine. Wear a lot of eye makeup and big earrings."

Kris caught Danni's eye in the mirror. "I don't wear large earrings."

Fluffing out Kris's shortened hair, she nodded. "Then start. Look, it's still long; comes right to your shoulders. I like it."

Kris reached up and put an arm around her taller friend. She looked at their reflections in the mirror. They were completely opposite. Danni's hair was short and the color of rubbed mahogany. Her skin looked as if it had a perpetual tan, dark and healthy. Behind her cosmetic contacts of deep green were naturally blue eyes. Whereas Kris had majored in communications in college, Danni had resisted any more formal education and had gone into retail merchandising. She was now the head buyer for the largest department store in the city.

"I can't believe we're standing here like this," Kris wistfully remarked. "Didn't we already play this scene in high school?"

Danni laughed. "No. That time it was my idea to cut your hair. I was sick of watching you iron it."

"But look at us," Kris insisted. "Here we are, after all those years, all grown up, reasonably attractive, and still huddled together in the bathroom. Something's not right."

Slipping away from her friend, Danni sighed with exasperation. "I must remember to thank you for this evening. I come over here to wallow in my depression and you turn melancholic on me."

Laughing, Kris turned off the light and headed down the hallway. "Let's open our fortune cookies," she said brightly. "Maybe one of us will meet a tall, dark, handsome . . . anybody."

Groaning, Danni reached the kitchen and rummaged amongst the white containers until she found the cookies. She threw one to Kris. "I saw your interview with Lynda Nolan tonight. That was a Valentino she was wearing."

Kris broke open the cookie and read a boring quotation about the virtue of patience. Throwing the paper on the counter, she popped a piece of the cookie into her mouth. "Don't remind me," she mumbled. "The woman actually lectured me on fashion trends."

Danni's face assumed an expression of mock horror. "You? Philadelphia's notorious slave to the tea length?"

Kris grinned. "Very funny, considering what you're wearing."

Danni looked down at her worn jeans and man's shirt. "It's comfortable."

Kris nodded. "That shirt was Brian's, wasn't it?"

"Dammit! If I wanted psychoanalysis, I'd see a shrink. Just give me a little tea and sympathy, all right?"

Kris stared at her friend. Danni was as close to a sister as she'd ever have. Walking to a cabinet, she asked, "Earl Grey?"

Without answering, Danni put out two cups. "I hate going home at night," she said quietly. "I hate the loneliness."

Kris nodded. "I know."

"But it's different for you. I lived with him for two years."

"You think I don't know what loneliness is?" A tightness started in her stomach and worked it's way up her throat, making it more difficult to say the words. "It's walking in that front door and being smacked with a silence so painful sometimes I want to scream, just to hear the noise. It's mus-

27

tering up the ambition to cook dinner and then eating tuna fish because there's no one to appreciate your effort." Kris poured the steaming water into the cups and sat down. Looking up to Danni, she said slowly, painfully, "It's going to bed alone and wondering just what the hell you did wrong in your life to have wound up that way."

Sinking down into the opposite chair at the kitchen table, Danni played with her tea bag. "God, I'm depressed. He was always there when I came home. Someone to eat dinner with; plan the weekend. I hate weekends now."

"I hate this weekend."

Danni smiled. "That's right. The big three oh. Why don't you tell your brother you can't make it, and stay home. We'll plan a huge party. Maybe rent a roller-skating rink."

Laughing, Kris shook her head. "The very last thing I want to do is celebrate. I plan to have the day pass as quietly as possible."

"But why go all the way down to Virginia? I can't believe Jack is turning that place into a restaurant. What's it called? River . . . something?"

"Rivanna. It used to be our family estate. Can you imagine that? A plantation house? Somehow I can't picture my great-great-grandmother as lady of the manor."

Danni sipped her tea. "I can if she was anything like your great-grandmother Ellena. God, she terrified me! She was always so proper. Don't you remember in eighth grade how she lectured us? I

28

can still see her—she must have been in her late eighties by then—leaning on that ivory cane of hers and telling us that ladies sit up straight, never cross their legs, and don't touch their faces in public. I remember thinking just what the hell were you supposed to do if you were stung on the nose by a bee? Watch your nostrils swell until you couldn't breathe?"

Laughing, Kris sat back in her chair. "That was the night we came downstairs in black satin bell bottoms. She didn't think they were proper attire for an eighth-grade dance. Of course, we thought we looked wonderful, sophisticated, and everyone at school was going to die with envy."

"Kristine, your great-grandmother said we looked like young women of questionable virtue. If you remember correctly, she made us go back upstairs and change. Then she gave those beautiful pants to her driver and told him to burn them."

Laughing even harder, Kris nodded. "She did, didn't she? She was certainly an eccentric. I wish I had known her better."

Danni grimaced. "I don't. The few occasions I saw her were enough. How old was she when she died?"

"Ninety-three, I think. The proper, gray-haired dowager to the end. I don't remember much about her, except she was always quoting her mother, Elizabeth, on how a proper female should conduct herself. And I don't know much about her

29

life, just that she lived with my grandmother, her daughter. Though I do know she gave my mother a hard time of it, too."

"God, I hope I never get like that," Danni vowed. "Of course, one must beget children to produce grandchildren, and so forth."

"Don't start," Kris interrupted. "I thought we had successfully dealt with the single condition and were onto another subject."

Danni issued a long, drawn-out sigh. "I'm glad I came over tonight. It is better than sitting home. Maybe we should move in together."

"We tried that, remember?"

Danni nodded. "That's right. You said I was a slob."

"You were. Why don't we just join a convent, and get it over with?"

"You're only saying that because you think the veil will hide your hair. And because you're turning thirty in four days."

"What a cruel person you are," Kris said. "I don't think the nuns would have you."

"I don't want them. I want Brian."

Kris could almost feel the pain in her friend's voice as Danni said those last words. "Why don't you come to Rivanna with me?" she offered. "Jack says he's found some old portrait. It could be fun."

Danni looked shocked. "Fun? Traipsing around an old house filled with antiques? Besides, I have no respect for that brother of yours, not since he overlooked me and married a woman with a certificate from the Cordon Bleu School. Imagine choosing someone whose hands are rarely out of dough—over me."

Giggling, Kris took her cup to the sink. "Elaine is a wonderful woman. And you only dated Jack twice. They're perfect for each other, and very happy."

"Exactly. That's why I couldn't bear to spend the weekend with them. After all that happiness, I'd come home and put my head in the oven. I'm refusing your invitation because I have a strong sense of survival."

Inwardly, Kris agreed with Danni. Seeing Jack and Elaine together always made her feel a lacking in her life. It was as if they had discovered a treasure of happiness, while Kris was still looking for the key. Why did she agree to go to Virginia? It was going to be a hell of a way to spend her thirtieth birthday. Turning from the sink, she mumbled, "Maybe I will look into a convent. Devote my life to a higher cause."

Shaking her head, Danni joined her at the sink and gently pulled on Kris's shortened curls. "Forget it," she advised. "Haven't you looked lately? Times have changed. Nuns are showing their hair now."

31

Chapter Two

Rivanna Plantation, Virginia — 1871

It was unquestionably beautiful.

Situated on the plantation highway paralleling the James River, Rivanna stood gracefully tall, proud to have served as a center of hospitality for one hundred years before, and even during, the American Revolution. The Mattson family had entertained the Byrds, the Harrisons, Washington, Jefferson, and other prominent Virginians who engaged in lively discussions of the important affairs of their day. Its three stories of red brick had served as a supply center for the Continental Army; a listening post in the no man's land, between the British at City Point and Lafayette's army at Malvern Hill. A century later, during the War Between the States, Rivanna again showed its strength by surviving the Peninsular Campaign and the struggle for nearby Richmond. It was a house built before the conception of this country, yet had assisted in its birth, participated in its growth, and grieved at its dissection.

Square in structure, its sixty windows had mirrored the long line of Mattsons that had matured and served their country. The women had married well, and the men had carried on the name and the heritage of Rivanna . . . until Silas. His union with Rachel Harrison had gained him the admiration of his peers, yet had withheld from him the one accomplishment essential to a Mattson—having a son to carry on the family name and inherit Rivanna. Rachel Mattson produced daughters, two of them, and Silas could never find it in his heart to forgive her; for through her he was the first to have failed the family. Disillusioned with married life, Rachel had easily succumbed to smallpox during the Civil War, leaving her daughters, Christina and Elizabeth, to the care of their father. Death had come as a release from a loveless marriage, and the other pestilence that threatened her home—the Yankees.

And so the responsibility to save Rivanna from the curse of Reconstruction fell to Christina, the elder daughter, a fragile beauty with a stubborn streak as wide as the James River; a spoiled flower of the South who'd heartlessly turned down Judson Taylor's offer of marriage, even though she had already given him her heart along with her body. A young woman with calculating eyes, she had seen her father's wisdom in marrying her to a stranger who could restore Rivanna to its former glory. Christina, embittered woman

33

who never learned from the mistakes of her parents. . . .

She watched him coming up the steps toward her. She could look at him with a dispassionate eye, for since the first month of their three-year marriage she had not allowed him entrance to her bedroom . . . and never to her heart. He was still handsome, his dark Irish looks having been enhanced over the years, and he was built like his race horses—tall, lean, sleek. In the beginning, before he'd realized what she and her father had done, she had seen dimples when he'd laughed. Now, he rarely gave in to that release, at least not in her presence. But then, neither did she. What a price she had paid for that deception, she thought miserably. But she wouldn't be defeated. The war hadn't done it to her, and neither would Sean O'Mara. What had started as tolerance had changed to loathing. Perhaps it wasn't his fault entirely. Perhaps if he hadn't appeared so naïve, if he hadn't been so eager to buy a heritage, as if it were a commodity, she might have taken pity on his Yankee soul. But what's done is done, she quickly thought. And never, never did she for one moment believe her condition was permanent. She'd been patient with her plans, slowly letting them build. . . .

Seeing him step onto the landing, she continued down the wide stairs. "You will not interfere with my orders," she stated in the heated voice that came so easily, so naturally now. "I'm sure you

34

wouldn't appreciate my interference with your little hobby, would you? Confine your directives. Issue them only outside this house."

He heard the outrage in her voice, yet chose to ignore it as he stepped aside for the young Negro servant who proceeded his wife down the stairs. "We have guests, madam. I suggest we finish this conversation at a more appropriate time." Sean O'Mara clenched his teeth as he stared down at his wife. "For now, I ask only that you find another to haul your skirts. Tisha is in no condition to be climbing these stairs."

Flinging back her hair, she glared at him through light brown eyes. "Let me remind you, sir, that Tisha was my servant before you ever stepped onto Rivanna soil. If I say she's to press off my gown, then shc'll do it!"

Angered, he grabbed her arm as she attempted to brush past him on the stairway. "Let me remind you, Christiana, that she is no longer yours. She is in my employ. If you want her to press your clothing, then bring it down to her yourself. She is not to climb these stairs, unless it is for a good reason."

Ignoring his command, Christina ran her tongue over her bottom lip and inhaled deeply, allowing her breasts to touch the side of his hand. She briefly looked down as Sean quickly withdrew his fingers from her arm, and upon raising her head, she looked at him with eyes filled with scorn. "You have a real soft spot for anything breeding, don't you, Sean? Nigras, or horses."

He straightened, as if slapped. It wasn't the

first time she had insulted him. "And you obviously have the manners of a stray cat." Glancing down to the two men waiting in the foyer for him, he then whispered in a low, angry voice, "Curb your temper, madam. We have guests."

Christina Mattson O'Mara issued a sarcastic laugh. "Guests? My daddy'd be turning over in his grave to know Yankee horse traders were foulin' up Rivanna's halls."

Hoping his company hadn't overheard her remarks, Sean smiled down to the men before lowering his head to his wife's strawberry blond curls. "I believe your father wouldn't've been in his element. Don't forget, my dear, he drove a hard bargain—you for this home."

Christina's eyes glittered, as cold as ice. "How I hate you. I wish to God you'd never set eyes on Rivanna."

There was no pain any longer. It was difficult to even recall a time when such comments had sliced through his soul. Now they inspired only resentment and a deep-seated urge for survival . . . and freedom. He stared back at her, his dark blue eyes mirroring the distaste in her gaze. Inclining his head, he said calmly, slowly, "So do I, madam. So do I."

He left her while he still had a thread of control, before he said aloud what was in his heart. While escorting the men to the stable, Sean attempted to wipe Christina from his mind. Christina, his wife. The word left a bitter taste in his mouth, like bile rising in his throat. For three years he had paid the price for his foolishness.

And for three years she had laughed at him, an Irish immigrant's son deceived into thinking he had found a home, a marriage. What he had found was a battlefield, on which the two of them engaged in a constant war of wills. Perhaps it was the price he must pay for marrying without real love. But he had wanted Rivanna so much that he'd fooled himself into believing the fondness he had felt for Christina would surely grow to that exalted state. It wasn't long before his dreams had been shattered by reality. He'd married a lady for respectability, and found her to be less than he'd expected. He'd dreamt of creating a dynasty, and been denied access to his wife. But he had bought Rivanna, paid for it with his own money and the misery of his marriage, restored it to its former glory with hard work and determination; and it was the one accomplishment since coming South that he could look back on with pride. Rivanna was his. Despite the constant arguing that would resume when he returned to the house, Rivanna was his home. . . .

"You've built quite a reputation for yourself down here, Sean. And in such a short time."

Acknowledging the compliment, Sean inclined his head and smiled. "Thank you, Thomas. I was fortunate to have acquired good stock, and —"

"And two consecutive derby winners," Bill Covington interrupted with a laugh. "You're doing something right here at Rivanna. You have close to thirty horses right now, don't you?"

Walking into the stable, Sean looked down the long corridor that separated the stalls. It never failed to fill him with a deep sense of accomplishment . . . and peace. Almost unconsciously, he ran his hand over the small white patch on the forehead of a chestnut yearling that peered over the half-open stable door. "Forty-two," he said quietly, his voice tinged with pride. "We've been very lucky."

"From what I hear, luck has had little to do with it," Tom Anderson spoke up. He looked about the stable and his face was transformed by admiration for the younger man. "You have a first-rate operation here, Sean. That's why we were so pleased by your invitation. We've been planning to come talk to you."

The three men continued their inspection of the stable. They passed and remarked on white Arabians with ivory coats, golden brown Morgans, black as night Tennessee Walking horses. And, finally, the Thoroughbreds. As if in silent agreement, all three stopped at the stall of a black stallion. They watched its high spirited beauty as the animal moved within the small confine, heard the power of its lungs as its breathing quickened with their presence.

"Celtic Star," Bill whispered, his voice filled with awe. "Is it true you can trace him back to the Three Arabians?"

Scratching behind the black's ear, Sean issued a small laugh. "Now, Bill . . . All Thoroughbreds can be traced back to the Three Arabians."

"Yes, but is it true you actually have the papers?"

Sean looked at the men. "It's true," he said

quietly.

Impressed, Tom Anderson and Bill Covington looked at each other and silently communicated. Finally, Tom addressed their host. "Sean, we've got a filly — PennyAcre. She's near ready to foal."

Anticipating Tom's next question, Sean held up his hand and led the men out to the stable yard. Pointing to a large rectangular building nearing completion, he said, "I have plans, gentlemen."

The two blood-stock agents glanced at the second stable, then back at the younger man. Their expressions conveyed intense curiosity.

Sean smiled, while slipping both hands into the pockets of his gray trousers. "I'm not racing the black again."

Tom's mouth dropped open with shock and Bill Covington appeared speechless. Both men continued to stare at the Irishman, as if he'd lost his mind. Celtic Star was in his prime, and widely acclaimed from New York to New Orleans. "Why?" Bill managed to get out. "He looked perfectly healthy."

"He is," Sean stated, the grin never leaving his face. "That's precisely the reason I'm letting him go to stud."

"But what about St. Andrews? We were told he was racing."

"I withdrew him."

Tom looked over at the construction of the second stable. "It doesn't make sense," he muttered. "Once, maybe twice, in a lifetime a horse like Celtic Star comes along. He's just reaching his potential. To take him out now . . ." Tom shook his head in sorrow over the loss.

"He's valuable now," Sean pointed out. "I have no guarantees that his value as a racer will increase. We all know anything could happen, at any time. Believe me, this is good business."

"Good business?" Bill Covington's bushy eyebrows nearly met over his doubting eyes. "Do you realize how much money he could make you in the next—"

Sean cut in. "I told you. I have a plan. Celtic Star has proved his worth. I want to take him out now—while he's still young and healthy, while he still has a winning record."

"But the money!"

Again Sean smiled, this time with patience. "What would you pay for a chance at a top-class foal, sired by a two-time derby winner? With the black's showing?"

Bill hedged, not wishing to drive up the price.

"Look," Sean said, wanting them both to understand, "a stallion might cover thirty-five, perhaps forty, mares in a season. I intend to sell nominations to Celtic Star. Thirty-five places at two thousand dollars apiece. That's seventy thousand dollars, without the risk of injury. Think about it, gentlemen. The black could only race for another two or three years. This way he will be in service for at least ten to fifteen. It's a much wiser investment."

Grinning at their astonished expressions, he added, "And that's far more than I could ever win off flat racing."

Both men came alive with questions. "Two

thousand? How will you sell the nominations? Will there be a lottery?"

Sean held up his hands. "There'll be no lottery. One of the reasons I've asked you both here is because the success of this venture depends on you. You're both valued stock agents, with the best contacts on the Eastern coast. You know which mares are ready to foal, and which owners with blood lines would be interested."

He could read the excitement in their eyes. "If you agree to act as my agent, your fee would be ten percent . . . and Celtic Star covers your PennyAcre."

Immediately, Tom's face broke out into a grin, but Bill Covington, the more serious of the two, still had a few questions. "Two thousand in stud fees is a lot of money. Not that the black isn't worth it, you understand. He's highly regarded, but still . . . What happens if some mares don't take, so to speak? I think we might run into a problem if we're selling for services rendered, regardless of results."

Sean nodded. "I intend for my policy to be: No foal, no fee. You see gentleman, I have no reason to believe the black will fail us. The fee is to be for a live foal. Alive, standing on it's feet and suckling."

Bill again looked to the second stable. "But can you handle thirty-five mares coming to your stallion within the next few months?"

Sean nodded. "That's why the fee is set at two thousand. I want the mares here at least a month before they deliver the foals they are carrying, so

41

they'll be near the stallion. There will be forty boxes for the mares and ten foaling boxes. You know the quality of my yard, my grooms. The mares will receive the very best care while they are here at Rivanna."

Both men looked at each other, again using a silent communication. It wasn't long before they turned to Sean and smiled.

"I don't think we'll have any problem selling forty nominations," Tom Anderson pronounced, thrilled that their mare was automatically secured.

Sean held out his hand. Shaking first Tom's hand, then Bill's, he said, "There will only be thirty-five places. The other five will go to my mares. Within three years I hope to have at least two more stallions sired by Celtic Star." He looked out to the paddock, the yards, the well-tended grounds surrounding Rivanna. "Then the promise will be complete," he said, more to himself than to his guests.

"Promise?" Tom asked, smiling with admiration.

As if shaking himself from a daydream, Sean returned his attention to the men. Walking back to the house, he said, "When I first saw Rivanna, I promised myself that within five years I would restore it to it's former prosperity."

"I would say you've surpassed that, Sean."

He smiled at Tom's words. They pleased him, the Irish immigrant's son. If only my father had lived long enough to see this, Sean thought. How proud he would have been. Rourke O'Mara had made his fortune in land—not by cunning, nor by

42

any other business expertise. It was pure Irish luck that he had bought forty-five acres in Titusville, Pennsylvania, to farm and raise horses. Neither Rourke nor any of his neighbors had any idea that under their rows of corn and potatoes was black gold. Oil. The O'Mara stubbornness came into play when Rourke held out against the new oil companies, refusing their offers to sell outright, instead he leased his land for a percentage of the profits and quickly became a wealthy man. With money came responsibilities, and Rourke had sent his son to the University of Pennsylvania to acquire an education and to meet the "right" people. But the war and the death of his father cut short Sean's education. Upon returning after serving in the cavalry, Sean knew he would never again call Titusville his home, not with its sea of wooden derricks. He came South, three years ago, searching for a place to call his own, one where he could raise a family and devote his time to his one true calling—raising horses.

When he had seen Rivanna, he'd known instinctively that he was meant to live in the large square home. Something inside of him, some strange force urged him to make inquiries, to investigate its owners. Upon hearing that Silas Mattson was on the verge of losing his plantation for taxes, Sean had requested an interview, and it was on his first visit to Rivanna that Sean had met Christina. Two months later he had married her, and it had taken one month more to know that he had made the biggest mistake of his life.

She could take away his dream of a family, of

providing his children with a place of permanence, a heritage; but she could never take away Rivanna. He had made the best out of a bad situation. And the best was that Rivanna took the place of the family that was denied to him.

And yet he still dreamed of freedom. . . .

"Christina, how thoughtful you are to give this little party for me." Pursing her lips, Lynette Taylor kissed her hostess's cheek. "Especially when I know the real reason has more to do with seeing my brother," she whispered in a bored voice.

Christina pulled back from her friend and smiled prettily. "Why, Lynette, I couldn't let your birthday pass without all of us getting together, now could I?" She gave Judson's sister a knowing look then turned to her other five guests. She barely noted the greetings of Mary and Elizabeth Hart, two sisters impoverished by the war and still unmarried, and she paid little regard to Corinne and Trent Cunningham, a couple she had known for years. All her attention was focused on one man — Judson Taylor. If his blond hair didn't seem to catch the sun, it was because he rarely had the time to ride under its warm rays anymore. If his step wasn't as quick, it could only be blamed on the tremendous pressure he was under to hold on to his home. She never saw fault in him, always made excuses. But now, she noted, his eyes had lost that preoccupied expression. They shone with excitement, and she smiled back at him with a love that bordered on obsession.

Judson Taylor had been hers since they were fifteen years old. In the woods that joined their two homes they had discovered the pleasure a man and woman could bring one another. When he'd gone away to war, Christina had thought she would lose her mind, and on each of his leaves from the fighting, they clung to each other and made plans for the future. She never doubted he would return, nor that their future would be together; for Judson adored her. But with the South's defeat, her plans had turned to ashes. She couldn't marry Judson, for he was as destitute as the rest of them. She had to marry the man who would rebuild Rivanna, give her back the style of living that was her birthright. Because he adored her, because she knew he would do anything she asked, Judson had promised to be patient. And he had. For three years he had waited for her to fulfill her promise. And now the time was ripe. . . .

"How good to see you, Judson." Her voice was low and seductive as she placed her hand in the crook of his arm and led him toward the tables and chairs she'd arranged near the old magnolia.

"You look beautiful, Christina . . . as always," he added, his eyes devouring her lips. How was it possible, he silently wondered, that this beautiful creature was still in love with him? She was his only reminder of a happier past, a time when life was easy and orderly, and everything was in its proper place.

"You're too kind, Judson," Christina murmured. "How any of us manage to look decent nowadays," she said in a louder voice, "is nothing short of a miracle." She smiled at the sisters as they settled themselves into chairs.

Mary and Elizabeth Hart returned her smile, yet couldn't hide the envy in their eyes as they took in Christina's beautifully embroidered white gown. How like Christina to wear the newest fashion—the bustle. Each young woman unconsciously smoothed the worn material of her own skirt in an effort to look more presentable. It was only right, Mary quickly thought, that Christina would appear untouched by the war. Since childhood she had always been the center of attention, and of any of the them, she would be the one to land on her feet. Christina would not have endured humiliation. Feeling somewhat better, Mary glanced at Elizabeth and silently congratulated her sister and herself for their strength of character. They had been through the fires of hell and had survived. Taking a deep breath, she then settled back in her chair to enjoy the afternoon at Rivanna. For just a little while she would pretend that it was like the old times, before the war had taken them away. It would be easy to do that here on Rivanna, where everything was the same. . . . She took a lemonade from a pregnant Negro servant and looked about the lovely grounds. The same, she thought except for that Yankee Christina had married. The poor woman had told them stories about Mr. O'Mara's treatment of her would curl your hair. Sipping her drink, Mary shuddered. Christina had paid dearly for keeping her home and her opulent lifestyle. Thinking of that, Mary was able to smile at her hostess with genuine warmth, the envy completely gone from her eyes. She would rather wear her brown skirt until it turned back into thread than live with that Irishman and his temper.

Standing in his study, Sean cursed and threw the paper onto his desk. *Twenty pairs of gloves!* Damn that woman! He picked up the bill and stared at it. After he had talked to her about her extravagant spending, she'd gone into town and had done exactly as she'd wished. What did he have to do to her? Her expenses were out of control. In three years of marriage to Christina, he had been more than generous. He had given her free rein to restore Rivanna's interior, had willingly paid for her sister Beth's education at boarding school; had silently watched as each season she filled her wardrobe with the latest fashions. But enough was enough! He had a new business venture to consider . . . and Christina had abused his generosity for the last time. Holding the itemized bill in his hand, Sean left his study to find her.

As he approached the group, he could hear the conversation slowly cease. It wasn't the first time it had happened. He was the outsider, the Yankee; he supposed that would never change. He politely smiled at the Hart sisters, nodded to Judson Taylor's older sister, and briefly acknowledged Corinne and Trent Cunningham. Taylor he ignored completely.

"I wasn't aware we were having guests, Christina." He stared at her, not believing she was threading her arm through Taylor's.

"It's Lynette's birthday. I thought it would be pleasant to spend the afternoon together and celebrate." She raised her chin, as if in defiance, and tightened her hold on Judson's arm.

The air was already thick with the mugginess that always preceded a thunderstorm. Corinne Cunningham looked at the married couple, and could feel their tension. She had no need to search the sky for confirmation that a storm was about to take place.

Sean glared at his wife's clinging hands, then allowed his gaze to travel up Taylor's jacket until they settled on Judson's face. The Southerner's expression could only be described as gloating. An intense white anger gathered at Sean's chest — not from jealousy, for there was none involved. He might have been naïve when marrying Christina, but he had quickly realized that his bride had given her body to another before the wedding night. No, after three years of marriage, Sean was full aware that his wife met secretly with Taylor, but he felt no jealousy. What provoked and incensed him now was that, for the first time, she was flaunting her lover in front of others. That was the one thing she had never done in the past.

He felt his throat tighten with rage as he observed Christina's fingers caress the material of Taylor's jacket, and he had to force words out of his mouth. "I wish to speak with you, madam . . . in private."

Christina continued to smile, her mouth hold-

48

ing a hint of satisfaction. "I'd rather not leave my guests, Sean," she said calmly. "Especially since we've just decided to move our little party into the house before the rain comes."

Sean glanced around him and saw the dislike in the women's eyes, the near hatred in the expressions of the men. He knew the stories Christina had been spreading about him, knew that a reputation as a loving and devoted husband was forever beyond his reach. Never once did he defend himself, for his pride demanded he keep silent. And never would he openly admit that he had been used.

He observed the servants as they hurried to bring the food back into the house, then turned to his wife. "I wish to speak with you immediately. This discussion will not wait."

Christina sighed in resignation and reluctantly let go of Taylor's arm. "What have I done now?" she demanded.

He waited until they had walked away from the others. Knowing they were being closely observed, he attempted to rein in his temper as he held out the bill to her.

"What is it?" she asked in a bored voice.

He ground his back teeth together, trying not to lose his control. "What it is, madam," he stated through clenched teeth, "is a bill for twenty pairs of gloves! Did I not tell you that you must stop this irrational spending?"

She took the paper in hand and read it. Shrugging, she tried to return it to him. "I can't believe you've disrupted my party for this."

"It must stop," Sean stated. "I've explained that to you—"

"Oh, yes." Christina interrupted, a sneer transforming her mouth. "Your little *breeding* farm. I haven't forgotten." She turned to walk away from him.

He grabbed her arm and pulled her back. "I'm cutting off your credit. I plan to write to each establishment and inform them that all purchases must first be cleared with me. If you won't stop, I'll do it for you."

Suddenly, her face crumbled and tears appeared at the corners of her eyes. "Please, Sean," she pleaded in a loud voice, loud enough to cause the others to overhear. "I promise I'll behave . . . only, please, don't do that to me!"

He was taken aback by her performance and immediately removed his hand from her arm. Never had he seen Christina cry. He stared down at her in disbelief, shocked that she would behave so in front of the others.

"Now, see here!" Trent Cunningham, ever the Southern gentleman, quickly stood up and started to walk in their direction.

Sean's head snapped up and his eyes blazed his anger. "Stay where you are, Cunningham," he ordered. "This doesn't concern you."

When confronted with O'Mara's fury, Trent Cunningham stopped dead in his tracks. He looked to Judson Taylor for help and was confused by the other man's expression. Judson seemed embarrassed by the scene taking place. Feeling powerless, Trent slowly returned to his chair.

"What are you doing?" Sean whispered down to his wife, his anger threatening to choke him. "Isn't it enough that we live a private hell? Must you now make it public?"

When she lifted her head, he saw that her tears had quickly stopped. Her eyes were dry and held a look of laughter. "You're just angry because Judson's here," she whispered back, her voice taunting him.

He sharply inhaled. "I don't give a damn anymore! Just have the decency to meet with your lover away from my home."

Her back to the others, Christina let her grin widen. "This is *my* home Sean. Rivanna will never be yours. You merely pay the bills. That was all you were ever good for, don't you know that?" Realizing he was incapable of answering, she quickly continued her ridicule of him. "And now you want to start a stud farm. *You,*" she emphasized, disgust written over her face. "who live the life of a gelding, unable to keep his wife in his bed!"

As lightning flashed in the sky, Sean was blinded by rage and instinctively brought up his hand to stop her words. From far away, he heard a woman scream and he fought to shake himself free of the fury that surged through his body with the speed of the instant lightning. Blinking, as Christina shielded her face with her arms, Sean slowly bought down his hand. He was breathing heavily, as though from exertion, and his eyes became a cold, icy blue. Never in his life had he

51

been so angry. Over the years she had tested his temper on every occasion, but never before had he attempted to strike her. Her scream had shocked him back into sanity.

Clenching his fists, he stared at her. Once he had thought she was beautiful, with her strawberry hair and dark golden eyes. Now she sickened him.

"You have provoked me for the last time," he growled, not caring if the others overheard him. "Even if I'm damned to hell for it, I'll finally be free!"

He straightened his shoulders, fighting to control the tremors of rage that coursed through him, and slowly walked toward the stables.

"Sean, wait! Please, forgive me!"

He wouldn't listen to her. He never wanted to see her again, let alone hear her voice. If he just kept walking, he would make it to the stables. There he could saddle the black and ride until his mind cleared. Just a few more minutes and he could leave them all behind, find whatever sanity was left to him. And then he would make his plans. . . .

Christina watched him walk across the yard, then turned back to her guests. Their shocked expressions clearly stated that they had overheard a good deal of the conversation. "I'm . . . I'm sorry," she stuttered, once more resorting to tears.

Immediately, she was enveloped in the arms of her friends. She allowed them to comfort her, listened as they voiced their sympathy for her bad marriage, and over Elizabeth Hart's shoulder she studied Judson's face as he continued to stare at the stables.

Like an accompaniment to the thunder, Celtic Star's powerful hooves pounded the earth as he shot out from the interior of the barn. Christina watched as Sean, atop the stallion, galloped away from Rivanna. Then she broke free from those around her.

"Wait!" She ran a few feet, but quickly stopped. Taking out a lace-edged handkerchief from her waistband, she turned back to her concerned guests. "I'm so very sorry for everything," she whimpered, while dabbing at her eyes. "I must go after him. I . . . I have to clear this up."

"You can't!" Mary proclaimed.

"Don't be foolish," Trent advised. "It's going to rain at any moment."

Corinne stood next to her husband and offered a more practical suggestion. "Let him cool down. But honestly, Christina, I don't know what you have to apologize for. He was so insulting."

"What *did* you say to him?" Lynette asked. "Whatever it was, it made him positively livid."

The two sisters began talking at once, expression their fears for Christina and their horror at Mr. O'Mara's actions. Throughout it all, Judson remained silent. Sniffling, Christina looked at him, and waited for him to speak.

He ran a hand through his hair and sighed loudly. "I think we should all leave."

Elizabeth was shocked. "No! We can't leave her here like this. Come home with us, Christina, until—"

She shook her head. "I can't leave Rivanna. I must go after him and make him listen!" Picking up her long skirt, she ran toward the stable.

No one could see the smile on her face.

Chapter Three

Rivanna — Present Time

"I can't blame you for not wanting to go tonight, Kris," Jack sympathized. "You know we wouldn't leave you on your birthday, if it wasn't important."

Kristine Gavin smiled at her younger brother and his wife. "You may find this hard to believe," she said, while sitting back on the leather sofa, "but this is exactly how I wanted to spend tonight." She raised her hand and waved it around the paneled study. "Alone, in a different surrounding, with no fuss over turning thirty. You two go and fight city hall. This place will make a fantastic restaurant."

Elaine picked up her sweater from the arm of a chair. "It isn't city hall we have to fight," she stated in a tired voice. "It's the historical society. When we applied for a variance, we were told there wouldn't be any problem. The place was so run down, it was an eyesore. Now that we've restored the outside, and are beginning in to work in here, all of a sudden this group of history buffs starts protesting." She shook her head. "No one seemed to care last year, when we bought this place, that Washington slept here."

Jack grinned at his wife. "He didn't sleep here. Just visited . . . at least that's what they're saying."

Elaine's hazel eyes turned a darker shade of green, as she ran her fingers through her brown hair. "Doesn't it bother you," she asked in a tight voice, "how much money we've already invested here? Not to mention the effort it's taken to get this far with the restoration?"

Kris watched as Jack quickly put an arm around his wife's shoulders. "Of course, it bothers me. Don't forget it was my idea in the first place." He looked out from the study and viewed the empty rooms across the foyer. "It seemed like the perfect investment. A gourmet restaurant in gracious surroundings with accommodations for a small group of overnight guests . . . very elite." He kissed Elaine's temple. "We'll give them a good fight, but if it doesn't work out . . . then we'll start again somewhere else."

Elaine turned to her husband and looked at him with so much love that Kris felt her stomach tighten. No one had ever looked at her with such devotion.

"Jack Gavin, I don't know why I ever thought you were nothing more than a rich snob," Elaine murmured, kissing his waiting mouth.

Uncomfortable with their show of affection, Kris cleared her throat and said, "That's all right, Elaine, he was forever making my life miserable with his teasing and practical jokes." She waved to the portrait leaning against the back of a nearby chair. "Tell me the truth, Jack. You had this thing painted. You didn't find it in any attic!"

They both turned to her as one. "No, it's true," Elaine swore. "I was with him when he found it. Neither of us could believe the resemblance."

"It's more than a resemblance," Jack said, walking up to the portrait of a beautiful young woman dressed in an old-fashioned white gown. "She looks exactly like you, Kris . . . the same coloring—hair and eyes—the same facial structure." He swung around to his sister. "If I didn't know better, I would swear it was you."

A chill ran through Kris and she quickly stood up. "Right. Sure, Jack," she challenged. "You never grow up, do you? What's supposed to happen now? You knew how I was dreading this birthday, so you arranged this mystery. Is there really a meeting tonight? Or am I supposed to be surprised when you waltz back in here with twenty people? I *said* I didn't want a party."

Jack and Elaine looked at each other and laughed. "Well, now you've spoiled it . . . as usual, Kris," he stated. He watched as she poured herself a glass of Harveys, and sipped the cream sherry. Shaking his head, he came up to her and placed a hand on her shoulder, as if in sympathy. "We've respected your wishes for a quiet evening." He sighed deeply and sorrowfully. "I once asked Mother why she was so hard on you, why she watched you like a hawk. I believe you are finally showing signs—"

Kris slapped his hand away. "Oh, shut up," she

giggled. "You're not pulling that on me again."

"What?" Elaine grinned at their playfulness.

Brother and sister looked at one another, each sharing a private joke, and again laughed.

It was Kris who leaned forward and kissed Jack's cheek. Gazing at her sister-in-law, she said affectionately, "Pray for a son, Elaine. And pray harder that he's nothing like his father."

"I don't get it," Elaine said, wrinkling up her nose as Jack took her hand and started to lead her from the room.

"I'll explain it in the car," he answered, automatically picking up an umbrella in the foyer as thunder sounded in the distance. "Oh, and Kris" — he turned back to his sister as he and Elaine reached the door — "I'll have you know I've never waltzed into a room in my entire life. Dipping," he pronounced as he gathered his wife in his arms and lowered her head to the floor, "looks ridiculous without music."

Leaning against the molding of the study door, Kris raised her drink in salute. "Try that down at city hall," she suggested with a laugh. "You'll really impress them, Jack."

Straightening, Elaine picked up her briefcase and pretended to swat her husband's arm. "Let's go, Fred Astaire," she ordered, grinning back at Kris. "If I don't get him out of here, the two of you will go on with this for hours."

"Good luck tonight." Kris smiled as they opened the front door. Elaine was right. When she and Jack started, neither of them knew when to quit.

Just as Jack was about to close the door behind him, he quickly reopened it and stuck his head back into the foyer. Winking at his sister, he said, "Happy birthday, old girl. Sorry about tonight."

Kris smiled, love for him filling her heart. "Thanks," she murmured. "Go ahead. Go fight for your restaurant."

A long sigh escaped Kris as she returned to the study. What a hell of a way to spend one's thirtieth birthday, she again thought as depression set in. Danni was right about Jack and Elaine. Seeing the love they shared was enough to make you feel ill with envy. She was happy for her brother, and she loved Elaine, but she felt cheated somehow that such a love had never once come into her life. She'd had several relationships, but never anything that she had wanted to make permanent.

Pouring herself another drink, she looked about the room. It was the only one downstairs, besides the huge kitchen, that had any furnishings. Jack and Elaine had started upstairs, with their bedroom, a guest room, and the main bath. Once their sleeping quarters were finished, they'd concentrated their efforts down here. This place would make a fantastic restaurant, she thought; though right now it was far too quiet to please her.

Uncomfortable with a silence, broken only by thunder and branches scraping the side of the house as the wind increased, Kris walked over and flipped on the radio. Immediately the room was filled with Mick Jagger's "Brown Sugar." She instinctively knew it was Jack's station, for he still kept his old rock posters in a trunk. Feeling it was a song more suited for a party than solitary listening, she quickly turned the selector knob until she came to an easy-listening station.

There, she thought as an old Kenny Rogers ballad came on, if you're going to drink all alone on your thirtieth birthday you might as well go all the way into depression. She stood in front of the stereo and stared at the machine as Rogers sang about his "Lady." It was an old song and, every time she heard it, it affected her the same way. Tears welled up in her eyes, and she was filled with an overwhelming sense of loneliness.

"Where's my knight in shining armor?" she asked the room, mimicking the song. She experienced a moment of dizziness from turning her head too quickly, and blinked several times as she held her drink up before her eyes. Three gin and tonics before and during dinner, and two Harveys afterward, were taking their toll. She was getting drunk, alone, on her thirtieth birthday!

Giggling like a young girl, she walked through the room thinking it was probably the best way to handle the night. With any luck she would be sound asleep when Jack and Elaine came home. On her way back to the bottle of sherry, she came to a sudden halt before her birthday present. Picking up the portrait, she placed it on the sofa and refilled her glass. When she returned to the painting, she sat down, kicked off her shoes, and curled her legs under her as she studied the woman's picture.

It is a good likeness, she admitted, wondering which of her pictures Jack had given the painter to copy. Everything looked right . . . except the eyes. Sipping her sherry, Kris scrutinized the woman on the canvas. The eyes bothered her. They looked different from her own, almost calculating, and she hoped that wasn't the way Jack saw her. She knew her brother thought she devoted too much energy to her career. And the smile . . . that, too, bothered her. It held a hint of arrogance, as if this woman knew she was lovely and used that knowledge to her advantage.

It wasn't Kris's smile. She didn't think of herself as lovely, or even pretty. God, she was always being told she was too short, wore the wrong clothes or the wrong makeup. Curious to see who had painted the picture, she leaned closer to it. The frame was old, perhaps five inches of scarred cherry wood with a gilt border. Putting her glass on a nearby table, she took the painting to Jack's desk. Flicking on the lamp, she shined the bright light on the canvas.

She could only make out a scribbling in the bottom right-hand corner, nothing legible. Shaking her head, she turned the frame over and saw that the backing was also wood, with two nails holding the chipped thin panels together. Kris grinned. All she had to do was take off the back. If the other side of the canvas didn't show age, then Jack's little prank was over. Quickly, she picked up a letter opener as a flash of lightning made her shudder. She'd always hated storms, for they filled her with a primal energy that begged for release. And tonight there would be no release. She concentrated on the frame and within less than a minute, she had worked the nails out of it. Slowly, and with a great deal of anticipation, she lifted the old panels away.

She just stood, staring down at the old newspaper that cushioned the canvas behind it. It was yellowed with age and falling apart at the edges. With infinite care, she took the painting and frame back to the sofa and left it there, forgotten in her excitement over her discovery. Gingerly, she removed the paper and carefully spread it out on the desk. She was fascinated by the ornate type, the hand-drawn picture depicting a riverbank with a large hat lying by the shore. Excited by her discovery, she pulled the chair out and sat down to inspect this old treasure.

It was called the *Richmond Gazette*, and was dated April 13, 1871. The headline was "LOCAL WOMAN MISSING, PRESUMED DROWNED." Intrigued, Kris grinned as she started reading the story that followed:

Mrs. Sean O'Mara, the former Christina Marie Mattson of Rivanna Plantation, was reported missing by her husband late Wednesday night after Mrs. O'Mara's lathered horse was found wandering in the woods that border the estate. On further investigation by Sheriff Vern Loftis, it was determined that Mr. and Mrs. O'Mara had been involved in a violent argument prior to Mrs. O'Mara's disappearance.

"Christina went after him (Mr. O'Mara) to discuss it," Elizabeth Hart of Coventry Plantation explained: "We were having a party for Lynette Taylor when Mr. O'Mara came up to Christina and started arguing with her. I don't know what it was all about," the distraught Miss Hart declared. "But it was terrible. At one point I thought he was going to strike her!

And he said such terrible things! We were all afraid for her when she went after him, and we decided to remain until Christina returned from her ride."

This reporter had to wait for Miss Hart's crying to subside before she could continue. "Christina never came back! They found her horse with whip marks all over it and her hat was lying on the riverbank. The sheriff said there were signs of a struggle. I can't believe this. . . . Poor Christina!"

The other guests — Miss Hart's sister, Mary; and Mr. and Mrs. Trent Cunningham of Jamesburg; Mr. Judson Taylor of neighboring Everleaf Plantation, and his sister, Lynette, (upstanding citizens of this county) — have all corroborated this account of the day Mrs. O'Mara was last seen. According to Sheriff Loftis, because of the severity of Wednesday's thunderstorm, they are waiting to see if a body is washed up before any arrests are made. Sheriff Loftis would only remark at this time Mr. O'Mara is under suspicion of having committed foul play.

Slowly letting out her breath when she finished the article, Kris shook her head. It sounded like a soap opera! And talk about yellow journalism! Today, if a paper reported that someone was "under suspicion" without an arrest having been made, it would surely be sued for libel. The lamps in the room once again flickered during lightning, and Kris hurriedly brought a candle to the desk just as thunder shook the old home. Once more settled at the desk, she searched its drawers for matches — just in case. She remembered Jack had said that it wasn't unusual for the power to fail during a storm. Placing the matches next to the candle, she was about to read the advertisements on the opposite page of the newspaper when a blinding white streak of lightning stabbed through the room, causing Kris to shut her eyes against its intensity. Immediately, the house shook violently from the magnitude of the roll of thunder. Kris's heart pounded against her rib cage, her fingers turned inward into fists of terror, she waited for the assault of nature to cease.

The thunder slowly rumbled away, and Kris let out her breath as she opened her eyes. The room was dark. She could see the shadows of furniture, but nothing more. Searching the top of the desk with her fingers, she found the box of wooden matches and quickly struck one while congratulating herself on being prepared. She waited for the wick of the candle to catch, for the flame to illuminate the room and push away the frightening darkness. As the small flame grew larger, she shook out the match and lifted her head.

She didn't move; she barely breathed, yet was acutely aware of the sudden pounding of her heart. It was wrong . . . the room was wrong! Terrified, she forced her eyes to search for the leather sofa, the furniture that should have been there. It, too, was missing. In it's place was a small green couch. Even the paneling was different, more ornate, and hanging from the once-naked walls were numerous paintings of horses.

Fighting terror, she exhaled her tightly held breath and leaned back in the chair. Immediately, her body tensed and she sat upright. Gone was the comfortable wing chair. She was sitting in a large leather chair, its covering worn and buttery with age.

Oh God, she prayed, what's happening? Where's Jack's couch? The table that served as a bar? Slowly, she let her eyes lower to the desk and couldn't suppress a startled gasp. It was larger and scattered papers were littered across it. But what had truly shocked her was what was lying on top. The old newspaper had lost it's yellow tint of age. As if by magic, the frayed edges were mended; the pages were no longer brittle, but soft and pliable. Lying before her was a fresh newspaper!

She could hear the hammering of her heart, was aware that her breath left her mouth in a shocked rush. It was the same article about the missing woman! The same ink drawing of the hat on a riverbank!

Instinctively, her arms wrapped about her shoulders, as if protecting her from the unknown. What the hell was happening? How could this room be different? How could it have changed so? Afraid to move out of the chair, she tried to think clearly.

She was drunk . . . that was it! What else could explain this insanity? As soon as the word entered her mind, she moaned aloud. *Insanity.* Jack had made a joke of it — they both had laughed about it since they were teenagers and Jack had had a talk with their mother. Explaining why she was more strict with her daughter, than her son, their mother had revealed that generations ago a female member of the family had been "ill." Kris felt that paranoia had been handed down through the women of the family, each watching their daughters for any signs, as she had been watched. Her grandmother had been the definitive matriarch, a little pompous maybe, but not crazy. And her mother was strict, remembering the talks of her own grandmother, who Kris believed had started this ridiculous fear. Yet her mother was the most stable person Kris had ever known. She herself had treated the whole thing as a joke, for no one would tell her any details, just that the females of the family must be very careful with their daughters. And even if someone did become insane generations ago, she'd never believed it was hereditary. But, now this . . .

A frightening chill ran up her spine and settled at the back of her head. What else could explain this? She wasn't really drunk when the lights had gone out. And she had never in her life hallucinated. What other reason could there—

Her search for an explanation quickly ended as she heard footsteps outside the door to the study. Her eyes widened in fear as she watched the large doorknob turn, and she automatically gripped the edge of the desk as if to ward off the evil she knew was on the other side.

"Christina!"

He stood in the doorway, staring at her as if he'd seen a ghost. Then, he seemed to find his senses, and she watched as the tall, handsome man's face was transformed with hatred. He entered the room slowly, and Kris had the distinct feeling she was being cornered; yet her mouth refused to move, to explain. . . .

She watched as his lips hardened into a sneer of disgust. "I see you're up to your old tricks again, aren't you? What did you hope to accomplish this time?"

Her tongue felt three times too large for her mouth, and she could feel the sweat of fear popping out all over her body as the man in the old-fashioned clothes came even closer to her.

When he again spoke, his voice was filled with bitterness and contempt. "You weren't happy just making me miserable in this marriage. Did you intend to see me hung for murder?"

Her lower jaw dropped open with shock. What was wrong with the man? Knowing she had to speak, she swallowed several times before muttering, "My name's Kris . . . Kristine."

He merely stared at her, and Kris watched as he stood on the opposite side of the desk, his knuckles turning white with rage as he gripped its edge. He continued to look at her with revulsion, as if the sight of her made him ill. When he leaned into the desk, she could see his jaw moving as he ground his back teeth together, hatred gleaming in his blue eyes. And when he again spoke, it was to say only three words.

"You selfish bitch!"

Chapter Four

Suddenly, she found her voice. "I beg your pardon?" she demanded, outraged that anyone would speak to her like that.

The man straightened and smiled evilly. "You heard me. What was the plan? To blame me for your murder so you would inherit everything? How long would you have waited before you married Taylor? Did you hate me that much?"

"I don't even know you," Kris muttered, shocked by his suggestions. "Who *are* you?"

His eyes narrowed. "What new game is this?" he challenged. "Now, to explain away your actions, you claim loss of memory? Do you really think anyone will believe you can't recognize your own husband?"

"Husband?" The word rushed out of Kris's mouth. "I'm not married." Dear God, what had she walked into?

His laugh made the hair on her arms stand straight up. "You may wish you had never married, Christina. What I can't understand is why you came back. Did you forget something, something that would incriminate you?"

She'd had enough, and held up her hands in supplication. "Look, mister, I don't know who you think I am, but I'm not your wife. My name's Kristine —"

With the speed of a panther, he came to her side and slammed his palm on the desk. "Read it," he demanded. "It's written plainly . . . Christina Mattson O'Mara, of Rivanna Plantation, was reported missing by her husband. Me!"

Kris glanced down to the newspaper in shock. He was the one under suspicion of foul play! Dear God! She was standing next to a man suspected of murdering his wife! This man dressed in black trousers and vest, his white shirt open at the collar, was very probably a madman. Suddenly, she laughed at the absurdity of the situation and fell back into the chair. Looking up at the infuriated expression on the man's face, she grinned.

"This isn't happening," she declared in a light voice. "You're not real, and this room isn't real. I invented you." She let her breath out slowly in relief. "This is nothing more than a nightmare. I think I'll just sit here until it's over."

"Do not push me, madam," he ordered, his breath reaching the hair on top of her head. "Your little tricks don't work any longer. Tomorrow I'm personally escorting you into the sheriff's office and putting an end to this public humiliation."

Kris's head snapped up. Her face was inches away from his; her breath just as labored. "Go away," she forcibly whispered. "You don't exist."

The man's eyes widened. "You're drunk!" he accused. "Your breath reeks of liquor."

Immediately, Kris's hands covered her mouth. "I am not," she muttered from behind her fingers. "I only had a few drinks." She popped up from her chair and glared at the man. "Why am I even defending myself to you? Who *are* you?"

They glared at each other. As if she'd never asked the last question, he pulled his eyes away from hers and studied her head.

"What have you done to your hair?"

Kris grabbed the side of her head and curls wrapped around her fingers. "I . . . I cut it," she answered stupidly. "Why are you asking me these questions?" Not waiting for answer, she backed away from him and around the desk. "I'm getting out of here," she said, hoping if she left the room everything would miraculously clear up.

Before she reached the door, a hand grabbed hold of her arm. "Oh, no you don't," O'Mara said. "I'm not letting you out of my sight. You, madam, are spending the night with me—quite a novelty, don't you think?"

Kris felt the strength of his hand on her arm, and lifted her chin in defiance. "You must be joking! Spend the night with you? I don't even *know* you!"

O'Mara grinned evilly. "Tell that to the sheriff tomorrow morning. Tonight, I'm not letting you out of my sight." With that, he pulled her toward the door and into the foyer.

She jerked away from him, but it was not to run in the opposite direction. She stood, very still, and stared out into the once empty drawing room. Even in the faint light coming from a lamp in the room, she could see it was completely furnished in beautiful shades of gray and rose and green. Two large sofas faced each other, separated by a high butler's table. There were numerous chairs and paintings and plants, and her eye caught the glint of heavy silver coming from a table against the wall. It was all beautiful . . . and none of it should have been there.

She felt frightened, numb, alone with this absurd dream; and allowed the angry man to lead her upstairs. It was only when they were in a bedroom, that he released her.

"You may exchange those trousers for suitable nightclothes," he said, his voice losing some of its edge. "But I will remain in this room. I do not intend for you to be out of my sight for one moment. Not until I deliver you to the sheriff in the morning."

Staring at the huge, postered bed with its canopy of heavy lace, Kris spun around to face him. "The sheriff? I haven't done anything!"

O'Mara startled her by throwing back his head in laughter that sounded more sarcastic than amused. "Haven't done anything? Madam, you have arranged a despicable hoax. Didn't you read that paper in the study? It's all over Richmond, all over the county that you are presumed drowned . . . and I am presumed to have murdered you! Have you any realization of the damage you have done to both our reputations? And for what? So you and your lover could claim Rivanna? The absurdity of this is that you thought you could get away with it!"

His words seemed to shake her out of her numbing fear. This was no dream. He was real. This home was real. She was living a damned nightmare. *"I'm not her!"* she screamed. "I'm not your wife!" She gulped several times before continuing. "My name's Kristine Gavin, and I come from Philadelphia. I was visiting my brother, Jack, when—"

"You think," he interrupted, "that by changing your hair, losing your accent, and wearing men's clothes that you won't be recognized?" He looked at her with disbelief. "We may have wound up hating each other, Christina, but I never doubted your intelligence, until now."

She sat on the edge of the bed and gripped the white satin comforter. "Look, Mr. O'Mara, I read that newspaper article. Your wife spells her name with a C and it has an a at the end. My name is Kristine." She spelled it for him. "I'm afraid your wife is still missing," she said softly, not wanting to anger him further.

He merely stared at her, before again laughing. Sitting down in a large, overstuffed chair, he crossed his legs and pulled out a thin cigar from his vest pocket. He seemed to ignore her until it was lit. Blowing out a slender stream of gray smoke, he raised his head and smiled. "No matter how you spell your name now, you're my wife. A fact I was not too happy about, as you well know, until tonight. But I intend to take you into town tomorrow morning and claim it to the world." His smile was more like a leer. "My neck feels better already, now that it's free from the hangman's noose."

He's mad! He actually thinks I'm this woman! Kris didn't know whether she should laugh or cry.

Deciding on doing neither, she looked away from him and studied the room. It was a woman's bedroom, probably his wife's. Everything was decorated in shades of rose and white. It was overly feminine, with yards of lace and ribbons everywhere. It reminded her of a young girl's room, rather than that of a mature woman. She let her gaze slide to the large dressing table and her expression froze.

Slowly, she rose from the bed and walked over to it. Standing before it, she stared down at the small framed picture that rested behind crystal bottles of perfume. The knot of tension in her stomach tightened as she viewed a smiling woman that could have been her. She recognized the woman in the old-fashioned clothes . . . it was the woman in the portrait.

"Your wife?" she asked in a frightened voice.

"You commissioned that last year," the voice behind her stated. "Are you telling me now that you've forgotten that, also?"

Kris touched the heavy comb and brush with its ivory handles, and turned back to him. "This is Rivanna?" Even to her, her voice sounded tiny and afraid.

The handsome man across the room merely smiled, as if not dignifying the question with an answer.

She didn't want to ask the next one, but her brain was screaming for her to do so. Gathering her courage, she lifted her chin and took a deep breath. "Could you please tell me what year it is?"

His smile broadened. "This act of yours is very

good, Christina. If I didn't know better, I would actually think you had a loss of memory." He ground out his cigar in an empty candy dish. "What am I supposed to say now? Am I supposed to refresh your memory?"

Kris walked back toward the bed. "Please, just tell me."

"I'll play along. After all, we still have at least five hours before dawn and this little game of yours will keep me awake. It's April fourteenth, eighteen hundred and seventy-one. Two days since your disappearance."

She felt her chest cave inward with shock as she quickly expelled her breath. Sitting heavily on the bed, she stared at him. It couldn't be real! These things didn't happen to real people! Her head began to ache, and she was suddenly very tired. Climbing up onto the bed, Kris piled the pillows behind her and propped her head on them. She would close her eyes, she thought, and go to sleep. When she woke up it would all be over. She would be back in Jack's study, and would laugh when she told her brother and Elaine about this insane—

"What a disappointment! No more questions? I would have thought someone who didn't know the year would at least have a few more."

She slowly opened her eyes and stared at him. If sleep wouldn't banish him, she would stare away this nightmare. She realized that to talk to him only made him seem more real, so she clamped her lips together. No matter what he said, she wouldn't answer.

"Where were you hiding for the last two days?" he

74

asked. "At Taylor's place? I'd be amazed if Lynette could put up with you for that long." Sensing he wasn't going to get a response, he changed subjects. "I'm very surprised to see you in trousers, Christina. When Beth wears them riding, you bloody well have an attack."

It was on the tip of her tongue to ask who Beth was, but she bit back the question. She refused to enter into more conversation with a dream. But what a dream, she thought, as she continued to stare at the man in the chair. Now that he was across the room, and looked like he intended to remain there, he was less threatening and she didn't fear him. She had thought she was immune to beautiful people, having interviewed so many in the last three years, but O'Mara was different. She didn't think he knew just how attractive he was. She guessed him to be in his mid thirties and he looked to be over six feet tall when standing. He was lean, sinewy, built like a runner; and with his black hair and blue eyes he reminded her of Pierce Brosnyn, the actor. The slight Irish lilt to his voice completed the image. Kris mentally giggled, then congratulated herself on inventing such a fantastic-looking dream man. Now if she could just make him disappear . . .

Sean watched her dozing, and noticed how her eyes would slowly close then flutter open as if she were surprised to find him still there. He smiled grimly. He had no intention of moving from the chair until morning. Settling himself more comfortably against the cushions, he continued to watch her. What was she up to now? When he thought about what he'd been through in the last two days, his body tensed with anger. He'd gone over it in his mind a hundred times since she'd disappeared and he still couldn't believe it. She hated him, he knew that, yet she must have been planning this for a very long time. And he had played right into her hands, had let her get away with it . . . almost. Christ! When her horse had come back with the marks all over it, he'd searched into the night for her. And when they'd found her hat by the river, he'd actually grieved. It had surprised him that he wasn't immediately overwhelmed with relief, for it appeared he had finally gained his freedom. But his grief was real . . . for what could have been, for all the anger of the past three years. He now saw how she had planned everything. Christina had purposely provoked him in front of others for weeks, and the final showdown at the party was a stroke of genius. With her back turned to the others, no one could see her laughter or hear her hateful remarks to him. She had positioned him just right, so her witnesses could watch as he exploded with rage. She was the consummate actress and she'd counted on him to ride off his anger as he had done in the past. He could just imagine her delight when he'd yelled about his soul being damned, but he was finally going to be free.

He shook his head, remembering how Trent Cunningham had related that outburst to the sheriff. No one had seemed to believe that at the time he'd been thinking about a divorce. It was against his religion, yet he'd known two days ago that he would have endangered his soul to gain freedom from Christina.

He looked at her, asleep on the bed. She was different. Her hair was shorter, to her shoulders instead of down her back. And she'd done something to it to make it appear like a cloud of curls around her head. Somehow, she'd lost her Southern accent, had acquired a low Northern one. And he'd noticed right away that she wasn't wearing her wedding ring. It was his one gift to her that she'd treasured. He grimaced, thinking that Judson Taylor was probably selling the diamonds and emeralds to salvage Everleaf.

He had to give her credit. It was a flawless performance. In a perverse way, he had to admire her, for she hadn't yet made a mistake in her role as poor, little lost Kristine—with a *K* and an *e* at the end. He chuckled under his breath. She should have come up with a better name. Yet it did make him stop and wonder how she had accomplished such perfection in acting. Her speech pattern was impeccable; not once had she reverted back to her own Southern drawl. Nor did she show any familiar habits, any nuances that would have given her away. It puzzled him that tonight he had seen a vulnerability in her that had never surfaced before. And her eyes . . . it was her eyes that startled him. They didn't look cold and calculating, as before. They showed no hatred . . . only fear. And that was most surprising, for Christina had never feared him. She had delighted in ridiculing every single threat he had made. All that had mattered to her was money. Nothing else.

Money. What had it brought him, but tragedy? Immediately, he thought about his plans for Rivanna, for the breeding farm. No, he quickly

77

revised his thoughts. Money had enabled him to devote himself to what he most enjoyed. He realized, as he glanced up to make sure his wife was still sleeping, that unconsciously he had needed to channel the love that was within him. Was he a fool? What would another man do when his wife rejected him, held him up to ridicule by meeting with her childhood lover? He had devoted himself to his horses, rather than go crazy from the day to day existence in a failed marriage. He thought back, trying to think of a way he could have stopped her. Outside of physical restraint, which he'd rejected, he knew there was no way to keep Christina from doing as she wished . . . even if that meant being unfaithful.

She looked so innocent, asleep in her bed, yet he knew otherwise. He'd known, in fact, every time she'd been with Taylor. He could tell by her face. The muscles looked relaxed; her lips appeared bruised; her eyes were filled with a mocking satisfaction. It had hurt, the first few times, and he had tried talking with her, then arguing with her; and finally she'd told him the truth — she didn't love him, never would. She'd only wanted to save Rivanna and recapture a way of life that the Yankees had taken away. It was then he'd closed his heart to her . . . and it had never reopened.

Letting his head rest against the back of the chair, Sean sighed aloud. This time she had gone too far. After he cleared his name tomorrow, Christina was going to learn that he was the master of Rivanna. If she intended to remain until they had settled the divorce, then she was going to have to learn a few new rules.

He watched her awaken, flexing her arms above her head and stretching her legs, then curling back to hug a pillow against her chest. He glanced up to Tisha and nodded. Immediately, he noticed the servant's look of apprehension as she approached the bed.

"Miz Christina? It's mornin'. Mr. O'Mara says you best get up." The black woman glanced to her employer, then back to the bed. She watched as her mistress opened her eyes, then squealed along with Miz Christina as they stared at each other.

"That's enough!" Sean jumped up from the chair as the two women shrieked at one another. He was exhausted from his vigil, and impatient to take Christina to the sheriff. Looking at his wife, he noticed that her eyes, wide with shock, stared at him and Tisha as if they were ghosts. Not looking forward to another scene, he cleared his throat and said, "I will give you forty minutes to prepare yourself. Tisha is here to assist you. However, if you choose to meet the sheriff in your present attire be forewarned that it will only support the story I intend to tell."

Her mouth remained open, her voice lost somewhere in the frozen muscles of her throat. She could only blink as she watched him walk out of the room and shut the door behind him. Breathing heavily, she slowly turned her head and faced the frightened woman named Tisha, who looked as terrified as Kris felt.

Holy Mother of God, the nightmare was continuing. They were real! *He* was real! She could feel her lips trembling as the panic that started in her stomach quickly traveled through her. Her hand shook as she pushed her hair away from her eyes. Staring at the pregnant black woman, she could easily read her nervousness as the servant clutched her long brown skirt. Remembering how, upon awakening, she had screamed when confronted by the strange face, Kris tried to make her lips resemble a friendly smile.

"Are you real?" she asked in a tiny, pleading voice, knowing how ridiculous she sounded. "Because if you're not, I'd really appreciate some little sign, something that would tell me it's okay to go back to sleep until this is over."

It didn't help to see the woman cross herself, as if for protection, and back away from her. "Miz Christina . . . you . . . you feelin' poorly?" the younger woman asked in a frightened voice.

They continued to stare at each other, until Kris muttered aloud, "This can't be happening . . . . Where the hell am I?"

Chapter Five

She sat beside him in the carriage, quietly biding her time until they reached town. Sean glanced at her from the corner of one eye and saw she was staring straight ahead. When she'd met him in front of the house, he'd had a moment of shock. She was still dressed in those damned black trousers, and had glared at him with defiance, as if daring him to make any comment. He hadn't. but as she'd turned away from him to look at the house, her eyes had appeared haunted, as if not believing what they were seeing.

Flicking the reins over the horses' rump, Sean grinned as he remembered the reactions of those on the plantation. Until they had reached the main road, everyone they'd passed had stopped work and stared, astonished . . . the mistress was back. He couldn't recall a smile, or a relieved expression. Now all he had to do was get through the next few hours and he could put this behind him. Already the mares had started to arrive. He thanked God that news of this fiasco hadn't reached the majority of his business associates. If he had to make the trip himself, he was determined that news of Christina's reappearance would reach the *Richmond Gazette* by noon today.

And then it was over.

Once more, Sean stole a glance at the woman next to him and sighed audibly. Well, almost . . . God only knew what plans were hatching inside that head.

Kristine Gavin thought she was in the hands of a madman, and in a world gone mad. She tried very hard not to think about the woman named Tisha who seemed to think of her as the mistress of Rivanna. Nor would she allow her mind to linger on the beautiful clothes Tisha had laid out on the bed for her, old-fashioned trappings from a time long ago. Yet she couldn't deny the expressions of those working on the plantation. They were shocked to see her, and not exactly pleased. She shook her head in confusion. She wouldn't think about any of it, for there would be no answers until she reached Chestfield, the town O'Mara was taking her to. Then she would ask the sheriff, for what had frightened her last night had now become her salvation. This person in authority, this sheriff, would surely listen and help her to escape from the nightmare. And until she stood face to face with him, she wasn't saying another word.

Men and women stopped and stared as the carriage passed; children started running ahead of them, laughing and shouting at each other as if a circus had arrived. When O'Mara pulled the horses to a stop in front of a small building a crowd gathered and whispered among themselves as they watched her every move. O'Mara came around the carriage and offered her his hand, and she stood up on shaking legs and listened to the laughter of the children when they saw her pants. Immediately, she raised her head and glared at the crowd dressed in old-fashioned clothes. A hush spread over them, and they made room for her to precede O'Mara into the building.

Sean watched her, not able to believe she'd risked ridicule by coming into town in those trousers. Even her white cotton blouse was soiled and wrinkled. Christina had always prided herself on her appearance, usually to the extreme. But maybe this was all part of her plan . . . . Had he just done something stupid by bringing her here? Had he again played into her hands? Either way, she was in town, alive and well, without a mark on her. As he opened the large wooden door, he swore that to regain his reputation he'd tear the clothes from her, if he had to, to prove he hadn't harmed one inch of her. Christina's days of lying were about to come to an end.

"Mrs. O'Mara!" A large man with a red beard rose from his chair as they entered the office. Quickly, he came around his desk and stared at her appearance. "What happened to you?"

Sean closed the door on the curious faces of the townspeople, all as eager as the sheriff to find out where the mistress of Rivanna had spent the last two days. Clearing his throat, Sean took his wife's arm and led her to a chair. "She wandered back to the house. I found her to be incoherent. She couldn't explain where she'd been, nor did she seem to recognize anything familiar." There. No lies yet.

Vern Loftis's eyebrows came together as he stared at the confused woman. Miss Christina had never looked so untidy, or so frightened. He'd never really liked her, or her kind—always looking down their noses at those who worked to put bread on the table—but he had a job to do, and he was good at it. "Can you add anything to this, Miss Christina? Can you tell us what happened."

Kris smiled. The sheriff appeared to be friendly, and right now he was her only hope. "This man," she said, jerking her head toward O'Mara, "is mistaken. My name is Kristine Gavin. I live in Philadelphia, Pennsylvania. And I work for a television station. I'm the entertainment reporter." Even though her mind registered the startled expression on the sheriff's face, she continued, hoping to make him see that O'Mara's story was false. "Look, I don't know how all this happened, I just want to go home. Well, back to my brother's home."

"And where is that?" Loftis asked softly, sitting back down in his chair. Jesus Christ! Her story was absurd. She didn't even have a brother. "Where is your brother's home?" he repeated, afraid of her answer.

Kris lifted her chin. "Rivanna."

The sheriff looked up to O'Mara and Kris gritted her teeth as she watched the younger man shrug as if to say I told you so.

Standing up, Kris leaned over the desk. "Listen to me. This guy here, O'Mara"—she threw back an arm to point him out—"thinks I'm his wife! He's

84

living in my brother's home with a lot of people, and expects me to believe *I'm* the one with the problem?" She gave a nervous, sarcastic laugh. "He's trying to make me think I'm crazy. Tell him! Tell him what date it is."

Loftis's mouth gaped open. He looked from husband to wife and muttered, "It's April fourteenth, eighteen hundred and seventy-one. You don't remember that either?"

Sinking back into the chair, Kris tightened the muscles around her eyes. She would not cry. She would not let them do this to her. "What's going on?" she asked aloud in a tiny voice. No one answered, and she looked across the room to the windows. Pressed against the panes were dozens of faces, each with a different look. Some of the faces that leered at her were weathered, those of young men looking too old for their years. And some were truly old. These gazed at her with a sadness, a wise understanding that said she was somehow a disappointment. Still others were framed by old-fashioned hats or bonnets. These had eyes that were glaring, almost gloating over her predicament. This couldn't be true! These people just couldn't be real. . . . What had happened during the storm? Where the hell was she? She closed her eyes and prayed for sanity to return.

"She looks fine, Mr. O'Mara," the sheriff finally pronounced. "Physically, that is. I think it might be a good idea to take your wife into Richmond, to seek professional help there. I don't know what more—"

Kris's eyes shot open. "I'm not crazy! I know

who I am! I just don't know *where* I am. Damn it! I don't belong here!" Tears streamed down her face and she gripped the arms of the chair to stop her hands from shaking. "Will someone please listen to me? Can't you understand this is a nightmare? None of you are real. I'm from the future. *This is supposed to be nineteen hundred and eighty-eight!*" she yelled to anyone who would listen.

Hearing the commotion her last remark had caused outside his office, Sheriff Loftis tore his eyes away from the madwoman and hurried to lower the shades and close out the spectators. "Calm down, Mrs. O'Mara," he said sternly. "Haven't you caused enough scandal for your husband, without this?"

Kris's face crumpled. "He's not my husband," she cried softly. "Why won't anyone believe me?"

Sean felt a twinge of pity for her as he observed her misery. It seemed so genuine. But then he remembered just what an accomplished actress she really was. What he found hard to understand was that she seemed to be playing right into his hands now, with this madness routine. Confused himself, he looked away from her as Loftis began speaking.

"After you take her home, I'll personally go into Richmond and speak to the paper. I know you've been wronged, and I'll try to clear up this mess. I don't see any point in involving the military in this, though. It's bad enough the Federal Government doesn't think we can handle ourselves in political matters. This," he said sadly, while looking back at the silent woman, "is a family matter. I promise I won't give out any details. As far as I'm concerned, the case is closed."

Sean took his wife's arm and led her to the door. She appeared to be in shock, allowed him to lead her. Before facing the town, he glanced at the sheriff. "I appreciate this, Vern. I'd like to keep this as quiet as possible. I'm sure it's only a temporary condition."

Vern Loftis met O'Mara's steady gaze. It surprised him to find out he liked the man. It was all that gossip he'd listened to over the years. Like a woman in a rocking chair, he'd believed the rumors about this man, this Yankee, and had wanted to accept them. He saw now that O'Mara was a man of honor and decency, wanting to protect his crazy wife from others. Holding out his hand, he indicated those still waiting outside. "I just hope they didn't hear much. If you'd like, I can ride over to Rivanna and give you a report when I come back from Richmond."

Sean shook the man's hand. He looked directly into his eyes and replied, "I believe, Sheriff, that you'll do everything possible to repair my reputation, and protect my wife's. There's no need for you to report back to me. I'm only glad this is finally over." Taking Kris's elbow, he opened the door. "But if you ever find yourself out by Rivanna, please know you'll be welcome," he added, as he guided Kris out of the office.

She heard a buzzing of voices when O'Mara led her back to the street. Her mind could only register whispers and shocked faces that glanced at her with embarrassment. From somewhere deep in her subconscious, she knew these people were frightened of her. They turned to O'Mara with sympathy, as if silently commiserating with a man saddled with a mad wife. Once in the carriage, she kept her hands tightly clasped in her lap. Staring down at them, she felt O'Mara sit next to her. She would not look up at the crowd, for no longer could she raise her chin in defiance. If she was to believe everything that had happened, everything that had been said, then she was somehow living in the past . . . taken back in time. She closed her eyes tightly to shut out the insane thought. It was easier to believe that she was crazy than to accept — A sudden, sharp pain exploded in her shoulder, and she snapped open her eyes to see dirt and mud falling onto her lap. The shrill voice of a woman forced her to look up.

"Harry Gentry! Your momma's going to make you eat that mudball when I tell her what you just done!"

Kris looked at the young boy standing beyond the crowd. His thin arms were crossed over his chest and his expression was rebellious. He couldn't have been more than thirteen or fourteen, yet he ignored the reprimand and continued to stare at Kris.

"I don't care," he finally said, his mouth quivering with barely contained anger. "I'm glad she's balmy. Maybe now they'll put her away for good!"

Never had anyone looked at her with such contempt, such hatred; and Kris felt her body begin to shake. Almost immediately, she saw O'Mara reach into his jacket and pull out a handkerchief. With a surprising gentleness, he began to wipe away the remaining mud from her blouse, then handed the hankie to her when he was finished. He picked up the reins and pulled the carriage forward until he was in front of the boy.

"When your manners return, Master Gentry, I will expect you to make an appearance at Rivanna and apologize to Mrs. O'Mara." The boy looked down to the wheels of the carriage in embarrassment. In a lower voice, O'Mara added, "I had thought better of you, Harry."

The young boy lifted his head and tears could be seen at the corners of his eyes. "I . . . I only done it 'cause of everything she did to — "

"I want you to go home," O'Mara interrupted, "and tell your mother what you did. And then I want you to think about what a gentleman would do to rectify this. I'm very disappointed, Harry."

Kris watched as the boy seemed to cringe under O'Mara's scrutiny. Then, without any further word, O'Mara flicked the reins and pulled away from the boy, leaving the town of Chestfield and its crowd of spectators behind.

Sean's mind was churning with unanswered questions when he pulled up in front of Rivanna. Christina had remained quiet throughout the short trip and he hadn't had the desire to initiate any conversation. When he helped her out of the carriage, he again felt a twinge of pity, and scolded himself for it. Didn't she deserve the treatment she had received? How many of those people had she insulted over the years? What he couldn't understand was why she had taken such treatment in

89

silence. It wasn't like her not to retaliate. He looked at her face, and could see a mixture of fear and confusion in it as she walked up the front stairs. As he opened the door, he couldn't keep a fleeting thought from crossing his mind: Was there any truth in the story being spread around Chestfield at this moment? Had Christina lost her grip on reality? Was she truly mad? Or was all of this an elaborate lie, something that would prove useful to her later? God in heaven, he thought, this isn't going to be over until I figure out what she is up to. . . .

He led her to the wide curving staircase and stopped. "You'll want to change now," he advised, looking at her soiled blouse. She just stared at him, as if he were speaking a foreign language. He noticed Tisha as she hesitantly walked into the foyer. "Tisha will take you upstairs and assist you. I'll tell Louis to have the girls prepare a bath." He looked to the servant and nodded, waiting for her to take his place next to Christina. When the young black woman reluctantly came forward, he backed away, saying, "I'm already late getting to the stable and there's much to be done. The first mare is ready to foal."

He was turning to leave the house when she stopped him with her voice. It was a shock for him to hear the fear and dismay in it.

"Who was he?" she asked, holding back the tears.

Sean spun around. "Who?"

Kris looked at him and swallowed down the burning in her throat. "That . . . that boy. Who was he? Why does he hate me so much? I . . . I don't even know him."

He couldn't believe the instinctual urge to comfort her that raced through him. Perhaps it was he who was losing his mind, wanting to console the woman who had done everything in her power to destroy him. Shaking away that feeling, he said gruffly, "We'll speak of this later. There's too much work I've had to postpone already."

He left the house, and breathed a long sigh of relief. What magic, what deceit, was she working on him now?

She looked at the photograph, so like her own image, then let her gaze wander to the mirror as Tisha brushed out her hair. She allowed the maid to pamper her this way. It was expected. Since coming back to Rivanna this morning, she had done everything she'd been told. She'd allowed herself to be led into this bedroom, had permitted Tisha and another servant to remove her clothes, and had gotten into the old-fashioned copper tub when she'd been instructed to do so. She had allowed them power over her, knowing this was another attempt to banish the nightmare. Perhaps, she had been wrong in fighting them. Maybe, if she went along and permitted the dream to reach its conclusion, it would finally end. And, in truth, she didn't have the energy to resist any longer.

She wanted to scream forth her denial, cry out against whatever force had carried her to this time; but she kept her emotions tightly coiled within her.

She'd seen their faces, had felt their apprehension. They thought she was mad. To survive this, she must be very careful, must never let them see her desperation, for to do so would mean giving up control of her life. The one fear—the terror—that took hold of her mind, was that O'Mara would lose patience and do something drastic. There were no psychiatrists in this time, no understanding of mental illness. If she became too irrational, too emotional, she would be put away in some institution . . . and Kris knew she would never survive that horror.

So she sat in front of another woman's dressing table, wore a stranger's white gown, and contemplated another woman's husband.

"Mae was wonderin' what to plan for supper, with you being back and all. . . ."

Kris looked at the maid through the mirror. Tisha was waiting for an answer. Slowly letting out her breath, Kris said, "I'm sure whatever she prepares will be fine." There. It had started. She wouldn't fight them any longer. She was about to assume the role of Mistress of Rivanna. Good Lord, she thought, and I have trouble managing my checkbook. How in the world will I ever pull off this deception?

Tisha's brush stopped in midair. "You're not comin' down to oversee, like always? You're leavin' it up to Mae?"

From the servant's surprised expression, Kris could see she had made a mistake. She tried to smile and slowly rose. "Why don't we go down together? We can see if Mae has any suggestions."

Please God, she prayed, make her stop staring at me like that!

Who was this woman, Christina, that elicited such strong reactions from everyone around her? What had she done? And where was she? It was the last question that chilled Kris's heart.

Where *was* Christina O'Mara?

Chapter Six

She no longer noticed the dreariness of the cabin, the mustiness that rose from the old furniture like a decaying perfume. He was with her. Finally, after all the years of yearning, she could embrace him without fear. It was going to happen, she silently vowed. It was her last chance.

She almost cried aloud as she flew into his arms. "Thank God, you've come! I thought I'd go mad with waiting . . . and wanting you." She tried to kiss him, to claim him, but was only rewarded by a brush of lips against her cheek.

Pulling back from him, she attempted to hide her disappointment. "What's wrong? Everything went as planned. Didn't it?" Her stomach tightened with apprehension.

He pulled a newspaper from his luggage and spread it out on the scarred table top. Shaking his head, he looked down at the headlines. "I don't know, Christina. It all happened exactly the way you said it would, but . . ." Again, he shook his head, as if regretting his part in it.

Barely controlling her impatience, she reached for the paper. "Let me see it." Reading about her disappearance, her suspected demise, brought a strange thrill, an excitement, as if somehow she had actually cheated death. She laughed aloud several times while reciting Elizabeth Hart's quotes. "Didn't I tell you the Hart sisters would be perfect witnesses?" She placed the paper back on the table and looked at him. "What's wrong, Judson?" she asked, trying to keep the impatience out of her voice. She'd done everything, the planning, the execution—all he'd had to do was keep silent and support her. Couldn't he see how close they were to having it all?

Judson sighed audibly. "I just wish it were over. Everyone's talking about it. I still don't know how I managed to convince Lynette that I needed to get away for a few days."

"Lynette would do anything for you, and she's known about us for years. Of course you'd be upset about my disappearance. I bet she encouraged you to get away from it all." Secretly, Christina knew her only rival for Judson's affections was his older sister. Ever since the war, Lynette had given up looking for a husband and had concentrated on making Judson the center of her world. It was sick, Christina thought. And it wasn't going to last much longer.

She looked at him as he silently unpacked his things. His conscience was bothering him. Judson was too good for this world, out of place with his time. And his sense of honor was a disadvantage when the Yankees were stealing their homes and destroying their way of life—all in the name of Reconstruction. To survive, you had to change. She'd learned that early in life. Though she had never experienced motherhood, a strange, maternal urge to protect Judson had developed in her since the end of the war. If he was weak in dealing with life's unpleasantnesses, she would be strong for him. And if his conscience made him feel guilty for what they had done, she knew how to change that. She had waited two days, alone in this horrible cabin, for him to join her and she wasn't about to waste the five days to come. Five days with him, waking up with him, loving him . . . No matter what she'd done, it was worth it.

"Judson . . ." She whispered his name and waited for him to turn around. When he did, she smiled and slowly brought her fingers up to the buttons of her blouse. With infinite care, she pushed each button through its hole, all the time watching the transformation in his face. He was hypnotized, unable to tear his eyes away from her. Leaving her blouse tucked in the waistband of her skirt, she licked her lips and allowed the material to fall around her hips. With an agonizing laziness, she pulled her chemise down to join the blouse. She never took her eyes away from his, yet her fingers slid up from her waist to gently caress her breasts. She deliberately took her time, aware that his arousal was heightened by watching her. She knew just what he required, had known since they were fifteen years old. He wanted to see her bring her fingers up to her mouth, then allow them to slowly draw moist patterns down her chest and finally circled each breast, narrowing until the points were hard with excitement. It was a rite of adoration, one that she'd indulged in many a night without him, standing before her bedroom mirror and pretending he was there.

His breathing was labored, and she looked up to see desire in his heavy-lidded eyes. "I'm going to paint you like this," he whispered, "so I can always remember . . ."

Her laugh was low and seductive. "Soon, Judson, you won't need a painting to remember me. We're finally going to be together . . . just the way it should have been." She pushed her breasts together, as if in an offering. "You've got five days. You can paint something to show Lynette later. I need you now."

He came to her quickly, kneeling before her and replacing her fingers with his mouth. She looked down to his hair, and gently ran her hand over the dark blond strands as she held him close to her. Letting her head fall back, she closed her eyes to the rough wooden ceiling and allowed excitement to surge through her.

She'd waited so long, and now it was going to happen. In a short time, she was going to have it all. Rivanna . . . and Judson. An overwhelming sense of victory mingled with the heat of their passion, and Christina cried out with pleasure as Judson carried her to the bed, his conscience completely forgotten.

Kris heard the laughter, the good-natured teasing

that was taking place in the kitchen as she and Tisha walked toward the back of the house. Taking a deep breath, she fixed a smile on her face and prepared to meet the other servants.

It happened quickly, the cessation of laughter, the silence. Kris stood by the door and watched the old black woman's eyes turn cold as she returned to her work at the stove. Another woman, younger, nervously look away and pulled at the brightly patterned kerchief on her head. Kris felt a knot in her stomach as she observed an older man vigorously polish a silver tray that already sparkled in the sunlight coming through the window. More than ever she felt like a stranger, an unwelcome presence. And not for the first time, she wondered what had Christina done, what kind of person she was to make everyone so dislike her. Realizing that she was going to have to take the first step, Kris broadened her smile and entered the room.

This is acting, she told herself. She'd reviewed hundreds of performances. She could do it. All she had to do was pretend this was her house, the clothes she wore were her own. If she really looked so much like Christina, then she could pull it off. She had to succeed, for the alternative was too frightening . . . she had to prove to all of them that she wasn't insane.

She looked at the woman in front of the stove. "Tisha said you were wondering about supper, Mae." Please God, she prayed, let it be her.

The older woman glanced up and nodded. "Mista Sean's gonna be mighty hungry after that filly drops her foal. Once you decide on somethin', I best be startin'."

Kris returned her nod. "What about chicken?" she asked politely. "That shouldn't take too long. A nice roast chicken."

"By the time Louis killed it and Riva, here, plucked it, I'd be—"

Kris held up her hand. "Forget the chicken," she said quickly, realizing that after Mae's description of the preparation she'd never be able to eat the fowl anyway. She searched her mind for an alternative. Wasn't Virginia known for its hams? She smiled. "What about a ham?"

Everyone stared at her in astonishment. "You never eat ham, Miz Christina. You said it makes you too thirsty, and it's bad for your digestion." Tisha looked to the others for confirmation.

As she watched the servants silently agree, Kris took a deep breath. She'd never thought assuming this woman's identity was going to be easy, but it was unnerving that *everything* she said or did was questioned. She realized it was ridiculous to think she could be Christina—she knew nothing about her, except that everyone seemed to dislike her. Whatever resemblance she shared with the woman, it was only physical. She decided it was time to put a little of herself into this character, for that was the only way she could convincingly pull off playing the part. Besides, she couldn't live with everyone's unvoiced fear, not even for another hour. It was unnatural to her, foreign, to be so disliked.

"I've developed a taste for ham," she announced to the room. "Doesn't Mr. O'Mara like it?"

Mae nodded and Kris grinned. "Well, then, I'd

99

say we've settled that problem, haven't we?"

They continued to stare at her, and Kris could almost hear them asking themselves if she'd lost her mind. What do I have to lose? she thought. I might as well make Christina someone I can live with until I am taken back to my own time. As though a heavy burden had been removed from her shoulders, Kris felt pounds lighter now that the decision had been made. "Mae," she asked, "this is your kitchen, isn't it?" She watched the woman nod, could see the alarm in her large brown eyes. "Then from today on, why don't you just plan our meals? Who knows better what's available? Or, how long it will take to prepare? I trust you."

Mae's mouth dropped open, and the older man deftly caught the large tray that had slipped from his fingers. Kris turned her attention to him. "Louis, how long have you taken care of Mr. O'Mara and this house?"

Louis looked directly at her. She could see he wondered if she was testing him. "I've seen to Master Sean's needs since your marriage, three years ago. And it must be going on thirty years since I've been working in this house."

Kris continued to smile at him. Again, she nodded. "I believe, Louis, that proves you certainly don't need my direction either. Just continue with whatever you've always done. You wouldn't be here thirty years if you didn't do a good job." She hoped he could hear the sincerity in her voice, for her statements seemed logical to her.

She now focused on the younger woman, Riva. She was considering how to draw her out when

100

Tisha spoke softly behind her. "Riva's doing real well here at the house. She's apprenticin' in here with Mae and helpin' me and Sada with the house work."

Kris cast Tisha a grateful smile. She felt Tisha appreciated the change she was seeing in her mistress and had decided to become an ally. Kris looked back to Riva. "Then you might be just the person to tell me what I can do to help out around here." She put her hands on her hips and nodded to the bowl of apples in front of the maid. "Do you need a hand peeling those? I'm a good worker, if you point me in the right direction."

Riva looked shocked and swallowed several times as she glanced at Mae and Louis for help. "Beg pardon, missus?" she squeaked out, dropping her paring knife onto the table.

Kris observed the startled expressions, the utter shock. Maybe I'm going too fast, she thought. But it was what she wanted. She didn't wish to see another person cringe away from her in fear. She wanted, somehow, to fit in.

Slipping her hands into the pockets of her dressing gown, Kris said, "I'm going upstairs to dress. When I come back down, let me know what I can do to help."

She turned to leave, and heard Tisha follow her. Here was another decision. She stopped and faced the pretty woman. "You don't have to come," she said in a low voice. "When are you due to have your baby?"

Embarrassed, Tisha cast her eyes to the floor. "Can come any day now."

Kris was surprised, for although Tisha's abdomen was large, she didn't look nine months' pregnant. But then, what did she know about such things? Tisha's bone structure was small, fragile. Maybe that made a difference. "Then you're definitely not taking those stairs again. Really," she assured her, "I can dress myself. Find a chair and relax."

She turned away from the startled maid and hurried to the stairs, anxious to get dressed and return. If she allowed herself to get into this charade, she might find out she enjoyed it. And anyway, she silently giggled as she sought out her room, keeping busy would make the time pass until the real Christina returned and found out what she'd done! It would be almost worth it to stick around and observe the woman's reaction. One way or another, Kris was going to make sure everyone believed Christina Mattson O'Mara had had a change of heart.

She experienced a moment of guilt while rummaging through Christina's drawers in search of underwear and suitable clothing. It was so personal, like going through someone's belongings after they'd died. Picking out a plain white cotton blouse, Kris grabbed some old-fashioned underwear and then went to the closet. From it, she selected a lightweight skirt with tiny pleats below the knees. As she placed her white costume on the bed, Kris untied the belt of her dressing gown and shook her head. She didn't feel quite so uncomfortable any longer about wearing this woman's clothes, for she was sure Christina was alive. She didn't know why she had that certainty, but it was a deep-seated intuition that she couldn't shake. Whatever happened during that storm hadn't killed her. As she stood before the mirror in the long frilly underwear, Kris giggled. What if Christina had taken her place? She could just imagine her brother's reaction to such a woman! Reaching for the white skirt and blouse, she tried to picture Jack dealing with Christina.

Kris's smile slowly faded as she tied a large bronze-colored ribbon around her waist. What if Christina was doing the same thing she was? What kind of havoc might she be creating in Kris's life? A knot formed in her stomach when she thought of her brother and Elaine, of Danni, of all those she'd left behind. They had been the core of her life, her nucleus of love, friendship, and support. How could she go on without them? How could she . . . .

She forcefully shook her head. She refused to believe she had lost them. If she allowed herself to think otherwise, she'd surely go crazy. She was going to return to her own time . . . and to them. It was going to happen. She just had to be patient and wait.

Leaving the bedroom, Kris explored the house. She was delighted by the intricate carvings, the detailed workmanship, the rich furnishings; and tried to memorize everything so she might describe the place to Jack and Elaine. As she left the drawing room, she passed O'Mara's study and paused at the doorway. An eerie chill passed over her. It was here that she'd discovered what had happened to her, and it was here that she'd first set eyes on Sean O'Mara.

She stepped into the room and looked around. Oil paintings of horses hung from the paneled walls lined by shelves of books. Picking up a cloth-bound volume, Kris opened it to see writing on the inside cover:

Property of Beth Mattson — 1862

Beth? Now who was that? Hadn't O'Mara mentioned that name last night when he'd been hounding her with questions? She thought of the tall, handsome man who was supposed to be her husband. It had been obvious from the way he'd badgered her the night before that O'Mara and his wife did not have the best of marriages. Thank God, she thought as she replaced the book and walked out of the study. It was certainly to her advantage that the couple were having problems. The very last thing she needed to deal with was a loving, concerned husband. Kris decided that her best course of action was to be pleasant and not antagonize him.

Opening the front door, she walked into the fading sunlight and looked around. How she wished Jack and Elaine could see Rivanna as it looked now; they could congratulate themselves on how they'd restored the plantation. The only thing they hadn't duplicated was the white fence that bordered and separated the property as far as the eye could see — and, of course, the grazing horses. It seemed to her that though the house was occupied by a family Rivanna really belonged to the horses — so many of them appeared to be in possession of the numerous yards. Picking up the hem of her skirt, Kris descended the wide marble steps and walked across the grass. There were two stables and she picked the one that looked older, the one in which she knew O'Mara would be working. As she entered it, she was surprised by the clean fresh scent of hay, the strong aroma of grain. Since so many of the horses were outside, most of the stalls were empty as she made her way down the center aisle looking for the master of Rivanna.

How strange, she thought, to be thinking of a man as master of anything, but she would allow him that title. Right now, she would let him call himself anything he wanted . . . as long as she could convince him that she hadn't lost her mind.

She'd made the wrong choice. He wasn't in the older stable, but in the newer one where, she was told by a hand, foaling boxes had been built. As she entered the barn, she heard whispers and slowly approached the sounds. Standing outside a large, square, wooden stall, Kris peeked inside. A huge brown and white horse was lying on its side, breathing heavily; its eyes wide and frightened. A black man was sitting in the hay behind its head, crooning to the animal, while Sean worked at the rear of the horse, laying a hand on its side.

"Okay, Eli, here we go . . . another one's coming. Get ready to hold her if necessary."

Kris observed Sean's anxious expression as he urged the horse on, quietly murmuring his encouragement while stroking the animal's side.

"C'mon, girl! This is it. Let's get it over with . . . one more good push."

As if the communication had been understood, the mare gave a grunt and her swelling sides heaved.

Kris stood silently by, unable to tear her eyes away. A glistening, near transparent membrane appeared. The small hoof showing within it was followed by the long slim shape of the head. Very rapidly, the whole foal slipped out onto the straw. The fragile membrane broke open, steaming with the heat of the mare, and fresh air reached the newborn's head, filling its lungs and beginning a new life.

Kris was amazed by what she had seen, and very close to tears from witnessing this emotional moment. She blinked several times to clear her eyes as Sean knelt next to the foal, which was already making its first feeble efforts to move its head. Sean picked up a clean rag and wiped the small creature's head and body, a smile breaking out over his weary features.

"He's beautiful . . . ." The whisper slipped out before she could stop it.

Sean's head snapped up and he stared at her. His smile quickly disappeared. "How long have you been there?" His voice was low with irritation, as if her presence had spoiled the moment for him.

Kris felt his resentment immediately. "Not long. I . . . I came to find you. Ask you about dinner . . ." Her palms started perspiring as he continued to stare at her. "I've never seen a birth before," she said feebly, glancing at the foal then back at the man. His shirt was open, almost to the waist, and his sleeves were rolled above his forearms. A black lock of hair fell onto his forehead, and she could see the sheen of sweat across his brow. He looked exhausted; and she remembered that he must not have slept the night before while guarding her.

It was then she realized that nothing that had happened was his fault. He was caught in the middle. And he didn't really resent her. He resented his wife, Christina. In that instant she made up her mind that the newspaper was wrong in painting him to be a monster. Anyone who cared so much about bringing life, any life, into this world could never take it — even in anger.

She smiled as the foal attempted to stand on its delicate legs, and the mare turned her head to nuzzle her offspring. Kris's smile widened as she lifted her eyes to Sean's. He was watching her and his face held the strangest expression, as if he were looking at her, Kris, and not the woman he had married. A sudden unexpected thrill shot though her, and she found herself in a totally ridiculous state of embarrassment, her cheeks flushing with an out-of-place pleasure. Not able to believe she was actually blushing, Kris quickly cleared her throat.

"I'll tell Mae to hold dinner for you," she said, wanting the sound of a voice, any voice, to break the strange silence.

He shook his head as if trying to recapture his train of thought. "Hold dinner?"

Kris nodded and smiled to the man named Eli before turning back to Sean. "Whenever you're through here, we'll have dinner. I'll wait."

His eyes narrowed with confusion. "I might be some time yet. I want to get these two settled," he pronounced, indicating the mare and foal. "You go ahead. We'll dine as usual."

He was testing her. She could sense it. What was *usual* between a man and woman who hated each other? Did they eat together? Not knowing the proper response to make, Kris returned his gaze and said quietly, "I don't mind waiting."

It wasn't what he expected to hear. Sean forced his eyes away from her and continued to wipe the foal's shining coat. He could feel her looking at him, knew she was waiting for him to answer. The problem was he could find no reply. Christina had never postponed anything for him, especially dinner. Even in the beginning of their marriage, if he was tied up elsewhere she sat down to eat at precisely six o'clock each evening. In the last year, they hadn't eaten a dozen meals together. Only when Beth was home did they make any pretense of being a family. Now, she was saying she'd wait until he was ready. It wasn't right. But then nothing seemed normal since she'd disappeared. Whatever happened to Christina had changed her . . . and he admitted he was frightened of the transformation. He could deal with her coldness, her anger. He wasn't sure how to handle this altered version of his wife. Nor was he comfortable with the look in her eyes. Something very unusual was going on, for he would swear when he'd first looked up to find her at the door there had been tears in her eyes. And for a moment, when their eyes had met, he'd felt a connection—a fraction of time they had communicated their awe, their amazement at the beginning of life.

Mentally shaking his head, he thought himself twice a fool if he believed in this strange metamorphosis. Christina was incapable of change . . . but she was a very good actress. Raising his eyes, he was relieved to find that she was gone. He looked to Eli who was helping the mare stand and said, "Once we get her up and about, we'll put them both into a new stall. This is our first, Eli. Let's take good care of them."

The black man smiled at his employer as he urged the mare upward. "If they're all as smooth as this one, we're gonna be building another new barn next year." He patted the mare's jaw as she finally stood. "Yes suh, Mista O'Mara. This here's gonna be one fine yard."

Sean smiled at Eli's enthusiasm, and stood next to the foal. Suddenly, he was very tired . . . too tired to sit across from Christina and match wits with her. The thought of dining with his wife held little pleasure, yet he knew he shouldn't miss this new performance. Perhaps, he would finally be able to catch her up, to detect something that would give her away—for soon he must talk about freedom, about the divorce.

She had supervised the setting of the table, personally arranged the spring flowers for its centerpiece; and was proud of her accomplishments. Kris felt almost like a wife waiting for approval. As Sean sat down opposite her, she noticed that his hair was still damp from his bath and she smiled at his surprised expression.

He didn't return her smile. "You did this?"

She nodded.

"Why?"

Kris's grin slowly faded. What was wrong with him now? "What do you mean *why?* I thought it would be nice. I thought . . ." She let her words trail off. She'd thought it was how they should dine . . . how he was used to dining. Angry with him for spoiling the mood she'd created for dinner, she clasped her hands together and looked at the glazed plate in front of her. Just when she was giving him the benefit of the doubt, just when she had decided he was a decent person, he insisted on being miserable.

She lifted her head and attempted to smile at Riva as the maid offered her a silver platter that contained ham, scalloped potatoes, and string beans. Serving herself, she quietly thanked the woman, then watched as Riva walked toward Sean. She could see he was puzzled by the entree, yet he remained silent as Riva placed the tray on the long mahogany sideboard and started to leave the dining room.

"Thank you, Riva," Kris said, smiling in response to the maid's nervous curtsey. "Please tell Mae she did a splendid job."

Ignoring the man at the other end of the long table, Kris concentrated on her meal. She was starved. And to think that she'd waited for him out of courtesy! Why in the world was she so afraid of him? It would take weeks before he could certify her insane and lock her in an asylum. And by then she had every intention of being in her own home—in her own time.

"Ham? I've never seen you eat it before."

Her chin lifted in defiance as she continued to chew the meat. Swallowing, she wiped her mouth and claimed, "I love it! Anything else you haven't

110

seen me eat? I really do have a great appetite."

He stopped chewing as he stared at her, and she could see he was startled. Grinning, Kris said, "I don't have to put up with your bad mood, you know. You're not going to make me feel guilty, because I wasn't the one who set out to frame you for murder."

He nearly choked on his food. Just as she was about to rise and offer assistance, he reached for his water goblet and drank half of it. Slamming the fragile glass back onto the table, he gasped, "By God, woman! Is there no end to your boldness?"

Kris shrugged her shoulders and very calmly cut another piece of meat. "I don't consider it bold to tell the truth." She raised her head and innocently stared back at him. "Unless, of course, you're using the word bold to denote courage or bravery. Then, I suppose, I should thank you for the compliment. As I told you last night, I'm not your wife. I'll go along with the charade for your servants and neighbors, but I want you to know that I don't deserve your resentment. I'm the innocent in this."

"Innocent!" His color was even darker than when he'd been choking. "Whatever tricks you are up to, madam, they'll not work with me. You're a good actress, Christina, but you forget I know you too well."

Kris chewed her food and nodded. "I'm not going to get angry. You can say whatever you want, but it's directed at the wrong person. My name is Kris, not Christina. I just look like her. Whatever problems you have with your wife are your business. I prefer to be kept out of them."

111

She was prepared for another outburst of anger; she was not prepared to see him sit back in his chair, look to the ceiling, and burst into laughter. When Mae rushed into the dining room, Kris was as bewildered as the cook. They both looked to O'Mara, then at each other. Kris shrugged, saying, "I have no idea why Mr. O'Mara is consumed with laughter. Do you?" Mae glanced once more at her employers and quietly backed out of the room.

As Sean wiped at his eyes, his grin widened. "You know, Christina . . . ah, Kris . . . I intended to speak to you about a divorce. Then, when you started talking a moment ago, I saw my way out. You've gone over the edge. You're completely irrational. Even the sheriff heard you this morning. I'm just going to give you a little time and let you hang yourself." He picked up his knife and fork and smiled. "In the meantime, I have to admit I'm beginning to find this transformation quite amusing. Please," he gestured with his knife, "keep speaking. This is definitely better than eating alone as we usually do. What other startling information do you have to impart?"

She was breathing deeply, trying to bring her anger under control. She'd tried being honest with him and he'd done exactly as she'd feared. The threat of being forced into an institution was the one thing that terrified her, especially since asylums were so primitive in 1871. So she'd play the role of his wife, be mistress of Rivanna, and face whatever surprises awaited her, but she would not let this man defeat her.

She looked at him as he ate, grinning and waiting

112

for her next words. Admitting that he was attractive didn't come easy, but what came even harder was the admission that she was attracted to *him*. He was old-fashioned, chauvinistic, and sarcastic. But she had seen him with others, and he could be kind. And, damn it, when he had laughed he'd been so appealing that she was shocked by her body's response. But she vowed that he wouldn't defeat her . . . neither by his sarcasm, his threats, nor his damned good looks.

Feeling his eyes on her, she picked up her water glass and sipped. As she replaced the crystal on the starched tablecloth, she raised her eyes to his and smiled.

"Do you prefer pizza, or Chinese food?"

He narrowed his blue eyes. "I beg your pardon?"

Kris picked up a forkful of potatoes, making him wait for her answer. Dabbing at her mouth with the napkin, she continued as pleasantly as if their previous conversation had never taken place. "Today, Mae was concerned about selecting menus for dinner. I was just wondering whether you liked Italian or Chinese food."

He stopped cutting the thick slice of ham on his plate and stared at her. "I've never had Chinese food. What —"

"That settles it," she interrupted, grinning like a fool. "Tomorrow, we have Italian."

Chapter Seven

Kris awoke the next morning, filled with determination. She was going to go into town to shop for dinner. After she told Mae how she wanted the chicken prepared, she was going to find O'Mara and ask for money. Last night as she'd fought for sleep, it had occurred to her that she really had nothing to fear. She could act any way she wanted. If she was pleasant to everyone, even Sean O'Mara, then he would have a hard time trying to convince anyone that she should be put away. Everyone might think she had changed, that she was a little absentminded, but she was going to make sure that they thought it was a change for the better.

Smiling, Kris hurried to get washed and dressed. She couldn't wait to start her new campaign to clear Christina's name. By the time she was through, O'Mara was going to be doubting his own sanity.

"Good morning, Sean."

His head snapped up from the ledger he was reading and his cup rattled back onto its saucer. He was dressed casually, his white shirt open at the collar and suspenders coming up from the black trousers he wore. He looked, she reluctantly admitted, very handsome in his old-fashioned clothes. Giving him a quick smile, she walked to the sideboard, poured herself a cup of coffee, and placed a cinnamon bun on a plate. Bringing her breakfast to the table, she sat opposite him and grinned.

"You're up early," he commented, closing the ledger and looking down the length of white linen. "Are you unwell?" He asked the question out of curiosity, for she had never looked better. The pale yellow dress highlighted the blondness of her hair and made her eyes more brown. And she looked . . . happy. He couldn't remember ever seeing her like this, not even before they married. There was definitely something different about her this morning.

Kris laughed. "Just because I'm awake when the rest of the house is up you think I'm unwell?" She shook her head, causing her curls to brush her shoulders. "I'm fine, Sean. And I'd like to talk to you about something before you go out to the stables."

He raised his eyebrows questioningly. "I can hardly wait to hear," he commented, bringing his cup to his mouth and resting against the back of his chair. Already, he looked amused.

She continued to smile, unwilling to let his superior attitude anger her. "I'm going to need money. I haven't any of my own."

115

He no longer looked amused. "Money? For what?"

"I'm going into town this morning to shop for food, and I'll have to pay for it somehow. Don't worry, I'll bring you back the change."

Ignoring her last comment, he leaned his elbows on the edge of the table and stared at her. "You're going into town? After what happened yesterday?"

Biting into her cinnamon bun, Kris nodded. She sipped the hot coffee and said, "I'm prepared. And anyway I'm just going shopping. It's not like I'm marching in there like Rambo. I intend to be very nice."

"Like who?"

She saw his confused expression; it was becoming increasingly familiar. "Rambo. A character from the movies. You see, he'd . . . Never mind. Look, can I have the money or not?"

He appeared startled. "Why do you talk like that? You know you don't need money. You've already established accounts at each store in Chestfield. Who is this Rambo person?" His eyes appeared to darken as he leaned against the table. "And what are movies?"

Kris laughed and finished her coffee. Standing up, she wiped her mouth and smiled. "Forget about Rambo, and you'll find out about movies in about forty years." Just before she disappeared through the doorway that led into the large kitchen, she turned back to him and grinned. "You're nothing like Rambo, Sean. You're more Remington Steele." She shook her head, as if daydreaming. "Too bad you'll never get the chance to see him . . ."

Quickly slipping into the kitchen, she closed the door behind her, but not before she heard Sean's annoyed command, *"Christina, get back in here and explain yourself!"*

Ignoring him, she stopped chuckling as she took in the surprised looks of the servants, and hurried to explain to Mae what she wanted done with the chicken.

An hour later, she found herself in Amos Mortrey's General Store. She held the baskets Tisha had given her close to her stomach as she slowly walked up the center aisle. The buzzing conversation of the shoppers had ceased at her appearance, and she could feel a dozen pairs of eyes following her every move. Kris had to admit she would feel better if she had allowed Tisha to accompany her, but she had refused to permit the pregnant woman to make the trip over unpaved roads. Instead, she had enlisted the help of an old black man named Walker, who served as her driver.

She had already asked the bewildered Walker to help her over her confusion by identifying anyone that approached them. As a small gray-haired man walked in their direction, she was grateful to hear Walker's whispered explanation that this was the proprietor of the store.

Kris raised her chin and smiled at the man. "Good morning, Mr. Mortrey. I hope you can help me," she added, placing her baskets on the polished wooden counter.

Amos Mortrey looked startled as he wet his lips for the second time and swallowed deeply. "Why, I certainly think we can, Miss Christina," he said, though there was a definite note of uncertainty in his voice. "What is it that you're looking for, ma'am?"

Kris's smile widened. He might have heard about yesterday's fiasco in front of the sheriff's office, he might even think she was a little bit crazy; but he was more than willing to do business with her. It was a beginning. "The first item I need is tomatoes—lots of them. Then olive oil, oregano—"

"But it's too early for tomatoes," Mortrey politely cut in, a look of confusion appearing on his face. "It'll be another two, three months before they come in." He gazed to his right, as if asking the other customers for affirmation.

Kris looked down the counter and saw an elderly woman nod her head. "Vile things," the woman muttered. "Poisonous—that's what they are!"

Turning back to the shopkeeper, Kris sighed. "Yes, well . . . despite all this, I still need tomatoes. Don't you have them canned or stewed or something?"

Mr. Mortrey again looked to his other customers. He scratched his chin, then snapped his fingers, as though magically finding the solution. "Mrs. Coscia! She came in here some months ago asking for them Eye-talion herbs. Had to order them clear from New Orleans for her. I'll just bet she can help you."

It was getting more complicated, yet Kris refused to give up. "And where can I find Mrs. Coscia?" she asked politely.

"The Coscias live over their shop," Mortrey said, his tone indicating that she should have known

118

that.

Picking up her baskets, Kris nodded to the man. "Well, thank you for your help, Mr. Mortrey." As she turned to face the other shoppers, she noticed a number of children hiding behind their mother's skirts and staring at her as if she were a curiosity. Knowing that stories must be being spread about town, Kris forced her lips into a smile and walked to the glass case that contained a wide assortment of candy. Looking back to the owner of the store, she called out, "Mr. Mortrey, please give each of the children whichever candy he or she chooses . . . . and charge it to the O'Mara account."

She heard childish gasps of delight and turned to gaze down at the blond-haired boy standing closest to her. "Jawbreakers used to be my favorite," she whispered to him. "You could make them last for an hour."

The boy giggled and pointed through the glass to the first row of candy. "Oklahoma Taffy's like that. You can chew on it till bedtime, then take it out, sit it on the windowsill, and pop it right back in when you wake up."

"Timothy Hendry! Mind what you say!" An embarrassed mother pushed her son behind her and tried to smile at the mistress of Rivanna. "Thank you for offering the candy, Miss Christina, but it's not necessary."

Kris smiled back at the young woman. "You're right. It isn't necessary, but it would give me pleasure to do it. Please let your son have his taffy. As a matter of fact, I think I'd like to take one with me."

She called to the shocked owner of the establishment. "Mr. Mortrey, may I try one of these Oklahoma Taffys? Mr. Timothy Hendry highly recommends them." She looked down to the child and winked. At least she had made one friend in Chestfield, she thought, taking the thick caramel-colored candy and placing it in one of the baskets.

"Mornin', Miz Amelia." Walker's voice called out the nervous greeting.

Slowly turning around, Kris faced the older woman who had pronounced tomatoes to be poisonous, vile things. Taking a deep breath, she plastered a smile on her face and extended her hand. The sour-faced woman's mouth dropped open as Kris pumped her gloved hand up and down. "How wonderful to see you again, Miss Amelia. I must say that springtime agrees with you." Letting go of the woman's fingers, Kris backed out of the shop, saying, "Now that the weather is pleasant, you simply must come to tea at Rivanna." She was amazed at how easily this acting was coming to her. All you had to do was get into character.

Miss Amelia hurried after her, following Kris out of the store. "Christina!" Something about the woman's voice stopped her. It had the same tone as the voices of the nuns who'd taught her and Danni at Villa Victoria.

Taking a deep breath, Kris turned back. "What can we do for you, Miss Amanda? Walker and I were just on our way to Mrs. Coscia's home."

The older woman was dressed entirely in black, which further enhanced Kris's comparison of her to a stern nun, and the deep frown lines around

Miss Amelia's mouth sharpened the impression. "Christina, for the sake of your parents' memories, I do wish you'd explain yourself! You're acting most irrational!"

Kris looked back through the window of Mortrey's store and saw the man handing out candy to a line of children. "Is it irrational to buy taffy for a few children?" she asked, wondering why the woman thought it was any of her business.

Amelia Markhem shook her head, causing her small hat to tilt to one side. "Well, I've never seen you do it before, but that isn't all I'm talking about. Where in heaven's name have you been? Why do you talk like a Northerner? And what was that scene about yesterday at Sheriff Loftis's office?"

Kris continued to stare at her. Not anticipating that anyone would be so rude as to directly question her, she hadn't prepared an answer. And what could she say? Especially to this woman, who Kris instinctively felt was the town gossip.

The entire community was speculating on the mystery of Christina Mattson O'Mara, and Amelia was sorely disappointed when she realized that the young woman wasn't about to reply. "The Mattson family was always held in high esteem in this county, even in the state," she muttered, her lips pursed with bitterness. It would have been such a coup to be the one with the answers, she thought. Even the Hart sisters didn't know where Christina had been, though the Lord knew they'd been regaling everyone in earshot with their description of the day she'd disappeared! For the first time in years,

Amelia Markhem felt her position of influence in the town was in jeopardy — and all because the high and mighty Christina had chosen not to invite her to Lynette Taylor's birthday party. If she'd disliked Christina before, her ill feelings for the younger woman were now intensified.

Amelia's eyes narrowed. There was something very different about Christina, something she couldn't identify yet. "I suppose we can only be grateful that Silas and Rachel aren't here to see what you've done to their good name, missy. This scandal you've caused is shocking to us all."

Kris had to bite back a smart answer. Exactly what gave this woman the right to scold her? From everything she had learned, Christina had had a bad temper, but she was determined not to let this woman bait her. Kris smiled a little sadly. "I'm sorry you feel that way, Miss Amelia, but thank you for sharing your observations with me."

It was with a certain degree of satisfaction that Kris watched Miss Amelia's lower jaw drop down to the black bow that was tied under her chin.

"I suppose this means you won't be coming to Rivanna for tea," Kris stated, while motioning to Walker to move on. Just before they turned, she added, "Oh well, perhaps another time. Do have a pleasant day, Miss Amelia." And then she presented her back to the woman.

Walking in front of the store windows, Kris could see the townspeople watching their progress. It wasn't going exactly as she had planned this morning, for it took a supreme effort on her part to smile and act the part of a normal woman when everything about her was abnormal. She didn't know these people, or this town. She didn't even know how to shop in this time. As she and Walker stood in front of store named Coscia's Bootery, she wondered if it was possible to obtain the ingredients for an Italian dinner from a shoe store.

Shaking her head, she looked to her companion. "I don't have any money, Walker. Ah . . . do you?"

The older man shrugged. "Not with me, ma'am."

Kris looked at the display of leather boots and old-fashioned shoes with hooks and eyes. "Do you know if we have an account here?" she asked, glad that the man was with her.

He scratched the side of his face and looked down to the wooden-planked sidewalk. "You and Mista' Sean get your shoes up in Richmond, I think; but it seems to me that Miz Beth had some ridin' boots made up here. Yup, I'm sure of it," he announced, a smile brightening his whiskered face. "Musta' had an account here then."

"Wonderful! Do you need boots, Walker?" she asked, looking down to his feet.

"Ma'am?"

Seeing that his boots were worn, the leather starting to crack, she took hold of his arm and led him to the shop door. "Well, I have to buy *something,* don't I, before I ask to charge the tomatoes, oil, and oregano to Rivanna's account. After all, this is not exactly an Italian market. C'mon, let's go order your boots, Walker. I have dinner to make!"

Two hours later, Kris had Rivanna's kitchen

smelling like the finest Italian restaurant in New York City . . . thanks to Mrs. Coscia. With Mae's help, Kris had forced the preserved tomatoes through a meat grinder screwed to the edge of the kitchen table. Riva was busy grating cheese, while Sada stood over a skillet and fried day-old chunks of bread in olive oil to make croutons.

Stirring the tomato sauce, Kris inhaled and grinned. It had worked. She knew it was a small thing, making a dish unusual in this place and time, but she hadn't been defeated — not by the town or by the time in which she found herself. It was a minor victory, but it did prove to her that she could survive, that she could make her way in the past if she had to. And she felt good, almost happy, for the first time in days.

"Now, after we let it simmer for a few hours," she told Mae, as she picked up a washed bowl and began drying it, "we'll pour it over the prepared chicken, sprinkle the cheese on top, and bake it. It wasn't so hard, was it?"

Mae looked up from her basin of dirty pots and pans. "Miz Christina, when'd you learn how to cook?" she asked. After spending the afternoon with her mistress, Mae actually found herself taking a liking to the young woman. It surprised and shocked her. If Miz Christina had hit her head on a rock or something, and this friendly person was the result, she only regretted that it hadn't happened years ago. Or better yet at birth, for Miz Christina was a handful right from the start. Though since Miz Rachel had passed on, her daughter had become even more spoiled and bossy than before.

This new agreeable mistress was a welcome change for the better.

"I . . . ah, I decided to experiment with foods from other countries," Kris quickly answered. "Wait until you taste the pasta Mrs. Coscia sold me. She'd just made it this morning."

Mae looked to the thin, hard noodles lying on a piece of brown paper. "Mista Sean don't like noodles. He likes his potatoes."

Kris placed a large empty pot on the stove. She would use it later. "This isn't just noodles, Mae," she said, picking up her long dish towel. "This is *spaghetti* . . . everyone likes spaghetti. You'll see. I bought enough for all of us."

Mae and Riva glanced to one another as if to say they doubted her words, yet neither wanted to upset their mistress, especially when the afternoon was going along so well.

Catching the exchanged look, Kris grinned. "I felt the same way about Chinese food, until I'd tasted it. Now I love it."

Mae's head jerked up from her washing. "You gonna be cookin' Chinese food next?" she asked with a note of horror.

Kris laughed out loud and threw her dish towel over her shoulder. "Don't worry. I wouldn't even know where to begin to shop for *that*. You'll get your kitchen back tomorrow, Mae. I won't bother you again, except on occasion." Once more she inhaled the fragrant herbs that seasoned the tomato sauce. God, it smelled terrific, and her stomach was already rumbling in anticipation of dinner.

"I do think I'd like to experiment with pizza, though," she speculated aloud. "I'll bet Tisha would like it. I remember reading once that pregnant women have a peculiar fondness for pizza." Kris looked up to her companions. Ignoring their astonished expressions, she asked, "Where is Tisha? Has anyone seen her this afternoon?"

Sada cleared her throat. "She'd be pressin' off in the laundry." The young woman nodded her head toward a hallway that led away from the kitchen. "That's where I seen her last."

Telling the others that she'd be back in a minute, Kris left them to search for Tisha. She found the pregnant woman in a small room that was filled with the aroma of strong soap. Several large tin basins stood empty while Tisha picked up a heavy-looking iron from a narrow stove and applied it to the blouse Kris had been wearing on her birthday.

"Tisha! Are you all right?" Kris ran up behind her as the small woman dropped the iron onto a metal plate and grabbed her back, as if in pain.

Breathing heavily, Tisha tried to smile. "Just . . . just one of them spasms again. I'll finish in . . . in a minute, Miz Christine."

Kris was horrified that Tisha, obviously in distress, still felt she had to work. What kind of monster was O'Mara? Angry, she pulled a chair up behind Tisha and slammed her hand down on the ironing board. "Don't you dare touch this blouse," she ordered in a voice shaking with fury. "Just sit in the chair and wait until I get back. Damn it! This is too much!"

Storming out of the house, she crossed the lawn

126

in long, angry strides until she reached the newer stable. When she found Sean, he was leading a horse into a large stall, coaxing the animal with a softly accented voice.

"Ah . . . little lady. To be sure you're a bit nervous about all this. Come along. . . . We've prepared the very best —"

"I want to speak with you," Kris stated, her lower lip and chin beginning to quiver with a tightly held fury. My God, the man talked to the animal as if it were human! And she couldn't help noticing that his Irish accent became thicker, more pronounced, as if he thought his Celtic charm would prove irresistible to the beast.

Sean looked over his shoulder and gave her an impatient shake of his head. "It will have to be later. I'm in the middle of settling this mare into —"

"Now!" Placing her fists on her hips, she held her ground. "This won't wait."

He nodded to the groomsman, and watched as Eli urged the mare into the stall. Turning around to face her, he pushed his hair back off his forehead and demanded, "Exactly, what is wrong, Christina? I'm very busy right now."

"You're busy? With your pregnant horses?" She grabbed the dish towel that still hung over her shoulder and snapped it against the side of the stall. "Well, what about Tisha? Do you value a human life less than that horse in there?"

Sean could feel the muscles in his neck tighten with indignation, and he ground his teeth together to control his anger. "I think you had better explain yourself, madam!"

She ignored the darkening of his blue eyes and the twitching of the muscle under his cheekbone. She wouldn't back down. "I am talking about Tisha . . . and about maternity leave!"

Again, he pushed his black hair away from his forehead, as if the gesture would help him understand what she was saying. "I beg your pardon? Tisha? What's wrong with her?"

Kris watched as Eli's head popped out of the doorway of the stall. Looking back at O'Mara, she raised her chin. "What kind of monster are you to demand that a pregnant woman, a *very* pregnant woman, continue working? I found her ironing my blouse . . . and she was in pain! She should be off her feet, not slaving over a hot iron."

Sean turned to Eli. "Go find her, Eli, and take her to your cabin," he told the anxious man, before turning back to Kris. "Is she in labor?"

Kris watched Eli break into a run; then she spun around to again face O'Mara. "I don't know. She said she's having spasms. I . . . I suppose it could be labor." She shook her head to clear it. She hadn't expected him to be so concerned. "What I want to talk to you about is the way you treat your employees," she declared, striving to get back on track. "Demanding that a member of your staff work this far into her pregnancy is unconscionable. If I had wanted that blouse ironed, I'm perfectly capable of doing it myself!"

Sean's head jerked back, as though from shock; then, unbelievably, he burst into laughter. He was actually *laughing* at her! Infuriated, Kris instinc-

128

tively reached for the closest weapon at hand. She brought up the dish towel and began thrashing him about the head and shoulders.

"You insufferable idiot! What the hell is so funny?"

Chapter Eight

Still laughing, Sean crossed his arms over his face to protect himself and backed away from her. Even though the towel could do little damage, she was wielding it like a saber, slashing at him like a trained swordsman. When he heard nervous sounds coming from the mare, Sean reached out and grabbed his wife's shoulders, rendering her arms immobile.

"Stop this, Christina," he whispered, still chuckling. "What's come over you?"

Kris looked up into his eyes, those startlingly blue eyes, and stopped struggling to break free. It was an unconscious response. Her body just refused to move. It is his touch, she thought frantically. He had touched her for the first time. Breathing in deeply, she tried to ignore the manner in which his black-Irish hair fell over onto his forehead, the astonishing way his eyes reflected the same laughter that she heard coming from his mouth. But in truth, she knew it was his smile that had stopped her dead. It was genuine . . .

and it was the very first time she had seen it directed toward her. Dear God, he had dimples! What was even harder to admit was that the closeness of his body was arousing very unpredictable emotions in her. From somewhere deep in her subconscious, she heard a small voice tell her that the situation was dangerous, that somehow she had lost control of the encounter. Her conscious mind shouted at her to ignore everything and concentrate on how well his white cotton shirt defined the muscles of his arms and chest, how his smile slowly left his mouth, how his beautiful eyes lost the laughter and became darker, almost haunted, hungry.

She knew that look; she felt that way herself. Blinking several times, she gasped as he abruptly released her and stepped back, away from her, as if distancing himself would break the spell. Kris felt the invisible wall immediately go back up between them, and fought to regain her own composure. "I . . . I'm sorry," she said in a low, unsteady voice. She feebly waved the dish towel between them. "I should never have struck you. I don't know why I . . . What I mean is, I'm not usually that—"

"I suppose I might have used more caution in laughing at you," he interrupted, pushing back his hair. He expelled his breath in a frustrated rush and lifted his chin. "Would you care to explain more calmly what the problem is with Tisha?"

She could see he was embarrassed, and decided the best way to handle the situation was to pretend that it had never occurred. Clearing her

131

throat, she took a deep breath. "As I explained earlier, I don't think you should ask someone in your employ to work this late in her pregnancy. Especially at something like ironing, where she's on her feet the entire time. I think Tisha should be given maternity leave." Why did she feel so foolish? Where had all her anger gone? Her mind tormented her with a dozen accusing questions.

He checked on the mare, then closed the door to the stall. "Maternity leave?" He motioned for them to leave the stable. "You wouldn't mind explaining that term, would you? What exactly are you trying to say?"

She kept her distance, a good two feet separating them as they walked down the long corridor that divided the stable in two. "When a woman is pregnant," she said slowly, wishing she could regain some of her former indignation, "she should be given time off early enough so that she can prepare."

"Prepare what?" Sean asked, squinting in the sunlight as he turned his face to look into hers.

Walking toward the house, Kris shrugged her shoulders. "Whatever she has to prepare . . ." Why did she suddenly feel so inadequate? So dense? "For all the changes," she quickly added. "The changes in her body, in her home, in her life! Tisha says she's due any day. She shouldn't have been working for the last month — at least. She should have been resting."

He stopped dead in his tracks and stared at her back. *"You're* saying Tisha should be resting? That she shouldn't have been working?"

Kris turned around and nodded her head. "And you shouldn't have expected it of her," she said. "It isn't right, Sean."

His mouth dropped open as he continued to stare. Made uneasy by the look in his eyes, Kris quickly turned back to the house. She could hear him following her, yet neither said another word until they had entered Rivanna and walked through its rooms. "Tisha's in the laundry," Kris commented, as he silently followed her into the deserted kitchen.

They could hear a commotion and exchanged glances before quickly moving down the hallway to the laundry. Kris stopped at the doorway and looked at the bizarre scene. Tisha was crying hysterically. Still seated in the chair, she had buried her head in her arms while hanging onto the ironing board. Eli stood behind her, feebly patting her back, while Riva, Sada, and Mae stood off to one side, shaking their heads.

Immediately, Kris entered the room and hurried to Tisha's side. "What's wrong, now?" she demanded. "Are the pains worse?"

Tisha's eyes were a liquid brown, as she lifted her face, and her tortured expression tore through Kris's heart.

"Please, Miz Christina, don't send me away! I'll do just like you say . . . only *please* let me stay!"

Kris stiffened. "What are you talking about? Why would I send you away?"

Tisha sniffled and wiped her eyes on her arm. Her lips trembled as she tried to control her tears. "You said you'd send me away . . . without . . .

without Eli. You said if me and my baby caused any trouble, you'd . . . you'd send me away from Rivanna. I couldn't take care of this baby alone, Miz Christina! Not without Eli!"

Kris felt everyone's eyes on her. She could sense the unspoken accusation, the condemnation. In that moment, she hated Christina far more than anyone in that room. What kind of monster was that woman to manipulate everyone? Swallowing several times, she straightened her shoulders and brushed a tear off Tisha's chin.

"I want you to listen to me, Tisha," she said in a low, controlled voice. "If I ever said that to you, I apologize. I don't remember. I've explained to Mr. O'Mara about maternity leave . . . time off for you to get ready for the baby. I don't want you working until after the baby is born and you've had time to recover. I want you to rest. Do you understand what I'm saying?"

She lifted her head and looked to the others in the room. They were literally gaping at each other in surprise. Turning back to the pregnant woman, she smiled. "Do you understand, Tisha?" Kris repeated. "You'll still have your job. It'll be waiting for you when you're ready to return."

"I can't come to Rivanna no more?" The crying had stopped, but there was a look of banishment on Tisha's face.

Kris smiled. "Don't be silly. Come to the house anytime if it makes you feel better, but I don't want to see you picking up an iron. I don't want to see you doing any housework. When you come, just sit at the kitchen table and talk to Mae and

Riva and Sada. No more working until after the baby is born. All right?"

Amazed, Tisha looked up to her husband, and Kris watched as Eli's mouth broke into a smile.

"Thank you, Miz Christina. I'll take her back to our cabin now, if that's all right." Eli helped his wife to stand.

Satisfied with the outcome of the incident, Kris nodded. "You do that, Eli." She lifted her nose and inhaled. "Right now, I think I'd better check on that sauce."

Turning to leave, she heard a soft "Thank you."

Looking back, she smiled at Tisha and winked. "You just take care of yourself and have a healthy baby." Grinning, she followed Mae, Sada, and Riva from the room. As she passed Sean, she noticed the bewildered expression in his eyes and added, "Wait until you taste what we're having for dinner!"

He stood just inside the deserted laundry and stared at the empty room. It's like she's another woman, he thought, totally confused. Was that really Christina telling a servant *not* to work? *Christina?* What could have happened to her to alter her personality so drastically? He shook his head and walked farther into the room. Unconsciously, he picked up the blouse Tisha had been ironing. Was it all an act, part of her plan to disarm everyone? Dropping the blouse back onto the ironing board, he noticed a satin tag at its collar and again picked it up. His eyes narrowed as he read: Liz Claiborne. Underneath it was a smaller tag, the material of this one not as expen-

sive. It, too, had printing: 100% Pima Cotton—
Machine Washable—Line Dry.

He looked around the room, completely confused. This was the blouse Christina had been
wearing the night she'd returned, for at the bottom of the board were her trousers, neatly folded.
What in the world was Pima Cotton? And *machine* washable? What kind of machine would
wash clothes without ripping them to shreds?
Shaking his head, he threw the blouse back and
jammed his hands into his pockets.

She was a mystery.

Something had happened to her during her disappearance, causing her speech, dress, and behavior to undergo a drastic change. Was it true she
was not in her right mind? If that were so, how
could he ever hope for a divorce?

Immediately, and without conscious thought,
he pictured her in the stable, slicing the air with
her dish towel. She had looked magnificent, her
riotous curls floating about her face as she'd advanced on him. Instinct had driven him to stop
her, to grasp her shoulders and halt her attack.
Yet the moment he had touched her, quieting her
as he would one of the horses, he had realized his
mistake. A foreign, nearly forgotten, emotion had
surged through him, rendering him incapable of
any thought—except how adorable she looked.
Studying her, he'd been shocked by the sexual pull
of her small body. In that moment, that fraction
of time, he had wanted her. Even now, it amazed
him that he'd managed to break her spell before
he embarrassed himself.

She was right to have called him an idiot. Only someone devoid of intellect would want a woman like Christina. Why had it been so difficult to summon up his aversion? His resentment? Yet there had been something so different about her . . . then. In a brief flash, he had recognized the vulnerability in her eyes, the surprise, the desire. . . .

"Damn her!" He issued the muffled curse while striding from the room. Avoiding the kitchen, he slammed the back door and told himself that it had been too long since he'd been to Miss Aggie's establishment in Richmond. What other possible reason could there be for him to be desiring his own wife? Surely, even God was laughing at his foolishness.

"What do you call this?"

Summoning up her patience, Kris smiled at the man seated at the other end of the table. "It's called Chicken Parmesan. And that's called spaghetti," she said, pointing to his plate. "Try it."

The look on his face said he doubted that he would enjoy it. He picked up his knife and fork, and was about to cut into the chicken, when he seemed to have second thoughts, and stopped. "We don't usually have foreign food," he pronounced, as if that would explain his hesitation.

"It's Italian!" she countered. "What are you afraid of? Don't tell me you think tomatoes are poisonous?"

He sat up straighter. "Of course not!" Challenged, he vigorously cut into the chicken and jammed a forkful of food into his mouth.

She watched him chew, her fingers nervously lacing together while waiting for his verdict. She had already tasted the meal before dinner and knew it was delicious. She found herself swallowing with him as he turned his attention to the pasta. He didn't say anything, just struggled with the spaghetti until he managed to place a few strands in his mouth. He looked helpless and she couldn't help smiling as she watched him suck in the remains of a long noodle. Impatient, she let a reckless giggle escape her when she saw the smudge of tomato sauce on his chin.

Ignoring his glare, she asked, "Well? What do you think?"

With a refined ease, he picked up his napkin and wiped his mouth and chin. Raising his head, he replied, "Please ring for Mae."

"But did you enjoy it? I *knew* you'd like it!"

He ignored her and nodded to the crystal bell in front of her plate. "Please. Call Mae."

Confused, Kris gave the bell a shake and placed it back on the table. "Is something wrong?" she asked in disbelief.

Before he could answer her, Mae entered the dining room. "Mae, have we any ham left from last night's dinner?" he asked calmly.

The cook nodded, then looked to Kris.

"Would you please make me up a plate of that and any other leftover food you can find? I don't think Italian food agrees with me."

138

Both women stared at him in amazement. Unsure of what to say, Mae quickly left the room and returned to the kitchen.

Breathing deeply in her anger, Kris asked, "Do you have any idea how difficult this was to prepare? Of the trouble I went through? There's nothing wrong with this meal . . . and you know it."

"That may be the case, my dear, but it doesn't appeal to me. My tastes are more simple—"

"I don't think you have any taste!"

His look was insulting, as if evaluating her worth. "You may be right, Christina."

How could she have thought him exotic or charming or sexy only that afternoon? She berated herself for falling for his Irish blarney. Sean O'Mara was nothing more than a chauvinist boor! She tore her eyes away from his and forced her attention to the plate in front of her. With sudden determination, she then squared her shoulders and began to eat.

It's good! *Damned* good, she thought viciously. He is only saying differently to be spiteful, to be mean. Her stomach knotted with anger as she twirled the spaghetti around her fork. Damn him! He wanted to incite her. He wanted to see her lose control. Well, if she had survived this afternoon's crisis with Tisha, she could manage to get through dinner . . . and somehow enjoy it.

Ignoring him, she continued to eat, making appreciative noises to further annoy him. She smiled at Mae when the older woman brought in the ham and then told herself that nothing more could go wrong this day. All she had to do was endure this meal and retreat to the frilly bedroom upstairs. There would be time enough, when she was alone, to let out her frustration.

It was as if God had heard her thoughts, for through the open window she heard the sounds of a horse and carriage. Both she and Sean looked up from their dinner and stared at one another, each wondering who could be visiting Rivanna . . . and each dreading the prospect of company.

The heavy front door burst open and they could hear a young female voice echoing through the foyer.

"Sean! Sean! I'm home! Where are you?"

Sean O'Mara's expression relaxed and he sat back in his chair. "It's Beth," he pronounced, grinning.

Kris felt a heaviness in her chest. "Beth?" she said weakly.

He nodded. "Your sister . . . she's come home."

Chapter Nine

She stood up with Sean, her heart pounding against her rib cage, an intense cluster of dread knotting in her stomach. God — Christina's sister! Clutching the edge of the table, she waited. . . .

Beth reminded Kris of a whirlwind as she ran into the dining room and flung herself against Sean's chest. She was a flurry of dark brown curls and green and white material.

"Oh, Sean! I'm so glad to be back!" The young girl lifted her head and looked at Sean's face. "I left the academy as soon as I got your telegram. But I heard Christina's back. Wayne Saunders, down at the station, said that she was craz—"

Sean looked up and turned the young girl around. "Christina returned two days ago."

Kris watched as Beth's face was transformed with surprise. It was difficult to stand at the table and look at the girl . . . *it was like staring into a mirror!* Although Beth's hair and eyes were dark brown; the thin, freckled face was the one that she had grown up with. It was more than familiar; it was frightening.

"How are you, Beth?" she asked in a low, nervous voice. It took a supreme effort to force her lips into a smile.

Beth stepped away from Sean and slowly walked down the length of the table. Her eyes seemed to bore into Kris's, as if searching for something. Her movements were gradual, deliberate, as though she had to force herself to come forward. Standing next to Kris, Beth leaned toward her and kissed the air by Kris's ear. "I'm fine, Christina. You look . . . different."

Blinking several times, Kris smiled at both Beth and Sean. "It must be my hair. I . . . I cut it." She sat back down in her chair and motioned to the empty seats at the table. "You must be starved, Beth." Her voice sounded excited, impulsive; and she tried to control it. "Why don't you join us for dinner?"

Seeing the young girl approach a chair closer to Sean, she watched as he pulled it out for her, then patted Beth's shoulder before returning to his own seat. As she picked up the crystal bell and rang for Mae, Kris filed away the gesture. It appeared that Sean and his young sister-in-law got along far better than Sean and his wife.

"I'm not going back to Wescott's," Beth blurted out as soon as Sean was seated. "I figured I'd better tell you that right off."

Kris looked at Sean, hoping he would handle the girl. She wasn't exactly sure what Beth was talking about. She might have meant that she didn't intend to return to school, but rather than make a mistake, Kris decided to remain silent.

"We'll talk of this later, Beth," Sean advised as Mae entered the dining room and squealed her delight over the youngest Mattson's homecoming.

"Oh, child! You're home?" Mae fussed over the teenager, filling the girl's plate and asking a dozen questions.

Grinning, Sean said, "I'm sure Beth will tell us all about her journey after she's eaten. You are hungry, aren't you, lass?"

Kris watched as Mae rushed to the sideboard and opened a drawer. Taking out a napkin and silverware, the cook hurried back to the table. "I'm goin' to send Riva and Sada right upstairs to get your room ready. You come in the kitchen for a visit now, after you get settled. I'll have somethin' special waitin' for you, like always."

"I'll be there, Mae," the girl promised. "Right now, I can't wait to taste this dinner. I could smell it as soon as I opened the door. What is it?"

Mae glanced at Kris.

"It's called Chicken Parmesan." Kris held her breath as the young girl tasted it.

Beth looked up at Mae. "Why, it's delicious! So colorful and exotic!"

"Miz Christina cooked it, not me, child."

Beth looked past Mae and Kris could see her happiness turn into surprise. Quickly, the girl's amazement became a sullen scowl. "It's very good, Christina."

Closing her eyes briefly, Kris managed a smile, Oh God, she thought, not her, too! Christina's own sister dislikes her. Her appetite completely lost, Kris felt isolated from the animated conversation at the table. She tried to listen as Beth told Sean about her trip from the academy, how the headmistress of her school had found a chaperone in South Carolina who was traveling to Virginia, how the older woman stayed with her on the train the entire time. She really concentrated, but couldn't seem to focus her attention on the conversation. If there was anyone who could call her a fraud, an imposter, it was this young girl . . . the sister of the woman she was impersonating. With ever-increasing panic, Kris knew her time was running out.

"If you'll excuse me," she murmured, pushing herself away from the table and standing up, "I think I'll go upstairs."

Seeing Beth and Sean look at her with surprise, she tried to smile. "Ah . . . I have a headache," she said feebly. Before leaving the table, she added, "Welcome home, Beth."

Kris stopped outside the dining room and leaned her head against the wall for support. What was she going to do now? How long could she hope to fool Beth, when there wasn't any way to avoid her?

From beyond the wall, she heard the girl's voice. "She seems so different. Her voice . . . it sounded strange. What happened? What's wrong with her, Sean?"

Kris's stomach tightened when she heard his reply. "I don't know yet, lass. But you can be sure I'm going to find out."

The sweet spring breeze blew over her body, caressing it like the soft fingers of a lover. Inhaling,

Kris turned to the window and reluctantly opened her eyes. For a few seconds she was able to pretend that everything was normal . . . that the dream had been fantastic, but was only a dream. Then her brain kicked into gear, her heart beat more rapidly, and she turned away from the window . . . immediately depressed. Hugging the pillow to her chest, Kris stared out at the room. She was starting to hate Christina's bedroom with all it's frills and ribbons and lace.

Ever since she'd left last night's dinner table, she had been holed up in this room, avoiding Sean for Beth, trying to sort out her thoughts. But there were too many things to remind her of Christina here, too many personal reminders of the woman she was supposed to be impersonating. Kicking back the covers, Kris suddenly decided to get dressed, to get out of the house and think everything through . . . for something instinctual, an unexplained inner sense, again told her it wouldn't be long before someone found her out.

He saw her walking toward a pasture and wondered what she was doing outside so early. He leaned against the open stable door and watched her. She had on a skirt and blouse and riding boots, and even from this distance, he reluctantly admitted that she looked appealing. It was strange to think that he could find her fascinating. He told himself that he was only interested in seeing how she was going to handle herself now that Beth was home. Christina and Beth had been at odds with each other since he had first come to Rivanna. And although Christina had been the accomplished actress for the last few days, now that Beth had returned if she was going to show her true face and slip up, it would happen soon. Christina had never been able to fool Beth—that was why the older sister had resented the younger—and Beth was genuinely liked by all who knew her.

From the corner of his eye, he saw young Harry Gentry walking in the direction of Christina. A wry grin appeared on Sean's lips. He crossed his arms over his chest and watched Christina stop by a fence to gaze out over the pasture as the young man came closer. Now, this should prove interesting, he thought, wishing there wasn't such a great distance between them. He would dearly love to overhear this confrontation.

Kris inhaled the fresh morning air and stared out at the beautiful scene before her, trying to clear her head. Spring at Rivanna was a sight to behold. As far as the eye could see lay a patchwork quilt of green pastures surrounded by an endless chain of white fence. Horses nibbled the grass, grazing on the dew-laden sprouts. It looked serene, genteel—

"Miss Christina?"

Spinning around, Kris saw the teenage boy who had thrown dirt at her in Chestfield. She watched him jam his fists into his pockets and kick at the ground with the tip of his boot. Knowing he was uncomfortable, Kris found it easier to smile. "Good morning."

The boy cleared his throat. "I've come to apologize to you for what I did in town."

Kris nodded. "Your name's Harry, isn't it?" She saw his eyes narrow, as though she should have remembered his name. He inclined his head. "Well, I'll tell you, Harry, there are some things that I can't recall too easily. But I do remember that day," she added with a small laugh. "Do you want to tell me why you did it?"

He looked beyond her to the grazing horses and Kris could see he was a little older that she had first thought—maybe fifteen or sixteen. And he was proud. "I'd really like to know, Harry."

Harry Gentry's young mind was totally confused. Coming here to Rivanna had taken every ounce of his courage, for if he had hated Miss Christina before, he had been terrified to stand face to face with her since she went crazy. Everybody in town was talking about it. You couldn't even walk into Mortrey's and check on mail without hearing a new story about Crazy Christina. That's what everybody was calling her behind her back. Now, looking at her, she seemed so normal, even nice. She didn't even seem mad about what he'd done. How could he explain it to her? He'd thrown that mud ball for a lot of reasons, but he guessed the main one was what she'd been saying about his family.

His anger returning, he took a deep breath. "You hadn't any right to call the Gentrys no-accounts! My father was a hero! Died at Gettysburg a hero! And he was the best lawyer around these parts, even practiced in Richmond. Everybody knows that if it wasn't for the war, my father would have been elected to public office . . . maybe even been governor or senator. We're as good as the Mattsons!" He would not wipe at the tears forming in his eyes. He was the man in his family now. "Even better," he

147

added in a trembling voice, " 'cause we'd never look down our noses at neighbors who fell on bad times. If it wasn't for Mr. O'Mara, you'd be no better off than the rest of us—and everybody knows it!"

"Harry!" Kris reached out to touch his arm, but the boy flinched away from her. She shook her head in sorrow. What a bitch Christina was . . . and now *she* had to listen to Harry's anger and somehow apologize for the horrible things the woman had said. "I'm sorry. I don't know what else to say."

It was the truth. Kris was at a loss for words. "She . . . I must not have been well. You see, there's so much that I don't know or remember right now. Please, Harry, can you possibly accept my apology?"

The young man was shocked. It was not what he had expected to hear. "Your apology?"

Kris nodded and tried to smile. "I think perhaps you were justified in throwing that mud ball." Her smile widened, and she couldn't help adding, "You have a pretty good arm there. Ever think about playing professional baseball?"

Shaking his head, he refused to crack a smile. "I'm going to be a lawyer, like my father. That's why I work here three days a week. Whatever I save, Mr. O'Mara's going to match it. Going to go to William and Mary, like all the Gentrys."

Kris nodded, as though she really did remember. "You like Mr. O'Mara, don't you?"

Looking to the stables, Harry finally smiled. "Besides my uncle, I guess he's the best friend I have now . . . 'cept Beth, of course." He looked at the ground and again let his toe scrape the earth. "I heard she came home last night. She staying long?" Once more, his voice sounded defiant, his words challenging. He was testing her.

Kris could only surmise the other reasons why Harry Gentry disliked Christina O'Mara. From the look on the boy's face, it was obvious he had expected her to be upset by his words. Christina must have tried to stop Harry from seeing Beth, telling him that the Gentry's were not good enough any longer to associate with—No wonder Harry was so angry.

She looked back at the large home. "Beth joined us for dinner last night. I'm sure she's awake by now." She had to hide her grin. "I suppose I should have told Mae that I was going to take a walk before breakfast. You know, Harry, you'd be doing me a favor if you would stop by the house and tell her for me."

He took a step backward, toward the huge mansion. "I don't mind," he said, trying to sound casual.

Kris could see the eagerness in his face as he waited for his dismissal. Knowing he had to go to work in the stables, she realized it would only be more cruel to detain him. Taking a deep breath, she nodded toward the house. "Just tell Mae I want to stay out here for a little while longer."

"Yes, ma'am."

"And, Harry. I'm glad we talked," she added.

"Yes, ma'am." Properly discharged, Harry Gentry ran across the lawn as fast as his young legs could carry him.

Kris chuckled. So that was the way it was—Harry

149

Gentry had a crush on Beth. And she would just bet that Beth's refusal to return to school had something to do with Harry. Grinning, Kris shook her head. Young love. It can be so painful and confusing. . . .

She turned back to the picture-perfect scene of the grazing mares and foals. It was the ideal backdrop for an interview. For a few seconds, she imagined herself in her old life—microphone in hand, ready for the camera. Who would she most like to speak with? Who would give her the best interview? Her mind immediately told her the answer—*Christina*. How she would love to see the woman, speak with her, find out what had driven her to become such a hated person. She sighed with resignation. Maybe Christina didn't recognize her problems, or fathom the solutions. Perhaps, the woman would never be able to provide answers to her behavior, but Kris knew she would sacrifice her grandmother's Monet painting to be given the opportunity to find out. What an interview that would be! Poor Irv wouldn't know what to do with it. Her smile was sad as she thought about her boss. What was happening right now in Philadelphia? What were they doing to find her? She could just imagine her friends, especially Danni, flying down to Virginia and tearing up the state in search of her. God, she missed them!

"I'm surprised you didn't have the lad kneel down and beg your forgiveness." For the life of him, Sean couldn't explain it. It was as though he had been drawn like a moth to the flame of her strawberry blond hair. He couldn't tell himself why he had left the stables and walked in her direction. He only felt foolish for doing so.

She turned around at the sound of his voice. Her hair, shining in the early morning sun, was pinned up on top of her head with combs, making her seem even younger. It didn't help him that the slight breeze had freed a number of curls to delicately frame her face. Looking at her, he felt that same unnamed emotion that had caused him to seek her out. It was also what had caused him to speak sharply to her, hoping somehow he could regain his dignity.

He felt the tightness in his stomach spread lower as she smiled, not only with her mouth, but also with her eyes. Although a little sad, it was a genuine smile.

"I know what you're trying to do, Sean O'Mara, and it isn't going to work. I won't let you provoke me."

She said it quietly, and with such conviction, that he was taken back. Again she smiled, and it was annoyingly serene. He felt compelled to speak. "Christina . . . let's be honest; let's drop this charade. No one can hear us down here." He tried to intimidate her with a piercing look. "Why are you doing this? And how long do you expect to keep it up?"

He was much taller than she was, stronger and more powerful, yet he no longer frightened her. She was far more concerned with a young teenaged girl. Looking back out over the tranquil pasture, Kris decided that to survive the next few days she must know what had happened right before Christina's disappearance. Not what the paper had reported.

She wanted to know what really had happened between Sean and his wife. Now was as good a time as any to find out.

"I know you don't believe me, but I really don't know what happened at the party, not any of it." If only she could absorb some of the tranquillity around her. She was so tense, her entire body felt like a mass of rigid muscles. But, with continual practice, she was becoming a better actress. It was important now to appear calm, for she had just stated that she wouldn't let Sean provoke her again. The only way to remain composed was not to look into his eyes, or to avoid looking at him altogether. No, she wasn't frightened of him any longer, not physically. It was what she felt emotionally every time they were together that made her very afraid.

"Would you tell me your version of what really happened the day of the party?"

He let his breath out in a rush. "I'm not going to waste my time here. I just wanted to know how you handled Harry, that's all. I have work to do."

"Please." The word came out as a desperate request.

He stared at her profile. "I can't believe you're asking me to indulge you in this!"

Kris looked down to the ground. "I have no memory of that day. If I know what happened, maybe then I can answer some of your questions, make sense out of what took place." She shook her head. As if anything could explain time travel! "Please, Sean, I have to know."

His voice was hard, angry. "I don't have time for this."

She turned her head and met his glare. His eyes were filled with bitterness. "I wouldn't ask you to go through it again if it wasn't important, Sean. I need to hear it. What was the argument about?"

He admitted it, if only to himself. She was beautiful—tiny, fragile-looking. Her eyes pleaded with him, something he had not seen in three years. She was so feminine, so soft, so vulnerable that he could feel his body responding to her. And he hated himself for the betrayal. It was a totally new Christina that had come back to Rivanna a few days ago. The small woman who stood before him was a stranger . . . and she was also a bitch, he reminded himself, needing to stop the pull of charged energy that was passing between them. It was a question of survival.

"If your interest is so keen," he said sarcastically, "perhaps you should speak to your lover. Did he tell you what to say? How to verbally castrate a man?" He laugh was ugly, harsh, and dangerous. "No, Judson Taylor is barely a man himself. The venom that came out of your mouth was all yours. Calling me a gelding . . . questioning my manhood. As if I actually *wanted* you in my bed! You're nothing more than used goods. You were when I married you."

His breath was labored, a formidable expression marring his handsome features. He refused to recognize the horrified look on her face, to note that her hand came up to cover her mouth as though she were about to be ill. All he could see was the woman who had taken his life and turned it into a living hell. "Goddamn it, Christina, I will not allow you to do this to me twice!"

She didn't try to stop him as he walked away from her, his back rigid with anger. She was incapable of speech. No wonder he hated his wife. *Wife!* Christina was no more his wife than she was! She tried to overcome her shock as something started to click at the back of her brain. It was important; she felt it. And she was, after all, a good reporter. What was happening was familiar. Attempting to shut out all distractions, she tried to remember everything she had heard in the last few days and let her thoughts take over.

Christina and Sean had a marriage that was beyond salvage. It had never had a chance. She'd married him for money, to keep Rivanna. And she was not a virgin—a minor thing to Kris, but she knew it was important to Sean. Christina had made more enemies than Alexis Carrington. She was spoiled, malicious, vindictive, and manipulative. No wonder her own sister didn't love her. And she had also taken a lover . . . Judson Taylor. This last bit of information brought a smile to Kris's face. At least now she had a lead, a place to start.

She was getting extremely tired of holding the same pose, over and over again. Having her portrait painted was not turning out to be as enjoyable as she had expected. All Judson did was paint. He was annoyed by even the slightest diversion. Sighing, Christina tried to entertain herself by recalling the glorious nights they had spent together. Even though she was bored to distraction during the daytime, spending so much time in this dreary cabin posing for Judson, he had rewarded her patience with wild, intense lovemaking at night. That was the only time he would let her go outside, for fear of discovery. He had taken her with abandon under the stars, by the river, making her body come alive as only he could. Just thinking of their lovemaking made her breasts harden with desire. . . .

"Judson, where will we go tonight?"

"Be still."

She sighed impatiently. "I am extremely weary of being still, Judson. I want movement. Do you hear me?"

Judson Taylor looked around the canvas. "I've told you the light in this place is atrocious! I have to capture it while I can." His leg was aching this morning, a reminder from the war. He propped it on the small stool next to his chair.

"You can paint outside. But let us get out of here!"

He looked back to his canvas. "Need I remind you why we are confined to this cabin? It was never my idea in the first place. You know I was against this from the—"

"Oh God! Please, not again!" Christina pressed her fingertips to her temple in exasperation. "Your virtue is beginning to wear thin, Judson. What I did, I did for both of us. How many times do I have to explain that?"

He continued to paint, not looking at her. "Yes, I know. I'm just not exactly comfortable with a man standing trial for murder. You know what will happen to him."

155

Christina realized a smile would upset Judson, so she adjusted her lips accordingly. "Don't you worry. His trial and . . . disposal will be swift. A Yankee murdering a Mattson! How many Southerners will think twice?"

"Do be quiet, Christina," Judson ordered, his voice tinged with annoyance and regret. "And remain still. How many times must I ask? You're worse than a fidgety child!"

She grinned and stretched her arms over her head. Slowly standing up, she walked over to him and stared down at the man she loved. She never said a word, never explained her actions. It was the way he wanted it, and she knew him better than he knew himself. Her look was indolent; her movements lazy. Slowly, she lifted her skirt and straddled his outstretched leg. It was so easy now, especially since she had invented a whole new identity for herself. When she went to New Orleans to wait out Sean's trial, she would be known as Marie Delacroix. In Christina's mind, Marie was a courtesan, a woman who knew how to please a man, and she imagined that she would be very good at that profession, for wasn't Judson's jaw becoming slack, weren't his eyes becoming heavy with desire as she continued to rub against his leg, moving her hips in a deliberately seductive way. She took the paint brush away from him and placed her hands on his chest, letting her fingers trail down to his belt.

Pushing away the voluminous material of her skirt, Judson couldn't keep back a small laugh. "Perhaps, you should have brought along a pair of those trousers that Beth is always wearing. Or did she take all of them to Wescott's? A pity. There are times when they're very convenient."

She wasn't smiling. "I don't want to talk about Beth. I don't want to talk, at all, " she added, grinding harder against him as Marie Delacroix would do. It was shameful the way she enjoyed imagining herself, a lady, as a whore. It was as if she'd been given permission to act out all her fantasies, and nothing excited her more. "I leave for New Orleans in three days. I won't see you or hear from you until you send me word that it's over." She bent her head and kissed him on the mouth. Letting her lips trail down his throat, she murmured against his neck, "What am I going to do, all that time away from you? I want to fill myself with you now, and take my memories with me. Finish your painting after I'm gone . . . ."

"My God, Christina, you're insatiable!" Judson buried his face in her hair. "You have no shame, do you?"

His breathing was labored, and she could feel his pulse beating rapidly. Biting her bottom lip, she lifted her head and gazed into his heavy eyes. "No Judson. Where you're concerned I have no shame at all."

She proceeded to demonstrate to him the truth of that statement.

Beth watched as her older sister entered the kitchen. Already filled with suspicion, she couldn't help the resentment that surged through her. Why did Christina have to come in just when everybody

157

was having such a good time? Tisha had been showing them the tiny cotton gowns she'd sewed for the baby. Mae and Riva and Sada were laughing and telling her everything that had happened since she'd left for Wescott's—everything, that is, except what had taken place at Corinne Cunningham's birthday party. Even Beth knew better than to ask about that.

It had been just like old times until Christina came into the kitchen and proceeded to have her breakfast right at the table with them! Everyone fell into an uncomfortable silence and Beth looked to her sister as the reason.

"We're going to have to send for the rest of my things," she stated abruptly. "Mrs. Bridely will be expecting an explanation when I don't return."

Kris heard the defiance in her voice, and understood the young girl's rebellion. "We'll have to talk to Sean about it this afternoon," she answered as pleasantly as possible. She sipped her coffee, then smiled to the rest of the women. "Tisha, that gown is adorable."

Actually the tiny gown was made of plain, unfinished cotton, and Kris thought it would be too rough for a baby's skin. She thought of the many nightgowns upstairs in Christina's bureau and decided to clean house, so to speak.

Beth stood up to take her plate to the sink. Standing in front of a basket of biscuits, she picked at the edge of one. She was so angry! Christina was doing it again. Taking away her friends. She'd seen how Tisha and Mae had smiled at her. By God, even Riva and Sada weren't as frightened of her as before. "Mary Kay Reardon told me at school that

158

there's a very strong suffragette society in Richmond, she said casually, knowing Christina was going to scream when she said her next words. "I think I'm going to join it."

Kris looked at the girl and almost smiled. It was still easy to remember when she was Beth's age and the need for independence had been a burning one. She also remembered what a challenge she had been for her own mother. "Really, Beth?" she asked, appearing very interested. "Tell me when you're planning on going to Richmond. I'll go with you. I think woman's suffrage is an important issue."

"What?" Beth placed her hands on her hips. "When have you ever cared about anything except Rivanna? I don't believe you give a damn whether women are granted the right to vote!"

Kris kept her face expressionless. Was there *anyone* who didn't want to pick a fight with her this morning? "Really, Beth, I don't think anyone's impressed by your use of profanity. But I do think you've recognized a valid cause. Women will definitely have the vote soon."

"Oh, really?" The sarcasm was dripping from Beth's voice. "How would you know that?"

Kris looked directly at the young girl. Her voice was low, almost riveting with its authority. "I know, Beth. Take my word for it."

Beth and Kris continued to stare at each other, neither willing to be the first to lower her eyes. It was a startled cry that tore their attention away. Tisha was staring at the kitchen floor, already wiping away fresh tears.

"I'm so sorry, Miz Christina . . . I think my

baby's comin'!"

Kris's mouth dropped open. A baby! *Now?* She looked at Sada. "Go get Eli," she almost screamed, already nervous. All she could think of was Butterfly McQueen's famous line from *Gone With the Wind*. Well, she didn't know nothin' about birthin' either!

Patting Tisha's back, she looked toward the hallway. "Damn it! Why the hell don't they hurry up?" she demanded of anyone.

Catching Beth's shocked expression, Kris shrugged her shoulders. "Well, sometimes the situation demands a touch of profanity," she explained. It was a feeble excuse, and she knew it.

But, damn it, where the hell was everyone? You'd think this was an everyday occurrence. . . .

Chapter Ten

"Let's get her upstairs."

Eli and Walker stared at each other and then at their mistress. It was Tisha who spoke up. "If I can just get to my cabin, Miz Christina, I'll be fine."

"Don't be silly," Kris protested, feeling more nervous than anyone in the kitchen. "Why in the world would you go all the way to the cabin when there are all those empty rooms upstairs?" Not waiting for an answer, she ordered, "Eli, Walker, make a seat with your hands and carry her upstairs."

At her command, the men looked appalled, but they quickly followed her instructions. Both remembered what it was like to be on the receiving end of Miz Christina's wrath.

Kris refused to listen to Tisha's protests, and proceeded the men from the kitchen as they carried the pregnant woman between them. "Did someone call a doctor?" she yelled back to Mae.

Beth answered for the cook. "Louis went over to Everleaf to get Sophie. Christina, what are you *doing?*"

She had forgotten about Beth, and looked over the heads of the trio that separated them on the stairs. "I'm getting Tisha upstairs to bed. Who's Sophie?"

"A midwife," Eli answered, stopping as Tisha experienced her first real contraction.

Unconsciously, Kris folded her arms over her own abdomen. It was as if she felt the pain along with the younger woman. "We want a doctor, not a mid-wife!" She stared at Eli.

Resuming the climb, Eli strained to respond. "Nearest doctor's in Richmond. I don't think we can wait, ma'am."

Almost to the second floor, Kris spoke with authority. "Don't be ridiculous! There must be a closer doctor. What about all those people in Chestfield? They can't have to travel all the way to Richmond every time they're sick!"

No one answered her as she led the way to an empty bedroom. While Eli helped his wife sit on the bed, Beth detained Kris in the wide hall. "Will you think about what you're saying? Dr. Carney is *white*. You can't ask him to tend Tisha!"

Kris looked at the girl in front of her. "Are you saying a white doctor wouldn't come?" A tight coil of anger started to build in her stomach.

Beth's mouth hung open in shock. "What's the *matter* with you?" the girl demanded of her sister, as they both moved aside to let Mae and Riva into the room. "Why are you acting like this? And you sound so different, as if a stranger's voice is coming out of your mouth. You know the way it is. . . . And, anyway, Tisha would be more comfortable with one of her own."

She knew Beth didn't make the rules or encourage the prejudice, yet she turned away from the young girl. How could she be so vehement about woman's rights while thinking it was perfectly acceptable to deny Tisha proper medical care? Hadn't the Civil War been fought to ensure the rights of *all* people, regardless of race? But that didn't really happen for a long time, she realized. A long, long time . . .

"Christina!"

Both she and Beth turned to the sound of a woman's voice. It was coming from the foyer. "Oh no," Beth moaned. "Lynette Taylor."

Preceding an older black woman up the curving staircase, Judson Taylor's sister nodded to Beth, then stared at Kris as if she were a ghost. "I had only heard yesterday that you'd returned." She walked down the hallway and stopped in front of Kris and Beth. "When Louis came for Sophie, I rode back with him. Goodness, Christina, where in heaven's name have you been?"

Kris held her gaze, fighting not to look away. Dressed in an old-fashioned gown of navy and white, Lynette appeared to be in her mid thirties. She was attractive, not pretty, and her face was already lined, showing how difficult life had been for her in recent years. And she looked strong willed. A navy bonnet was tied under her chin, and white lace mitts encased her hands. Oh, God, Kris thought as she returned the woman's hard gaze, why did she have to come today?

Realizing she had to make some reply, Kris said, "The last week has been very confusing, Lynette. Is

163

this Sophie?" Finally, she looked to the older black woman.

"Of course," Lynette answered slowly, her expression clearly revealing that Kris should have known the midwife. "Is something wrong, Christina? Everyone's saying—" She stopped when a long, agonized moan came from a nearby bedroom.

Kris sprang into action. "Sophie, would you please go in to Tisha?" she asked, steering the older woman past Lynette. After closing the bedroom door, Kris turned back to Lynette Taylor. She could have laughed at the woman's shocked expression.

"You're letting that baby be born here, at Rivanna? *Upstairs?*" Lynette clutched at the high collar of her dress. "Have you lost your mind?"

Shaking her head, Kris issued a small sarcastic laugh. "I'm beginning to think so," she muttered, while steering Lynette back toward the stairs. Leading her down to the foyer, she was aware that Beth followed them. "Lynette, right now isn't a good time to visit. I appreciate you coming, but perhaps we can do this another day. . . . I'll find Louis and have him drive you home."

Lynette's back became rigid as she stopped in front of the door. "Do you have any idea of the talk this is going to cause? A Negro baby born inside Rivanna! My God!"

Kris tried to smile at her. "Lynette, there won't be any talk . . . unless you start it."

"That's right," Beth piped up. "No one has to know."

Lynette looked at the sisters, sudden allies, and frowned.

164

Slowly turning her head, Kris grinned at the young girl standing at her side. This time, Beth's smile was genuine and there was a different look — perhaps respect — in her wide brown eyes. Kris returned the look in a silent communication. "Beth, would you find Louis and ask him to take Lynette home? I'm going back upstairs and see if I can help."

Beth was shocked by the rush of admiration that ran through her. She was actually proud of Christina! Her older sister had not only insisted that Tisha's baby be born in Rivanna, but she'd stood up to Lynette Taylor. And, earlier, Harry had said that Christina had sent him to look for her. Christina! A truly remarkable day!

Turning back to the older woman, Beth squared her narrow shoulders. Just as she'd been taught at Westcott's, she placed her hand, very lightly, on Lynette's back and gently led her through the open door while distracting her. "How is Judson?" Beth asked, not really caring. She had always resented the power the Taylors held over Christina, especially Judson. "Is he still painting?"

Lynette stopped on Rivanna's steps when she saw the carriage waiting for her. She looked down at Beth Mattson. This child was actually dismissing her! "He left after your sister disappeared. He was very upset, as all of us were, thinking that Christina was . . . well, that she had possibly drowned. He said he needed to get away." Lynette's mouth pursed in anger. "What's wrong with your sister, Beth?"

Standing in front of the carriage, Beth shook her head. "I'm afraid I don't know what you mean." She

165

couldn't help smiling. She was defending Christina, doing something totally foreign to her. "If you'll excuse me, I'll see if I can find Louis." She turned back to the house before the woman could recover and question her further.

Left alone, Lynette Taylor looked back at Rivanna. Her jaw was set in anger. The hair on her arms actually bristled as she indignantly straightened her bonnet. She had spent years fighting Christina's hold over her younger brother, and just when she thought Judson was free of her, the woman reappeared like a deadly fever. Well, this time she would save her brother. No more would Judson think of Christina as a martyr, as someone sacrificing herself for Rivanna. She spun around and looked over to the stables. This time she would take matters into her own hands.

"I beg your pardon? I don't think I could have heard correctly." Leaving the stables with Lynette, Sean stopped walking and stared at the woman.

Lynette raised her chin and repeated her request. "I said, Mr. O'Mara, that I do not want Christina harassing my brother again. Please see to it that your wife stays away from Judson." She would not be deterred by the fury she could see building in his eyes, nor the delicate subject of their discussion. Embarrassment didn't even enter her mind, for she had waited too long to say these words.

"You want *me* to keep Christina away from Judson? Have you had this discussion with your brother?" My God, the gall of the woman! Sean gritted his teeth as he waited for her answer. The very last thing he needed was to lose his temper again!

"I have every intention of speaking to him. This . . . this situation has gone on for too many years. Your wife is becoming an embarrassment to all of us." There! She had said it. Feeling righteous, Lynette waited for his reaction.

Sean relaxed his facial muscles. "Christina is an embarrassment for you and your brother? I'm afraid I don't understand." Let her explain it, he thought. Let her be forced to say the words.

Lynette started to feel uncomfortable. Why was the man being so dense? Surely, she didn't have to spell it out for him! The Irish— What could you expect from a country of peasants? Annoyed, she cleared her throat. "This . . . this attachment Christina has for Judson must be stopped. Especially now, in view of what I've just witnessed. Lord knows what Christina will come up with next! The Taylors don't want to be a part of it."

Sean leaned against the stable, studying the woman. What the hell was she talking about? What had Christina done now? "Exactly what is it that you've just witnessed?"

Lynette jerked her head toward the big house. "Do you know that she's put one of your maids into a guest room? If you don't stop it, there'll be a negra born under Rivanna's roof!"

Seeing O'Mara's shocked expression, Lynette grinned at Beth who was running across the yard. So much for Beth Mattson getting rid of her, she thought with satisfaction. No youngster still in

167

school was going to usher her off Rivanna land.

"Lynette! Louis is waiting to take you back to Everleaf." Beth stopped in front of them and caught her breath. "Sean, what's wrong?"

He looked at his young sister-in-law. "What's going on in the house? Where's Tisha?"

Resisting the urge to stick out her tongue, Beth glared at Lynette. The woman couldn't even keep her mouth closed for five minutes! "Christina insisted that Tisha stay at Rivanna. She wouldn't hear of her going back to the cabins."

"Eli's with her?"

Beth nodded and breathed a little easier. He didn't appear angry. "Louis brought Sophie over and now he's ready to take Lynette home." The smile she directed at the older woman held more than a hint of satisfaction.

Annoyed by the child's obvious gloating, Lynette turned her attention back to the man. "What are you going to do about this, Mr. O'Mara? How are you going to handle your wife?"

Sean forced himself to smile. "If there is a problem here at Rivanna, Lynette, then it's our problem. And we'll take care of it."

"Well, you better do *something* about Christina very quickly! She needs to see a doctor; it's obvious. There's something very, very wrong with her." Lynette pulled on the lace of her mitts in agitation. "I can't put my finger on it, not yet. But it seems like it's her, then it isn't. She's different: her eyes, her mannerisms. And listen to the way she talks . . . like a Yankee!"

Suddenly realizing her mistake, Lynette brought

168

her hand up to cover her mouth. If she hadn't incensed O'Mara before, her last remark had certainly done it. The look on his face told her he had understood the insult. And Beth's little gasp of outrage hadn't helped matters any.

It took a supreme effort to control his anger, for Sean felt like throwing the Taylor woman off Rivanna, bodily. Instead, he said tightly, "I believe Louis is waiting to return you to Everleaf. Good day, Miss Taylor." He bowed stiffly and walked toward the house.

Beth hurried to keep pace with him.

"What is going on in here?"

Along with everyone else in the room, Kris looked toward the opened door. Leaving her place at the foot of the bed, she quickly walked in Sean's direction. "Please! Can you help her? Why can't we send for a doctor? My God, Sean, she's in such pain!"

He glanced at Tisha, then back at his wife. "And what do you think I can do for her that Sophie cannot?"

"I saw you with that mare. Remember? If you can help an animal, surely you can attend Tisha."

Sean was dumbfounded. Christina was pleading with him to help another! He shook his head in amazement. "Christina, Sophie is quite competent to care for Tisha. She's been helping to bring babies into this world far longer, I should think, than Dr. Carney."

"That's jus' right, Mista O'Mara," Sophie pronounced, giving Kris a righteous look. "Everybody

169

asks for Sophie, always has, at Everleaf, Coventry Plantation, and right here at Rivanna. Been this way for the last forty years now. Ain't gonna change jus' 'cause we's in this fancy room. Babies is babies, and I know all there is to know about gettin' 'em here!"

Not quite convinced, Kris watched as the old woman turned her attention to her patient. "Can't you check her?" Kris whispered, tugging on Sean's shirtsleeve.

Unconsciously, he answered in the same hushed voice. "What do you want me to check? Tisha's not a mare, you know."

"Really? How kind of you to point out the difference!" She wanted to slap his arm. Instead, she continued to whisper, "Find out some information . . . like how far apart her contractions are . . . stuff like that!" She shoved him forward.

He resisted her thrust and pushed back. "Now wait a minute!" Suddenly aware that he was still whispering, Sean cleared his throat. "Madam, you are behaving in a most peculiar fashion."

Seeing the others look in their direction, Kris smiled back and tried to speak without moving her lips, "Go on—find out how Tisha's doing."

Cautiously, he made his way to the bed. Smiling into Tisha's frightened face, he patted her arm in a futile gesture of comfort. "You'll do just fine, Tisha," he said, then turned to the midwife.

"How far apart are the pains, Sophie?"

The old woman rushed to grab Tisha's hand and apply counter pressure as the young maid started to moan. Looking up to Mr. O'Mara, she frowned.

"Well, we had one a while ago, and here's another. You want it timed better'n that, you get yourself somebody else."

Seeing the pain and alarm in his wife's eyes, Eli spoke up. "No, Miz Sophie! We don't want anyone else." He looked toward his employer, silently pleading with him.

Nodding, Sean stepped away from the bed and grabbed his wife's upper arm. Pulling her through the doorway, he announced over her shoulder, "We'll wait out here, Sophie. The room is yours!"

Just before the door closed, both Kris and Sean heard a muffled chorus of "hallelujah" come from inside the room. It took ten more minutes for Eli to be thrown out and five more hours for Naomi Mae Weaver to make her entrance into this world.

"I think I hear her crying! Do you hear her?"

Sean and Beth glanced at each other, then at Kris. It was Beth who answered. "Christina, Tisha will tend the baby. Finish your tea before it cools."

Kris looked down to the cup in her hand. "I suppose you're right," she admitted. "Tisha and Riva can handle everything until I go back up."

"That's not your child," Beth protested. "You've been very generous, giving Tisha nightgowns and ribbons and lace for the baby, but you shouldn't keep interfering. It isn't right."

Kris looked at the teenager. What wasn't right? "I only gave her a few things . . . this is a special occasion, you know. This is Tisha's first child." Thinking of the beautiful baby upstairs, Kris put down her cup of tea and grinned. "And she is pretty, isn't she, Beth? Did you see her chin? It's so tiny!"

Sean couldn't believe his eyes or trust his hearing. His wife was positively gushing over a baby — a servant's baby! He had stayed on after dinner to accompany Beth and Christina into the drawing room. Only when Beth was home did he and his wife make any pretense of being a family. Now he was glad he had made the effort, for the scene before him was incredible. Christina and Beth were engaged in a lively discussion, and their talk was frequently punctuated by streams of giggles and tides of feminine laughter. Christina and Beth, who had never claimed to like each other, appeared to be enjoying each other's company. He'd already heard about Christina's generosity toward Tisha and her child; that in itself was astounding. What in the world was happening at Rivanna? More importantly, what was happening to his wife?

It was the last question that bothered him the most, for no answer was forthcoming. He had thought that Beth would find her out, bring out the real Christina; yet his young sister-in-law sat across from him now and giggled with his wife. He had seen them argue over which way the wind was blowing; he'd never expected to see the two of them huddled together, agreeing that Tisha and Eli's daughter was adorable. Sean sighed and shook his head. There was no understanding women.

Standing up, he excused himself and left for the stables. It bothered him that his departure was barely noticed by the two females. Christina is winning over everyone, he thought with disgust as

172

he crossed the lawn. She is endearing herself to the servants, to her sister, to all those on Rivanna. It seemed to him that the others had very easily forgotten how superficial Christina could be, how calculating, how cold and devious.

Entering the stable, he stopped and looked down to the stone flooring. That no longer seemed like an accurate description of his wife. In fact, in the last few days he had heard her referred to as open, friendly, generous, and good natured. He continued walking to the foaling box. How could one person change so? And why was she more than ever on his mind?

Better to bury yourself in work than try to find the answer to that question, he thought as he entered the stall in which a mare was in early labor. Kneeling before the animal, he scratched behind her ear and grinned into her large brown eyes. Christina's eyes are a much lighter shade, he thought and quickly cursed himself for the comparison. Trying to banish her image from his brain, he again shook his head.

"I must be possessed," he whispered to the mare. "That's how she's done it." Then he thought of Lynette Taylor, of her accusations, and of how he had stood up for Christina, even defended her. He had told himself at the time that he'd spoken up because no matter what, Christina was still his wife and no one, especially Taylor, was going to run her down to his face. Now he admitted that he'd actually been defending the woman who had returned to Rivanna, not the one who had left it the week before. The Christina who had shown up in the library was a different person . . . someone to be frightened of, for there was a magic in her smile, a promise in her eyes — and a vulnerability that startled him. Damn it all, how much more was he supposed to endure? Was he being punished for considering divorce? Was it God or the devil who was laughing at his predicament?

The cool water that he used to clean himself did nothing to rouse him. He was much too tired; all he wanted was sleep. As Sean wiped his face and hands he glanced at his bed with yearning. It had been a long night and a particularly difficult birth. Again, he counted his blessings for having Eli as his head groom. The man had an uncanny ability to calm mares. Sean smiled as he pulled his suspenders down and unbuttoned his shirt. Another healthy foal born on Rivanna, and tomorrow he would be putting the first mare that had delivered to Celtic Star. It was finally going to happen . . . his dreams were about to be fulfilled.

Sean's grin froze as he listened to the soft crooning noise. Walking over to the door, he leaned his head out into the hall and listened. There! He heard it again. It was too close to be Tisha, for the maid's room was at the far end of the hall. Whoever was singing was much closer. Curiosity got the better of him, and he ventured down to investigate.

She was totally captivated. There was no other way to describe her fascination with the infant. Naomi Mae Weaver was the most adorable child Kris had ever seen. Sitting on the settee in her room, she held the little girl out before her to admire. Naomi Mae was perfection. Soft black curls framed a delicate face with cheeks that begged to be kissed. Kris gave in to the urge. The child stirred in her sleep, and Kris again smiled before unconsciously singing the only lullaby she knew.

"Hush little baby, don't say a word; Momma's gonna buy you a mocking-bird. . . ."

Sean stood in the doorway, dumbfounded. Christina was sitting in her nightgown, singing to Tisha's baby! He blinked several times. Surely he was dreaming this vision, for wasn't he exhausted? Yet Christina looked so beautiful, so soft, so feminine. . . . He took a deep breath and listened to her gentle voice, his own breath catching in the back of his throat as, her face so filled with love, she bent and softly stroked the infant's cheek with her own. My God, this couldn't be his wife!

"Christina?" His voice was a whisper of disbelief.

When she lifted her head, she wasn't surprised by his appearance. It was as if she had been expecting him, but perhaps it was only that she didn't wish to startle the child. Sean was confused when Christina smiled at him and quickly whispered an invitation to approach and look at the infant. He should have refused, made some excuse about being tired; but he didn't. He realized as he ventured into her room that he lacked the power to turn away from her. This night, she exuded a strange energy, a force so powerful and subtle that he found himself drawn into the

175

room and seated at her side. In some part of his brain that functioned normally, he realized she had just come from a bath, her hair was still damp, and she smelled of jasmine.

"Now you must admit it," she whispered. "Isn't this the most beautiful baby you've ever seen?"

Sean looked at the child in her arms. "She's very pretty," he said dumbly. Why, he thought wildly, can I feel the heat from her body? Perhaps he should move away, adjust his thigh so that it wasn't touching hers.

"Look at her hands! Absolute perfection. Isn't it amazing?" Her smile was brilliant.

Sean found himself clearing his throat. "What is amazing? Her hands?" He must be losing his mind to stay here in this room. The child was no barrier, for his mind was racing with forbidden thoughts, thoughts that were completely inappropriate.

"Life. Isn't it amazing that I'm holding a child whose life has just begun . . . and she's perfect." The tiny fingers that she had been admiring curled around her own larger one and Kris sighed with contentment. She was in love with the child. She giggled at the thought. At every opportunity, she had sneaked into Tisha's room to check on the baby, and as soon as Tisha was done feeding her, Kris volunteered to walk her. She absolutely loved the feel of the child in her arms. It was the strangest thing, but she was enjoying it too much to try and figure it out. Maybe it was because she had never been around an infant before. At the christenings of her friend's children, the babies had always seemed so engulfed by immediate family that she'd never paid too much attention to them. Naomi Mae was different . . . this child was life. For the first time Kris pondered that miracle, vowing never to take it for granted again.

Sitting next to her, watching her face, Sean caught his breath. It was as if he had suddenly seen the woman in her, the real woman inside of her, the one she was always meant to be.

"Would you like to hold her, Sean?" Her smile was warm as she looked up from the child.

Automatically, he held out his arms and Christina placed the infant in them. He felt stiff and embarrassed, and very uncomfortable as his wife told him how to hold the child. He watched as she placed her finger inside the baby's palm and heard her giggle as the infant clasped it and held on tightly. He inhaled the intoxicating fragrance of Christina's hair as she bent her head and kissed the baby's hand. He found himself blinking rapidly as she turned her face up to his and laughed so lightly that her breath caressed his cheek. And he thought he would groan aloud when she leaned against his arm to see the baby and he had felt the firmness of her breast.

He was entranced by Christina. She was weaving a spell over him, and his arousal frightened him. How could he allow her to control him? After everything! Sensing a closeness between them that had not been there before, Sean handed the baby back to Christina and stood up.

"I think I should say good night. It's been a very long day."

Why did she look confused? Why did she appear hurt by his abrupt words? Sean quickly retreated to

177

his room.

He never should have left it.

Three hours later, with sleep eluding him, Sean O'Mara tossed in his bed and stared out into his shadowy room. He couldn't stop thinking about her. She had bewitched him, taken over his thoughts, and she was robbing him of sleep. He pictured Christina when they had courted, even after their marriage, and he had to admit to himself that he had never, ever, desired her as he did now. What a terribly humiliating admission that was. But it had been so easy then, in the beginning, to bury any feelings he had for her. Later, after her blatant infidelities, he was devoid of feeling. Yet now, for the past two days, he'd found himself in a near-constant state of arousal. It was humiliating. He cursed as he turned onto his side and pounded his pillow in frustration. It was disgusting. A man his age, in his thirties, unable to control himself . . .

His jaw hurt from clenching it, yet he continued to grind his back teeth together. He must avoid her. He quickly nodded in the dark room. That was it! If he didn't see her, she couldn't tempt him. He relaxed his jaw and smiled for the first time since returning to his bedroom. He could handle this, he vowed, now that he had a plan. Happy with himself, he closed his eyes and, letting the tension leave his body, finally relaxed against the soft pillow. It was going to be all right. . . .

Suddenly, without warning, his mind painted a picture of Christina in her bedroom, holding Tisha's daughter, her hair still damp and curling around her face, her body smelling like jasmine.

178

"Ahhh!" He pounded his fist against the mattress in frustration. Throwing the light cover off, he then left the bed and took the silver flask from the top of his dresser. Desperate, he quickly unscrewed it while walking over to the window. Gazing out at Rivanna bathed in moonlight, he tilted his head back and swallowed the Irish whiskey. His eyes watered as the heat of the strong drink burned down to his stomach. Leaning his forehead against the window, Sean wished that it was as easy to burn Christina from his mind.

Bringing the flask back up to his lips, he sighed, already feeling defeated. It was going to be a very, very long night.

Chapter Eleven

She told herself that she didn't care. She reminded herself that he had been obnoxious, overbearing, and condescending. She tried to picture him dragging her into town and submitting her to public ridicule. She tried . . . More often than not, her mind would display a vivid recollection of Mr. Sean O'Mara smiling down at the baby, crooning to a pregnant mare, grinning at one of Beth's outrageous remarks. Kris shook her head, trying to force his image out. Surely she was losing it, if O'Mara could invade her thoughts so frequently. Granted he was good looking, in a dark, Irish sort of way, but he could also be the most infuriating man she had ever met. She should be glad that he was ignoring her, instead of trying to figure a way to capture his attention. There was no explaining it. She was attracted to Sean O'Mara, a man who didn't even exist in her own time. While she admitted that he was fantastic looking, he also had a foul temper. Even though he could be gentle with others, he was positively chauvinistic with her. Except last night with the baby, she thought. Then, he was warm and friendly and when she had looked into his eyes, something strange had passed between them. Whatever it had been, it had kept her awake for half the night with the most peculiar fantasies. It was laughable! She had absolutely no reason in the world to be falling in love with Sean O'Mara. She couldn't think of one single reason why such an incredibly stupid thing could be happening. She only knew it was . . . and it was frightening.

Adjusting Naomi Mae on her shoulder, Kris continued to burp the infant as she walked around the large bedroom. Sean O'Mara! How could something like this be happening to her? She shook her head with disbelief and thought about Beth. At breakfast this morning, Beth had told her about the conversation she'd had with Lynette. It seems Judson Taylor was away. Beth told her that Lynette said her brother had needed time to get over the shock of Christina's apparent death. The reporter in Kris thought the story was entirely too pat. Christina disappears and now Judson leaves. She shook her head as she walked to the window and looked out. She would bet anything the two of them were together out there somewhere. The baby burped, and Kris grinned as she watched Beth run across the lawn to meet Harry Gentry. It appeared spring at Rivanna was affecting everyone . . .

Suddenly, Kris' smile froze as she continued to

stare out to the young couple. Realizing she was clasping the baby to her chest, she forced herself to place the infant on her bed. Quickly, she turned back to the window and stared at Beth and Harry.

Beth and Harry . . . The hair on her arms rose up; she felt a chill race down her spine. She shook her head, as if the action could deny the crazy thought. Beth and Harry. Elizabeth and Harry Gentry.

Elizabeth Gentry . . . her . . . her great-great-grandmother?!

Kris's mouth opened in shock. Was it possible? Was Beth the ancestor who had started all those horrible rumors of insanity? Could Beth Mattson, the young suffragette, Rivanna's own hoyden, possibly be the person Great-grandmother Ellena was always quoting when she lectured on how a proper lady should conduct herself? Ellena's mother? The one named Elizabeth? *Her Great-great grandmother Elizabeth?*

Kris covered her mouth with her hands and forced herself to blink as she continued to watch the teenagers. If Beth marries Harry, then she's Elizabeth Gentry, Kris thought, and I know, I remember, hearing that Elizabeth's husband was a lawyer! Closing her eyes, she took a deep steadying breath. And if Beth was her great-great grandmother, then Christina was her aunt! Her eyes snapped open as her lower jaw dropped in shock. It all made sense! That's way she looked like the woman. Dear God! She was related to these people. It was insanity . . .

182

and she was living it.

The baby stirred and Kris hurried to the bed, picking the child up and walking back to the window. Beth and Harry were gone. Again she shook her head in disbelief. It can't possibly be real. None of this can be happening! As Naomi Mae's mouth rooted for nourishment, Kris hurried down the hall to Tisha's room. This was one time she didn't mind returning the infant, for she needed to sort out her thoughts.

"She's hungry again," she said to Tisha, as she placed the child into her mother's waiting arms.

Tisha smiled, adjusting the fine material of the nightgown that she wore. Bringing her daughter to her breast, she looked up at her mistress and said in a small voice, "I'm real grateful for everythin', Miz Christina. I hope you know that."

Kris absently returned her smile. Tisha, who lately had been looking almost radiant, now appeared worried. "What's wrong?" Kris asked, hoping that Tisha would shake her head in denial, for the very last thing she needed right now was a distraction.

"It's time, Miz Christina. I best be takin' Naomi Mae home. Me and Eli, we want to be a family."

Take the baby? "Eli can come here, can't he? Why don't you just stay a few more days? Until you're completely well again." Kris wanted to beg her to bring the child up in this house, but she knew how ridiculous that would sound. Already feeling the loss, Kris swallowed back the tears and nodded.

She tried smiling. "You're right," she admitted. "You and Naomi Mae belong with Eli. It's just that I'm going to miss her. Thanks for . . ." What could she say? Thanks for filling a void in my life that I didn't even know existed? "Thank you for letting me be a part of her birth. She's a beautiful baby."

Just then Beth came into the room, a look of happiness on her face. "Oh Christina! Sean says I don't have to return to Wescotts. Isn't it wonderful? He says we can look into a school closer to home. In Richmond."

Kris could only stare at her. It was all so clear now. She saw her mother's eyes in Beth's, even Jack's smile resembled the ecstatic expression on the teenager's face. Although their coloring was different, when she'd first seen the young girl, hadn't she thought Beth looked just like her?

"What's wrong, Christina? Why are you looking like that? Sean said he was going to talk to you about it."

She couldn't hold them back. It was too much. Blinking away the tears, she glanced at Tisha and the baby and fled the room.

No sooner was she back in her bedroom when she heard the door open behind her. Hugging her waist, she spun around and saw Beth standing in the doorway.

"Tisha said she just told you about going to her own home," Beth stated, closing the door behind her. "Is that why you're so upset? You knew they were going to leave, Christina. You couldn't have

184

expected Tisha to just give the child over. Is that it? Is that why you're crying?"

Kris shook her head. She stared at Beth as she came closer. Dressed in riding pants and a white blouse, Beth looked almost modern as she stood before her and waited for an answer. Instinctively, Kris reached out and hugged the girl to her chest. She felt Beth's body tense in surprise and Kris stroked the long braid that fell down Beth's back.

"What's wrong?" Beth whispered.

Even though she was crying, Kris managed a smile. Still holding the young girl, Kris murmured, "I'm not her, Beth. I'm not . . . Please, listen to me."

Beth straightened and looked into Kris' eyes. "What are you talking about?" she demanded. "You're not her? Who? Honestly, Christina, I haven't –"

"I'm not Christina," Kris interrupted. "I'm not her."

Beth stared at her, her eyes searching, before abruptly pulling away. Putting a small distance between them, Beth looked back. "What are you saying?"

Kris wiped the tears from her cheeks and attempted to appear calm. "Please," she implored, holding up her hand. "if you'll just listen to me . . ." Taking a deep shuddering breath, Kris said, "My name is Kristine Gavin. I come from Philadelphia, in the year nineteen eighty-eight. I'm not your sister, Beth. I come from the future. You, Beth . . . I think

185

you're my great-great grandmother."

"Stop it!" Beth's eyes reflected her fear. She backed up toward the door. "They said you were— you weren't right, but I didn't believe them. Then you were acting so nice. I was hoping whatever happened to you while you were away was permanent. But now this! My God, Christina! Do you even realize what you're saying?"

Kris nodded, taking a step in her direction. She had to make Beth understand. "I know this sounds crazy to you. Believe me, I would feel the same way if you had appeared in my time. But we are related. Not as sisters. Christina is my great-great aunt and you're my grandmother—"

"I said stop it! I don't want to hear any more!" Beth brought her hands up over her ears and raced for the door.

Kris felt desperate. "Beth! Listen to me. I was brought back in time. I don't know why. I don't even know how to get back, but I have to have someone who believes me. I've been acting. This isn't my room. These aren't my clothes," she cried, grabbing the skirt of her dress. "Please . . . I'm not Christina. Your daughter was my great grandmother—"

Beth ran out of the room and slammed the door behind her. Looking at the painted wooden door, Kris slumped onto the bed and bit her lip to keep from crying out.

"Her . . . her name was Ellena," she whimpered, though no one could hear her, "and her daughter was Grace. And her daughter was Margaret. And

186

her daughter is me . . ." Kris continued to stare at the door, hoping that Beth would walk back in, believing everything she had said. Shaking her head, she wiped away the tears from her cheeks. How could she expect a fourteen year old child to understand? *She* couldn't understand it, and it had happened to her! Sighing, her shoulders sagged in defeat and she covered her face in her hands. Please, God, she prayed, get me out of here. Bring me back. I don't belong. Please, let me go home.

"I'm not quite happy with the mouth, Judson." Christina lifted her chin as she viewed the painting. "do you really see me like this?"

"Yes." He shrugged his shoulders. "Next month I might see you differently. For now, this is my impression."

Placing her hands on her hips, Christina walked in front of the painting. "Well, when all of this is over, I want you to paint another. I'll have a gown made up especially for it, don't you think?"

He placed his shirt into the carpetbag. "Whatever you want, Christina."

She looked over her shoulder at him and found herself unclenching her teeth. Forcing a smile, she walked up to him and slid her arm through his. "What's wrong, Judson? You aren't still upset because of the money, are you?"

He untangled his arm from hers and continued his packing. "For the last four days I have listened to

187

you congratulate yourself on your brilliant plan. I would think you could have managed to bring enough money to take with you to New Orleans."

She made herself ignore the sarcastic tone to his voice. "How many times do I have to tell you? I forgot. Everything else went exactly as I had planned. This is something you'll have to help me with, Judson. I'm sorry."

He looked down at her. She was asking him to betray his family. To take the money he and Lynette had put away for this quarter's taxes and finance her trip to New Orleans. She was supposed to have taken the money from O'Mara, who could well afford it. They had argued last night and this morning. He had promised to wire money each week to her, but she had said it was too risky and that it would never be enough. Knowing she was right, he had even offered to steal the money from O'Mara himself. In the end, he had agreed to return to Everleaf and get the money for her trip. God help him

"I have to be at the train depot at eight tomorrow morning, but I don't have much packing to do," she said, watching him close his bag. "While you're gone, I'll get things ready. Close up the cabin, and everything." She pressed herself against his arm. "This is our last night together. I don't want to waste any of it."

He found he could do no more than kiss her forehead, as he picked up his bag and paints and brought them outside to his horse. It was strange, but he felt almost relief in leaving her. Perhaps the time she spent in New Orleans would be good for both of them.

Christina followed him outside. "What about the painting? You'll need it to show Lynette."

He saw that she had wrapped it in a cloth. Holding out his hand, he fastened it to the saddle. With everything in place, he turned to her. "It takes at least an hour and a half to reach Everleaf. And that's in daylight. I must visit with Lynette before returning here for you. Don't expect me before nine or ten this evening."

Christina sighed and reached up to play with his collar. "I don't know what I'm going to do with myself until tonight," she pouted.

"I thought you said you had work, packing. I don't think we want any evidence that we've been here." He checked the horse's bridle and adjusted the cinch on the saddle. "We'll have to leave early in the morning to get you to the depot. You did bring the correct clothes? Didn't you?"

Christina looked annoyed. "For goodness sake, Judson. Of course, I did. Tomorrow I'll look like the most grief stricken woman in Virginia. Even you don't recognize me with my widow's weeds. I swear you can't see through the veiling at all!"

Judson nodded. "Then I'll see you tonight," he stated in an emotionless voice. He bent his head and lightly kissed her lips.

Christina watched him ride away. As Judson disappeared into the woods, she thought of how much she was looking forward to New Orleans . . . and Marie Delacroix. Yes, she was going to enjoy this holiday until "justice" was done here in Virginia.

Her smile widened as she turned back to the cabin. It really was too bad that Judson was having trouble accepting responsibility. She needed that money. She certainly wasn't going to New Orleans and living like a pauper. Why, Sean's trial could go on for months! And she had an image to protect. Marie Delacroix was going to arrive in New Orleans in style.

Closing the cabin door behind her, Christina wondered if everything she had heard about Creole men were true. French and Spanish blood mixing together . . . Leaning against the planked wood, she closed her eyes and grinned.

"You what?"

"I want a horse." Kris lifted her chin and stared back at him as she repeated her request. "To go riding," she added, as if it were necessary.

Sean's gaze traveled down her body, taking in the laundered blouse and freshly pressed trousers. It was the same costume she had been wearing when she'd returned home. Why did it look so much better on her now?

Kris hated the way her body reacted to his presence, and resented the way his one eyebrow rose up in question as he viewed her pants. She had no right to want him like this. And he had no right to look so damn handsome, so attractive. He was her great-great uncle . . . or something! All she wanted was a horse to go riding. She had cried for a good half hour, cried for herself, for her family, for *this* family, until the room had closed in on her. She'd known then that she had needed an escape to get away by herself, away from Rivanna.

She looked up at him, met his stare and forced herself not to look away from his fantastic blue eyes. Why had she never noticed before that they were so astonishingly blue? Brushing her unbound hair back from her face, she cleared her throat. "Well? Do I get the horse, or not?"

Judson Taylor looked at his home in the distance. At one time, not really so very long ago, Everleaf had been a showplace on the James River. Yet, it was hard to remember . . .

He stopped his horse on the hill overlooking his home, deep in thought. Even from this distance, he saw a number of shutters hanging off and fence posts that were never replaced. Everleaf was in disrepair. Why did he never notice it before? Oh, to be honest, he had vaguely marked the gradual decay of the plantation, but hadn't concerned himself with it. He had been distracted. He realized that he could have easily fixed the shutters and the fence. Even without any help, he knew he was still capable of taking care of his home. Poor Lynette! He had allowed his sister to live in the past, giving up her chances for happiness to cater to him. He shook his head in disbelief. How could he have let it all happen? He had blamed the War for everything, for the loss of their workers, the idle fields . . . even Christina. How blind he was. How convenient his excuses.

He was on the verge of losing the home, the family that he had fought to save. Sitting on that knoll, he pondered the wasted years. Was it all for nothing?

Moments later, he was distracted by a rider exiting the woods near the border of his home. He could tell by the amount of hair that it was a woman. She wore trousers and he unconsciously shook his head as he watched her slow exploration of the countryside. How women had changed! Before the War, no respectable woman would have worn such a riding outfit. Now, women were demanding equal rights in the courts, the right of franchise, and God knows what else. The War had brought about so many changes—

He straightened in the saddle and his entire body became rigid with disbelief. No! It couldn't be! Surely his eyes were playing tricks on him. It had been a long ride, and he was tired. He'd done so much thinking on the ride back, thinking about Christina. And now he was more confused than ever. That had to be it, for what he thought he saw made his stomach clench with fear. He blinked, hoping the vision would change. It didn't and he called out her name as he kicked his heels into the horse's sides.

"Christina!"

Kris jerked her head toward the sound of the yell. Seeing the man racing toward her, she quickly urged the horse back into the woods and prayed that she would remember the direction she had come. Crouching down, she tried to protect her face from branches as she and the horse followed a worn path through the woods. It wasn't until she could see Rivanna in the distance that she slowed up and listened for the sound of the rider. He hadn't followed, or he'd given up when he had seen in what direction she was heading. She didn't know why, but instinct had told her to run away from the man. Shaking her head, she tried to regain her breath as she led the horse more slowly toward Rivanna.

Right now, the house was a welcome sight.

"Judson! I'm so glad you've come— What's wrong?"

Lynette watched as her brother threw his things in the entryway. As he walked up to her, the expression in his eyes was frightening . . . He looked haunted.

Grabbing his sister's upper arms, Judson demanded, "Have you seen her? Was she here?"

Lynette could only blink. What was wrong with him? "Do you mean Christina? I saw her a few days ago." Suddenly, she relaxed. "Of course, you've been away! You have no way of knowing—Christina's returned, Judson. She wandered back to

Rivanna last week."

His fingers dug into her arms and he shook her. "What are you talking about? Tell me!"

"You're hurting me," Lynette said in a falsely calm voice. "Stop this!"

Brother and sister looked at each other. Lynette watched as Judson's face started to crumble and, slowly, as if it took a great amount of effort, he released her. He turned, looking about the dusty rooms, as if seeing them for the first time in years. Stumbling, as though drunk, he made his way into his father's library. He knelt in front of the old desk, and fumbled with the combination to the safe.

Lynette followed him, frightened, shocked by his actions. It was as if something had happened to him while he was away. He was obsessed. Never had she seen him like this. When she realized what he was trying to do, she knelt down next to him.

"Judson! Why are you doing this? Tell me!"

He opened the safe and withdrew the precious money, holding it before him, as though he'd never seen it before.

"What are you doing?" she again demanded, her voice shrill this time. "That's tax money, Judson. You know that. If you take it we'll lose Everleaf. Everything!"

To him, that moment, that statement, was like someone thrusting him into the daylight, into the fresh air. When Lynette had told him that Christina was back, he had felt like the ground itself was swallowing him up, stifling him. But it was impos-

194

sible! He had left her only two hours ago. How could she be here? Impossible!

Still, something inside him, some small part of him felt unsure. More confused than ever, he thrust the money into his pockets and ran from the room.

Chapter Twelve

Still frightened, Kris walked the horse back into the stable. She expected to see Sean and tell him of the rider, the intruder; but no human being was about. Finding an empty stall, she led the horse inside and removed the saddle. Hurriedly, she grabbed a handful of straw and began to wipe her mount's glistening brown coat.

"There," she whispered to the animal. "It's the best I can do right now." If she couldn't find a groom, she would come back later and finish the job. She patted the horse and left.

Since there was no one in the stable, she decided to check the newer building. Probably one of the mares was ready to give birth again. Between Tisha and the mares, in the last week Rivanna was a regular hive of reproductive activity. She looked at a beautiful foal over the half-door of a stall. It was lying on the thick straw, all long nose, huge velvet eyes, and folded legs. Its dam eyed her with suspicion. Kris smiled as she moved on toward the back of the stable where she could hear voices. Wouldn't it be wonderful if she could witness another birth? She would never forget the thrill of first seeing a foal being born.

The closer she came to the back of the stable, the more agitated the mares in the stalls were acting. She could hear the excited noises made by horses coming from the large room at the rear of the building. Stopping at its door, she looked in.

From somewhere in the back of her brain a voice told her to turn away, to go back outside. But something much stronger kept her rooted, gripping the heavy wooden door as she watched with fascination a mating ritual more primordial than man.

The mare was nervous, her tail held high as she danced with excitement. The huge black stallion, the one Sean was leading, had a definite presence about him. Celtic Star held himself imperiously, as if certain of his effect on the mare. Kris stood by unnoticed while the men brought the horses together. The joining was swift and untamed. Celtic Star bit the mare's neck in a show of passion that was violent and tender, and Kris found herself digging her fingernails into the wood of the door. The breeding was savage yet filled with a grandeur; primitive yet somehow sacred. It was a copulation of thrust and vigor and pleasure. It took Kris's breath away and made her weak with longing, and she found herself staring into Sean

O'Mara's intense blue eyes, communicating with him—telling him of her need, her arousal. Even at a distance, she could read the hunger in his answering gaze.

As Celtic Star brought his forelegs to the earth with a resounding jolt, Kris quickly looked to the floor of what she now knew was the breeding shed. She was breathing heavily as if she had actively participated, and she wished she could hide in the thick blanket of hay and soft brown peat that covered the floor. My God, she thought, what have I done? Acutely embarrassed, she started to turn away, but not before catching the look on Sean O'Mara's face. Although busy with the horses, he appeared as shaken by the experience as she.

Kris ran through the stable, passing the dams and their foals, not seeing anything but the exit doors at the end of the long corridor. Once outside, she stood with head thrown back, gulping the fresh, calming air. Her hands on her hips, she waited for her breathing to return to normal, her heartbeat to settle to a more comfortable rhythm.

"Christina? Is it you?"

Her head jerked in the direction of the muffled male voice. Within seconds, a man came around the side of the stable and walked toward her. His actions were secretive, as though he knew his presence would not be appreciated. In that fleeting moment, she knew the sandy-haired man was the rider who had chased her. She also knew he was

198

Judson Taylor.

He stood before her, not three feet away, staring at her as if she were a ghost. Suddenly his eyes narrowed and his voice was an anguished whisper. "Who are you?" he demanded. "What are you doing here?"

Kris found she couldn't answer him. He knew! Everyone else expected her to be Christina, yet Taylor knew immediately that she wasn't . . . and he hadn't even heard her voice, her Northern accent. From somewhere came a silent warning: Judson Taylor knew she was an imposter.

Brushing the curls back from her face, Kris lifted her chin and stared at the man. "Where is she, Judson?" she asked impulsively. "Where's Christina?"

She realized the stupidity of asking when Taylor seized her upper arm and tightened his grip. "What are you talking about? Who are you? Why did you come here?" Looking desperate, he shook her. "Who *are* you?"

Kris pushed him away and took a step backward. Before she could think of an answer, she saw Sean at the stable door, staring at her and Judson, a look of pain on his face. He held the reins of the huge stallion. Even from a distance she could see muscles twitching in the animal as sweat dripped from its gleaming black coat. The aura of sexuality that followed the mating was still powerful. She watched as the pain in Sean's face was swiftly replaced by anger. Quickly looking up at the man in front of her, Kris ordered, "Go away! Get away from here, *now!*"

Judson turned his head to take in her line of vision. Seeing O'Mara's expression, he moved away from the small woman who, through some magic, some twist of fate, looked like a replica of Christina. "I'll be back," he whispered, almost as a threat. "I want answers."

Remaining silent, Kris turned away from Judson Taylor, away from Sean O'Mara, and ran for the safety of her room. It only added to her depression to hear the warning sound of distant thunder.

She couldn't face them. Beth thought she was mad to have claimed her for a great-great grandmother. Kris shook her head, remembering the scene that had occurred earlier in the day. And Sean . . . She closed her eyes, remembering, seeing him in the breeding shed. My God, it had been so powerful. Then later, when he'd watched her and Judson . . . the pain in his eyes . . .

Pacing in her bedroom, Kris hugged herself to ward off an imaginary chill brought on by the impending storm. It had been better to take her dinner here than to face the two of them downstairs. What could she say to either of them? What were they saying to each other about her? She told herself she wasn't hiding—not exactly. She needed this time to sort out everything. Today had been extraordinary, beginning with the discovery of who Beth really was, who Kris thought she really was. Then being chased by the rider who'd turned out to be Judson Taylor; the astonishing experience with Sean in the stable and finally the confrontation with Judson.

Taking a deep breath, she looked at the ceiling, searching for some answers. One thought kept running through her brain: She'd been playing games with this family—and she didn't have that right. She was pretending to be the wife of a man she found herself falling in love with; she was posing as the concerned older sister of a young girl who was probably her great-great grandmother. It was madness! It didn't matter that she had tried to explain who she really was. She had ignored the fact that they both had dismissed her explanations as lunatic ravings. She was playing with the lives of these two people . . . and in her heart she knew it wasn't right.

She also knew what she had to do. It was the only answer. She'd tell him her suspicions about Judson and Christina. She would try, one last time, to make him believe the truth. And then she was leaving Rivanna. Tonight. Before she changed her mind or lost her courage . . . or allowed anything foolish to happen. Kris looked down at her clothes, and her lips formed a melancholic smile. She had yet to change from her afternoon garb. Ah well, she'd never really liked voluminous petticoats and skirts. Her slacks were much more practical. This isn't my time, she thought sadly, and those clothes belonged to Christina. Just like the tall Irishman downstairs.

She was going to leave this house exactly as she'd come to it.

It was his father's. From Ireland. Holding the precious bottle in his hands, Sean blinked several times while focusing his eyes on the fading Irish Whiskey label. Over one hundred proof Irish Whiskey . . . as fine an ambrosia as ever passed a man's lips. He had been saving it, planning to open it on the birth of his first child. When it became clear that the whiskey would forever go unopened, he'd revised his plans. Ordinarily he would have waited until next year, on the occasion of Celtic Star's first foal, to taste of the precious heritage. Instead, he sat in his study and squandered the exquisite blend, hoping it would blot out her image and his disgust with himself.

He was besotted, and not just from the whiskey. It was a sad thing to admit, if only to himself, that he desired the one woman who had done everything in her power to destroy him.

Sean reminded himself of Christina's cruelties, but his heart forced him to recall her face that afternoon in the breeding shed. Quickly, he poured half a glass of liquor and brought it to his lips. Throwing back his head, he swallowed it with little regard or restraint. Would that the whiskey had the power to burn the memory of her face from his brain, he thought.

Jesus! He had scarcely believed it when he'd seen her standing by the door. He had wanted to shout at her to get out, to leave them, but he was caught up with Celtic Star and the mare. He admitted now that it had been the first time he'd been so affected by a mating. This time it hadn't been just a business, an occupation. This afternoon it had been an encounter to stir his soul, to inspire in him fantasies of loving Christina. Would he ever forget the astonished look in her eyes? The way she had bit her bottom lip? The fever in his own body, or the wild need he'd had for her? In the moment that their eyes had met, Sean had admitted that he wanted Christina more than he had thought possible. Sweet Jesus! How had he let it happen?

And what of her and Judson? When he'd seen them together, he was seized by such jealousy and pain that for a minute he had been immobilized. He knew there was something wrong with the encounter, something decidedly different, but he hadn't been able to put his finger on it, not earlier. Now he knew what it was. Christina had pushed Judson away from her as though she wanted to put a distance between them. She had seemed frightened of him. From the expression on her face, it was very hard to believe that she had once loved Judson Taylor.

Once loved him? The flooring beneath his feet

203

rumbled from thunder, and he looked to the darkness outside the window for signs of accompanying lightning. Within seconds, its momentary brightness filled the room. Shaking his head, Sean laughed at himself before bringing the whiskey to his lips. "Surely you're a drunken fool, Sean O'Mara," he muttered aloud, setting the glass onto the table. Less than one week passes, and you think Christina is a changed woman! That she might have—

Hearing the knock on the door, he jerked his head upright. He pushed his hair back off his forehead and sat up straighter. Another knock. Clearing his throat, he yelled, "Come in then!"

She ignored the fact that he sounded annoyed. She had made up her mind and would act on her decision. Gathering up her determination, Kris turned the doorknob and walked into the study.

As soon as she entered the room, he stood up and moved to the front of the desk. He leaned against it, casually observing her as she stopped at a wing chair and rested her hands on it's back, as if for support.

"I'd like to talk to you, if you have the time," she said, her voice sounding strange even to her. Why was he looking at her like that? His eyes were devouring her every movement and she felt as if she were to be his next meal.

"Would you like a drink? I'm celebrating."

She tried to smile. His voice was low and seductive, and it sent a shiver of warning down her

204

back. "What are you celebrating?"

He poured her a small portion of the whiskey. Handing the glass to her, he waited until her fingers almost touched his own before answering, "Life. The beginnings of it, anyway."

She blushed. She could actually feel herself flush at his words. She knew exactly what he was talking about. This afternoon. The breeding shed. She didn't think she would ever be able to forget it. Clearing her throat, she sipped her drink and walked about the room.

"I really do have to talk to you, Sean." When he didn't answer, she turned around. He was right behind her, staring at her with those fantastic blue eyes. She backed up. Realizing he wasn't going to say anything, Kris continued. "There are some things I have to tell you . . . you must listen to me this time. I've done some thinking and . . ." She unconsciously bit her bottom lip as he advanced on her. Why was he stalking her like this? And why did her brain suddenly turn to pulp? Why the hell couldn't she remember what she was about to say? And why did she keep imagining her fingers playing with the curling black hair at his temples? My God, she was acting like a teenager! Worse, she was unable to stop herself from doing it.

He thought his voice would betray the terrible craving inside him — a hunger so deep, so sharp, that he was drawn to her like a starving man. And so he remained silent. His mind refused to remember her years of betrayal. Instead, he saw before him a beautiful woman—soft, seductive, even a bit vulnerable. Before he knew what he was doing, he reached for her waist and drew her against his chest. He looked into her eyes, those incredible tawny eyes that stared back at him with surprise.

Leaving one arm around her waist, Sean took the glass from her and placed it on a small table. He watched her astonished expression as he lifted his hand and allowed his fingers to be caught by the riot of curls that surrounded her face. He stared at the curls, examining them as they weaved around his fingers like fine silk. Then slowly, ever so slowly, he applied pressure to her neck and brought her mouth closer to his.

She knew she should stop him, say something to break the spell. She also knew if he kissed her, she'd be lost. No sooner did she think those words than he did just that. Softly, his lips grazed her right temple. The tender caress was far worse than if he'd kissed her on the mouth, for her entire body became inflamed with the need to feel those warm lips upon her own. Beyond reason now, she forgot consequences and pulled his mouth down to hers.

It was wild and tense. There was a mixture of anger and passion as their lips met, fought for a few uneasy moments, then became demanding, exacting a response. It was easily given, for each knew the other had waited a long time. Kris threaded her fingers through the black silk of his hair, wanting somehow to hold on to him, to bring him closer against her. There was so much that she wanted to remember: his scent, the feel of the muscles under his shirt. Her mind refused to concentrate on anything but his mouth as it left hers and traveled to her neck.

She was all nerve endings, exposed to his tongue and his mouth. Everywhere he touched, she felt the most exquisite sensations. While he unbuttoned her blouse, she fumbled with the material of his shirt and pushed the cotton away to reveal his chest. She had an overpowering need to feel his flesh against her own, and cried out as the heat of his body seared her inflamed skin. She was flushed and frantic with desire as, together, they discovered each other. They stroked, fondled, scratched, and tasted. To Kris, what was taking place between her and Sean was as wild and primordial, as urgent and pleasurable as what she had seen this afternoon. And she wanted him. . . . Throwing her head back as his mouth finally arrived at her breast, Kris freely admitted it. She had been waiting for this moment.

Sean couldn't get enough of her, and thought surely he was dreaming or he'd conjured her up in his drunken state. But her skin was soft and scented — she was real, and in his arms. How many nights had he wished for just this moment? To see her desire and feel her arousal . . . How many nights had he imagined her in his arms, exactly like this? And how many nights had he been left alone with his empty thoughts?

207

He tried to brush them away, the nagging accusations . . . but they crept back inside his head. He was to be pitied. What kind of man was he to want her after everything she had done? Could he live with himself? Breathing heavily, he straightened and held her head between his hands while staring into her eyes. He had to be so careful not to let her gain power over him.

"You are a witch, Christina." His eyes searched hers, looking for the woman he had married.

When he spoke, Kris felt his breath on her lips and saw the accusation in his eyes. Her eyelids closed and her shoulders sagged when she heard him address her as Christina.

"I'm not her," she whispered, trying to gain control over her breath and the tears welling up at the corners of her eyes. He wasn't making love to *her!* He thought she was his wife. Her hands quickly drew the edges of her blouse over her still-exposed breasts. Knowing he thought her to be Christina was like a slap in the face. It made everything that was beautiful tainted.

Kris opened her eyes and stared back at him. She looked at his dark blue eyes, the black lashes that ringed them. She took in his straight nose, the slightly flaring nostrils . . . his chiseled, patrician features. She could love him so easily, but he belonged to another. It was so simple and so painful. "I . . . I came down to tell you that I'm leaving Rivanna. And that I think Christina is alive." She couldn't stop the tears from sliding down her cheeks. "That's what I was trying to say to you."

She could feel the pressure at her head as his hands tightened in her hair. His face was filled with pain and anger.

"I could easily break your neck. Do you know that, my dear? And make it look like an accident."

She felt the strength in his fingers, saw the fury in his eyes. "But you won't. You couldn't hurt me." Her smile was sad. "When I came in here, you were toasting life . . . it means too much to you, Sean." She felt his grip gradually lessen until he released her. From the look on his face, she didn't know who he was more disgusted with — her or himself.

"I don't know what to make of you anymore." His voice was raw, anguished, and she heard him pour himself another drink as she fumbled with the buttons of her blouse.

"I don't know what to make of her either, but I damn well intend to find out a few things!"

Startled by the new voice, both Kris and Sean looked toward the door.

Christina!

Accompanied by Judson Taylor, she moved into the room and closed the door behind her. Strangely, Kris's first impression was that the rain must have started, for Christina's hair was damp, her curls falling in tight ringlets. She watched as the hateful woman threw a long cloak onto a

209

nearby chair. When Christina turned to those in the room, her smile was iniquitous, evil, as she looked at Kris and then let her gaze slide to Sean.

"Who is she?" Christina demanded. "Who is this woman you've brought into my home?"

Staggered, Sean held onto the edge of the desk for support. *"Christina?* My God, is it you?"

Christina threw back her head and laughed. The sound was wicked and angry, a fit accompaniment to the thunder and lightning, Judson thought. Somehow, he'd known it would never work out for him and Christina. It wasn't as hard now to allow relief to flood through him. Ever since he had found Christina back at the cabin and told her about the imposter, she had been like a woman possessed. She actually frightened him.

Christina walked closer to her husband. "Of course, it's me." Her voice was sarcastic and condescending as she watched Sean quickly look at the woman who stood between them. "Don't tell me you were fooled by this imposter!" She turned to the one Judson had told her about and studied the face so like her own. "You must have known it wasn't me. We're nothing alike . . . any resemblance is only superficial."

Kris backed up, going closer to Sean. She didn't like the look on Christina's face as Sean's wife advanced on her. She knew now why everyone on Rivanna feared the woman. Christina seemed to be enveloped in an aura of malevolence. Kris felt that if one got beneath her outer layer of control one might find a very disturbed woman. Kris tried not to show her fear as Christina came closer to examine her face.

"Leave her alone, Christina. Get away from her."

Ignoring Sean's orders, Christina glared at the woman who had crushed all her dreams. "What is this game you're playing? Did someone put you up to this? What's your name?" Each question sounded like a sharp rifle crack.

Kris swallowed several times. She looked at Sean, at Judson Taylor, then at Christina. The woman was breathing deeply as if trying to control her rage. Kris watched as her fingernails curled up into her palms, her hands becoming tightly clenched fists.

"I asked you a question," Christina stated in a strangled voice as lightning again flashed. "I want to know the name of the person who's ruined my life . . . all my plans . . . everything."

Kris raised her chin. We look nothing alike, she told herself. This woman, even if she is an ancestor, is nothing to me. Nothing! She desperately searched within herself for courage. "My name is Kris. Kristine."

"Liar!" Christina took another step in Kris's direction and Kris stepped back.

"You're wrong. It is the truth."

The only warning Kris had was the low growl of outrage that came from Christina as the woman lunged at her. It was an unnatural sound, and she threw her hands up to protect herself, blocking the strike. She caught Christina's wrists and fought to keep the clawing, grasping hands away from her body. The strength of the woman was unbelievable.

They stood together in mental and physical battle, facing each other, their eyes inches apart. She could hear the voices of the men, but they were fading fast. In that moment, that span of time and space, Kris looked into the mirror image of herself and saw the face of insanity. Somehow, she knew none of this was supposed to have taken place. She didn't know how this knowledge came to her. It was instinctual. Just as she knew that she and Christina should never have met, have touched, or made a physical connection. It was as if they had committed a transgression against nature.

When the lightning came, it entered the room with such velocity that Kris close her eyes against the blinding brillance. Turning her face away from the blaze of light, she let go of Christina to shield herself as she felt a white hot current surge through her body. There was pain at her chest and her breathing was labored. She heard a scream. Was it her own? Vaguely, as if it were happening to someone else, she felt hands at her waist, strong hands clinging to her. Someone was pulling her backward. She opened her mouth to scream, to command whatever force was in the room to leave her alone; but no sound came. She felt herself slammed against the wall, and the air in her lungs rushed out of her body. As she slid down to the floor, she knew that whatever was in the room was not of this world. This was her punishment for meeting Christina, for loving another woman's husband. . . .

Before she lost consciousness, gave herself over to the comforting darkness, she heard her name cried out from very far away.

It was Sean's voice . . . and he was calling to her.

"Please . . . Kristine. Wake up, lass." He placed her head back on the floor and looked around them. "Ahh, God help us."

Sean stared at the room with its strange furniture and its even stranger music, and panic filled him. Light magically spilled out from odd lamps and flooded the space. The music continued, though he couldn't tell where it was coming from. Everything hurt his eyes. His skin still tingled from the lightning. If he knew where he was, he would call out for help.

Was this Rivanna? Where the hell was he? Finally, his gaze rested on the portrait of his wife, propped up on a chair.

Even from across the room, it looked very old. . . .

Chapter Thirteen

There was music, distant familiar music, and from very far away she heard her name being called. Slowly, forcing herself to ignore the ache in her upper body, Kris opened her eyes. Immediately, she recognized that the light in the room was brighter, more artificial, and she squinted from the glare.

"Where are we?"

Turning her head at the sound of his voice, she saw Sean kneeling beside her. She had heard the alarm, the awe in his words. As she attempted to sit up, she felt Sean's hand at her shoulder, supporting her while she looked around the room. Her heartbeat quickened, her fingers tightened on his arm as a slow smile spread over her lips.

Tears of gratitude welled up in her eyes as she looked with wonder at her brother's unfinished study. It was all there, just as she had left it . . . the black leather sofa, the makeshift bar, the desk. Even the stereo. It was playing Whitney Houston's "Didn't We Almost Have It All."

"I'm back!" she exclaimed, her voice filled with reverence. She didn't know how it had happened; she didn't even care. *She was back in her own time!*

"Back where?"

In the joy of having returned, Kris had almost forgotten him. She now turned to look into his face. "It's all right, Sean," she whispered, trying to be reassuring as they both attempted to stand. "Don't be frightened."

"I am not frightened," he insisted, though the expression on his face said otherwise. "I would like to know where I am." He looked around the room, his eyes wide with dread.

Feeling the slight trembling in his arm, she took his hand and led him to a chair. "This is my brother's home. Rivanna. Sit down—"

"Rivanna? What are you talking about?" He dropped her hand and searched the room for something familiar. "If this is Rivanna, then where are my paintings, my books, my furniture?" Frustrated, he spun around and stared at the stereo. "Where is that woman's voice coming from?"

Kris hurried to the radio and shut it off. "It's a machine, a stereo, very common in this time, Sean." She couldn't help looking at him with pity. There wasn't any way she could hide it. Knowing

215

from experience what he was feeling, she softened her voice, for she also knew what had to be said. "This is nineteen eighty-eight, Sean. Somehow, you've come with me to my time."

Kris watched as Sean flinched, almost as if he had been struck by her words. Then he straightened his shoulders and she could see he was trying to compose himself. "Why don't you sit down? I'll get you a drink," she offered. Quickly, she walked over to the bar and found the bottle of Harveys. It was just where she had left it . . . how long ago?

Handing him a glass of sherry, Kris noticed that her hands were still shaking and she smiled weakly. "I know what you must be feeling. Remember, this happened to me, too." She knelt in front of him, watching him as he stared off into the distance. "It won't be as hard on you, because I'll help you. I'll be here for you. I'll—"

"This isn't Rivanna!" He stood up and walked away from her.

She watched as he brought his drink to his mouth and swallowed. It was only natural that he fight it. Hadn't she done the same? she thought as she gazed around the room. But he had to face it, and the sooner the better, for how in the world was she going to explain him to Jack and Elaine? Slowly, she rose and stared at the desk. "Look, Sean," she said, making her way to it. "This is what I was telling you about. The newspaper article." She allowed her gaze to take in the room. Everything was just as she had left it. "I don't

216

think I was gone very long . . . from my time," she whispered. "Nothing's changed, not even the newspaper. At least look at it, Sean."

As he turned to her, she could sense the battle going on inside him. He didn't want to hear her explanations, to see any proof; but she knew his curiosity would win out. Soon he placed the empty glass on a table and walked in her direction.

He stood next to her and stared at the yellowing newspaper pages, the ink drawing. "How?" Confused, he shook his head. "It can't be!" He reached out his hand, and his fingers trembled as they touched the frayed, fragile edges of the paper. "What happened? What happened to all of us? Who *are* you?"

She felt the muscles in her body tightening almost defensively as his voice rose. "Calm down and listen to me, because now you know — for the first time since we met, when you thought I was Christina — that I've been telling you the truth." He was staring at her, his eyes desperately searching hers for a sane explanation. Taking a deep breath, she knew there wasn't any.

She said it slowly, as if that would make it more real for him. "This is nineteen eighty-eight. Look at this newspaper. It's old. I found it behind Christina's portrait, just like I told you." She took his hand and led him to the painting. It still lay on the chair, exactly where she had left it. "This, Sean, was Christina. Only I didn't know it when I first saw it. This painting was a present from my brother. He said he found it in the attic of this house. And when I took off the back, I found the newspaper with the story of Christina's disappearance. Remember me trying to tell you about a storm? About the terrible lightning? And, then . . ." She shook her head in disbelief, finding it hard to comprehend all that had happened since that night.

"I was taken back to the Rivanna of your time." She looked at him again, hoping he would understand. "That's when you found me in your study. I tried to tell you who I was . . . I did try. I can't blame you for not believing me."

Sean's eyes searched the painting, then he quickly looked up at Kris. His gaze returned to the canvas. As he studied it, he said slowly, "I remember. You said your name was Kristine, with a *K*, and *e* at the end." Without looking up at her, he whispered, "I never believed you, not ever. But when I saw you both together, you and Christina, in the same room . . . I thought I was losing my mind, that somehow I had entered your nightmare or Christina's nightmare." He shook his head before raising it to stare at the strange furnishings that surrounded him. "God help me, now I am living someone's nightmare—I'm actually in it! This isn't my home. This *is not* Rivanna!"

She reacted instinctively. She took his hand and led him to the study door. Flinging it open, she pulled him into the foyer. "Look at it, Sean!" she pleaded, gesturing to the once beautifully furnished drawing room. "It's all gone . . . all of it.

This isn't the Rivanna you know. My brother lives here now. He's turning it into a restaurant. This must seem cruel to you, and I'm sorry. I just don't know how else to convince you."

He felt like he had been physically abused. His legs were shaking and perspiration was slipping down the center of his back. Using the partially painted foyer wall to support him, Sean dragged his eyes away from the empty room. "A restaurant! But where's my home, then? Where is everything? It can't all just be *gone!*"

She wanted to hug him, to hold him close and wrap him in her arms, almost as she would have comforted a child. She wanted to brush back the black hair that fell over his forehead, to kiss his temple and tell him that everything was going to be all right. But she knew no amount of comforting would take away the pain that was so evident in his expression and voice. He was confused and shocked, suffering from a terrible loss. Hadn't she gone through that herself? What wouldn't she have given for someone to have held her and told her that she didn't have to handle the nightmare alone?

Knowing she was right, Kris reached out to him. But before she could embrace him, before she could offer support and consolation, the front door was flung open. Both she and Sean jumped in fright as a crowd of people, her friends, burst into the foyer and immediately surrounded them . . . laughing, shouting, bending their heads to kiss her cheek.

"Surprise! Happy Birthday, Kris!"

She had forgotten. It was her birthday. Her thirtieth birthday. Her frightened grin froze on her lips as she backed up against Sean's chest. Feeling his hand protectively clutch her shoulder, Kris watched the faces of her friends. As the group made their way into the study, familiar, friendly faces laughed at her shocked expression. Soon, Jack shouldered his way through the crowd and kissed her cheek.

"I did it, didn't I? You really were surprised." Grinning, her brother glanced up at Sean before looking back down at her. "Happy birthday, old girl. Are you going to introduce us?"

Jack had never looked so handsome, and Kris quickly hugged him, needing to touch — physically touch — family again. She could feel Sean's fingers tighten on her shoulder. Taking a deep breath, Kris turned to him and mouthed, *"It's all right!"* Smiling, she said aloud, "Jack, this is Sean O'Mara. Sean . . . my brother, Jack Gavin."

She moved slightly so the men could shake hands and watched as Sean stiffly extended his to her brother. As soon as their hands had disengaged, she casually took Sean's fingers in her own. She knew Jack saw the possessive act and realized she would have to explain.

"Isn't it wonderful? Sean flew down here to spend my birthday with me. I was . . . shocked . . . to see him," she added nervously, unable to

220

stop a silly giggle from escaping her lips. Oh God, she prayed, help me get through this night!

"Really?" Jack asked while walking with them into the study where the rest of the party was already in full swing. Rock music blared from the stereo, people were opening bottles of wine, and Elaine and Danni rushed into the room from the kitchen carrying trays of intricate-looking canapés and hors d'oeuvres. "I didn't see a car outside when we drove up," Jack shouted over the music.

Kris stared at her brother. "He took a cab from the airport," she said in a loud voice that sounded strained, even to her.

Jack looked from his sister to the man at her side. Smiling at Kris, he nodded. "Too bad we didn't know. We could've picked him up along with the others." Jack smiled at the stranger who stayed close to his sister. "We'll talk later, Sean," he yelled over the noise of music and laughter. He shook his head toward the stereo that was blaring popular songs. "This is my house and I'm giving this party, you'd think I could listen to decent music. I say it's time for a little of the Stones, don't you Sean?"

Sean blinked several times. "Well, yes, of course," he agreed, not sure what exactly he was agreeing to.

A look of pleasure on his face, Jack slapped Sean's arm. "All right! A fellow Stones fan!" He winked at his sister, but her shocked expression did not change. "I approve of him, Kristine," Jack said, and just before he moved away from them, he reached for Sean's hand and again shook it. This time in friendship. "Welcome to Rivanna," Jack said with a grin; then he hugged Kris and left to take charge of the music.

Kris immediately turned to Sean and motioned for him to bend his head closer to hers. She could see he was both hurt and shocked by Jack's last words—a stranger welcoming him to his own home. "I know this is confusing," she said directly into his ear. "You're doing great. Play along until I can get us away from here, okay?"

Sean nodded as a tall dark-haired woman carried a tray in their direction. Although her hair was closely cropped, she was attractive in an exotic sort of way and had a grin that, even across the room, signaled she was delighted over something. Instinct told Sean he was the cause of her delight, but he had no idea why.

The woman stopped directly in front of him and let her eyes roam over him. Her gaze was bold, yet not offensive. Sean felt she was assessing him. Her grin widened as she shifted the tray to rest it on her hip and loudly ask, "Who *is* this man? Talk about a fashion statement! I love it!"

Spinning around, Kristine squealed with pleasure and rose on tiptoe to kiss the dark-haired woman on the cheek.

"Danni!"

Pulling back from Kristine, Danni extended the tray to Sean and smiled. "Try one of these phyllo filled things Elaine made. Everyone's raving about them." Still grinning at him, she said to Kristine,

222

"Introduce us, Kris."

Sean watched as Kristine grimaced. "Danielle Rowe . . . this is Sean O'Mara. Danielle is my oldest friend."

Danni's smile widened. "Not oldest, Mr. O'Mara. She meant dearest."

Sean bowed slightly. "How do you do, Miss Rowe?"

Danni's eyes widened. "I'm doing fairly well . . . I think." She glanced at Kris. "Very polite."

Knowing Danni would say anything that came into her head, Kris nodded hers. "We'll talk later," she promised, giving her childhood friend a familiar, forbidding look.

Danni understood immediately. Smiling at the handsome man with the accent, she held up her tray. "Sorry I can't shake your hand, but duty calls." She looked to Kris. "Elaine insisted that I serve everything hot. I've never known anyone to be so passionate about food!" Almost in the same breath, she continued, "Are you in architecture, Sean? Your name sounds familiar."

He automatically shook his head. "I raise horses. Thoroughbreds — "

Nodding, Danni interrupted. "Then that explains the way you're dressed. Actually, it looks good on you."

"Danni!" Kris wished she could stuff her friend's mouth with canapés.

Sean, looking down to his black trousers and white shirt, wondered what the woman was talking about.

Danni continued, as if he'd voiced his question. "I swear if I see one more man in an Armani suit I'm going to scream. And they've done the thirties to death. Long jackets, shoulder pads you could land a plane on . . ." Seeing Kris's startled expression, she explained, "The newest trend right now in men's fashions is period clothing. Like Sean's." Once again she surveyed his clothes, this time with a critical eye. "Baggy pants. Suspenders. Collarless white shirt, made of really good quality cotton." Her eyes narrowed. "Have you ever thought of modeling?"

He blinked several times. "I beg your pardon?"

Kris stepped up and linked her arm through his. "Don't be silly, Danni!" She looked up to Sean and explained, "My friend's in the fashion business. She automatically critiques everyone she meets."

The dark-haired woman shrugged. "I can see the black and white glossy: Sean, dressed just like he is, standing in front of a horse . . . at the racetrack . . . giving the camera a drop-dead faraway stare." She took a deep, regretful breath. "Oh, well, it was just a thought. Listen, you two, if Elaine catches me letting her little phyllo things freeze up, she'll find a way to run me through her Cuisinart. I'll come back later and we'll really talk." Again, she smiled at Sean. "So, you're from Philadelphia . . ." She shook her head as if the idea were amusing.

Sean, not knowing what to say, yet feeling as though the situation called for something, said over the noise, "It was indeed a pleasure to have met you, Miss Rowe." He picked up a canapé from the silver tray she carried. "Thank you for the phyllo . . . thing."

Danni laughed out loud. Looking at Kris, she said, "I like him. I don't know where you found him or why I haven't heard of him before, but I do like him!"

Kris's smile was embarassed as she watched her best friend gracefully maneuver her way through the room, offering gourmet tidbits to those in her path. She turned to Sean and immediately felt sorry for him when she viewed his shocked expression. She had to pull on his hand to draw his attention from her cousin. Barbara, dressed in a red and black mini, was lighting a cigarette.

"It's all right, Sean," she whispered, leading him to the bar. "Women have been smoking for a long time now. It may not be healthy, but it isn't shocking."

"But her attire!" he whispered back. "Surely, that's shocking!"

Kris looked across the room at her cousin, and shrugged. "Personally, I don't think a woman should wear a mini anything when she's past the age of eighteen, but what do I know? Fashion is definitely one area where I feel insecure." Finding a newly opened bottle of Harveys, she poured him a glass without asking if he wanted one. "You should hear Danni on the subject of my individual fashion statement."

"She's a very confusing woman."

225

Smiling at those who turned in their direction, Kris leaned closer to Sean's shoulder. "Look, I know this is sort of like a baptism by fire into the twentieth century, but try to be patient." She led him to the desk chair and motioned for him to sit down. Carefully folding the old newspaper, the one containing the story of him and Christina, she said, "In less than a minute, people are going to be surrounding us and asking questions. I know you're confused. I don't blame you. Just let me do most of the talking until we can get out of here, okay?"

As a short man approached them, Sean looked at her and nodded. "All right," he answered, "but then we must talk." He looked around the room. "I have so many questions. . . ."

Kris couldn't keep the sick grin from her lips. "I don't doubt it, Sean," she murmured, before plastering a wide smile on her face and greeting the short man and his wife.

"Irv Handleman! Peg! I can't believe you both came all the way to Virginia for a birthday party! Who's minding the station?" As Kris accepted her boss's hug and then introduced him to Sean, she couldn't help wondering if this was how Alice had felt after venturing into Wonderland.

He didn't believe he was dreaming, for he could never dream up anything so bizarre as what was happening to him now. He was encircled by people and machinery that seemed from another world. He was dizzy and his head pounded from the loud music and everyone shouting to be heard over it. For the life of him, he couldn't understand why someone didn't just turn it down so those around him could hear one another. He was tempted to do so, but feared to appear ill mannered. Besides, he wasn't sure how to control the machine. He wasn't sure of anything tonight, except that he was frightened.

There were seventeen people present. He knew, because he had counted them. He also knew he must appear unfriendly to the laughing crowd because his answers to their questions were short and did not invite conversation. He had responded to inquiries about horse breeding with as much politeness and patience as he was capable of displaying at the moment. He was afraid to say too much, for fear of contradicting what Kristine was saying about him. How was he to get home again? he wondered. This was surely an advanced time and if Kristine—Kris, he corrected himself—was able to travel to eighteen seventy-one, then somehow she would be able to help him get back. He would just have to wait until this party was over, until Kris was able to leave her guests and talk to him, tell him what he must do to go home. It was absolutely unthinkable that he should never return to Rivanna. Sean looked about the room and a chill of dread ran up his arms. He must return to *his* Rivanna, not this foreign home stripped of everything familiar.

Looking across the room as the others surrounded Kris, Sean watched her cut a large birth-day cake. As he leaned against the wall, he could clearly see the difference between Kristine and his wife. Kris possessed a genuine warmth and kind-ness that Christina had always lacked. Even though the crowd surrounded her and demanded her attention, Kris's eyes sought his own. To Sean, it appeared that she was telling him to be patient, that soon they would escape this madness.

Hoping no one would approach him, Sean sipped his drink, nursed his headache, and waited. He had so many questions to ask Kris about this aberration, this deviation from the nor-mal and sane order of things. Surely, those couples moving to the rhythm of the loud music were not actually dancing? He shook his head and thought how naive his questions would seem to Kristine. Even someone new to this time would not call what he was watching dancing. It was a parody. That was it, he decided, the couples standing in front of each other and making those strangely seductive moves were actually ridiculing the dance. This time he nodded and smiled with satisfaction at having figured out by himself ex-actly what they were doing. Now their wild gyra-tions made sense . . . though for the life of him he could not determine what all the shoulder and neck movements were supposed to signify. The continual snapping of the fingers and clapping of hands was much easier: it was a maneuver, a means to draw attention to themselves, as were the particularly intricate foot movements. The neck and shoulder effects, however, remained a mystery, and looked positively uncomfortable.

Entertaining was much simpler in his time, Sean decided, though when he recalled an endless series of young women stumbling through Stephen Foster compositions, he changed his mind. Watching these couples parody the dance was definitely more interesting, though he would never allow a female of his acquaintance to participate in such primitive entertainment. It was a positively scandalous activity.

He sipped his drink and wished for something stronger. Less than a half hour had gone by, but the night seemed interminable. He knew that no amount of alcohol would dull his mind and make the absurd appear rational. Not tonight. Tonight the only person with explanations was making her way across the room to him—now. Despite his bizarre situation, being in this room in the wrong century, Sean O'Mara realized that he was very happy she was who she was . . . and that everything he had sensed about her—the warmth, the kindness, the shy sensuality—was real. His heart soared as she smiled up at him and weaved her arm through his.

"You seem so interested, I thought I should ask you to dance."

Sean's answer was a look of absolute fear and disbelief.

"They look like they are alive, with angry eyes."

Standing next to him on the porch, Kris nodded. "That's because it's night and those who are driving need light to see in the darkness. The noise comes from an engine. When you see the cars in the daytime, Sean, you won't feel like that." She waved to Peg and Irv Handleman as they drove their rented car down the circular drive.

"Just a few more guests to get off to the hotel, and then we can really talk," she said. She was determined to stay next to him, for his reaction when he'd come outside had been frightening. Yet it was to be expected, she thought. Seeing Rivanna in the present time, even at night, must be terrifying for him.

She was tired, and her emotions were too close to the surface right now. On the one hand, she was thrilled to be back in the present. On the other, she admitted that a small part of her grieved over having left the past. Beth. Harry. Riva and Sada. And God, Tisha and Naomi Mae. What was going to happen to them now? She tightened her grip on Sean's arm to stop the tears and the memories. Don't, she silently scolded. If only she could sleep for a few hours, renew herself . . . But she knew Sean had waited all night for his answers. She must reward that kind of patience with honesty.

Standing under the light at the front door, Kris kissed her cousin's cheek. Her smile was strained as she listened to Barbara's suggestive remarks.

"Good night, you two." Barbara looked at Kris

230

and Sean, and her smile held a trace of smugness. "Why, Kris, you kept this man all to yourself tonight. I guess I'm going to have to wait until brunch tomorrow to find out what's really going on between the two of you."

Kris had to force the smile to remain at her lips. It was only within the last hour she'd learned that her brother had invited everyone for the weekend. "Just don't come too early, Barbara. You know how Jack loves to sleep in on Sunday mornings."

"That right, isn't it? Especially after a party. But Elaine's so organized she'll have everything under control." Satisfied that she had solved all problems, Barbara stifled a yawn, threw the end of her shawl over her left shoulder, and walked to her waiting car.

"That does it!" Kris exploded as her cousin drove off into the night. "C'mon, Sean. We're getting out of here. I'll explain everything on the way to Philadelphia." She took his hand and led him back into the house.

Pulling back from her, Sean quickly said, "What are you saying? Philadelphia? Surely, you can't mean that I should leave Rivanna? I must go back to my own time."

Quickly checking around to make sure no one had heard, Kris pushed him back out onto the porch. "For God's sake, look around you, Sean! Haven't you figured it out yet? This isn't your Rivanna. I wish to God I could give it back to you, but it doesn't exist anymore. There isn't anything for you here in Virginia, not now." She didn't realize that her hands were grabbing the front of his shirt. "Come home with me, Sean. At least until we can talk about this without interruption. You heard Barbara. Half of the people who came tonight are returning for brunch tomorrow."

Closing her eyes, she slowly shook her head. "I'm so tired, Sean. I can't face another day of this."

Under the artificial light that flooded the porch, he could see the strain and fatigue in her face. He felt guilty, remembering now that she, too, had been forced to mask fear and anxiety. How hard it must have been for her in his time . . . all alone. He admitted, if only to himself, that he was terrified to leave Rivanna, yet he was more terrified not to be with Kristine. He couldn't let her go away without him. Everything here was foreign. She knows, his brain insisted. She can explain it all.

He wanted to run away, to hide himself, until sanity had returned, but he knew that he wouldn't leave Kristine. As he agreed to go with her to Philadelphia, he couldn't help but wonder how he would ever have survived losing her . . . if he had stayed in his own time. The thought of sacrificing Kristine for Rivanna was not to be entertained, for in truth he wouldn't know how to choose between them.

Sean decided to put his own worries aside for the moment and lend Kris the support she needed. Following her back into the house, he watched as she whisked her friend Danielle into the deserted study.

"I need your help, Danni."

Danielle Rowe looked from the anxious face of her best friend to the handsome man standing behind her, and then back again to Kris. "I take it you're not thrilled with Elaine putting me in the guest room."

Shaking her head, Kris asked, "You rented a car, didn't you?"

"Yes. Where are we going? It's almost two in the morning."

"You're not going anywhere. I need your car."

Danni's eyes narrowed. "This isn't one of those mystery weekend parties, is it?" When she didn't receive an answer, she almost whined, "Oh, Kris, you know I hate those kinds of things. I'm simply not competitive in that way. Believe me, after being 'in service' to Elaine tonight, my sympathies will always extend to the hired help. I could have easily murdered your cousin Barbara when she—"

"I need your car, Danni," Kris declared impatiently. "I'll leave it at the airport. You can always get a lift from Jack tomorrow."

Danni calmly reached for Kris's hand. "If you'll excuse us, Mr. O'Mara, I think I need a moment alone with her." Giving Sean a false smile, she pulled Kris back into the foyer.

"All right, what's going on? I feel like I'm on 'Miami Vice' and at any moment men who don't speak English very well are going to burst in through the front door carrying machine guns.

233

Who *is* this Sean O'Mara? And why haven't I ever heard of him before?"

Kris had to think quickly. She was so tired, and lying to Danni didn't come easy. "Don't be silly. I . . . didn't tell you about Sean because I didn't have the chance. Everything happened so quickly between us. That's it! That's why we have to get away from here before tomorrow. We need some time together." She looked at her friend's skeptical expression. "I didn't know about the party. You remember Jack and his surprises."

"I'm not letting you go with him, Kris. You're acting strangely." Danni sighed heavily. "Besides, if you leave and I stay, I'll be Elaine's little drudge. And I'm not even on retainer. The only reason I agreed to play kitchen maid was because this was for you."

Kris hugged the taller woman. "You know I appreciate everything you've done. And Elaine does, too."

Danni shrugged. "Actually, I like her. It's just that she's so damn good in a kitchen, so controlled. And I feel so inferior." She sighed. "Wouldn't the National Organization for Women love that remark?"

Kris pulled back and, despite her fatigue, laughed. "Oh, Danni, and I feel inferior to you! You always look so *perfect!* Even now. You give class to that apron."

"Right!" Danni's laughter ended abruptly. Shaking her head, she said seriously, "You aren't in trouble, are you, Kris?"

234

"No, I'm not. But I still need to take your car. We really do have to get away."

"It's that serious? The two of you? So quickly?" Danni's eyes were wide with shock.

"I don't know," Kris said honestly. "That's why we need time."

Suddenly feeling like an accomplice, Danni grinned. "The keys are upstairs in my purse, along with the rental papers. You'll need them, I think."

"Thanks. I'm going to run up and pack. Then I'll talk to Elaine. Thank God, Jack's asleep."

When she saw that Danni was about to reenter the study and confront Sean, Kris grabbed her arm and pulled her toward the wide stairs. "Leave him alone, Danielle. He's not ready for you yet. Come help me pack and I promise I'll explain as much as I can."

When they returned less than ten minutes later, Kris looked into the study and saw that Sean was staring at the portrait of his wife. His face looked tortured.

She cleared her throat and he spun around. A slow smile appeared at his lips when he saw that she had changed into a skirt and sweater. Her legs showed, and she looked lovely and . . . of this very time. Like her friends tonight.

"Are you ready?" she asked with a catch of laughter in her voice. She handed him a man's sweater. "You're about to take the ride of your life."

Sean hoped it was only his imagination that detected a hint of pity in her expression.

235

"I don't think I can do this! The car was one thing, even exciting once you explained how it worked. But this airplane, as you call it, is entirely different, Kristine." Sean pulled on the seat belt, as if trapped. His eyes were filled with fear, as he stared at Kris. "I must get off this thing immediately."

Sensing the near panic in him, Kris quickly looked around the first-class compartment and was grateful that the early morning flight to Philadelphia was almost empty. "You're all right. Calm down. Really, Sean, it's natural to be nervous the first time you fly."

He made a strangled sound in his throat, and she hurriedly added, "Well, actually, you don't fly. The plane does. Or, the pilot flies the plane." Nervous for him, she shook her head. "It doesn't matter—"

"It doesn't matter!"

She couldn't help it. She laughed. "Don't worry so. Honestly, they know what they're doing. See." She pointed to the window by his shoulder. "It's backing away from the terminal. Sort of like the car, don't you think? Only larger?"

"A lot larger, Kristine!" His eyes were glued to the window, staring at every light and vehicle that they passed. "When you were purchasing my ticket, I saw the size of this airplane. It will never lift off the ground." His voice sounded haunted.

She wound her arm through his and patted his

236

hand as they headed for the runway. "Then you must have seen other planes taking off and landing."

"They weren't as big as this one."

"Of course they were. They just appeared smaller because you were farther away."

Sean shook his head. "It will never leave the ground. And if it does, it will never stay up."

Before she could reassure him, the flight attendant began her safety lecture and though Kris tried to distract him, Sean hung onto the young woman's every word. When the attendant explained the procedures to be followed should the plane be ditched in an emergency, Sean turned to Kris and fiercely whispered, "See! I told you! This is suicide."

Kris then tried talking about everything and anything to take his mind off his surroundings. But as the attendants took their seats and the captain announced that takeoff was eminent, Kris was totally unprepared for Sean's reaction.

He put his head back, held it stiffly against the cushion, closed his eyes, and totally ignored her. As the plane gathered speed, Kris immediately became aware of a low moan increasing in volume as the plane raced down the runway.

"Ahhhh . . . !" Suddenly the plane lifted into the air, and the noise at her side abruptly stopped. She looked at Sean. His jaw was rigid, his knuckles were white, and perspiration had popped out all over his face.

A wave of pity washed through her, and she

leaned closer to whisper, "You can open your eyes now, Sean. It's all right. We're in the air."

There was another moan before he muttered, "Then God help us! We're doomed."

Chapter Fourteen

The plane banked sharply to the right and Kris placed her hand over Sean's. His was still clutching the arm of the seat. "Look out the window, Sean. That's Richmond. Isn't it beautiful from up here?"

She could tell he was reluctant to open his eyes, and had to smile as he slowly lifted his lids and looked from side to side. "We're still alive?" he asked in an uncertain voice.

Kris sighed. "Yes, Sean. We're still alive—and we have to talk."

Sean bent his head and looked out the window, his fingers touching the glass. "God in heaven . . . I'm dreaming!" He turned back to Kris. *"That's* Richmond?"

Smiling, she nodded. "From a few thousand feet up."

He looked out at the multitude of tiny lights. "It reminds me of a drawing I once saw in a book of fairy tales. This is preposterous, Kristine. I simply can't be up in the sky looking down at the entire city of Richmond!"

"You are, Sean."

His breath came out in a rush, and his voice was awed. "This must be a dream."

As the plane leveled off, the attendant rushed to serve the six passengers in first class, offering them an early breakfast or a late dinner. Ordering breakfast for herself and Sean, Kris waited for the steaming coffee before drawing his attention away from the window.

"Have something to eat, Sean."

He turned toward the food, then looked up at her. "How did it happen?" he asked. "How did we leave my time and come here?"

Swallowing her coffee, she shook her head. "I wish I knew. I think it had something to do with the lightning. The storm. Remember there was a storm the night I was taken to your time."

"And there was lightning and thunder last night . . ." His eyes were searching hers for an answer.

"I don't know if you are supposed to be in this time, Sean. I don't think so. When Christina was about to strike me, you pulled me away and I . . . I must have taken you with me." He was looking at her so intently that she attempted to explain. "We never should have met, Christina and I. Or touched. Somehow I sensed it. There was something not . . . right about it. I can't explain what that moment was like when Christina was so close. I could feel her breath on me." She shivered. "I know it sounds crazy," Kris admitted. Confused, she shrugged her shoulders. "I wish I knew what to say to you."

"You mean you don't know how to send me back to my own time?" His voice was strained from the effort not to raise it.

She swallowed down her dread and tried to smile. Shaking her head, she said, "No one knows how to get you back to your time, Sean. If we told anyone about this, they'd think we were mad. What happened was an accident. I don't know how I came to be in your study, and I haven't the slightest idea how to get you back into it. I know you think this is an advanced time, but we haven't come that far yet. We have to talk about what we're going to do now."

He was staring at the miniature croissants, the grapes and slices of melon. He hadn't touched his food. "You are saying that I can't return to Rivanna? My Rivanna, not your brother's. That I have to stay here in this time?"

She wet her bottom lip, then captured it with her teeth. What could she say to him? "Would that be so terrible? Oh, I know," she rushed on, "everything you've worked for you've left behind, but you really haven't seen what the twentieth century offers." He wouldn't look at her and she could feel his pain. "I don't know what to say to you to make it easier. But I do know how you feel. It happened to me, too. Remember?"

He slowly turned his head. "That's right. And then it corrected itself and you were returned to your time. That can happen to me, can't it?"

She blinked several times. What was she supposed to say to him? Should she tell the truth? Admit that she didn't want him to go back to eighteen seventy-one? Should she tell him she secretly hoped he would have to stay with her. Could she be that cruel? That selfish? Instead, she whispered, "Anything's possible, Sean. I just don't know. . . ."

He stared at her. She was so lovely. So different. "You look so much like her, and yet now that I know there are two of you, I can't imagine why I didn't see the difference before."

His voice was low, husky; and he cleared his throat as if embarrassed by his words. Picking up his croissant, he tore off a small piece. "And now she's back there, with no one to stop her. What frightens me is that she has a free hand on Rivanna. What's going to happen to everyone there when there's no one to protect them from her?" He turned his head and stared into her eyes. His expression was tortured. "Rivanna is in Christina's hands now. Who's going to stop her?"

Thinking, Kris rested her head against the cushion and looked at the ceiling of the cabin. "Beth will stop her," she said with more confidence than she actually felt.

"Beth? She's a child."

"She's more than a child, Sean. She's definitely

on her way to being a woman. She's strong, with a firm sense of responsibility." Kris looked at him. "I told her, Sean. About me. She didn't believe me, of course, but she isn't going to believe Christina's story either. Is there someone she'll turn to? Somewhere she can go for help?"

He thought for a moment. "Once I'm discovered missing, if Beth confides in Harry Gentry, then his uncle, Matthew, will step in and take over."

In answer to Kris's confused look, he continued, "I've been using Matthew as my lawyer for the last two years. A copy of my . . . my will is filed in his office." His eyes were wide with shock. "I can't believe I'm talking about this."

Kris stiffened. "Sean. Who inherits Rivanna?"

"If . . . if I were to die without any children of my own, I wanted Beth to have Rivanna. She loves it almost as much as I do, for the same reasons."

"And what of Christina?"

He shook his head. "I've established a trust fund for her, until she remarries. I made sure she would have enough money to live comfortably, but no: Christina would never inherit Rivanna. The house, the land—all is in my name. And I wanted Beth to have it. I trust her."

Kris nodded and looked across him to the window. Staring out into the night, she said, "I think I can tell you what happens, Sean, at least part of it, and put your mind at ease." It would be so easy to say nothing, to keep the knowledge to herself. But she knew it would eat away at her, until she lost all self-respect. Besides, Sean had a right to know.

She closed her eyes, concentrating, wanting to get it right. "Elizabeth Gentry's daughter—Beth's daughter—is named Ellena. And she's my great-grandmother."

"Kristine? . . ."

She didn't open her eyes. She had to continue before she lost her courage. "Ellena's daughter is Grace, my grandmother. And Grace's child is Margaret." She opened her eyes and held his vision with her own. "My mother."

"What are you saying, Kristine? I don't understand."

"I'm saying that Elizabeth Gentry takes control of Rivanna. I've never heard of Christina. No one in our family has. The money in our family came from my mother's side, at least in the beginning. The women all married well, to men who added to the family fortune, either by their own wealth or their financial talents."

He was staring at her.

"Don't you understand? If Christina and Beth were related to me, then my family's wealth was based on your money—money Beth inherited from you."

He was slowly shaking his head. "I'm confused. How do you know this?"

"Beth is my great-great-grandmother. I'm sure

244

of it." Kris massaged her temples. "I even told her so. My God, she was so frightened of me."

"I wouldn't wonder," Sean whispered. "That poor child . . . what she'll have to go through."

Kris turned her head and held his gaze. "She's strong, Sean. And she makes it. We know that. Elizabeth Gentry was the matriarch of my mother's family."

"And will I meet your mother, Kristine? Perhaps we can find out from her what happened to her grandmother, to Beth. And maybe she might have a recollection of Christina, or Rivanna."

Kris shook her head. Her smile was sad. "My parents were both killed in France. A car accident."

She suddenly looked like a small girl to him, alone and trying very hard to be brave. For the first time he could see a resemblance to Beth. He wanted to put his arm around her and offer comfort. "If your brother lives in Virginia, and you live in Philadelphia, does that mean you live alone? Or do you have other brothers or sisters?"

The sadness disappeared and was replaced with tenderness. "No. There's just Jack and me. That always seemed enough."

His eyes widened. "You *do* live alone? In Philadelphia? You must be very brave."

Kris giggled. She was so tired that any emotion, even laughter, came quickly to the surface. "It's very common for a woman to live alone. So much has changed in the last hundred years, Sean.

245

There's a lot you're going to find strange. Women living alone is minor compared with the other changes you'll see."

Interested, he began eating the food on the tray in front of him. "What changes?" he asked as he held the small cup of coffee to his lips.

She shook her head. "You'll find out soon enough," she promised, closing her eyes and slowly letting out her breath. "I'm so tired," she murmured, relaxing for the first time since . . . since when? Since she'd come to Rivanna? Jack's Rivanna? And Sean thought *he* was confused! Well, she wouldn't think about it now. She wasn't asking for sleep. She knew she had to stay awake for Sean. All she wanted was a little rest. Just a few minutes without questions. Or searching for simple answers to impossible questions.

He watched as her cheek came closer to his shoulder and knew the moment she fell asleep by the way the muscles in her face relaxed. Listening to her even breathing, Sean sat back in his seat and smiled at the young woman who took away their trays. He watched as she returned and opened the compartment where Kris had put her luggage. When the woman brought down a blanket and draped it across Kristine's shoulders, Sean smiled his thanks and closed his eyes. Slowly, letting his jaw rest against the top of her head, he inhaled the sweet scent of her.

If he was dreaming, did he really want to wake up? Stifling a yawn, he admitted that he was too tired to search for an honest answer.

Philadelphia International Airport was a blur of wondrous sights, from the glass-enclosed bridge that was suspended over traffic to the moving stairs that took them down to street level. Dawn was about to break as he and Kristine rode in a hired automobile to her home, which she called a townhouse.

Placing her luggage on the foyer floor, Sean straightened and looked around. It was tiny compared to Rivanna, but he immediately liked her house. Even at dawn, it felt comfortable and inviting.

"You have a very nice home, Kristine. Where would you like me to put your bag?"

Flipping through her mail, Kris looked up. She smiled and walked back to him. "I'll take it into the bedroom."

"Direct me and I'll carry it for you."

Reaching out, she picked up the small overnight bag and said, "Honestly, Sean. I carried it to Virginia. I think I can manage the few feet into the bedroom."

When she straightened, they were staring at each other. "I'm not certain that it's proper for me to stay here with you . . . unchaperoned as you are."

"Oh, Sean." She laughed lightly. "How am I going to explain this to you? Look, why don't you make yourself comfortable while I put this away and check my machine."

"Your machine? Do you mean your automobile?"

She shook her head. "My answering machine. On second thought, why don't you come with me and see for yourself. After a plane trip, this is going to seem minor."

Less than five minutes later, in Kris's small library, Sean looked up from the metallic box. "This is amazing, Kristine. Do you mean to say that people can communicate all over the world with this? And you don't even have to be home to receive the messages?"

Nodding, Kris felt the pleasure of his discovery and her grin widened. "Would you like to try it out? We can call Danielle's machine."

All she needed to see was his answering smile.

Kris called out the phone numbers to him and she watched as his expression changed to amazement when he heard Danielle's message. Taking the receiver from him she said into it, "It's just me, Danni. I wanted to let you know I got home safely, and I'll call you in a few days. Take care. . . ."

She replaced the receiver and looked up at him. "There's a lot to learn, Sean. Almost everything's different now."

"It must have been very hard for you, Kristine . . . in my time. You left behind so many wonders."

She stared at his mouth, the shadow of his beard under his cheekbones, the emotion revealed in the expression of his eyes. "I don't know about that, Sean. Your time is so uncomplicated—so much simpler."

Neither said anything. They continued to stare at each other, thinking private thoughts. Finally, Kris cleared her throat. "We both should get some rest, a few hours' sleep. The naps on the plane don't count."

Sean nodded and stood up.

"That way," Kris continued, "we can make some definite plans this afternoon. After we've rested." Why did she suddenly feel like a young schoolgirl?

Again Sean nodded, looking more uncomfortable. "Where would you like me to sleep," he finally asked when she didn't volunteer that information.

Kris's mouth went dry and she swallowed several times before answering. "That's right. I'm sorry. I should have told you." She hurried to the couch in the back of him. "This . . . this thing opens up into a bed," she mumbled, while throwing cushions onto the library rug. "Since there's only the one bedroom, I got it for overnight guests." Thank God, Kris silently added.

Sean quickly lent a hand, again marveling at yet another discovery. "A bed inside a sofa! Amazing! Very ingenious."

Kris straightened and backed out of the room.

"I have to get the linens, but I'll be right back," she promised.

As she left she heard him whisper, "What other wonders await me? It'll be most difficult to sleep."

Kris shook her head as she walked down the hall. Poor Sean. Even in his wildest dreams, he couldn't imagine what was ahead of him. He didn't know it, but he was going to need his sleep. He'd need strength to survive the twentieth century.

Two hours later, Kris slipped from her bed and padded barefoot down the hallway to her library. Tired as she was, she couldn't sleep. As she peeked into the room, she could see Sean sleeping on his side, the pale yellow blanket high on his shoulder. She could hardly believe he was here. Right here in her home. A man from the nineteenth century . . .

Crossing her arms over her chest, Kris stared down at him. She knew why she couldn't sleep. It had been over fifteen months since she'd been with a man. And she wanted this one. Frightened, she shook her head as if the action could wipe out the memory of them together in his study—before they had stopped and Christina had appeared. Dear God, it had been so long since she was with anyone. Fifteen months of suppressing nature, of pretending that sex wasn't that important. Thank God they had stopped, for she would have surely frightened him. She'd been so successful in building a dam against her emotions and needs, but it was so different now, she reminded herself as she looked down to Sean. Her fingers itched to brush back the hair from his forehead, but in this time of this century one practiced monogamy, celibacy, or stupidity.

Since she had never really loved before, and no one had ever accused her of being stupid, Kristine Gavin had remained celibate for the last year. She had over one year of raw emotion locked up behind that dam, and she feared what would happen when it finally broke. Already she could feel huge cracks in its foundation.

She would scare the hell out of Sean O'Mara, proper Southern gentleman from another time. . . . That's exactly what would happen. If she ever let her guard down, if she ever allowed him to make love to her, she would shock him — for it couldn't be slow. She didn't have the patience for a courtship. Not after fifteen months. It would be fast and hard and primitive. Like Celtic Star and the mare. That's why the mating had affected her so. And she knew instinctively that he would never understand. A man of his time would be scandalized by such behavior from a woman.

She closed her eyes briefly and shivered. There was so much inside her that she wanted to share, but she knew that Sean had a monumental adjustment awaiting him. For her to add to his confusion right now would be selfish.

251

Let him get used to the twentieth century, she thought, before he has to contend with a twentieth-century woman. She opened her eyes and gazed down at him. She wanted to claim him, protect him from what he would find outside her home. But she knew in the end she would have to let him go; she would have to allow him to make his own choices.

She had no rights to him, for in his mind he was still Christina's husband. It would take time for everything to sink in, especially the fact that everyone he had ever known was gone, that they no longer existed. As Kris closed the library door, she noticed the sun shining off her crystal chandelier and sending prisms of color to the ceiling and floor of her dining room. Her lips slowly lifted in a smile. Was it only yesterday she had flown to Virginia to spend her birthday with Jack? The very concept of time confused her now, for it seemed two parallel worlds were existing simultaneously. Two Rivannas. Yawning, Kris headed back to her bedroom. It was too confusing to contemplate without sleep. Right now it only mattered that she was home and Sean was with her.

It was a new day, and a new beginning.

Chapter Fifteen

"It's called a bathroom."

"A bathroom? You bathe in here?"

Slowly letting out her breath, Kris nodded. This was not going to be easy. It had dawned on her that Sean was going to have to be led, literally, through the twentieth century. And since he had awakened shortly after she had showered, it seemed the best place to begin was right here. But, how?

"Think of it as a combination bathhouse and outhouse—in the house." She waited to see that he understood.

"*In* the house?" he asked, looking around the room.

"Okay, I can see I'm going to have to be more specific. That," she said, pointing to the toilet, "takes the place of a chamber pot." She pressed on the handle. "And you can't even begin to imagine how hard *that* was for me in your time." To cover her embarrassment, she turned on the water in the sink. "You can get hot or cold water here, or in the shower." She walked around him and opened the glass doors. "It works on the same principle as the sink. Hot. Cold. Adjust them for warm."

He came closer and stuck his head in the shower. Running his finger over the tiles, still damp from her use, he said, "It's absolutely amazing! Everything is here, in this one room. You can even grow plants in here."

Kris's mouth dropped open. "Plants?"

He nodded and pointed to the grouping of ferns that hung from the skylight.

She smiled. "Ahh, yes. Plants. Actually, Sean, they're just here for decoration." Why did he have to look so eager, so handsome? Suddenly feeling self-conscious in her robe, Kris pulled it more tightly to her chest and hurried on to explain. "There's soap in the dish here, along with a razor. And I've already laid out fresh towels. Do you think you'll be all right?"

He stood, hands in his pockets, and looked around the bathroom. "I think I can manage, Kristine. If you'll show me where the razor is, I'll start."

She pointed to it.

He shook his head.

"This is a razor? How do you open it?"

It came to her that he was used to an actual

blade and she chuckled. "No, Sean. This is it. Watch. . . ."

She turned on the water and picked up the soap. Lathering the skin right above his wrist, she held the razor under the water and then brought it to the dark hairs on his arm. Very lightly, she stroked the blade across a small patch of skin. Before she could shave any more, Sean took the thin razor from her fingers and rinsed it under the flow of water.

Holding it up to see, he said, "Ingenious! Who does it belong to?"

She looked at him and wished she had applied a little makeup. "It's mine. Well, really it's brand new. I have an entire bag of them." She could feel herself blushing. "They're disposable, Sean. You throw them away when they're dull."

He continued to stare at her. Was she only imagining that his eyes were a darker blue in this brighter light?

"It's your razor? I don't understand."

She actually groaned and didn't care that he heard it. Taking a deep breath, she said in a hurried voice. "Women in this century have the option of shaving certain . . . ah, certain . . . body hair. Like on their legs, for example. Some do. Some don't. I do. Therefore, the razor." The blush at her cheeks was actually making her feel warm. She refused to look at his face. The very last thing she wanted to see was his reaction to her words. "Now," she quickly continued, "here is deodorant, an extra toothbrush and toothpaste. Please read everything for directions. I have to finish dressing and then prepare lunch." She reached for the door, anxious to get away from him and the small room. A bathroom was a far too personal a place to be with a man, especially when you hadn't actually *been* with a man for well over a year. "Just read the directions," she repeated.

"I will. Thank you, Kristine."

She looked up and his expression made her smile. He was totally confused. "Just follow the directions. You'll do fine, Sean. You've already flown in an airplane. This is a piece of cake."

"A piece of cake?"

"An expression, meaning it's easy. Now, hurry up. We have a lot to do today."

His look of alarm made her laugh out loud. Laughter—thank God for it. It relieved some of the tension in her body.

"Nuclear Arms Treaty with the Soviets a year ago? What is this, Kristine? A new Indian tribe from the West? And what are nuclear arms?" As he pored over a paper called the *Philadelphia Inquirer,* Sean looked up as she giggled once again. It didn't annoy him, for she was trying so hard not to do it. He found her fascinating, delightful, and totally feminine, despite the fawn-colored trousers that she wore. Sipping his coffee, he liked the way her white blouse and copper sweater high-

256

lighted the reddish streaks of blond in her hair. Once more he wondered how he could ever have thought she was Christina? They were nothing alike; the difference in them was so obvious to him now.

"Soviets are Russians. That treaty dealt with bombs, enormous explosives that could decimate an entire city." She stacked dishes into the dishwasher. "And depending on your politics, nuclear arms are either a necessity for protection, or they should be eliminated before we destroy the entire world."

Sean looked down to the huge newspaper. "I am a Republican, and I believe they should be eliminated."

She straightened and stared at him. Her lips broke into a slow smile. "Good for you. Too bad you can't vote."

"I can't?"

She shook her head as she dried the skillet she had used to fry his eggs. "You aren't registered. And you can't register without proof that you're a citizen. We're going to have to work on that," she added, before putting the frying pan away. "What else have you read?"

Sean had the feeling that she was trying to distract him, and he allowed her to do so. Today was so special to him that he decided, for just a little while, to enjoy this trip into the twentieth century. Surely, he was going to be taken back to his own time, and while he was here in the future,

257

it would be foolish not to partake of its pleasures and surprises.

"I have read these colored pages with drawings—"

"The comics," Kris said.

"Some of them are very strange. Like this one called, 'The Far Side.' I don't understand it."

Standing next to him, Kristine patted his arm. "You couldn't possibly," she remarked, grinning at the comic strip. "You'd have to understand this time period to grasp the absurdity of it. You've been reading since I gave you the paper over an hour ago. Anything else strike your imagination?"

He looked down and waved his hand over the newspaper. "Everything! It's so big. You say this is published every day? How do people accomplish anything if they read newspapers of this size each day?"

She shrugged her shoulders and he could smell the fragrance of her perfume. It was light and feminine.

"I suppose people only read the sections that interest them: the headlines, local news, their horoscope, Ann Landers. Who knows?"

"I saw those listed in the index and looked them up. Why do people write to this woman and ask her to solve such personal problems?" He wanted her to look at him again. He wanted to make sure the gold flecks in her eyes were really there.

"I don't know, Sean. I suppose people are lonely. I *know* people are lonely," she affirmed.

"Maybe they don't have anyone to talk to. Or maybe, the anonymity appeals to them—telling about problems and then seeing them in print, without fear of being found out." Again, she shrugged. "You see some pretty strange letters in there."

She could feel his gaze on her, and Kris found herself warming under his scrutiny. Talk about confusion! Any man who read Ann Landers on Sunday afternoon, thought the Soviets were a new tribe of Indians, and was a Republican who'd vote against nuclear arms had to be worth his weight in gold. And she had him! The hitch was what to do with him.

She quickly flipped through the paper until she came to the insert for Danni's store. "Here. Look through this while I finish clearing the table. It will give you an idea of what people are wearing today and what to look for this afternoon."

He raised his head from the colorful booklet of advertising. "This afternoon?"

She smiled. There was so much to do before she returned to work tomorrow. Somehow, before morning, she had to settle Sean into the twentieth century. Sighing, she knew her work was cut out for her. "This afternoon," she said with a grin, "we're going sightseeing. And, we're also going to do a little shopping for clothes."

He looked at her sweater, which was a shade darker than her hair. "Clothes? For whom?"

"For you, of course. Danni might think the way

259

you're dressed is the height of fashion, but these are the only clothes you have. Unless you replace them, they're going to get old very quickly."

He thumbed through the ads, skimming over the photographs of women in revealing lingerie, skimpy bras, and daring underwear. When he came to the pictures of men's fashions, he studied the pages. "Ninety-five dollars for a sweater! This is how men dress today?" he asked.

Kris nodded. "The sweater's on sale. I'll explain about inflation later. But, look, this is what Danni was suggesting that you do—model clothing for her department store." She watched him as he studied the pictures, seeing what Danni had seen: an extremely attractive man, who didn't know the power he would convey to a female audience. "You'd probably be very good, Sean," she remarked absently.

Once more he glanced at the pictures, then shook his head. "I could never do this—stand around in clothing and have someone photograph me! If I do stay here, I'll get a proper job until . . . until I return to my own time."

She wouldn't argue with him, nor could she tell him that the thought of his leaving brought an actual pain to her chest. It was so selfish to want him to stay, yet she knew it would take a supreme sacrifice to let him go. Not knowing if she could do it, she tried to smile.

"Well, until then we'd better find something else for you to wear. C'mon, let get started."

"But it's Sunday," Sean protested as he stood up. "What stores are open on a Sunday?"

"We'll go to the Bourse." Picking up her purse, Kris handed him Jack's sweater. "You'll enjoy it. It's a beautiful old building that used to be a stock exchange." Linking her arm through his, she led him toward the front door. "Come along, Mr. O'Mara, you're about to enter modern times."

She'd lived in the city for three years, and had grown up in its suburbs. Suddenly, everything was different. The city was different. Kris never realized that she had taken Philadelphia for granted all her life until she'd seen it through Sean O'Mara's eyes.

They spent the afternoon sightseeing and Sean was thrilled to see many of the buildings he had known were still standing in the twentieth century. They toured Independence Hall like the rest of the tourists; visited the Liberty Bell Pavilion, where Sean informed her that originally the bell was known as the Old State House Bell or Old Independence and that it was recast from the original and rung every year until it broke in the mid eighteen thirties. He told her about living in this city when he was young . . . how his father had sent him from Titusville to acquire knowledge and manners from the cream of Philadelphia society. He knew more about the history of this city than she did. And so she listened, for he told her of it

261

with more interest, more passion, than any tour guide.

They took a cab to see the University of Pennsylvania, Sean's alma mater, and he was shocked by the school's expansion. Returning to the Society Hill section of the city, they walked through Elfreth's Alley and even for Sean it was as if he were taken back in time to the Colonial period of the city. Wanting to see it more slowly, Sean insisted that they hire a horse-drawn cab. He was more comfortable with this familiar mode of transportation, and Kris, forced to leisurely observe the city from the leather seat of a wagon, marveled at everything she had missed or taken for granted.

They walked over Interstate 95 to get to Penn's Landing, and Sean insisted that they stop as he stared down at the lines of traffic that were leaving Veteran's Stadium after a Phillies game. Seeing his childish innocence, his awe at the endless snake of automobiles, Kris knew she would never view a traffic jam in the same way again.

They saw the tall ships at permanent anchor, and toured one that was open to the public. When they came upon a replica of a sailing vessel from the mid eighteen hundreds that was in Philadelphia for the weekend, Kris stood back and watched as Sean questioned the crew for over fifteen minutes. When he thanked the men and turned back to her, his face was flushed with excitement.

"Kristine! They take passengers for weekend cruises to Baltimore or Charlestown. Wouldn't it be wonderful to sign on for the weekend?"

She grinned. "Sign on? Like in work on the ship?"

Nodding, he turned around for a final glimpse of the long wooden vessel. "I've always wanted to find out what it would be like to go to sea. This is perfect. One pays for the experience, and if he doesn't like it . . . well, then he has his answer."

She linked an arm through his and steered him back across the concrete bridge. Feeling him slow down, she looked at him as he stared off to their right.

"What is it?" he asked, pointing to the long, black wall of marble with scenes etched into it.

She let her breath out. "It's a memorial to veterans who died in the Viet Nam War."

He turned to her. "What war did you say?"

"Viet Nam." She allowed him to pull her toward it, feeling the power of the wall as she came closer. "Don't ask me about it, Sean. Not yet. You have so much to learn about history. So many wars, since the one you fought in. So many men have died. . . ."

He could sense her sorrow as they silently walked in front of the marble. Occasionally, he would stop and read the name of a fallen warrior before continuing to the next panel where a wreath or a wilted bouquet of flowers would be propped up in a show of remembrance. Saddened,

Sean led her away from the memorial and back toward Society Hill and the Bourse Building.

Kris was glad she had saved this for last, for there was something very satisfying about going shopping with Sean. As she sat in the exclusive men's store and waited for him to emerge from the changing room, Kris admitted that she was thoroughly enjoying dressing Sean O'Mara. It had taken fifteen minutes of whispered arguments to convince him to let her pay for the clothes. But what fun it had been when he had finally consented!

She felt a little like Henry Higgins with his Eliza Dolittle, realizing that all she had to do was nod her approval and Sean would add the garment to those already acceptable. She decided what kind of underwear he would wear, whether or not he would need a suit, what style of shoes he should buy. She chuckled when explaining that two pairs of jeans were a necessity, that denim had been elevated from work clothing to everyday fashion. And since it was early spring and the night air was still cool, she couldn't resist the sale of a bomber jacket. When they were through, Sean O'Mara turned the head of every female as they left the Bourse. Dressed in tan tweed pants, a forest green sweater, and his bomber jacket, he was casually elegant and every woman's fantasy.

The best part was that he didn't even know it.

They decided to have dinner at City Tavern, the oldest eating place in Philadelphia and in existence since before the Federalist period. In it, Ben Franklin had sat down to read newspapers and drink ale. And in it, Kristine Gavin looked across a table laden with Colonial meat pies and plates of oysters, and knew she was falling in love with Sean O'Mara.

Sipping her warmed punch, Kris couldn't stop smiling at him. She loved the way he looked when he spoke. He was so earnest, so excited by each new discovery. Dear God, she thought, while watching the candlelight warm his eyes, please don't take him back. Please leave him here with me.

She knew that was part of what held her back from him, for she honestly didn't know if she could survive the loss. If the last few days had taught her anything, it was that nothing could be taken for granted. He might be returned to his own time. To Christina. And if she did lose him, she knew she'd lose a part of herself.

Confused, and more than a little frightened by acknowledging her feelings, Kris looked down to her watch. "We should be leaving soon. I have to work tomorrow."

Wiping his mouth with his napkin, Sean's eyes narrowed. "Work? Where do you work?"

She signaled the waiter for their check. "I did tell you once, though I can't blame you for not believing me then. I work at a television station. I report on entertainment: movies, celebrities that come into town to publicize their work, you name

265

it. If it can be labeled entertainment, then I report on it."

"I don't understand," he said, watching as she used her credit card and signed her name . . . just as she had done in the clothing store. "What is a television station?"

As she stood up, her grin widened. "Now, *that's* going to take a bit more explaining. Let's go home and we'll begin that phase of your education. I've purposely saved it for last."

As she helped him gather up their packages, he thought her expression was positively mysterious.

A half-hour later, Sean listened as she described the feast she was setting on the low table before the sofa: popcorn, fudge-ripple ice cream, and diet Pepsi. He watched as she hurried about the room in which he had slept, saw her open the small wooden doors under a large machine. It was something he had examined earlier, a complex apparatus that had numbers and many buttons. Numerous wires connected it to the larger glass area. The buttons had tempted him when he had awakened. He had wanted to push the one marked on/off, but had been afraid to touch it in case it would break. It appeared he was about to find out just what they did. And from the look on Kristine's face, it must be something exciting.

"Just sit down," she ordered, while rummaging through the stack of videos. After a minute, she held two in her hands. *Gone With the Wind* or *Lady and the Tramp?*

Deciding the Civil War epic should be viewed later, she inserted the animated *Lady and the Tramp* and sat down next to him on the sofa bed. "Now watch what happens," she giggled, more excited than Sean. "Watch the screen."

She felt like Houdini as she held out the remote control of the TV and pressed the play button. Hearing his cry of astonishment, Kris joined in, "I know! I know! Just sit back and enjoy it. I'll explain it all later." She kicked off her shoes and brought her feet up on the cushion. "Oh, look! I love this part . . . Jim Dear and Darling. I'm so glad I gave in to that moment of nostalgia and bought this tape."

Handing Sean his dish of ice cream, Kris picked hers up and sat back on the sofa. Poor Sean was spellbound. He didn't even taste the fudge ripple that he automatically brought to his mouth. Kris took a deep, satisfying breath, letting the ice cream slowly melt over her tongue. All in all, she decided, this had turned into a terrific day.

Laughing at the puppy's pranks, Sean turned to her. "But how is this possible?" he demanded, quickly turning back to the screen before he missed anything else.

"I'll explain later," she promised, watching the wonder on his face. She'd picked the right movie after all. She couldn't wait until they got to her favorite part, the Siamese Cats.

He smiled at her and his expression told of his pleasure. "I'll never forget this day, Kristine," he said sincerely.

She returned his smile. *Neither will I, Sean O'Mara. When asked someday what was the best day of nineteen eighty-eight, I'll think of this one. This beautiful day in April.*

It had been a long time since she'd felt this content, this happy. Now if she could only make it last . . .

Perhaps there is a time, a precise second when a person knows she is not dealing with reality, when perception has been altered to an unrecognizable state. As Christina looked up from the filthy, littered street, she met the young man's insolent gaze and knew she had crossed that boundary.

There could be no other answer for this insane experience, she reasoned. At one moment she was in her father's study, at Rivanna, and in the next instant she was in the midst of a strange city, fighting for her sanity. Richmond. That's what the shamefully dressed woman had said to her. But it wasn't Richmond—not this loud, raucous place where screeching vehicles roamed the streets; bright, colored lights hurt the eye; and frightening night noises terrified the soul. This Richmond knew nothing of gentility. Here a lady was not respected and could not seek the aid of a gentleman. There were no gentlemen here, nor, it seemed, were there any woman of quality.

In her first moments of panic, Christina had

268

attempted to find assistance, but it was obvious that those she'd approached were as afflicted with madness as she. The women were attired without a thought for modesty, in skirts that rose above the knees, garments that barely covered their breasts. Why, even their faces were painted in garish colors and every single one of them had unbound hair. Some wore it even shorter than a man's. Their laughter and ridicule mocked her and she backed away, for it became obvious that they were women of easy virtue. Within seconds, she was forced to acknowledge a reluctant curiosity on her part, and openly stared back at them. She also had to admit a thrill of excitement as a few men directed coarse, suggestive remarks toward her.

"You're new."

The low, lazy voice sounded behind her and she quickly turned around. It was the young man who'd been staring at her earlier. He wasn't tall, not much taller than herself, nor was he as handsome as Judson or Sean; yet there was an air of worldliness about him that no other man of her acquaintance had acquired. Instinctively, she knew the stranger was crude, common, and dangerous. It was as if the madness gave her the power to look into his heart and read it. But she was attracted by the aura of raw sexuality that radiated from him. Despite his strange but expertly tailored suit, he exuded provocativeness, male instinct, and she knew that he had sought

269

her out from all the others.

"What's your name?"

She hesitated for only a moment. "Marie Dela-croix," Christina answered, giving him the name she had planned to use in New Orleans.

"You're new," he repeated in a low voice. He stared at her face, as if looking for something. "I would have heard about you . . . remembered that hair." He slowly reached out his hand and wrapped a curl around his finger. "Pretty hair," he said to himself.

Looking back up at her, he smiled. "You got a place? Somewhere to go?"

She shook her head. Her heart pounded against her rib cage and a warmth quickly spread through her. He thought she was one of the prostitutes. Maybe . . . maybe she could live out her forbidden desires. Maybe she could be Marie Delacroix while she waited for sanity to return.

"Come with me, then," he whispered, his attractive smile turning into a seductive grin. "You don't belong out here. You're different from them." Running his fingers through his brown hair, he cast a sneering look at the garish prostitutes.

She was pleased. "You're right. I'm not . . . like them at all."

"Then let's go."

She pulled back when he took hold of her wrist. "Why, I don't even know your name, sir! I couldn't walk off into the night with someone I'd just met, now could — Why are you laughing?" she demanded, as she watched him throw back his head and burst into a shout of laughter.

Seeing that he had attracted the attention of those on the street, he controlled himself and whispered, "I knew you were different the moment I saw you. I didn't care about the way you were dressed or the crazy look in your eye. I felt it. Right here." He emphasized the remark by touching his stomach. "I'm going to take care of you, Marie. You ain't never gonna need another man again."

It was the most he had said. As he spoke Christina smelled alcohol on his breath. It wasn't unpleasant, just a reminder that she still didn't know his name. "Who are you?" she asked, presenting her hand to him.

He looked down at her extended fingers, as if puzzled, then chuckled when realizing what she intended. Seeing the hurt look on her face, he raised her hand to his lips and placed a kiss upon it. As he lifted his head, his eyes sparkled almost unnaturally, the pupils dilated so that they looked black.

"My name's Bobby Ray Evert."

She smiled. It was a good name. Finally, she had found a gentleman in this insane world she'd entered. "I'd be most grateful for your assistance tonight, Bobby Ray," she trilled, bestowing on him her most coquettish look.

He shook his head, as if not believing his luck

271

in finding her. "C'mon, Marie, let's get out of here before it starts raining again." He took her arm and led her down the street.

Christine couldn't help giving the prostitutes a superior look as she passed them by. Let them settle for the dregs of society, she thought, still smarting from their ridicule. She, now Marie Delacroix, had attracted a gentleman . . . a protector.

Had she not presented them her back, Christina would have seen their looks of pity.

Chapter Sixteen

Kris worried about leaving him alone, but knew she had no other choice. "Now remember," she said calmly, "don't answer the telephone. Just let the machine pick it up and take the message. And don't touch the stove. Use the microwave, like we did this morning. If you read the directions on the boxes, you'll be fine." She wiped the counter that separated them. "And what do we never put in the microwave?"

Sean answered like a schoolchild. "Anything metal." He was fascinated with the small box that hung from a cabinet. It was much easier than trying to adjust to the hot coils that were on top of Kris's stove. Electric, she had said, but he thought the microwave oven was far superior, even if Kris couldn't explain how it worked. There were so many new inventions to explore that he couldn't wait for Kristine to leave—but that wasn't the only reason he wanted to be left alone this morning.

"If you want to watch *Lady and the Tramp* again, I'll leave the tape on top of the television," Kris said as she picked up her purse and walked to the television that she had taken from the library. It had seemed logical to bring the set into the living room. She wasn't exactly comfortable camping out in the room where Sean's underwear and clothes were stacked in neat piles on the corner of her desk.

Making a mental note to clear out a drawer in her filing cabinet for him, Kris placed the tape on top of the TV. "Remember, twelve o'clock, turn on the set to channel seven for the midday news. If you run into any problems, use the telephone. I've left a number where I can be reached at the station in an emergency. If not, I'll call on the answering machine every hour or so. If you need me, pick up the telephone. Just like we practiced last night."

Sean nodded, remembering how Kristine had left him after the fascinating story about the dogs had ended. She had told him she was going to use a public telephone. When the small machine in the study had started ringing, he had done exactly as Kristine had instructed and lifted the thin part to his ear. Even now, he was amazed that her voice had traveled that distance and that they had been able to converse so easily. "I remember," he stated, "though I don't think I should have any problems." When was she going to leave? Soon, it would be too late.

Like a mother unwilling to leave her child, Kris felt a tight knot in her stomach. She could only hope Sean would be able to make it through the day without a catastrophe. Leaving him alone was like leaving a six-year-old child. He might have enough common sense to see him through, but a child would be more familiar with technology . . . and probably safer.

Letting out her breath, she tried to smile reassuringly as she observed him glancing at the clock. Looking herself, she gasped, "I'm late! I really have to leave."

Sean kept nodding as he followed her to the door. He stood in the foyer and said goodbye, as she picked up a leather briefcase from a table. He held the door open for her and assured her that he would be fine—there were many history books that he wanted to read. When she finally left, he had to force himself to quietly shut the front door and lock it. As soon as he heard the tumbler of the lock set, he raced back into the room with the television and flicked on the machine. Using the remote control, he quickly tuned in the channel he had found that morning, while Kristine was in the bath—the shower—he corrected himself. He had been flabbergasted to see the advertisement for the story. The unseen person with the deep voice had said it would start at nine o'clock, and it had taken all his patience to wait this long.

A smile slowly spread over his lips as the music started and the show began. Although it did not have the realistic color of the other programs, this one held his interest more. He found himself shaking his head with astonishment. Surely, this was a miracle of science . . . a talking horse!

Mr. Ed never had a bigger fan than he did that morning.

Rushing into the five-story building of WKLM, Kris felt the excitement rising in her, as always. As she passed through the revolving door the air seemed to change, to become charged with an urgency. Waving to the security guard, she ran for the elevator and let her breath out as she leaned against the mirrored wall inside it.

"I wasn't aware that talent had its own hours."

Opening her eyes, Kris groaned as she saw the producer of the midday news shaking his head. "Oh God, Roger. Would you believe that Mercury is in retrograde? My biorhythms must be in a downward curve? How about I'm sorry? You know I hate to be late."

Unsure how he should handle the situation, Roger Scanlon did not stop shaking his head. A producer couldn't be too careful about what he said to talent. In most cases, talent was in stronger with management. Talent had clout—the viewing audience. And those behind the camera were more easily replaced than talent, whose contracts were worth hundreds of thousands of dollars. A producer had to be careful and weigh the risks. But then Kristine Gavin wasn't just talent. She was one of the good ones; everyone liked her. And she was going places in the business. That was another thing producers were especially smart about — spotting the ones that had a future. Kris Gavin's career was just beginning.

Hitting the button for the third floor, Roger said, "Look, I just don't want to see any trends starting here. Especially today. Irv's calling a big meeting this morning."

Hearing the news director's name, Kris wondered how angry Irv Handleman was going to be because she had left him and Peg in Virginia. At the time, she hadn't been prepared for explanations. As she stepped off the elevator, she realized that she still wasn't prepared. Not the best way to begin the day, she told herself as she headed for her desk.

As usual, the place was a sea of humanity rushing in various directions. Phones were ringing. Orders were being shouted over the noise, then quickly contradicted. The news room was a state of organized chaos. Against one painted wall was a line of wire-service teletypes, loudly printing out the news coming in from around the world. A large assignment board hung in the middle of the room. It listed the names of reporters, their whereabouts, and the stories they were working on. To the unknowing eye, the desks of the reporters were no different from those of their editors and producers. All were piled high with newspapers and wire copy. All were crammed together and in disarray. And God help anyone that touched another's clutter.

Dropping into the chair at her desk, Kris felt exhausted before she had even begun. She would definitely have to keep better hours now that Sean was with her, or the lack of rest would show on camera. As she placed her purse into a drawer, she turned to the man at the next desk. "What's going on, Steve? Roger said Irv's called a meeting this morning."

Looking up from a copy of the *New York Times,* Steve Santiago leaned back in his chair and picked up his mug of coffee. "The Nielsens and Arbitrons," he proclaimed in a somber voice familiar to the Philadelphia audience. Steve Santiago was the finest crime reporter in the city. "My guess is we've dropped."

Kris leaned her elbows on her desk. "How can that be? Your documentary on those kids dealing in crack down on Fisher Street ran just last week. You've even had inquiries from the Federal Government. It was one of the biggest exposes to hit this city in years."

Steve shrugged, then lifted his head. "I don't know, but it looks like we're about to find out."

Following his line of vision, Kris watched Irv Handleman walk to the front of the news room. He was accompanied by Arnold Brettin, head of the sales department. Arnie was carrying several graphs. It was not a good sign.

"Overall, it was a pretty good book," Irv said, referring to the Nielsens and Arbitrons. "The station itself is still in the number one position. Our public affairs, documentary, and programming placed well. But the news — our news — was down two rating points. Arnie and I are here to figure out why."

Kris silently groaned as Brettin brought out his graphs. He was a small man who, although he had lost almost all the hair on top of his head, could not seem to control the growth that sprouted from his ears. Kris could never remember seeing him without his pocket protector and the dozens of pens and pencils that rested there along with his calculator. He was a man who had no time for people. Somewhere in his life, he had lost any interest in humanity and had become fascinated with numbers. He was rude and narrow-minded. And he never failed to bore the news room to tears.

"Our bad news is . . . the news," Brettin stated, and was surprised that his joke was not appreciated. "You all know what that means," he continued, his voice building. "A drop of just one point can mean a thirty-second spot can drop five hundred to a thousand dollars."

He took out his pointer and used the graphs to depict the nuances of the ratings. As Brettin rambled on, Kris tuned him out and thought about

279

Sean. What was he doing now? How was he coping, all alone? She wished Brettin would hurry up so she could phone home, and rubbed her ear with her index finger. Not for the first time, she wondered why the man didn't cut that hair. Didn't it effect his hearing? And what must his wife think? Focusing her eyes once more on Arnie Brettin, she wrinkled her nose. He couldn't possibly be married.

Looking around the newsroom, Kris had to bite the inside of her cheek to stop from grinning. Here she was, amid some of the finest investigative reporters on this planet, and she had scooped them. She, Kristine Gavin, entertainment reporter, was sitting on the biggest story of the century. And she couldn't say a thing. She sighed and her eyes glazed over as Brettin droned on about the relationship of rating points and selling time. She had little interest in what he was saying. Instead, she wondered what her time traveler was doing.

Sean was disappointed with himself and very glad he hadn't asked Kristine about the program before she'd left. He *knew* it wasn't possible for animals to speak. Hadn't he spent enough time around horses to know that? Surely, if a horse had that capability he would have heard something about it in his years of working with the creatures. It had only taken a few minutes for Sean to realize that Mr. Ed was not doing the actual speaking. It had been a trick, just like the animated romantic story about dogs. This time period certainly had strange conceptions about animals and a peculiar desire to make them appear human. It was very odd.

Once more he was thankful that he had not asked Kris about the talking horse. She most certainly would have laughed. What a fool he must seem, he thought. Especially to Kristine. She had looked so different this morning, so independent. He wasn't sure whether he liked her applying color to her face, although yesterday he had seen that most women wear more. She was beautiful, his Kristine. . . .

Suddenly, he stopped thinking about Kristine and thought of his wife. A quick slash of pain ripped through his chest as he remembered that Christina now had the power to ruin everything he had worked so hard to build. Walking into the small room Kris used as a study, he browsed over the titles of the books lining one wall. Stopping, he no longer concentrated on the strange titles, but worried about his horses and the contracts he had already entered into. What was going to happen to Celtic Star? Would his wife dare to sell the stallion?

A shudder of horror ran up his back and he promptly reached for a book, any book. *What Color Is Your Parachute?* Now, what kind of book was that? And what was a parachute? Dropping the book onto the desk, he reached for the dictionary Kris had said would explain any foreign words.

His eyes narrowing, he read out loud: an apparatus of lightweight fabric that when unfurled assumes the shape of a large umbrella and acts to retard the speed of a body moving or descending through the *air!* He shook his head in disbelief and read the definition again. That was what it said. He would have to ask Kristine about this one. To retard the speed of a body moving through air! The picture he conjured up in his mind was ludicrous.

At that moment, the telephone startled him by ringing. Only twice, before he heard Kris's voice explaining that she wasn't available. Then the beep, just like last night, and he found himself sitting forward, waiting to hear who was calling Kristine.

"This is Mark. Sorry I missed your birthday down in Virginia. Couldn't be helped. Hope it was a good one. Are you really thirty? As your agent, I'd advise you to deny it." There was a low, masculine laugh that for some reason bothered Sean. Then, "Anyway, Kris, give me a call when you can. The word up here in New York is that Anne Jennings is resigning and KLM has got feelers out for new talent. Interesting, isn't it?"

The machine stopped and a red light blinked. Sean knew it was to show that someone had called. Kris had told him that. What she hadn't told him was who Mark was. The man sounded very familiar . . . and friendly. He wasn't family. Who was he? Sean realized that he knew very little about Kristine. He needed her, and was allowing her to treat him with condescension. He allowed it now, because everything was foreign and only she could explain this new time. Only she understood how frightening this world was to him, how he agonized over whether or not he was going back. How—

His thoughts were interrupted by the sound of the telephone. Surely this was Kristine, calling as she had promised. He listened with expectation.

"I think you know who this is. I'm not going to leave any record of my name on tape. You understand? Anyway, if you're still interested, meet me on Wednesday night. Eleven forty-five. City Line Diner. You don't show, I'll know you lost interest."

Sean stared down at the machine, picturing in his mind the type of man who would belong to that voice. It wasn't reassuring. What kind of woman was Kristine? Two men calling her, both overly familiar, in less than ten minutes? Sean suddenly felt protective of Kristine. He wanted to guard her from harm.

He shook his head and issued a self-deprecating laugh. Who was he deluding? Kristine was like a mother hen to him. And he had no other choice but to rely on her. Their roles had been reversed, along with the changing of times. Women were very strong in nineteen eighty-eight. Not only

Kristine. He had seen it yesterday on the streets of the city, and last night and this morning on the television. Women were . . . aggressive, he decided.

He wasn't sure he liked the change.

At the end of the meeting, Irv Handleman walked by Kris's desk and stopped only long enough to say, "Come into my office, please."

Kris didn't even watch him walk away. It was the please that had thrown her. That *please* had the same polite anger that Sister Marian Delores had used on her and Danni at Villa Victoria when they had been caught smoking. And Kris would never forget the dear sister's face when she'd interrupted them reading Danni's stolen issue of *True Confessions*.

With a feeling of dread Kris stood up from her desk and followed Irv through the news room and into his office. For a brief moment, she felt thirteen and doomed. Then she realized that she hadn't done anything. At least nothing she could remember. But then, it was hard to remember anything before Sean. Before Rivanna. As complicated as it was, life was simpler. . . .

"Have you any idea what was said out there?" Irv asked.

Hearing the annoyance in his voice, Kris closed the door and sat down in front of his desk. "I'm sorry. I'm still not over the weekend. I apologize for leaving you and Peg stranded in Virginia." She gave him a weak smile. "Is your wife speaking to me if I call and ask her forgiveness?"

"Actually, we both enjoyed ourselves immensely. You could take a few lessons in manners from your brother and Elaine."

Kris watched him settle himself behind his desk. He still appeared annoyed. She gave him a look of pained embarrassment. "I can't offer any excuses, only the truth. I was in a situation that demanded a quiet place to deal with it. Remember, I knew nothing about that party. And you have to admit, Jack and Elaine's could never be described as quiet."

Irv shrugged and then nodded. "Jack does have a blind fascination with the Rolling Stones. He says they can't be appreciated at a lower volume."

Kris chuckled and Irv, unable to help himself, joined in. "I enjoyed myself, but Peg nearly inhaled a bottle of aspirin on the plane trip home. She says Jack's hearing should be checked."

"I don't know how Elaine puts up with it," Kris stated, glad to be on friendlier terms with her boss. "She's a jewel."

Irv nodded. "I told Elaine that she should advertise getaway weekends. Between the gourmet meals she presents and Jack's knack for effortless entertaining, they're sure to be a success."

"Did they tell you about the problems they're having getting a variance? I'd hate to think that they might lose Rivanna."

285

Irv held up his hand. "Wait a minute. This isn't why I brought you in here. We need to talk."

Kris met his gaze. "As my friend? Or as my boss?"

"As your superior."

Kris felt the knot rebuild in her stomach. "Whoa . . . you know I'm going on at noon. If I'm fired, save it for afterward." She tried to read the expression on his face. "What the hell have I done?"

Irv shook his head. "Calm down. I was angry because I could see you daydreaming like a lovesick teenager during the meeting." He waited and was rewarded by a quick blush. "Look, you of all people should have been paying attention. There're going to be a lot of changes now that Anne's resigned."

Kris sat straight up in her chair. "I missed that? When?"

"It won't be announced until after four o'clock today. I'm telling you because an early meeting was called this morning and you've been chosen as the temporary replacement for 'Morning Forum'."

Her eyes widened. *"Me?"*

Chapter Seventeen

"Yes, you," Irv confirmed, breaking into a genuine smile. It lasted for a few seconds before he again appeared stern. "Remember what I've just said, Kris. This is only temporary. It's a chance to prove yourself."

She kept nodding, still shocked that she was to be given this opportunity. "When do I start?" she asked, her voice not yet steady.

"Day after tomorrow. The thing is, Kris, you're still going to be the entertainment editor for the news. At least for now. That means twice the work load for a few days, maybe more." He took the plastic bottle of Maalox from his drawer and brought it to his mouth. After taking a large gulp, he left the bottle on his desk and continued, "Naturally, you'll be compensated. The contracts department is going over your contract as we speak. Larry Goodman will be calling Mark this morning to negotiate." He stopped talking and smiled.

"I'm supposed to explain your duties and ask if you'll accept this challenge. I take it you will?"

She leaned forward in her chair. "You did this, didn't you?" she demanded, a grin spreading across her face. "You went to bat for me again."

Irv shook his head. "I'll tell you why you were my recommendation: because you are far more intelligent than the other candidates on the list. You're liked by the public. And you had the winning ace this morning, the one card that beat out the others. You're clean, Kris. There are no skeletons in your closets, no surprises, or scandals we have to bury."

Kris thought about the gossip in the industry — the affairs, the drinking problems, the conflicts of interest — and raised her head to look at Irv. Immediately, she thought of Sean. He was her secret and definitely a surprise, but he certainly wasn't a skeleton in her closet. "I guess I just haven't been around that long, Irv, to attract a scandal. Give me time."

"Don't even joke about it," he answered in a serious voice. "You wouldn't believe how much that matters upstairs."

She couldn't help looking at the ceiling that separated the floors of the building. Upstairs housed the vice presidents and the station manager — the people with real power. Looking back at her boss, Kris grinned. "I'll be good. I promise."

"You'd better be good. What I'm about to tell you is in confidence, because this really could

288

prove to be a once-in-a-lifetime opportunity for you."

Now he really had her attention. It wasn't like Irv to reveal anything. He was true management, and kept his cards close to his chest. This had to be something—

"If you had listened to Arnie a little while ago, you would be aware that KLM is taking the loss of those two rating points very seriously."

"The sales department is always complaining—"

"Listen to me," Irv commanded in an urgent voice. "One of the things that was discussed at the meeting upstairs is that we have a weak lead-in to the five-thirty news. The game show makes a profit, but not much. There is serious talk of replacing it with a new show."

Kris swallowed. "A new show?" she repeated, her mouth too dry to say more.

Nodding, Irv said, "You take the 'Morning Forum' and prove yourself. Make it your show. Intelligent, funny, controversial. And in a little more than a week that same show becomes 'Philly Live!' and hits the air at four o'clock."

Kris definitely had trouble speaking. "An hour show?" Her voice sounded like a squeak. "Against Oprah and Magnum?"

Irv had to laugh at her horrified expression. "The promotional department's ready to stand behind the new concept, and sales thinks it's a terrific idea. Even though I stand a good chance of losing you, so do I." He laced his fingers together

289

and brought them behind his head. "Look at the contacts you've made here in news. Chances are you'll already be familiar with most of the guests."

Kris shook her head in bewilderment. "I don't know, Irv. This sounds so . . . overwhelming. An hour show. And I'll still report entertainment for the news?"

He nodded. "For now. We'll probably do tie-ins. If someone comes into town to promote, you'll do the premiere, the book signing, whatever it is for the news department—and they'll run the spot again for the talk show. Believe me, it'll go over. This town is too important to settle for syndicated shows. Philadelphia wants a voice and it hasn't had one since the 'Mike Douglas Show.' And you know where that went. 'Philly Live!' will give it to them. It's either going to be your show . . . or they'll bring in someone new."

"I can't understand why you're so enthusiastic over this? It's only going to make your job harder. All that to coordinate—"

He dropped his hands on to his desk and leaned into it. "If we start to lose the five o'clock news, then the ratings for the six and eleven may start to erode. I won't let that happen." He sat back in his chair. "This new concept makes sense. It's going to be strong. And if it turns out as well as we think it will, then there's talk of syndication. Who knows, someday even Chicago might be listening to the 'Kristine Gavin Show.'"

She smiled weakly and just sat for a moment, thinking about what Irv had said. She was scared, really scared. This was what she had wanted, what she had been working for . . . but could she do it? Could she carry a one hour show all alone? If she failed, she would publicly make a fool of herself. Her humiliation within the industry would be unbearable. But what if she never tried? What if she let this chance slip through her fingers because of fear? Did she want to live with that degree of regret, always mumbling in the quiet corners of her life—What if?

She knew her answer and gave Irv his. "I accept."

Irv laughed. "Was there any doubt?"

Her own laughter was more nervous than joyous. "You may not believe this, but yes there was—serious doubt."

"Not on my part. You're going to surprise yourself. You're what is known in this industry as natural talent. I knew it the minute I saw your résumé reel. You have it, Kristine."

She felt her throat constrict with emotion and she blinked several times, while trying not to notice how embarassed Irv was with his admission.

"Now," he said, clearing his throat. "Let's talk wardrobe."

She groaned, remembering his lecture before the weekend. Oh well, nothing was guaranteed to be perfect.

"I don't care how you dress for the news. Keep

291

your long cotton skirts and bizarre sweaters. But," and he indicated the floors above his office, "they've already said that you have to dress more . . . well, glamorously. That includes high heels."

She made a face, knowing how uncomfortable an old newsman like Irv was with a fashion discussion. Then she nodded. There was no sense in arguing with him. "Who's going to be the director and producer?" she asked, hoping to get him off the subject.

It worked. "Don Averly and Mike Causson."

Hearing the names, she smiled. She liked both men and admired their work. Kris stood up, ready to leave. She wanted to find a phone and call Sean. "Well, I guess I'd better prepare for the twelve o'clock. It's only a forty-five-second spot with the results of that spring movie survey. I was surprised by the all the responses I received."

Irv stood with her and nodded. She looked at him and felt the tightness reenter her throat, closing it and causing an acrid burning sensation. She really didn't want to cry. But she truly cared for this man. And respected him.

"Thank you, Mr. Handleman," she whispered, forcing the words beyond the constricting muscles. "I know what you've done for me. The trust you given me. And this isn't the first time. I'll . . . try very hard not to let you down."

Irv kept nodding. "Just don't disappoint yourself. You've got a good record here, Kris. Don't do anything to jeopardize it. You are all right, aren't you?"

She knew he was talking about Sean and her unexplainable behavior this past weekend. He'd probably thought up fifty reasons why she had whisked Sean away from everyone. She didn't doubt that most of them were immoral or illegal.

She smiled. "I'm fine."

"Good. Then bring him over for dinner soon. You can't imagine the questions I've had to endure from Peg over your mystery man."

"I will," she promised, and opened the office door. She stopped, and turned around to her friend. "And, Irv? Thanks. I won't disappoint you."

"Pick up the telephone, Sean."

Looking down at the machine, Sean lifted the receiver and said in a loud, yet hesitant voice. "Hello? Hello? Kristine?"

He heard her laugh into his ear and an unexpected warmth traveled through his body.

"I can hear you, Sean. You don't have to shout. Are you all right?"

"Yes."

"What have you been doing?"

He frowned. He didn't want to tell her about the horse he had watched on the television. He remembered the books. "I've been reading," he said in a stilted voice. He was not comfortable using the machine. "I started to read about a thing called a parachute, but the book only gave advice on finding employment. It was very confusing."

Again she laughed, and this time Sean began to take offense. He tried to overcome the feeling as he listened to her speak.

"I can see why you're confused. I should have selected reading material for you before I left — something to ease you into the twentieth century. Actually, I thought you would be watching television."

He knew she was waiting for an answer by the silence on the line, and he cleared his throat. "I decided to read instead."

He could almost hear her breathe as she exhaled. "That's okay. In fact, that's great. But try the encyclopedia, instead of separate books. That way if something confuses you, you can look it up in another volume."

"Well, I was confused by the term parachute. I used the dictionary, just as you said, and read the most bewildering explanation. Why would people need this apparatus? How do they descend through the air?"

Kristine chuckled. "Oh, Sean, I wish I were there now. Listen, this is not going to make very much sense to you but people use them so they can land safely after jumping out of planes."

He didn't say anything for a moment. He was trying to imagine what she had said. "Do you mean people jump out of an airplane? Like the one we were on?"

"Well, not exactly like that one, but yes."

He thought about her answer. "Why?"

This time she laughed out loud. "I don't know," she managed to say. "I've never been able to figure that out myself. Try the encyclopedia. It might have a picture." There was a short period of silence before she added, "We can talk about this tonight when I come home. I have some wonderful news about my job."

She started to explain to him about something called ratings and news reports and a new show. He knew she was disappointed by his silent reaction. "You are to receive an advancement at your place of employment?" he then asked, not quite sure that was what she was talking about.

"Yes. That's exactly right!"

Now he could hear that she was pleased.

"Listen, I have to hurry. Make sure you turn on the television at noon, all right?"

"Yes. I remember."

"Channel seven. Do you remember how to use the—"

"Yes, Kristine. I remember how to use the control box," he said too harshly, annoyed by her maternal tone. Hadn't he used it well enough in her presence last night? Regretting his show of temper, Sean added, "At midday, I will watch the television."

"Sean, are you sure you're all right? Has anything happened that you're not telling me?"

He knew she was picturing an accident in her household, for it was obvious that she did not trust him to come through the day without a mishap. He tried to keep the annoyance out of his voice. "Two people called on the machine."

"Who were they?"

He thought she was brazen to ask him. "Two men." It was all he could say.

"Did they leave their names?" she asked in an innocent voice.

He found the muscles in his face tightening with indignation. "One was named Mark, and the other refused to leave his name. His attitude was very disturbing."

"I'll listen to it when I come home. I really do have to run, Sean. Are you sure you're all right?"

His set his jaw in annoyance over her continual questioning. "Yes, Kristine. I'm all right."

"Okay. After you hang up, push the on/play button again to reset the machine. And I'll call later this afternoon."

"Okay." He used her words.

"Goodbye, Sean."

He pushed the button, just as she had said. Just like a trained animal in a side show, he thought with disgust.

Forty-five minutes later, he watched Kristine on the television. At first, when he had seen her face, he had stood straight up and talked back to her.

She was only on for a short time, talking about something called movies, something she had briefly discussed last night. She had said they would see one tonight. But it was watching her on that glass screen that pushed him over the edge.

He was not a man to remain idle. He had no money and did not trust those strange credit cards that Kristine used. And anyway, her name was printed on them. He had no income, nor any prospects of finding employment. He looked around Kristine's front room. It was lovely, but it wasn't Rivanna. And he wanted Rivanna. His home.

The anger started to build slowly within him, anger that he had forced down while dealing with the panic of finding himself in the late twentieth century. Now he gave vent to his wrath, recognizing the cruelty of being ripped away from his home. There was yet so much that he had intended to do at Rivanna. Not sure where he should direct his anger, he bristled with indignation and, without time to think, picked up the receiver of the telephone. Kristine had told him to touch the zero button if there was an emergency. His life had fallen apart. This qualified as an emergency.

"Operator."

He listened to the woman's voice. It sounded like she was in a hurry, just like everyone he had met. Everyone in this century was in a hurry. No one, it appeared, had the time for grace and charm and patience.

"Operator. Can I help you?"

He cleared his throat. "Why, yes," he answered quickly. "I hope you can."

"What do you want?"

He winced at the brusqueness in her voice. "I . . . ah . . . I was hoping that I could talk to the courthouse in Richmond."

"Richmond, Virginia?"

"Yes. I need—"

"You'll have to call information."

"Information?"

"Yes. Dial four-one-one."

"Four-one-one? The numbers on the front of the machine?"

There was a moment of silence on the line. "Yes. On the front of the phone. Can you do that?"

"Yes I can do that. Thank you."

He started pushing the numbers, but heard the woman shout, "You must hang up first."

Sean stopped and stared at the telephone. "Oh." Replacing the receiver, he bent his head and whispered, "Thank you, Miss Operator." He shrugged his shoulders, not knowing if the impatient woman had heard him. It was a most queer sensation to speak with disembodied voices, especially chafing ones. Once more, he picked up the receiver and pushed the correct numbers.

After a few ringing sounds, he heard another woman's voice.

"Directory assistance. What city?"

Sean started to grin. It was working. "Richmond, Virginia, please." How easy this was. He really had no need to be nervous after all.

"To call Information in Richmond, you must dial one-eight-oh-four-five-five-five-one-two-one-two—"

"Excuse me," Sean interrupted, blinking furiously as he tried to find a pen. This was not going to be as simple as he had thought. He picked up something that resembled a pen, yet it had no nib or writing tip. As he pressed down, he was grateful to see a line of black ink on the paper. "Would you kindly repeat those numbers, please?" he asked, conscious that his heartbeat had increased with his anxiety.

This time he wrote down the numbers and, after thanking the woman, remembered to hang up the phone. He took a deep breath, then reached for the receiver with one hand, while pressing the quoted numbers with the other. Soon a man answered and this time Sean felt more confident. Surely, this man wouldn't be as impatient as the women when he explained his problem.

"Yes, sir. I would like to speak to someone at the courthouse in Richmond, please."

"The courthouse? In Richmond?"

"Yes, sir. I would like to speak with someone who handles the records for . . . say, the last one hundred and twenty years. A clerk, perhaps?"

He heard a click and then a woman with a strange singsong voice told him a different number. Thank goodness she repeated it. When he was sure he'd got it right, he hung up the telephone. Shaking his head, he decided the man was no different from the women. He hadn't even waited to be thanked. Everyone connected with this machine was in such a hurry.

In the next twenty minutes, Sean was introduced to bureaucratic red tape via the telephone lines. He was transferred from one department to the other. Even he, a gentleman, was becoming impatient with the inability of anyone to help him. Finally, it was decided that he should put his request in writing and he would receive his answer within two weeks.

When he replaced the receiver, he felt drained. He didn't even know if he was going to be here in two weeks! Why could no one tell him when Elizabeth Mattson took over ownership of Rivanna Plantation? And from whom? It appeared that Fate was deliberately keeping the answers away from him, denying him peace of mind.

Frustrated, he drew a clean sheet of paper from the box on Kristine's desk and began his formal request.

Sitting in the strangest vehicle, Christina Mattson O'Mara looked out the window and recognized Richmond's old courthouse as they sped past. The extreme speed at which they traveled created a sweet intoxication that only added to the excitement building inside her. She had entered this world yesterday, this strange new world of freedom, with liberty to indulge any daydream or fancy. And she had easily merged into it.

She grinned and closed her eyes, letting the dizziness carry her with the fast movement of the vehicle. The car. She must remember everything Bobby Ray told her, for he didn't understand her lack of knowledge about "simple" things. If only he knew . . . She silently laughed. And to think that last night she had thought she'd lost her mind. Why it had taken her hardly any time to figure out what had happened. Once in Bobby Ray's little rooms she'd seen a newspaper, had listened to the picture box — the TV — and had concluded that she'd been taken on a little time trip. It was nineteen eight-eight, and she, now Marie Delacroix, had been selected for this extraordinary travel. It was a sure sign that the fates had given her permission to indulge herself.

And who deserved it more?

Opening her eyes, she tried to look sophisticated as she watched the scenery speed by. She knew it was best that she not confide in Bobby Ray. Sweet though he was, he simply wouldn't understand that she had come to him from a hundred and seventeen years ago. He would never believe that everything around her was foreign. She simply had to learn the new ways quickly so

301

as not to disappoint him, for Bobby Ray Evert was proving to be everything she had hoped—and more. Why, she could almost blush thinking about the things he had done to her body last night. Even Judson had never come close to being so unbridled with his passion.

She glanced at the young man who drove the car so casually, as if the vehicle did not possess such great speed. He was certainly handsome, in a rough way. Dark hair and dark eyes . . . almost like the Creoles from New Orleans. Almost.

"I want you to stay in the car, Marie. You hear?"

She nodded as they slowed down and turned into a narrow street. "Whatever you say, Bobby Ray."

He turned the key and the huge motor was silenced. Reaching over her knees, he opened a little compartment and withdrew a small sidearm. It was much shorter than any gun she had seen, and she found it hard to believe that it could actually harm someone. But then, everything she had seen so far was hard to believe.

Bobby Ray smiled as he slid it inside the black jacket he was wearing. "For insurance," he explained.

She nodded. "Of course. A gentleman can't be too careful today."

He seemed to enjoy her words, for his grin widened. Suddenly, his hand snaked out to encircle the back of her neck and bring her face closer to his. Without asking permission, he kissed, forcing his tongue into her mouth to duel with her own. She allowed him to grind his mouth against hers, to bite at her bottom lip and slid his fingers up to cup her right breast. It was all part of the fantasy. And she had permission to taste it all.

When he slowly pulled back from her, she saw the desire in his dark eyes and smiled. "You hurry on back, Bobby Ray," she whispered, smelling the cologne he had used this morning after his bath.

He let his breath out in a long rush and brought his thumb up to rub her bottom lip. "You really are something, Marie. We're a good match, you and me. After this, I'm going to take you shopping for some clothes. Woman like you should be dressed in the finest."

He quickly kissed her again and got out of the car. Pushing her hair off her face, Christina watched him as he walked into a deserted building. She couldn't help smiling. He was dashing and mysterious and insatiable. And for right now, for however long she was here, he was hers.

Bobby Ray was right. They were a good match.

Chapter Eighteen

Driving back with her crew from Atlantic City, Kris kept to herself in the news van. It wasn't unusual for her to be tired after interviewing a major celebrity at one of the gambling casinos. She made the trip on the average of three times a month and it wasn't exactly a favorite assignment. However, this time she had obtained a firm promise from the hottest nighttime soap star to appear on next week's morning talk show. And that was an accomplishment, for Grant Adams had never gone live on the East Coast before. Even his one appearance on Donahue was taped. He had decided to be a singer, and it was her good luck to get to him while he was breaking in a new act at the Castle.

Exhausted, she rested her head against the back of the fake leather seat, grateful that the crew of technicians had decided on an agreeable silence. The guys sometimes knew when to leave her alone, and since they had teased her on the way to the shore about her "promotion," she felt certain that they'd leave her in peace on the return trip to Philadelphia. God, she was tired. So much was going on in her life that she didn't have the chance to calmly work things through. Like having a man from the last century living in her home . . .

Men can be such fools, she thought as she closed her eyes to make sure of her privacy. And Sean O'Mara was certainly no exception. He seemed to resent her going to work and leaving him alone. She had tried to talk to him about it, and had tried to get him to talk to her. It hadn't worked. In fact, they had come very close to arguing. She could still hear the offended tone in his voice. . . .

"Am I to understand that you'll be doing this every day?"

"Why, yes. I thought you understood that."

"Every day you will speak on the television? Like you did today?"

Although she was tired, she would once more attempt to make him understand. "Not every day, Sean. But most. Why are you upset?"

"I am not upset." He walked back and forth in front of the window, reminding her of a caged animal. "It's just that I would be interested in why it takes so long to prepare for a job that lasts less than a minute."

She found her shoulder muscles tensing in reaction to his words. "Sean." She said his name patiently. "There is a great deal of preparation for even one minute of air time. I know it's hard for you to understand this, but try to think of it on your terms. How long did you prepare for a birth at Rivanna?"

Immediately, she could see that she had chosen the wrong example. His eyes narrowed and he raised his chin an inch higher. "I don't see how the two can be compared."

Faced with the stubbornness the Irish are so famous for, she shrugged. "Just tell me how long."

"Each mare was a separate case. Each one was different."

She wasn't getting anywhere. "Never mind. Take my word that my job entails a great deal of preparation. And it will take more, once I begin hosting 'Philly Live!' "

"Yes," he had said. "Your work. It appears everyone has a job in this time, somewhere to go, work to be done. Well, almost everyone."

"Be patient, Sean. You've only just come to this time. Don't you think it's only natural that it will take time to adjust?"

"Adjust?"

She nodded.

"I don't believe that it will take a great deal of time to find employment. Even in this time, a man willing to work must account for something."

She wasn't sure how to explain it to him. "He does, Sean, but there are a lot of people out of work. And you'll need documents, a social security number." Raising her hands in a gesture of futility, she again shrugged her shoulders. "I'm not sure how to go about getting you one. You have no birth certificate."

He had looked tortured by her statement. "I will find a job. Someone will hire me, even without those documents."

That was two days ago and she knew he was frustrated by his inability to find employment. He had no experience, no job record; and although hired twice for menial jobs, he'd had to let these opportunities pass because of his lack of a social security card or a license. No one, it seemed, was will to take a chance on a man without any papers or past.

Opening her eyes, Kris looked out the van window and realized that they were approaching the Ben Franklin Bridge. Almost home, she thought, aware that she must have fallen asleep. It didn't surprise her, since most of her nights were spent thinking about the man sleeping in her study.

How many times during the last few days had she fought with herself over Sean O'Mara? How many times in the middle of the night did she reach for the knob of her bedroom door, only to stop herself as sanity returned? Something had to be done about their situation. It was as if they were lovers, yet were forced to live as brother and sister. But no one was forcing them; it seemed to have been determined by silent mutual consent. And they hadn't been lovers, not really. Not in the past, and certainly not in the present.

If that were so, then why did she feel so miserable, so deprived . . . so damned cheated? Suddenly it didn't matter that her career had just taken a colossal leap forward. The one person she wanted to share her happiness with was in pain. Sean's pride was seriously wounded. He came from a time when men ran the world, when superiority was strength, and he wasn't having an easy adjustment in the twentieth century.

"You're awake, are you?"

Smiling, Kris nodded to her sound man, then glanced out the window. Philadelphia. She wondered how Sean had managed today and what mood he would be in when she came home. At least he'd be there. There wasn't silence to greet her at night. Now there was Sean with his wonderful accent that became more deep, more Irish when he was upset or moved by emotions. And if he was cranky, well that was understandable. But he was there, waiting for her. And something was happening between them . . . she just couldn't define it yet.

As the van pulled in behind the station to the private garage, she issued a silent prayer, one that was becoming a litany. Please God, don't take him back. Please leave him here. Give us time. Please . . .

He was whistling as he opened the boxes of frozen dinners. How convenient, thought Sean, to have complete meals already prepared. He liked using the microwave oven, and these meals had been designed for it. It said so right on the box. They were expensive, outrageously expensive, but he hadn't wanted to purchase an inferior meal. Dinner tonight was bought with his money.

Grinning, Sean dug into his pocket and brought out the remaining bills and coins. Not much left after buying the meals, but enough so that he knew great satisfaction. He couldn't wait for Kristine to come home tonight so he could tell her.

Imagine! Three dollars and fifty cents an hour! And for washing dishes . . . He wasn't exactly proud of that — washing dishes — but the heavy set man had said he didn't care whether Sean had a social security card, because he was paying under the table. It had taken a minute or two to realize that the owner of the little restaurant was hiring him. He had started right away to see to the lunch trade and had earned the grand sum of fourteen dollars, minus the cost of the few dishes that he'd broken. He was finally employed. Just like everyone else.

As he placed the plates on the kitchen table, he wondered how long it would take to hear from

Richmond. Kristine had posted his letter for him, and, she'd said Richmond would receive it by today. Soon, he would get some answers. The thought cheered him, as did his independence. It was good to feel like a man again. Smiling, he heard the front door open.

"Sean? Where are you?"

"In the kitchen," he yelled back, hurrying to lay out the cloth napkins. The paper ones seemed incredibly wasteful, and Kristine rarely used them. Adjusting a fork, he quickly straightened as she came into the room.

"What are you doing?" There was amusement in her voice.

"Making our dinner," he answered. She looked lovely. Her hair was pulled up and back in the front and fell past her shoulders in waves of curls. She seemed happy, and there was an attractive flush of excitement on her cheeks. Grinning, he held out her chair. "Your seat, madam."

Smiling, Kris threw her purse onto the counter and walked up to him. As he pushed her chair in and then reached for a bottle of wine, Kristine couldn't help thinking that even the National Organization for Women would be proud of the progress he'd made. She shook her head in amazement. Imagine, Sean O'Mara had prepared a meal! Now that was a giant step toward woman's liberation.

"This is very thoughtful of you, Sean. Thank you."

"You're welcome. Would you care for wine?"

Nodding, Kris held up her glass. He was becoming familiar enough with her home to find the wine glasses. "Yes. Please." As she watched him pour himself a glass, she remarked, "I can't tell you how nice this is . . . to come home and not have to face cooking. I could certainly get used to—"

"But this is a celebration," he interrupted. The expression on his face revealed his confusion. "I wished . . . That is, I had hoped to celebrate my finding employment."

She nearly dropped the glass onto the table. "A job? You found a job?"

He nodded, very pleased with himself. "Yes. Today, and my employer doesn't care that I don't have proper documents." He couldn't keep the smugness out of his voice. "He's paying me under the table."

She could only stare at him. What kind of job had he gotten? Finding her voice, she asked the question aloud as the buzzer on the microwave sounded. "What will you be doing?"

Sean walked toward the oven and removed their dinner. "Right on time," he muttered, while presenting Kristine with Chicken Marsala on its own disposable plate. Ingenious! Bringing his own dinner to the table, he sat down and smiled before raising his glass in a toast. "To fame and fortune. And beginnings . . ."

She automatically raised her glass and murmured, "Congratulations."

Sean accepted her good wishes and sipped his wine. "Ahh . . . Now for dinner!" He bowed his head and concentrated on his food.

Kris looked down, trying to gather her thoughts. "Sean, where did we get this? I don't remember seeing it in the freezer." What was going on?

"I bought the dinners at the grocery store. The same one you took me to on Vine Street."

She raised her head and stared at him. "You bought them?"

"With my first day's wages." He felt very proud. "I am to be paid every day, in cash."

She watched him cut a piece of chicken and pop in into his mouth. He chewed for a very long time. "Sean, where is this job? What exactly do you do for this money?" Her stomach tightened even before he answered and she immediately wondered what kind of people he had met in her absence.

He swallowed and cleared this throat. "I am working in a small restaurant on Callowhill Street. It isn't much of a restaurant, though they do have a large lunch trade. They fry most of their food."

"Are you a cook?" Her eyes widened in surprise and disbelief. Sean working in a restaurant?

He shook his head. "No. I . . . wash the dishes," he said in a low voice. "Actually a machine does the washing—much bigger than the one here in your kitchen, Kristine. This one has

312

many belts and hoses. . . ." His voice trailed off, he felt embarrassed because it sounded as if he were making excuses.

She wasn't sure how to answer him. He was washing dishes! She wanted to cry at the unfairness. Sean O'Mara was a wealthy man, a gentleman . . . intelligent, witty. He'd made a fortune in his own time. And in hers, the best he could do was wash dishes and be paid under the table. Oh God, what had she brought him to?

Clearing her throat, she smiled. "Why, that's wonderful, Sean. Again, congratulations." She concentrated on her meal, trying to make it appear as if everything were normal. "What's the name of this restaurant?"

He looked up. "The French Court. I can't understand why it's so named. There isn't a single French item on the menu. They do a very good business with something called cheese steaks, though. It doesn't sound very appealing. Cheese and steak." He shook his head as if to say you figure it out.

She forced the overcooked chicken down her throat. She had to say something; he was trying so hard to keep up a conversation. "Actually, Sean, cheesesteaks are very popular in Philadelphia."

"Really? The city has changed so, since the years I spent here in college." He, too, seemed to be struggling with the Chicken Marsala. Giving up, he concentrated on the vegetables. "There's so much to get used to . . . like the loud music that is played even on the streets. The construction that seems to be going on all over. And why do people write things on the sides of buildings? It's very unattractive."

Picking up her wine glass, Kris smiled at the handsome man across from her. "What a guest you'd make on the talk show. If people could hear you speak and believe you, I think they'd take a second look at what they're doing to this town. What was it like, Sean," she asked with a dreamy smile, "before all this progress? What was Philadelphia like when you were a young man at the University of Penn?"

He sat back and his smile answered hers. "You're right about one thing. I was a young man then, and believed myself and my friends invincible." His laugh had a hollow ring to it as he stared down at the table. "There were many trees then. I remember that. And parks—many parks where we would picnic on Sundays. We would watch the ladies riding in their carriages, or walking the trails." He smiled with remembrance. "I'm afraid, we bothered them terribly as they passed by. James Appleton's parents had a home in the city and we, the six of us, were granted entrance into most of the city's better entertainments. I have to confess that one of the reasons we went was mainly to partake of the fabulous food that was offered."

He looked up with a sheepish grin. "We were all

living on allowances and none of us was managing too well."

She nodded, remembering similar situations in her past. "What happened to them—your friends?"

He exhaled and brought his wine up before his eyes. Studying the glass, he said, "We all enlisted when war broke out. Four of them never got to hear about Appomattox. Jim Appleton went West a few years later." He shrugged. "And I came South and bought Rivanna."

"And . . .?" They had never really talked about Rivanna and Christina. It was something that stood between the, making them both wary.

"And you know the rest. Or, I'm sure you've been able to piece together the rest. I bought Rivanna and married Christina—in that order. As you know, one turned into a successful venture. The other was a miserable failure."

"Is that what you thought marriage was? A venture?" It didn't sound like him.

He didn't say anything, just continued to stare down at the table. Finally, he whispered, "This is painful, Kristine. I have never enjoyed recalling memories, especially unhappy ones. Thinking about Rivanna only brings distress, and I can't change what has happened. For now, everything is lost."

He wants to go back, she thought, and the muscles in her face tightened. She was going to lose him. Soon he would leave her because she was the reminder of a better time—his time. She had to do something to change that, to make him want to stay. But what?

Ten minutes later, they both gave up on their dinners. Kristine had begun clearing the table when the doorbell rang. "I'll get it," she said automatically, her guard already up. She didn't want visitors tonight.

Looking out the peephole, Kris groaned aloud. She had to force the smile on her face as she opened the door.

"Danni!"

Danielle Rowe marched into the foyer, threw her purse onto the nearest table, and spun back around to Kris. Without warning, she slapped her friend's upper arm. "Where have you been? Why didn't you answer any of my messages?" She placed her fists on her hips and frowned. "I have to read about your promotion in the papers! What's gotten into you?" She raised her chin and stared down at the smaller woman, attempting to convey her annoyance. "And who was that Sean O'Mara character? How come I've never heard of him?"

Seeing that Kris was glancing over her shoulder, she followed the shorter woman's line of vision.

"Ahhh . . ." Danni said slowly, an embarrassed grin curling her lips. "I see you have company."

Kris swallowed. It'd been sheer stupidity not to have called Danni on Monday to explain Sean. Now it wasn't going to be easy to justify her reluctance to confide in her best friend. But how do you explain that a man from the past — a hundred and seventeen years in the past — happens to be living in your study?

Knowing it was hopeless, Kris tried smiling and led Danni into the living room where Sean awaited them. She gave Sean a pleading look before turning back to her friend. "Sean has been . . . staying here," she said, as if that explained his presence. Seeing the look in Danni's eyes, she added, "He's originally from Virginia, but he's thinking about settling in this city." She sat down, wishing that Danni would join her on the sofa, instead of staring at Sean as if he were another life form. You would think she'd never had a man in her living room before!

"I thought you said he was from Philadelphia. In fact, I'm sure — "

Kris watched in amazement as Sean quickly moved in front of Danni and inclined his head in a formal salutation. "How nice to see you again, Miss Rowe. I believe Kristine was referring to the fact that I attended the university here some time ago."

A little startled by the almost ceremonial greeting, Danni sank onto the cushion of a chair. She couldn't stop staring. "What university? What year did you graduate?"

"Danni!" Kris couldn't believe her friend's rudeness.

Sean only smiled. "That's quite all right, Kristine." He smiled at the tall attractive woman opposite him. "I attended the University of Pennsylvania. And that was . . . some time ago, longer than I like to acknowledge. Would you care for wine, Danielle? I was about to pour some."

Danni blinked several times. He was certainly charming, and she suddenly had the distinct impression he was a knight coming to the rescue of his maiden. She almost shook her head to push out the fantasy. This was Kris she was talking about, and this man seemed very important to her dearest friend. The least she could do was be pleasant.

"Why, yes. Thank you." She watched the tall, handsome Irishman walk away, then turned to her closest friend. "All right, what's going on? Is he living here with you?"

Kris glanced toward the kitchen. "My God, Danni, we're not living together, if that's what you mean. He needed a place to stay, and I . . . well, I like him. I wanted to help him out."

"What do you actually know about him? I thought you said he was an architect, that he breeds race horses. Why is he living here?"

"I know all I need to know," Kris whispered, refusing to answer any questions about Sean's past. "I trust him. It's been a long time since I've been able to say that and mean it," she added. "Now, you're going to have to trust me, Danni."

Danielle Rowe stared at her best friend. Together they had shared every disappointment and

318

triumph since they were young girls. Looking at Kris, she saw her plea for understanding, read the underlying look of happiness, and suddenly Danni felt left out. Alone. Kristine was in love, and very protective of the man who'd finally captured her heart. She probably doesn't even know it yet, thought Danni, for Kristine Gavin was usually a very cautious woman—especially in matters of the heart.

Taking a deep breath, Danielle knew she had a decision to make, and quickly. Her stomach tightened and her eyes burned with emotion. My God, was this how Kris felt when she'd visited her and Brian? For over two years she and Brian saw her almost every week. Why was it that until tonight, she had never thought about the pain Kris must have felt? How could she have been that absorbed with a man? And what a dear friend Kristine was to have put up with all her recent complaining about the breakup of that relationship. Now everything was reversed. If she nagged Kris about O'Mara, a man that even Kris herself didn't seem to know too much about, then he would come between them—and she refused to allow that. She and Kris were closer than some sisters. They shared a past, a friendship that was enduring, one that was valued. Now was not the time to test it because this man's past was obscure. The most she could do was to be happy for Kris and accept her decisions. Trust her, just as she had asked.

"Here you are, ladies," Sean said, as he

smoothly carried a silver tray into the room. Offering a glass of wine to each of them, he waited until all were settled before raising his in a toast. "To Kristine," he said quietly. "Thank you for your generosity. Thank you for opening up your home."

Kris looked embarrassed. "You would have done the same," she murmured, while avoiding Danni's questioning expression.

He smiled at both women. "No. I'm afraid you're wrong, Kristine. I would not have trusted as easily." His eyes locked with hers, and he knew she understood his words. "I won't abuse that trust."

Much to the relief of everyone, the ringing of the telephone broke the intimate mood. They listened as Kristine's message carried from the answering machine in the study and, together, waited to hear who was calling.

"I haven't heard from you about tonight. Look, I'll wait ten minutes. If I don't get a response, then we'll just call it off, all right?"

Before the man finished speaking, Kris shot off the sofa and ran into the study in time to pick up the phone before he hung up. Both Sean and Danni remained silent as they listened to her side of the conversation.

"I'm sorry! Of course, I won't use your name on the phone. Look, this has been a crazy week. I meant to get back to you the night you called. Certainly I still want to meet with you. Now more

320

than ever. I'll explain when I see you. Yes . . . fine
. . . all right . . . fifteen minutes. No more than
twenty-five at the most. Yes . . . I'll be there."

Walking back into the living room, Kris felt the
questions even before they came rushing at her.

"That was the same man who called on Monday, the rude one. Who is he, Kristine?" Sean was
almost glaring at her.

"You aren't meeting this person, are you?"
Danni asked, placing her wine glass on a nearby
table.

"Of course she isn't meeting him. At least not
alone,"

Kris raised her eyebrows in surprise and sudden
annoyance. "I'm not?"

"Not alone, certainly." Sean's glass joined Danni's on the table, and as he straightened he seemed
to notice the subtle change in the room, the electricity in the air.

Kris began slowly, as if trying to control her
anger. "This happens to be business, something
I've been working on for months."

Danni interrupted. "I have to agree with Sean.
This doesn't sound like anyone in the entertainment industry, Kris. Why not let him go with
you?"

"You both are ridiculous, do you know that?
This man happens to have valuable information
about corruption in the city's government. I've
been doing some investigative reporting, and Neal
happens to be the only contact I might ever have

inside the current administration. I've waited months for him to open up, and you both think I should be chaperoned?" She pushed stray curls off her forehead in an angry gesture. "I'm a grown woman. I make my own decisions. I'm going alone."

"Kristine . . ." Sean's voice sounded almost parental.

"Don't even start," she warned him. "I won't be gone long. If I'm not back in an hour and a half, then you can start to worry. Neal works in an office, for goodness' sake. He's not dangerous." She checked her appearance in the hall mirror and picked up her purse. Turning around, she said, "Stay here with Danni. I'm sure my ears will be burning as soon as I shut the door behind me." She saw that he was not happy. "Really, Sean, I'll be fine. This is part of my job."

They both listened as the heavy front door closed after her. It was Danni who first spoke. "Well, Sean, now you've seen why I couldn't live with her. I suppose I should wish you better luck, since it appears you're staying here." It was blunt and to the point. Danielle Rowe cared too much about her friend to waste time.

She had to give him credit. He had the grace to look embarrassed.

"Kristine has very kindly agreed to let me use her study until I decide what I'm going to do."

"That's the way Kris is—kind." Danni looked at him and was again struck by his presence. It was revealed in the way he carried himself, in his manner, his accented speech . . . in the way his dark blue eyes looked directly at you. The camera would love him. "She's also been my dearest friend since I was twelve years old," Danni added. "I want you to know why I'm concerned."

Sean nodded. "Thank you for being honest, Danielle. I'm not exactly comfortable with this arrangement, and I would like you to know that I would never do anything to compromise Kristine."

Danni's eyes narrowed. Where had Kris found him? When was the last time a man had worried about compromising a woman's reputation? Picking up her glass of wine, she smiled. "Tell me about yourself, Sean. Are you sure you wouldn't consider modeling as a career?"

She couldn't help laughing at the look of horror on his face.

Neal Koenig watched her as she hurried into the diner and recognized him. If it were possible, she was prettier in person than on the TV. There weren't too many patrons in the City Line Diner at this time of night, but every one of them stared as Kristine Gavin walked straight to his table. It gave him a rush of satisfaction to know that there wasn't a man in the place who didn't envy him.

"Neal, I'm so glad you could wait." There was a breathless catch in her voice as she greeted him before sitting down opposite him in the booth. He loved it. He'd read all about celebrities in a magazine once, even that Lynda Nolan that Kristine interviewed last week. Lynda Nolan said she liked a real strong man. He guessed all these woman were alike. He might be short, and he'd never visited a gym in his life, but he knew how to be strong. Yeah, look how she'd responded to him on the phone. He almost smiled.

"I was only gonna give you five more minutes and then take off. You act like you don't remember what kind of risks I'm takin'." There. Let her think he didn't care. Never let her know that he'd been at the diner for over an hour and had planned on waiting for as long as it took.

"I'm sorry, Neal. This has been a crazy week."

She looked up as the waitress approached. Neal watched her smile at the older woman and order coffee. She was smooth. Real sophisticated, but apologetic too. He'd been right to take the hard approach with her. It was just like Linda Nolan said: "A woman needs to know her limits. She really wants a man to show his strength."

When the waitress left, Neal cleared his throat. "So what is it that you want to know? I already told you I'm not gonna lose my job over this. All I'm willin' to do is point you in the right direction."

Smiling, Kris nodded. The man was small fish, bait to catch someone really big. But she did need him. "I understand, but before we get started maybe you can help me with some information on another story."

He seemed to sit up straighter, and Kris remembered that Neal Koenig had an ego that needed constant attention. "I mean, who knows more about licenses and departmental red tape than you?"

Neal shrugged. "I keep my eyes open. What d'you want to know?"

Kris leaned closer in to him. "How would someone go about getting a fake birth certificate? How do you get a social security number, Neal, if you have no records?"

He sipped his coffee. "Why do you want to know that?"

She attempted to look casual. "I told you. It's for a story I've been planning. Illegal immigrants, that sort of thing." She told herself she was only seeking information. She wanted to report on corruption, not contribute to it.

"It wouldn't be easy, but it's been done before. They'd have to go through the state capital for a birth certificate. There are ways. . . ."

"And you'd know them?" She couldn't help asking.

He smiled. "It'd cost."

"How much?"

Once more, he shrugged. "Maybe five thousand."

Kris's eyes widened. "That much?"

"Anybody that needs a new birth certificate is desperate enough to pay for it."

"But how would they go about it? Do you mean if I gave you a name, any name, you could have a birth certificate, a copy of a nonexistent certificate, issued?" The question was out of her mouth before she could stop it.

Neal could see that he had made an impression, a favorable impression. He'd prove to her that he wasn't only strong but smart as well. He'd show her that he could accomplish things a lesser man wouldn't know how to bring about. "Sure. I can get it. You'll have to pay though. Most of the five thousand goes up to Harrisburg."

He pushed his glasses back up his nose and grinned at her astonished expression. "It's one hell of an expensive project you're workin' on, you know that?" She was still speechless, and Neal was glad she'd asked about the birth certificate. It was more complicated than a few supervisors in the department accepting money under the table for granting building permits. If he could pull this off, he would really show her that he was more than a pencil pusher. He threw back his head and gave her what he hoped was a sexy, man-of-the-world kind of stare. "What name do you want on the certificate?"

It was strange, and decidedly distasteful. Looking down at the white powder lying in four tiny lines on the small piece of glass, Christina shuddered.

"Bobby Ray, how can you do such a thing?" she demanded in a strained voice. "The old people might have used snuff, but nothing like this." She turned her face as he inhaled another line through a slender straw. "I wish you never came out of that building with it."

He looked up, his eyes wide with excitement. "This here's white gold, Marie—cocaine. You have any idea how much I brought out of that warehouse? How much it's worth on the street?"

Confused, Christina shook her head. "All I know is that strangers keep coming here and you sell it to them. I'm just saying I wish you wouldn't use it yourself. It . . . well, it changes you."

Bobby Ray ignored her and bent over the glass. Sniffing several times, he shook his head as if to clear it, and wiped his nose on the back of his hand. He grinned up at her. "They're only strangers to you, babe. I'm conductin' business here. You wouldn't feel so left out if you'd just try, do some action—"

"No, thank you." Christina cut him off, as someone again knocked at the door. Watching him stand up to answer it, she thought this was certainly a side of Bobby Ray that she hadn't even considered. Even in her time, opium was regulated. Obviously, Bobby Ray was selling this drug illegally. As she watched him admit a nervous-looking man into the apartment, Christina realized that the thought of using the powder didn't excite her. She didn't even pay attention to their conversation. This was the ninth man who'd come since this afternoon. Not one of them had looked reputable, and they'd all said basically the same thing. . . .

"Snowman! I'm lookin' to score, man. Two bags now, maybe two more tomorrow."

"It's gonna cost," Bobby Ray said, as if already bored. He led him into the kitchen area. "This is some mean crush. You got to pay for the good stuff, you know? I'm just passin' along the increase."

The man scratched at the side of his face and nervously looked at Christina before following Bobby Ray. "Hey, we all gotta fly. Right?"

Christina gave him a withering look that would have quelled a less desperate person, then walked into the bedroom. She wouldn't watch the same scene played over again.

Chapter Nineteen

"You do like I tell you. Take that garbage outside and pick up everything around the dumpster. If we get one more violation, I'm gonna hold you responsible."

Sean looked at the man speaking to him. He was young, and took his position as manger of the restaurant far more seriously than was required. It was obvious that he had been told to utilize Sean in any position.

"Yes, sir," Sean said, untying the long apron that he wore when operating the dishwasher. "I'll get right to it."

The man nodded, obviously disappointed that he wasn't getting an argument, and walked away. Outside, Sean looked at the litter behind the restaurant. As he bent to pick up a tin can, he had to remind himself that this was the best the twentieth century offered to him. He was restricted here, unable to get other work or use his past knowledge to acquire a better position. Here, there was nothing. Nothing, except Kristine . . .

He continued to police the narrow alley, depositing bottles, newspapers, refuse from a modern, careless, society into the large metal bin. Shaking his head, Sean wondered what had happened to mankind. What had made it value the earth less? Surely in his time there'd been litter, but nothing to compare with this. And it wasn't just this alley. He'd noticed it all over the city. People didn't care. It was obvious in the little things. No longer did men tip their hats in greeting or as a courtesy to a lady. And woman tended to look determined and calculating as they quickly brushed past you. It was as if they were frightened, fighting for something. Maybe, it was recognition.

Women especially confused him. It didn't take him long to realize that warmth was a sign of weakness on the street, yet when he would hold the door open for a woman, she'd act so surprised that her face would be transformed by unexpected pleasure. It was definitely confusing. Kristine had told him of women's progress in the last century, and he was especially pleased that women had been given the right to vote, that they were also valued for their intelligence.

Secretly, he wished that somehow Bridget O'Mara could have seen this for, in truth, his mother was far more intelligent than most men he had met. The daughter of a teacher in Ireland, his mother had left her homeland with her new husband only to die fifteen years later on a field in eastern Pennsylvania . . . from a cut made by a rusted plow blade. It was so unfair. His mother's love of books, her thirst for political news, for current events—all of it had been wasted on that farm in Titusville. Bridget O'Mara would have earned a place in this society of women. She would have been valued . . . like Kristine.

Picking up a newspaper from the ground, he thought of the woman who now shared his life. Her lovely eyes were so open and revealing, showing all her emotions. He didn't think she was aware of how exposed she became in those moments. Perhaps that was why she had been chosen for this new job on television. Kristine Gavin invited warmth, a response; and at her best she was impossible to dismiss. As he again pictured her as she'd looked that morning, he immediately frowned. Something was wrong, different. Kristine was hiding something from him.

Before he'd left for work, he had heard the voice of that man again, on the answering machine. It was the one she had gone to meet. Sean admitted that he hadn't liked it then, and he was angry that Kristine had encouraged the man to call again. The coarse, nasal voice had said that Kristine was to meet him at the same place, and that she was to bring what they had discussed. All morning and into the afternoon, he had been incensed that this man should order Kristine about, and that she seemed not to take offense. And what was she supposed to bring to the meeting?

That thought alone consumed him. Ever since she had first met the man three days ago, he and Kristine were living with an undeclared truce. They didn't argue; they were actually cordial; but it was a strained arrangement—one they both knew was forced.

He would rather have sat her down and talked to her about the matter, about encouraging the man, but he knew he didn't have that right. She was part of this new society of women that answered to no one. And who was he to her, someone forced on her by fate? He was living in her home, yet not a relative. He had no proper reason for making any demands, except concern. Even her best friend, Danielle, hadn't been outraged by his presence in Kristine's home. No one, it appeared, questioned the fact that a man and woman were living in the same house, without the benefit of marriage. Much of propriety had been lost with the passage of time.

And then, too, Kristine was busy now with her job and its new responsibilities. She seemed so engaged, so preoccupied. But everyone's life seemed to be moving ahead—except his. He felt angry, with Kristine and with himself, and with the fates that had brought him to this time. He felt left out of life, almost like a beggar with his face pressed up against the window. He was on the outside. The worst part was that he didn't know how to gain entrance to this new world of the twentieth century. To be honest, he had felt it coming . . . this anger. It had started slowly, entering his system as aggravation. But aggravation had built into frustration, and frustration had now turned into anger. He felt battered for each day brought a new set of difficulties and he felt impotent against them all.

Glancing down at the newspaper in his hand, he saw it was the racing page. A knot formed in his stomach and slowly tightened as he read about his own profession. Here was something from his life. Something he understood, but again he was shut out. Damn!

"Hey, O'Mara! You ain't being paid to read. Finish up out here and then come back in. I want you to mop up in front before you leave."

The muscle in his cheek clenched with aggravation, and his fingers curled around the newspaper until they formed a tight fist. Slowly, and with great concentration, Sean let out his breath and tossed the paper into the dumpster. He couldn't afford to lose this job . . . and both he and the man behind him knew it.

He unclenched his teeth. "I'll be right there," Sean said with a calmness he didn't feel. "As soon as I'm finished here."

At that moment, he made a promise to himself. It wasn't always going to be like this. He didn't know how he was going to do it, but he'd be damned if he'd spend his life letting others order him about. If he could make a success of Rivanna, then there had to be something in this time that he could build on to make his fortune. It was hidden from him now, but it would come.

All he needed was patience.

The plane landed so smoothly Kris didn't even pay attention until they taxied to the private holding area of Philadelphia's airport. On the ride into the city, she went over her notes and finished the last few paragraphs of the Broadway piece. She wrote as legibly as possible, since there wouldn't even be time to have the script typed onto the Teleprompter. She'd be winging it live on the five-thirty report, and her stomach tightened with the inevitable butterflies. Closing her eyes, she tried to memorize as much of what she'd written as possible while her driver fought rush-hour traffic.

Thirteen minutes later, still mumbling to herself, she raced into the elevator at the station. There wouldn't be time for makeup. She could only hope that Philadelphia would develop a taste for the natural look. As the elevator door opened onto the frenzied news room, she ran to the night editor and quickly handed him the tape of her interview. Making her way to the studio, she met with the director of her new talk show.

"You're going to make me an old man, Kris," Mike said, while trying to keep up with her. "You've really got a piece of *Phantom* on film?"

Nodding, Kris smiled. It was a coup, at least in this city. "Charlie's got the release papers on it. The excitement on Broadway is less feverish, only frantic, now that tickets for the musical have been made more available. This show's going to run for years. I think Paine wants to make sure our fair city knows it's only an hour and a half to the Big Apple."

Mike opened the studio door. Within, it was a little less frenzied than the news room. As he helped Kris over cables, he couldn't keep the envy out of his voice when he asked, "Did you see it? The musical? I can't remember this much excitement since *Cats*."

Kris smiled as she attached her microphone to the lapel of her linen jacket. "I went up to New York this morning thinking all of it was just so much hype. But, Mike"—her smile widened.—"I only saw ten minutes of the first act before we did the interview and they had to drag me away," she whispered as the news started. "It's so elaborate. There's a pageantry—"

Mike sighed, as if in resignation. "With this schedule, the best I can hope for is to catch a touring company in about five years." Then, as if dismissing his situation from his mind, he nodded to her notes. "Are you going to be all right with those?"

Reaching into her jacket pocket for lipstick, she gave him the thumbs-up signal with her other hand, as the director signaled for her to take her seat. Just as they came out of a commercial, she managed to slide behind the desk at the same time as the anchor announced, "And now, with an exclusive report from Broadway, entertainment editor, Kristine Gavin."

335

"He's the hottest man in New York City. Women are falling in love with him and men are fascinated. He's also the toughest ticket in town. Meet . . . the Phantom."

The videotape began with scenes from the musical and then went to her interview with its creator. When the camera returned to Kris, she looked directly into the lens and tried to convey the excitement she had felt that afternoon. She didn't try to sell the musical, for a large portion of her audience might never see a live production of it, she just wanted them to see and hear what it was like to be drawn into a different medium. She wanted her audience to think, to imagine. . . .

"Broadway seems to run in seasons: seasons of mystery, adventure, comedy, or drama. This year, and perhaps for many years to come, will be known as the Season of Romance. . ."

Her delivery had been flawless. She walked off the set to join a smiling Mike Causson.

"You were terrific," he said while leading her off the studio floor. "Come with me. You've got a date with makeup."

She pulled back when they reached the hallway. "What are you talking about? I'm out of here. I've already cleared it with Irv to use the tape on the six o'clock and the eleven. You don't need me."

Mike looked confused. "He didn't tell you that you have to do promos for the new show?"

Her shoulders sagged with defeat. "Tonight?"

Mike nodded. "They want to start running them tomorrow morning. Sorry, kid. Big date?"

Her breath left her in a frustrated rush. "Something like that." She had really wanted to get home to Sean. There was an underlying tension between them and they needed to talk and clear the air. She'd hoped that tonight they might begin to get back that earlier feeling of closeness.

"Why don't you call him?"

"What?" She blinked a few times at the man who seemed to be reading her mind.

"The big date. Why don't you call him and explain." Mike winked as he led her toward makeup. "I've always found late dinners more romantic, anyway."

She grinned and pulled away from him. "I think I'll take your advice and call. Go on ahead. I'll be right with you."

She hurried to the wall phone and dialed her number. When the machine picked up the call, she realized Sean must not yet be home. She left a message for him, hung up, and dialed again; this time adding the code to play back any messages already recorded. When she heard Neal Koenig's voice, the hair on her arms rose with fear. Was she really going to meet with him again? She already knew the answer, for hadn't she withdrawn five thousand dollars from her account? It was lying in an envelope in her safe at home. If she was caught, it could mean her job, maybe even her freedom. Dear God, what the hell was she about to do?

Taking a deep breath, she replaced the receiver and stared at the phone. Right now her life was too complicated to figure out. There were no easy solutions. She was about to start a new show, and the responsibility for its success would sit right on her shoulders. But she was still expected to handle the entertainment segment of the news until management made its decision. She was living with a man from the nineteenth century, and even though she thought she was falling in love, he was barely speaking to her. On top of all that, she was contemplating, seriously contemplating, placing everything in jeopardy by committing a felony.

Maybe if she could just get through each day, until things calmed down, she might make it. But that didn't settle what she was going to do tonight. A little voice inside her said not everyone can have it all—there are always sacrifices. She shook her head and walked toward makeup. Now was not the time for an attack of conscience. First things first. Squaring her shoulders, she walked down the hall and prepared to fight. She would not let them make her up like an evangelist's wife.

"I'm sorry, Sean, but I do have to go out again. It can't be helped."

Was it only his imagination, or did Kristine already look guilty? Why was she lying to him? He knew in his heart that she was meeting this Neal person, that voice on the machine. "Where are you going?"

"I have to do a little more research . . . I'm meeting someone who can help me with it."

Sean thought she appeared nervous as she checked inside her purse for the third time in less than five minutes. What was she taking to the man?

"I'll go with you," he offered. "I have nothing to do tonight, and I'd enjoy the air."

He watched her swallow several times and he had the distinct impression that she was backing away from him.

"I have to leave right away, or I'm going to be late." She picked up her jacket and flung it over her shoulders as she headed for the door. "I'm sorry, Sean. Today's been insane. I never expected to stay late at the studio to do those promos for the new show. We'll go out tomorrow night. I promise." Without another word of explanation, she left the house.

The anger that had been building in him all day almost strangled Sean as he stared at the front door. Without the slightest hesitation, he grabbed the worn, brown leather jacket that Kristine had bought for him that first day in the city. If she insisted on meeting with this man alone and gave no thought to her protection, then he would look after her.

Slowly opening the door, he left the house.

It hadn't been easy. When Kristine had entered a taxi cab, Sean had thought he would lose her. It had taken a certain amount of courage to approach an idle driver and ask him to follow the preceding cab. The driver had thought Sean was joking until he'd had taken out his money. As he settled into the back seat, Sean was thankful that he had left his wages in his pocket. This could prove to be an expensive night.

Five minutes later, he prepared to leave the cab. "Please wait for me," he said to the driver as he paid him. "I'll be right back."

They both watched Kristine enter the diner. "Your wife?" the driver asked.

Not knowing what to say, Sean nodded.

The heavyset man shook his head. "Listen, I've been through this before. I can give you the name of a good lawyer."

"I beg your pardon?" Sean kept an eye on the glass doors of the diner.

"For the divorce. That's what this is about, isn't it?"

Confused, Sean shook his head and left the cab. No, thought Sean. This was about something entirely different. This was about trust. Walking closer to the diner, he looked through the windows and followed Kristine's movements. When she sat down across from the man, his jaw clenched.

Kris didn't order anything. As it was, she could barely swallow now. Her tongue seemed to have swelled to twice it's size and her heart was beating like a drum. She was living her nightmare of stage fright. Koenig was sitting across from her like a proud rooster. She didn't even have to ask. He had the birth certificate. Now, she thought, all I

340

have to do is reach into my purse and bring out the money. And when I hand it over, I'll be committing a felony. Was it worth it? Could she compromise herself, her career? Closing her eyes, she felt her whole life was hinged on her next move.

Could she make it?

He sat in the dark of her front room, sustaining the anger inside him, letting it build and take over. While waiting for her to return home, he thought over everything that had happened between them—remembered it all. Even when she had come to him at Rivanna, she had been stubborn. He had to give her credit for that. All alone, with no one to guide her, Kristine had managed to adjust. Looking back, he could see how she'd overcome her fear and assumed Christina's role. She had fought back, against him, against the entire town, and won.

So why did it surprise him that she needed no one, especially him? She was her own woman. It didn't matter to her that he thought her too familiar with men . . . like this Neal person. What mattered to her was her job, her position. Never had he met a more dedicated worker.

But living with her was not working out. The two of them were just too far apart. It didn't bother her to walk around in her robe as if he were made of stone. She didn't think that he might be aroused, like any normal man, that at those times he had to fight with himself not to touch her—that he waited, like a callow boy in his teens, for a glimpse of her body as she reached for her morning coffee. It was appalling, how far he'd regressed.

Since she now was the more experienced person, he'd allowed her far more control over his life than he'd permitted any other human being. She had dressed him, for God's sake! Like a simple-minded youth, he'd allowed her to mold him into her version of a twentieth-century man. How was he to have known that her idea of a modern man was one that remained silent and did as he was told? He now knew what she was doing, for it only took common sense to realize that Miss Kristine Gavin was playing God, rearranging his life to suit her own ideas of—

Hearing her open the front door, he stood up and listened as she entered the foyer. He watched her walk over to the table below the mirror and drop her purse onto it. She looked tired as she raised her head and looked into the glass. Slowly, she brought up a hand to brush back a stray curl, and she stared at herself, as if searching for something in her face.

"What are you looking for?" he quietly asked.

She spun around and clutched at the long, silky collar of her blouse. "My God! You frightened me. I thought you were in bed."

"Like a good child?"

Her eyes narrowed. "What are talking about, Sean?" She brushed past him and walked down the hallway to the kitchen.

He followed.

"I'm talking about your attitude. Perhaps you were looking for the woman you once were . . . back at Rivanna. Here, in this time, I think you disappoint even yourself."

She stopped at the counter and clutched its edge. "I beg your pardon?" Her voice held more than a hint of indignation.

"I think it's time we have the discussion both of us have been avoiding." He stood still, his chin held high and a look of determination on his face.

"Please, Sean. You wouldn't believe the kind of day I've had. We'll do this tomorrow." What was wrong with him?

"Just as we'll go out tomorrow?"

She nodded and held up her hand in supplication. "That's right. We'll go out and we'll have this talk tomorrow night."

"No."

"Excuse me?" The very last thing she needed tonight was a confrontation. Why couldn't he leave well enough alone?

He leaned a hand on the counter and looked down at her. "Listen to yourself, Kristine. You sound like a parent trying to pacify a child. *We'll do this tomorrow. We'll go out tomorrow. Be a good boy, Sean, and leave mother alone.*"

She snapped her head up and her mouth hung open with shock. "What is wrong with you?"

"Where would you like me to begin, Kristine? Shall we discuss how I've been stripped of everything? Including my self-esteem?"

343

She shook her head and backed away from him. "I can't do this tonight, Sean. Please . . . If you only knew where I've been—what I've done . . ."

He pursued her back down the hall. "Oh, but I do. You see I followed you—"

She spun around. "You what?"

"You heard me. Since you refused to protect yourself, I made the decision to do it for you."

"Well, thank you very much, Mr. Sean O'Mara! Weren't you the one that toasted me and said you wouldn't abuse my trust?" Sarcastic laughter issued from her.

He was breathing heavily as he kept pace with her. His earlier anger was fully renewed. *"Trust!* You actually have the brashness to speak of trust? After meeting with that man tonight? How many others are there? Who else do you meet, Kristine? The number of men that place calls to this house is staggering. What do they all want with you?"

She pushed at his chest. "Those are business calls. I think you'd better be careful about what you're implying."

"I know exactly what I'm saying. It was simpler, wasn't it? In my time?" He brushed back the hair from his forehead. "Even the short while you were there, you knew right from wrong. Here . . . you seem to forget the proper order of things."

"I haven't done anything wrong!" She spotted her purse on the table and quickly looked away. "And what is the proper order of things, Sean? This is a male-female, thing, isn't it? Would it have been proper if I had obeyed you and stayed home tonight?"

He turned on the lights in the front room and looked back at her. "A little more honesty, and a little less condescension would have been proper."

She moved into the living room. He might as well be waving a red flag to incense her. She couldn't back down. "I can not believe you're saying this. I've done everything I could to make this transition easier for you. Perhaps what's really bothering you is that you expect me to continue holding your hand."

She could see the muscles moving in his cheeks as he ground his teeth together. Ignoring that, she continued, "Except I had no choice in the matter. I came back to a job that demanded my attention, and to a once-in-a-lifetime chance to advance my career. I never ignored you. I tried to—"

"You *mothered* me, until I almost lost my own identity!" he hotly interrupted.

"Mothered you?" Kris mimicked him. "You don't know what you're saying—"

He didn't want her to finish her sentence. "Who chose my clothes?"

"But, I thought—"

"Who told me how to think? What television programs to watch? Which books to read?"

"Now wait a minute! That was for your own good. I didn't want—"

It was her turn to back-pedal as he relentlessly pursued her around the room. "Who told me that I couldn't get a job on my own? Who explained away the last hundred years as woman's struggle

345

against male supremacy? And who the hell believed *that?*" He glared at her, daring her to deny any of it. "Who has tried to mold me into someone I'm not? And who, goddammit, has been treating me like her own personal pet? Her damned trained animal, to be rewarded with a smile and a pat on the head if I perform correctly?"

When he exhaled, his breath was a long, drawn-out shudder. "Well, it's over. All of it. I won't allow you to control me any longer."

She stared at him, blinking furiously. Never would she admit to this stubborn Irishman that a few of his remarks had hit home. Instead, she thought back to what she had done only an hour ago. And for what? Because she was foolish enough to think she was in love? God, what is it that makes women believe in the happy-ever-after ending? Do we never grow up, thought Kris? Are we the eternal optimists, even in the face of doom?

"Now it's your turn to listen, Mr. O'Mara," she ordered, as she pushed him into a chair.

She paced back and forth before him until she had made her decision. Quickly walking into the foyer, she picked up her purse. Coming back, she threw it onto his lap and smirked when he grunted in response.

"Open it," she commanded. "You've made some pretty serious charges against me. I want you to see what I've been up to tonight." He hesitated to follow her order. "Go ahead," she urged. "I know it isn't proper for a nineteenth-century gentleman to open a lady's purse, but you're not in the nineteenth century any longer, Sean. This is the twentieth century, and I just gave you permission."

She watched him lift the leather flap and zip open her purse. He looked back up at her, as if asking a question. "The yellow envelope," she instructed, and observed him take it from the interior. Slowly, he opened the it and withdrew a folded light green paper with an embossed seal.

Raising his head, he said in an unsteady voice. "I don't understand. A birth certificate? There's no name on it."

She leaned down so her face was closer to his. She wanted him to see the anger in her eyes. "It's yours. I bought it for you—tonight. *That's* what I was doing in that diner! Five thousand dollars, so you could be legal . . . get on with your life. Do you think I've been blind? That I haven't seen the pain in your eyes, that I don't know the loss you feel? Do you have any idea what I've done? What I've put in jeopardy? You talk about honor and integrity as if only a man could lose it!" She straightened, refusing to let him see her cry.

"God damn you, Sean O'Mara!" Before she could even think about what she was doing, she slapped him soundly on the cheek. He had hurt her so terribly she'd wanted to strike back. Horrified, she stared down at him, aware that her fingers stung and tears burned at the corners of her eyes. My God, to be reduced to this! "Damn you to hell!"

He looked up at her, blinking back the rage that threatened to blind him. "Surely I'm there now," he said, a deadly undertone to his voice. "My only comfort is that I'm not condemned to remain here forever. I'll find a new place to live in the morning."

She felt as if he had returned her blow. "Then go!" Her lips, even the muscles in her face, trembled with emotion. "Take your stupid Irish pride and leave. Just remember this is your own decision. You are capable of making them, after all."

Kris ran her fingers through her hair and turned toward the hallway. If she could just get to her room before the tears reduced her to a blubbering idiot . . .

"Kristine! We aren't finished," Sean shouted to her back.

Hearing him stand, she ignored him as she muttered, "Oh yes we are. Quite finished." It was with a mixture of sorrow and relief that she closed the door of her bedroom behind her.

She only turned on the light in her closet, for she didn't think she could stand the sight of herself right away. Her breathing was unsteady and her stomach was clenching as if she were ill. Unable to hold back the tears, she threw her jacket onto the bed. Unbuttoning her skirt, she stepped out of it and left it on the rug. Nothing matters right now, except undressing and getting into bed, she thought as she dropped her pantyhose. Maybe sleep would shut out the ugly words, the loss of control. . . . Standing before her closet in her blouse and slip, she sniffled and reached for her robe just as the door to her room was opened.

Sean stood in the doorway, the light from the hall silhouetting him. He didn't say anything for a moment. He just stood there, watching her watch him.

"You were right," he finally whispered. "This is a man-woman thing, just as you said. You told me what to wear, how to think, even how to feel."

For the first time he crossed that threshold and came into her room, and she couldn't find the voice to tell him to leave. In truth, her pounding heart raced as she listened to his hypnotic whisper.

As he stood in front of her, his breath touched her face when he continued, "This is the one thing you can't control, Kristine, any more than I can. That was our problem. We tried too damn hard."

He reached out and gently wiped a tear away from her cheek. At his touch, she momentarily pulled back her head . . . until she felt the soft brush of his fingers. Unwillingly, her face turned into his palm.

"You . . . said . . . things." She couldn't stop the burning at her eyes, nor forget his words.

"Shh . . ." He drew his finger to her mouth to silence her. "We both said things," he whispered in a low, soothing voice that held a hint of his Irish background. "Together, we started something over a hundred years ago, lass. It's time . . ."

He traced her chin with his finger, curling it under her jaw and tilting her face up to his. She stared at him, this proud, handsome man; and felt the overpowering urge to touch him, to make sure this person who had come into her life was real . . . and not a fantasy.

As her fingers made contact with his arm, she felt his muscles jump under her sudden touch and her anger swiftly left her. In its place was an overwhelming desire to touch and be touched. The room filled with a tension that seemed alive. The air was charged with electricity, an aura of crackling sexuality, as they continued to stare at one another.

She wanted him. The admission was honest, painful, and illuminatingly true. Since the first time she had seen him, in the study at Rivanna, she had known this moment was going to come . . . had secretly wished for it. He had come into her life while she was alone, frightened in the crazy, mad world of the past. And she had shared more with him than with any other human being. They were linked together by fate and destined to love. She wouldn't think about forever—forevers were never guaranteed. She would think about now . . . while he was here with her. The thought that he might be taken back to his own time, stolen from her by fate, was too painful to even consider.

She would claim him. For now. For however long it lasted. Surely then he would be allowed to stay. Suddenly, her heart opened to him and admitted him inside. She loved him. Filled with a warmth that was both comforting and exciting, she lifted her lips.

It was the sign he had been waiting for, a response to the desire mirrored in his own eyes. With a wild desperation, he pulled her against him and felt the vibration of her heartbeat as it countered his own. With a moan, he curled his fingers through the maze of her hair and held her head gently between his hands.

"I'm so sorry I hurt you . . . didn't trust you." His voice was hoarse, raspy, as if he were having trouble speaking.

She shook her head. "Please, don't . . . I can't believe I actually did that to you." A look of sorrow crossed her face as she reached up and touched his cheek, the place were she had struck him.

"You did nothing," he breathed into her hand. "Nothing more than I deserved."

With a swiftness that was astonishing, he pulled her face toward his and devoured her lips in a feverish kiss. He wanted to be slow and gentle, to make up for everything; but it was not to be. Their denial had been too long, their longing too strong for denial. Finally, it was their time.

Their mouths melded in a searing union; their hands moved over each other in frenzied exploration. For so long they had imagined this moment. It was to be treasured and tucked safely into their memories.

Clothing became barriers that needed to be thrown aside. Neither thought, neither reasoned. Driven by instinct, they felt for bindings and stripped away material. Her blouse hung from one arm while he peeled his shirt over his head and threw it into her closet.

He kissed her face, her neck, her shoulders. His mouth roamed over her body, hungry to taste all of her. He pulled her slip over her head and watched in fascination as waves of coppery curls fell to her shoulders. He was enchanted and he couldn't hold back.

She wondered if it were only an illusion, something she had conjured up in her need. How many nights had she imagined him coming to her like this? How many nights had she fought going to him? But he was here, with her. She shuddered as he shoved down the straps of her bra and her breasts fell free into his palms. Her head dropped back as she gave herself over to him. She knew, in her soul, it was a gift he would cherish.

Sensing her abandon, Sean lifted her in his arms and took her to the bed. He placed her on it and stood beside the mattress, looking at her, spellbound, as his fingers began to strip away his remaining clothes. And when he joined her, there was no need for words.

Speech was impossible, for their joining was sweet and swift and as primordial as that of any of God's creatures.

They experienced power and strength and passion as teeth grazed skin and fingers stroked in fierce possession. It was breathtaking and exhilarating, inspiring and soul stirring. And it was their chance to partake of eternity, a moment of paradise, as Sean and Kristine mated more than their physical bodies.

Staring into each other's eyes as flesh joined flesh, they loved with their minds, their hearts . . . and, finally, their souls.

At that moment, they were alone together in the universe.

Lovers beyond time.

Chapter Twenty

She lay perfectly still, staring at his profile, as soft morning rays of sun filtered through the bedroom curtains. It was one of those magical mornings when for fleeting minutes or even seconds you and the world are in complete harmony. It never lasts. It always fades away. But while it's yours, for that precious time, you sense what perfection must be like.

Closing her eyes, she smiled at the notion.

They had come very near perfection last night, thought Kris. Both of them had been in a state of shock following their first, frantic lovemaking. As crazy as it seemed, they had felt shy after such intimacy, awkwardly uncertain as to what should come next . . . Finally, Sean had cradled her face within his palms and had apologized for his haste. His voice had been filled with tenderness, sincerity. He'd then taken her in his arms and again made love to her . . . this time leisurely, exquisitely, talking to her in a low seductive voice until she'd thought she would go mad from wanting. And sometime in the middle of that magical night, it had come to her. She had been waiting for Sean O'Mara her entire life. . . .

"I can't decide whether to kiss away that smile, or just lie here and watch it."

Hearing his gentle words, she opened her eyes. He looked sleepy and . . . well, contented. For the first time since she had met him, Sean looked relaxed and truly happy.

Her smile broadened. "I don't think you should kiss me."

"And why not, lass?"

She noticed that his accent thickened when he was emotional. It only endeared him to her even more. "Because," she whispered, letting her fingertip trace the dimple in his cheek, "then I wouldn't be satisfied with merely a kiss."

"Ahh . . . but I wouldn't want you to be."

"Ahh . . ." she mimicked him, pouring on the Irish intonation. "But then I'd be late for work. And so would you. You forget, Mr. O'Mara, we're a working couple."

He looked deep into her light brown eyes. "I have a confession, Kristine. I haven't been totally honest."

Her eyes widened. "You haven't?"

Shaking his head, Sean said, "I quit my job yesterday. You're not to worry. I'll find another."

"I never doubted that you could find a job. I want you to know that. I was only afraid that you wouldn't be able to work at something you enjoyed." She brushed back the dark hair from his forehead. "But tell me, why did you quit?"

Inhaling deeply, Sean said, "I'm afraid my temper got the best of me. I told the manager of the restaurant that he was a tyrant, with the intelligence level of a flea." He couldn't help smiling when Kristine broke into giggles. "Needless to say, I won't be returning to The French Court."

"Good for you," she cheered. "Now that we have a birth certificate, we can see about getting you proper legal documents. And another job."

His expression became serious. "About the birth certificate, Kristine . . . we never did have a chance to discuss what you've done—"

She quickly placed her finger against his lips to silence him. "Shh, don't say anything, Sean. I've thought about it, and I knew what I was doing."

"But—"

"But nothing! C'mon," she urged, pulling the sheet off the bed and wrapping it around her. "Bring the birth certificate into the study and we'll fill it in. Hurry, or I'll be late for work!"

Smiling as he watched her walk out of the bedroom, Sean knew that he'd never find another woman quite like her. Maybe he wasn't meant to go back to his own time. Maybe . . . He suddenly knew he wouldn't leave Kristine. Not now. Not ever.

Grabbing up his trousers from the rug, Sean O'Mara looked down at his bare feet and realized that for the first time in his life he was in love. In love? It was truly a shock, and he had to sit on the edge of the mattress to shove his legs into the pants.

He was in love with Kristine! It had to be, for he knew in his heart that he would give up everything to stay here with her. Somehow that thought wasn't as frightening as it might have been.

He knew with a certainty that he wasn't alone any longer. Now there were two of them. It was as Kristine had said. They were a working couple. Well, maybe for right now just a couple, but he was positive that he could find another job.

But did she love him? Last night, he would have sworn the answer was yes. He found himself growing warm as he remembered her passion and the thrilling hours they had spent exploring each other's bodies, then talking until they'd both drifted off to sleep.

He wasn't positive, for Kristine was still a very modern woman, but he would bet Rivanna that she cared for him. A smile returned to his face. Yes. He must be very careful with her, never push her for an admittance. He would be patient, at least he would try to be, and he'd wait until she was ready to tell him. There was, of course, nothing wrong with helping her to realize her feelings if she was confused. Yes, that's it, thought Sean. A campaign. He would make sure that Kristine realized they were meant to spend a lifetime to-gether.

Hearing a bird singing outside the window, Sean zipped up his pants and grinned. It was good morning to begin.

Kristine's fingers hovered over the keys of her electric typewriter. "No middle name?"

Sean shook his head. "Just Sean O'Mara."

She nodded, nervous as she typed his first name onto the birth certificate. There could be no mistakes. It had to be perfect. She spelled his last name aloud. "All right. That's done."

Hitting the return key several times, she spaced down to the next blank line. "Now. Place of birth." She looked up at Sean who was standing next to her desk.

"Titusville, Pennsylvania."

"You'd better spell it," she said. As he did, she typed each letter onto the green document. Spacing down to the next line, she groaned. "Uh-oh, here it comes . . . date of birth."

They looked at each other, neither one sure what to say. Finally, Kris spoke. "This is just a paper, Sean. Remember that. I don't even know your birthday. What month, or day?"

"December seventeenth."

She typed the numbers. "All right, now we have to decide on a year."

He nodded. "Why don't you put down nineteen

fifty-five? Thirty-three years ago. That would make sense."

She smiled and lowered her gaze to the typewriter. "One, nine, five, three." She counted off the numbers as she typed them. Finally, she carefully took the certificate out of the machine and, after examining it for a few seconds, handed it to him. "Here you are, Sean. It's the first step. You're on your way to being legal."

Taking the document from her, he looked down to it and said in a low, emotion-filled voice. "I don't know what to say to you, Kristine . . . how to express my gratitude for all you've—"

"Listen to me," she interrupted. "I was angry last night. We both were. And maybe a little frightened. But I want you to know that it was worth it. What I did last night wasn't wrong, because the law doesn't take into account a nineteenth-century man dropping into the twentieth century." She was glad to see him smile. "Believe me. It was worth it."

"What if this man, Neal, tries to make trouble? He could blackmail you." A worried expression came to his face.

Kris grinned and shook her head. "I told him it was for a story I was researching. That's why I insisted the birth certificate be blank. He might say I bought it from him, but without a name, it's just his word against mine." Standing up, she adjusted the sheet around her body and flipped off the typewriter. "Now, Mr. O'Mara, since you

359

don't have to go to work today, how would you like to come to KLM with me?"

He looked interested. "Accompany you to your job? Where they make the television programs?"

Her grin widened. "Sort of. Today's a slow day. I could take you on a little tour and then you could come with me while I give a short speech this afternoon."

"A speech?"

She nodded and made her way from behind the desk. She really was running late. "It's part of my job. It's called public relations, and most of the time I don't mind it. This afternoon I'm speaking to an organization called the Association of University Women." She started down the hallway for the bathroom and yelled back over her shoulder. "I have a prepared speech that I adapt for the group I'm talking to. It's all about women in communications. You might even find it interesting."

Reaching the bathroom, she turned and saw him standing in the hall, watching her. He was wearing nothing but his gray trousers, and she gasped when she remembered running her fingers through the dark mat of hair that disappeared behind the material at his waist. My God, she thought, I'm becoming obsessed with the man. A tingling warmth started churning in her belly and she quickly added, "I'll use the shower first, then you. Okay? But we'll have to hurry, or I'm going to be late."

360

Moments later, Kris was standing under hot water, just standing there, letting the heat envelop her. She knew she should hurry. She should turn on the cold water, for the hot only intensified her already arouse nerve endings. It was as if she were becoming insatiable, for she wished he were with her . . . touching her, stroking her. . . .

"I want you to know I'm only here because you expressly said we'd have to hurry. I wouldn't want you to be late."

She screamed as he entered the shower, and grabbed for the thick washcloth to cover herself.

"What are you doing?" she demanded, moving away from the water so she could speak.

He looked down at himself, naked and already aroused. "Why I'd think that was obvious. You said we were in a hurry."

"But, Sean. I said—"

"I know what you said, lass." He looked at the washcloth. "Are you still shy with me? Do you think I'd forget an inch of you, Kristine?"

They were both blinking to keep the water out of their eyes when he smiled. Pulling her to his chest, Sean ran his hands down her back and cupped her bottom. When she felt his arousal against her belly, she sighed and raised her face to his.

"I think I'm going to be late," she whispered with a strange mixture of resignation and anticipation.

"Aye, lass. I'm sorry."

361

Kris didn't think they fooled anyone. Though she tried to appear nonchalant as she introduced Sean to her colleagues at KLM, their looks told her she hadn't been successful. She simply could not stop staring at him, touching him, smiling at him. It was embarrassing . . . she was behaving like a schoolgirl. She could actually feel herself blush when one of the editors mumbled something about her being late. Oh God, she prayed, save me from making a complete fool of myself!

After finishing up some paperwork, she took Sean on a tour of a control room, an editing room, and the master control where he saw how programs and time were mixed and commanded. Next she took him to the studio where she would be shooting "Philly Live!" He marveled at the set and appeared hesitant when Kris invited him to sit next to her. Don Averly and Mike Causson wanted her to do a sound and light check and she readily agreed, hoping Sean would find it fun.

When she saw the red light—on camera—she smiled and said, "I'm here this morning with a most fascinating man, Mr. Sean O'Mara." She turned to the handsome man next to her and grinned, remembering that in the shower she had spent several minutes kissing the light sprinkling of freckles on his shoulders and arms. "Good morning, Sean."

She could have sworn his responding smile held

tenderness and . . . well, something else.

"Good morning, Kristine."

She blinked for several seconds as he mouthed the words: *I love you.*

"What?" Her voice cracked.

From somewhere to her left, she heard another male speak. "Ahh . . . that's great. Thanks, guys. You'll want to do something about that voice, Kris, before Monday. Sounds a little hoarse."

It was like waking from a dream. She felt disoriented as the bright lights were shut off and Don Averly, her producer, came up to her and Sean.

He shook Sean's hand. "Nice to meet you. Thanks for helping us here." Quickly, he turned to Kris. "We have a problem."

"A problem?" she repeated, still looking at Sean. Had he really said he loved her? Vaguely, she heard Don telling her that her first guest, the President's brother, had cancelled his appearance on "Philly Live!" Shaking her head, she turned to the producer. "I'm sorry, Don. I'm going where?"

"Garden State Race Track. Tonight. Lee Saunders is running another of his horses. You know what I mean. It's a joke. They always lose. He's got the number one-rated comedy show and can't pick a winner." Don shrugged. "I don't know why he keeps at it. That's what you're going to find out. Tonight we do one of those tie-ins that Irv was talking about. You'll take a mobile unit to the racetrack, do the interview; and Lee Saunders will agree to be your first guest on Monday morning.

It took some pretty fancy footwork but it's all been worked out."

Kris stared at her producer. "When was I going to be told about this? I've been preparing for a political show with a strong human interest story. Now, we're switching to comedy?"

Don looked uncomfortable. "Word is Cammeron cancelled because of pressure from the White House. Either that or we just weren't big enough for him. Probably wants to make his debut on national." Suddenly, Don grinned as if mentally shrugging off the President's younger brother. "Anyway, when you think about it, this is better. You're good with people, and your audience will feel comfortable seeing you mix it up with Lee Saunders. This is your first show as host at four o'clock. We want it to be as smooth as possible. Cammeron would have been controversial; Saunders'll be fun. Besides, the city loves him. He went to college here, and Philadelphia claims him as a native son. Everybody will be comfortable. You'll see."

Knowing there was nothing she could do about it, Kris let her breath out and asked, "What time do we have to be at the track?"

She barely heard the answer as she caught Sean's expression.

"May I come with you tonight?" he asked.

"Sure. I don't see why not. We'll take my car and meet up with the mobile unit." Kris could see how excited he was, and she smiled as they walked out of the studio. Now just didn't seem like right time to ask him if he'd just said he loved her.

But did he?

It was almost four that afternoon when they left the small suburban community college in New Jersey. Kris's speech had gone well and she was proud that Sean was with her. She'd had to smile a few times when she'd glanced toward the back of the lecture hall and had seen him leaning against the wall. He'd looked impressed, and she had to admit that she was pleased. She also remembered the attention of quite a few women was frequently drawn away from her and centered on the tall, sleek Irishman in the back of the room. She had to admit he was devastatingly handsome, and she'd felt a primitive surge of enjoyment . . . knowing he was waiting for her.

After signing a few autographs, she joined Sean and the two of them hurried toward her car. "I'm glad you're with me," she said as she started the engine and pulled out of the parking space.

"You were wonderful, Kristine," he said sincerely. "I was so very proud of you . . . standing up there . . . talking to those women. I would have been very nervous."

She laughed. "I used to be. The first time I thought I was going to die, literally. I could hear my heart beating in my ears, and my hands shook so terribly that when I grabbed onto the podium the tremors traveled to my legs and they started shaking." She shook her head, as the memory faded. "Anyway, it gets better each time, or at least easier."

"Well, you seem so poised and composed — Why are we stopping?" He looked around the deserted parking lot.

Slowly turning her head, Kris smiled. "Wanna learn how to drive?" she asked, leering at him like a shameless wanton. God, she wished they were home.

"Are you serious?" He ignored her brazen expression and grinned with excitement.

She nodded. "My brother taught me in a parking lot. I suppose I can teach you."

He was more than eager. "What do you want me to do?"

Amused by his impatience, she said, "Well, I think it would help if we changed places."

"Yes," he agreed. "I think that would be best."

She tried not to laugh as they got out and walked around the car.

"Are you sure I can do this?" He was staring at the instrument panel while maintaining a death grip on the steering wheel.

"If I can do it, you can do it. Let's just think of this as a first lesson. No one learns to drive in one day, Sean." She patted his right hand. "Why don't we talk about these buttons and gauges?"

They spent over ten minutes discussing the mechanics of the car. They practiced the gas pedal

366

and brake. And although he was trying to hide it, Kris could sense Sean's impatience to begin the actual driving.

"Okay, start the engine."

"I beg your pardon?"

She grinned. "Turn the key, Sean."

"Ahh . . . yes."

There was a hesitancy in his fingers as they slowly applied pressure to the ignition. Seemingly of its own accord, the engine came to life, and his fingers pulled back to the steering wheel, as if burned. Why was it that the roar from the motor sounded twice as loud when he was behind the wheel? thought Sean.

"Very good," Kristine said. "Now put your foot on the brake and shift the transmission into drive—the letter *D*. Easy . . . that's it. Lift your foot off the brake now."

Like magic, the car started to move forward and Sean was mesmerized by the power he had in his control. It was nothing like driving a carriage. This was a mighty force he felt beneath his fingers, and at his feet.

"Slow down," Kris advised as the car moved toward the exit of the parking lot.

Confused, Sean took his eyes off the road and looked at the panel for some direction.

Seeing he was in a near panic, Kris said, "The brake! Hit the brake!"

Lifting his leg, Sean jammed his foot onto the brake pedal as if he would push it through the

367

floor of the car. The car stopped with a screech, and Kris would have hit the windshield if she hadn't been prepared for the sudden halt.

Sean was breathing heavily, a frightened look on his face as he reached for her. "Kristine! Are you all right?"

She nodded and pushed her hair back off her face. "I'm afraid this is my fault. I forgot to tell you the number one rule when you enter a car: Fasten your seat belt." She pulled hers from the panel by the window and buckled up. "Now you do the same, just like when I was driving you here."

Watching him, she smiled and then broke into a giggle.

Fitting the metal locks together at his waist, he turned and glared at her. "Exactly what do you find so funny?" he demanded. "I could have hurt you!"

Holding up her hand, she shook her head and continued to laugh. "Oh, Sean, *everybody* does that the first time behind the wheel. Don't get upset. I should have remembered. At least you're not learning on stick shift, like I did."

"Stick shift?"

She explained the difference. "Poor Jack! I think I must have driven him crazy the summer of my sixteenth birthday. I'd throw it into any gear, as long as the car moved." Shaking her head, she giggled. "Once we got past the parking lot of the local school, that yellow Volkswagen convertible started making unexpected appearances on our neighbor's lawns, in their gardens. Jack insisted that the entire town begged my father to buy me an automatic." Still chuckling, she shrugged her shoulders. "Anyway, Mr. O'Mara, if I can do this, so can you. Just slide the transmission into park and take your foot off the brake before it becomes permanently attached. And then we're going to start again."

He was smiling now and beginning to relax. "Thank you for your patience, Kristine. I keep remembering when you were at Rivanna, my Rivanna, how unkindly I behaved toward you. And now here, in your time, you're warm and kind and . . . When I think about it, I'm ashamed."

She grinned. "There's a difference, Sean. I know what you've been through, and I know how difficult all this must be for you. You're doing great, though."

He was staring at her mouth. "I wish we weren't belted into these seats," he said with a grin.

She understood completely, for a familiar warmth was starting to spread through her. "Listen, if you do really well during your first lesson, I'll show you another modern tradition concerning cars . . . it's called parking."

He could see the desire in her eyes and chuckled. "Parking? Isn't that what we're doing now?"

"Oh, no. *Parking* involves much more than this. I think you'll pick it up very quickly." She swallowed several times, wishing that the late afternoon dusk would soon turn into night. Letting out her breath with a slow, controlled rush of air, Kris said, "We'll find a restaurant over here in Jersey before we meet the mobile unit at the racetrack tonight, and somewhere in between I'll definitely find time to show you parking. Don't worry, Sean, I have a feeling you're going to be a natural."

"Now, I'm really curious about this parking," he said, and turned his attention to the transmission. "But the sooner I learn to drive, the sooner I can learn to park."

She chuckled as the car started moving again. "Now you've got the idea."

Surrounded by impeccably groomed lawns and lit with a thousand tiny lights, it appeared to be a palace with walls of glass, a tall watchtower, and rows of flags. Sean couldn't stop staring as they drove through the winding blacktop that would bring them to the paddock area of the Garden State Race Track. He could sense it, smell it, feel it. This was as close to home as he could get. This was familiar ground. Finally . . . thoroughbreds.

They parked by the red and white van that served as KLM's mobile unit and Sean watched as Kris got out of the car and talked to her crew.

He was staring at the large metal dish on top of the van when she returned to his side.

"What is it, Kristine?" he asked, pointing to the van.

She grinned. "It's a satellite dish. It's going to feed our transmission—our interview—back to the station in Philadelphia."

Shaking his head, Sean muttered, "I don't understand."

Kris put her arm through his and led him toward the stables. "Don't feel bad. Most people don't. They just take it for granted that a picture is going to appear on their sets every day. C'mon. Let's find Saunders. You're about to meet the biggest star on television today."

Since she practically had to drag him away from the endless rows of stalls, Kris attached a press pass to his jacket and let him follow the crew more slowly. When she finally met up with Lee Saunders, he was surrounded by his entourage and already making jokes about his horse. The bay gelding wore green and yellow colors, and his handlers were trying to calm him as the comedian entertained those around him.

"The last time I saw my wife this excited," he joked, while pointing to the horse, "was when American Express sent her two cards, instead of one."

Kris groaned as she made her way through the men. Lee Saunders had been a stand-up comedian for the last twenty years, with moderate success. He got his start playing the Catskills, and as the saying went: You could take the comic out of the

371

Catskills but never the other way around. After so many years there, it was as much a part of Lee Saunders as his receding hairline. His routine had been heavily loaded with mother-in-law and wife jokes, and with the ascent of feminism, Saunders act had started to fail. It wasn't until he'd been teamed up with Gracie McDowell in a sitcom that his career spiraled into megastardom. All it took was two years, appearing every week on Wednesday nights, and Lee Saunders owned the weekly rating slot of number one.

Sometimes, the power of television flat out amazed Kris, its ability to make a superstar out of anybody—given enough air time. And there was so much waste. Television had to power to inform and enlighten, but most of the shows offered what ad men programmed the public into believing it wanted. Then there were the insecure egos, the hard-edged maneuverings of programmers and salespeople. All of these came together to create a schedule of game shows, soap operas, sitcoms, magazine shows specializing in how to serve cauliflower, cop shows, religious shows—and that didn't even include cable. Some of the programming was good, a lot of it could be better. Lee Saunders' show served its purpose. It was funny, and she had to admit that after a tiring day at work she'd tuned in on Wednesday nights herself.

Tall, browned by California sun, and sporting a slight paunch, Lee Saunders grinned down at her. "Kris Gavin, right?"

She nodded. "Right. It's a pleasure to meet you, Lee. I've heard you're going to be my first guest on the new show Monday. Thank you for that."

His smiled widened. "Hell, when they explained who you're going up against, I figured you deserved a shot. Glad if I can help."

She couldn't help chuckling. "Oh, you'll more than help. Philadelphia loves you. I don't think they're going to miss the chance to speak with you in person. Especially if we lead in with this." She nodded to the nervous horse behind him. "What's his name?"

"Margi's Misery. Margi's my wife and she names every one of my horses. This one's misery because the money I used for the horse was supposed to go for her new car."

"Wait!" Kris held up her hand and motioned to her crew. "Let's set up and get this on tape. Okay?"

"Sure." Lee Saunders was a professional and moved aside so the technician could set up the equipment. Looking at his horse, he yelled to the handlers. "Get him under control, will you? I have a feeling he's going to be on camera."

Within minutes Kris and Saunders were discussing his hit series, his visit to the Delaware Valley, and his years of horse racing. Even Lee made a joke out of his unusually poor luck in picking winners. From the corner of her eye, Kris saw that the horse was becoming more agitated by the lights and commotion. For a moment, when the gelding shied away from his handlers, she thought his owner might be shoved right out of camera range. But she and Lee managed to continue the interview, and were wisecracking about horses being more intelligent than critics when Sean quickly moved toward the gelding. With a gentle tug he grabbed hold of the bridle and brought the horse's face down close to his own. They could all hear Sean murmuring to the animal and soon, to everyone's astonishment, it calmed down. When the first part of the interview was wrapped up, both Kris and Lee turned toward the horse to see Sean handing the reins over to a groom, then watched the man lead the gelding toward the track. Kris could see the longing in Sean's eyes.

The KLM crew and Sean followed Lee Saunders to his box to watch the race with him. Kris wanted to record the actual running of the horse and capture Saunders reaction to it. In truth, she was thinking about her show on Monday, how her viewers would relate to a big-time celebrity losing at the track. That probably would endear Saunders to the public even more.

What happened in the next three minutes proved to be a shock to more than those gathered about the television star. Rounding the home stretch, Margi's Misery pulled away from the pack and gained on the horses in the lead, all heavy favorites. Lee Saunders forgot the cameras monitoring his every movement as his horse strained toward the finish line. He screamed and pounded his fist against the rail as he urged the gelding on.

Margi's Misery came in third, the best a Saunders' horse had ever done. In his excitement, Lee tousled the hair of the man in front of him, only to wind up with a toupee in his hand. Though the man was part of the entourage, Kris was sure none of this was planned and let the cameras record it all. Amid the celebration, she noticed a sly grin on Sean's face.

Later, at the stable, a camera captured a jubilant Saunders as he placed a wet kiss on the bay gelding's muzzle. Afterward, mugging for the lens, Lee noticed Sean behind the boom man and motioned for him to join them.

Now knowing what he should do, Sean was pushed his way toward Kristine and the popular owner of the horse. He wasn't sure he wanted to join those already the center of so much attention.

Lee slipped an arm around Sean's shoulder and actually hugged him. "Hey! What the hell did you say to that horse to get him to run like that?"

Sean was suddenly embarrassed by this show of affection from a man he didn't even know and he mumbled an answer.

Sean looked at Saunders, at Kris and the microphone in her hand. Not knowing why, except that he had seen others do it, Sean looked directly into the camera and said, "I just told him to run fast . . . and win. He did his best."

Lee Saunders threw back his head and laughed.

375

"You just told him to run fast?"

Seeing the horse, Sean moved toward it. Not knowing the camera had followed him, he stroked the horse's long neck and looked back at Kristine. "They understand," he murmured.

A half-hour later, Kris looked at the replay of the tape in the mobile unit before she left for home. When she came to the part where Sean appeared on the screen, she froze the tape and stared at him. A lump rose up in her throat, the hair on her arms stood up in alarm. She had to admit Danni was right. The camera loved him. He looked rugged and sexy and gentle and . . . plain beautiful. What's more, Sean O'Mara unconsciously played right to the camera. He'd thought he was looking at her, but the cameraman was at her shoulder. The lens had captured him making love to her with his eyes. And now every woman in Philadelphia was going to feel he'd been looking at her.

"It's pretty good, isn't it?" the cameraman asked. "Because of Saunders, I wouldn't be surprised if it didn't go network. That bit about the horse was sensational. We couldn't have planned it better."

Slowly Kris reached out and pressed the play button so the tape would continue. She nodded. "Right. Sensational." Inwardly, she groaned. Now every woman in the country was going to want him.

She sat in front of the TV and watched the blond woman speak of television stars and their hobbies. Entertainment Tonight. It was her favorite program, but this night she wasn't even listening; she had shut out the woman's voice. The last three days had been a nightmare that she'd somehow survived. Ever since he had gone into that warehouse, Bobby Ray had turned into a different person. It was the cocaine. He was like a frantic teenager in his demands, demands that she could no longer satisfy. Just thinking about some of the things he'd made her do, she shivered. She wasn't the one who was insane. It was Bobby Ray. She'd known that when he'd raised his hand to strike her. It was in his eyes. Frightening eyes . . . Somehow, she had to escape him. No longer could she stay here in these rooms with him, as his prisoner. Somehow —

She blinked several times when she saw them on the small glass screen. It couldn't be! Sean and that woman were on the television! No . . .

They were here? She forced herself to listen more carefully, to hear what they were saying. She read the words on the bottom of the screen: *Courtesy of WKLM Philadelphia.*

They were here! In Philadelphia!

As they disappeared from the screen, Christina rose from the chair and stared around the small room. Soon, without thought, she began pacing. Thinking . . . Sean and that woman, Kristine

377

Gavin the television voice had said, were also in this time, and they were in Philadelphia. And the way he'd looked at her! There was something, maybe love or devotion, that she'd never seen in his eyes. He actually loved that woman!

Somehow, she had to get to away. Without realizing it, she stopped pacing in the bedroom, directly in front of the oak dresser where Bobby Ray kept all those bags of white powder. She looked at the sleeping man on the bed and her mouth curled in distaste. How could she ever have thought he was exciting? All he cared about was cocaine, and the money that it . . .

As she turned back to the dresser, a smile formed at Christina's lips for the first time in days. At last, fate had decided to be kind and grant to her the means for revenge.

This time it would be twice as sweet.

Chapter Twenty-one

Kris knew the moment she had begun losing him. It was after the van had left the racetrack. All the races had been run and she had linked her arm through Sean's as they'd walked through the stables. They had been talking about horses — his very first and when he had decided to go into breeding. They'd been enjoying reminiscing when they'd come upon a group of horses being led toward a large trailer.

"What's going on?" Kris asked a young groom.

The teenager shrugged his shoulders. "They didn't turn out. Had their chance though. The lot's going on the auction block next week."

"They're being sold?" Sean was curiously looking over the group.

It was at that moment, when his arm stiffened under her hand, that she had begun losing him. She'd felt it as surely as she had felt his love the night before. She was losing him not to another woman, not even to the past. She found it incredible that it was to a horse by the name of Robbie's Folly. She didn't understand at the time that this particular horse had the same triangular marking behind its right knee as Sean's own stallion.

On seeing it, he was convinced that Robbie's Folly was a direct descendant of Celtic Star. All of his energies, all of his concentration, were now directed toward the purchase of the gray stallion.

He had refused her money, though she'd again tried to explain that all the Gavin wealth originally came from him. Instead, he had placed a telephone call to Danni, of all people.

Now, Saturday, Sean was meeting her best friend . . . and she wasn't invited.

It didn't matter that she had to go over her notes on Lee Saunders for Monday's show. Try though she might, Kris couldn't concentrate on anything but Sean and Danni. *Sean and Danni!*

What the hell were they up to?

"I really don't think I can do this, Danielle. I'm sorry I bothered you on a Saturday."

Danni laughed out loud, then brought the camera up to her face again. "All right, O'Mara. Just a few shots for the ad men on Monday. I'm not a professional photographer, but this will give them something to think about until you arrive. Ten-thirty. Monday. Right?"

"Right." Sean was feeling more than foolish for

calling Danielle and setting up a meeting. If only she hadn't made this job—modeling—sound like a way to make a lot of money in a short time.

"Now, smile. Look right into the lens. C'mon. You can do better than that." Danni was moving closer to him. "Remind me to tell you about the time Kristine glued Sister Marian Delores's gloves shut."

"She did what?" Sean grinned at the thought.

It was just what Danni wanted and she snapped the picture.

"I can't conceive of Kristine doing such a thing," Sean protested, while imagining a nun attempting to push her fingers through the glued gloves.

Danni continued to move around her living room, trying to maneuver Sean into better light. "You can't, huh? Well, nobody else could either. I can't tell you how many times we were called into Mother Superior's office. Everyone *always* assumed I was the guilty party." She had to laugh herself. "Of course, when they did, at least half of the time they were right. There. Hold it right there. Think Kristine. . . ."

They're going to love him, Danni thought as she snapped the picture and lowered the camera to her side. Besides being great looking, he possessed a unique quality, a combination of old-world charm and suppressed sexuality. Brubakers and the leading men's cologne manufacturer had signed a two-year contract to promote Thoroughbred. Until she'd met Sean, the name had made her cringe. It conjured up all sorts of sexual thoughts about the man who would wear the product: aristocrat, stallion, sleek lines, good breeding. All they needed was the right male model to project the image. Even though she was Brubakers' head buyer, not head of advertising, or even marketing, she had a voice in the promotion. This was going to be an intensive advertising campaign, both in print and media. They'd been looking for the right model for five months, and time was now of the essence. Danni knew they'd almost settled on a blond, out of New York. But that was just it. They'd be *settling* for someone who was almost right. Whoever was chosen to represent Thoroughbred, was going to be an overnight millionaire. And she couldn't think of a better person to be hit with instant success. Besides, the very minute she'd laid eyes on Sean O'Mara in Virginia, she'd known he was special. It was in his face, his clothes, his professed love of horses, his carriage. Damned if he wasn't a thoroughbred himself.

"I have a friend who's a photographer. He's down at the shore, but he'll be back tomorrow. And he owes me a favor." She placed the camera on her coffee table. "I'll take the film over to him in the morning and have prints by Sunday night. I'll bring the video with me on Monday, too. What a stroke of luck that we already have you on tape."

Sean visibly shuddered. "I looked so ridiculous on the television. I never knew that they would keep showing the tape. I keep making the same mistakes over and over."

Danni chuckled. "I hope you never realize what you do to the camera. Stay insecure, O'Mara." She poured them both a second cup of coffee. "So explain further why you decided to take me up on my offer. A horse, you said?"

Accepting the cup, Sean nodded. "His name is Robbie's Folly—"

"Doesn't sound real promising," she interrupted.

"Names don't mean anything," he said, before sipping the hot coffee. "He's going up for sale next week. An auction, like I told you. I have to have him. I can't explain it. One of the men at the racetrack said he was a fast starter, but couldn't finish. I know horses, Danielle. Maybe that's all I really do know. And this one is a winner. It's in the breeding."

Putting her coffee down, she grinned at him. "I'm telling you, O'Mara, you're a natural for this job. Just talk like that Monday morning." She picked up his bomber jacket and threw it at him. "Now get out of here. I'm sure Kris is like a caged lioness waiting for you to get back."

Catching the jacket, he slipped an arm into it. "You promised you wouldn't say anything to her about this."

"Well, if you get the job, she's going to find out."

He shook his head. "I know that. I mean now. If these people don't care for me tomorrow, I'd rather she didn't know anything about it. This is . . . embarrassing, to say the least."

383

Walking him to the door of her apartment, Danni put her hand on his shoulder. Ever since that night when Kris had left them alone, she'd felt a strange closeness to Sean. He loved her best friend, and he was a gentleman — a real gentleman. In her book, he was a rare find. "Look, Sean. Tell me now if you don't think you can do this. If you're embarrassed by the thought of being photographed by me, what are you going to do when strangers take your picture? And some of them are really strange."

He stopped at her door. "Whatever it takes, I'll do it. I might be embarrassed, but I can't afford pride any longer. I have plans."

She saw the determination in his expression. Whatever his plans, he would probably succeed. "Look, I shouldn't even say this to you, but if everything works out on Monday with the agency men and the Thoroughbred people, then you're going to need an agent, someone to negotiate for you. Come over Monday night and I'll have a list." She playfully punched his arm. "I might even make a few recommendations."

He took her hand, held it between his, and looked directly into her eyes. "You're a good friend to Kristine, and you've been more than generous with me, Danielle. I would value any recommendation you might be kind enough to make."

She could only nod as a lump formed in her throat. Pulling her hand away, she muttered, "You'd better get going. Kris is waiting." She watched him walk toward the elevator. "Remember. Ten-thirty, Monday morning in my office at Brubakers."

"I'll be there," he answered, as the steel doors opened and he disappeared behind them.

Back in her apartment, Danni gathered up his cup and poured the coffee down the sink. Where did you ever find him, Kris? she wondered. Sean O'Mara was one in a million.

Suddenly, she felt like crying, a really good female cry. It was hell being alone on a Saturday afternoon. . . .

On Monday morning Kris was all nerves as she attempted to apply makeup to her face. Of all the days in her life, why had nature picked today to make a pimple appear on her chin? Looking in the bathroom mirror, she wondered just how she was supposed to host her very first show of "Philly Live!" The more she stared at it, the bigger the pimple became. Before her very eyes it was growing to the size of a crater. By four o'clock in the afternoon, viewers in the Delaware Valley were going to wrinkle their noses and wonder why she'd been picked to host a new talk show.

"Because you can talk," she told herself as she washed off the two-year-old foundation that she had never once used before. "You're the host because you have brains. That's what's really important."

Not that damn zit, she silently protested as she threw the washcloth onto the black marble vanity. Still, she cringed at knowing she'd have to go into makeup and ask to have the blemish disguised. And after she had argued last week for a more natural look! Shaking her head, she let the damp curls dry around her shoulders. At least everyone had agreed that her hair should be left alone, though she'd nearly groaned when Mike Causson had said it would probably be her trademark.

"Kristine. I think I've managed to make the coffee correctly this time."

She looked toward the closed bathroom door. "I'll be right there," she said a little too impatiently. Sean! My God, she thought, I'm turning into a shrew! She had tried not to think about what Sean and Danni were up to, but her own insecurities had come rushing back Saturday afternoon when Sean had returned. He never said anything about meeting her friend, and she'd been afraid to question him. Everything was too fragile, and it was obvious that he was preoccupied. Even Sunday when they had resumed the driving lessons, she had sensed that a part of him wasn't in that car with her. His laughter seemed less natural, his mood less relaxed. And when they'd made love, it had still been an astonishingly powerful union, yet Kris had had the distinct feeling that he was holding back a part of himself from her. Something was happening with him, and it concerned her best friend. The possibilities were depressing.

386

Just a few weeks ago, she'd turned thirty, and now she was definitely turning paranoid. It was not the best way to begin the week, or a new job.

"They love you, Sean. What the hell do you mean you don't know if you can sign a contract?" Danni paced in front of the huge windows in her office.

Sitting in a chair opposite her desk, Sean tried not to appear as uncomfortable as he felt. "I'm very happy they like me, Danielle, but I'm afraid I can't sign a two-year contract with anyone, about anything."

She stopped pacing and stared at him. "Why?"

What could he say? Trying to look innocent, he muttered, "I honestly don't know where I'm going to be in two years."

Danni looked around her office. "So, who does? This doesn't mean you have to live in Philadelphia, you know. You can always fly in when we need you." Seeing that he wasn't convinced, she took another tack. "Look, I don't know if you realize what we were talking about in David's office. We're offering you a great deal of money. I shouldn't be saying this, but it could go as high as nine hundred and fifty thousand. That'll buy a lot of horseflesh, O'Mara. That is what we were talking about yesterday, isn't it?"

He sat up straighter. "Nine hundred and fifty thousand *dollars?*"

Grinning, she nodded. "That's right."

He stared at her, his mouth open in shock. "For taking photographs of me? This must be a joke."

Danni chuckled. "It's no joke, and believe me, they'll make you work for every dollar. What they were talking about was a little bit more than taking photographs. It's a two-year contract. There'll be the print work, the television commercials, an occasional public appearance—"

"Did you say television commercials?" he interrupted. "Do you mean I'll be on the television?"

"Of course." Looking confused, she sat on the edge of her desk. "That's what we were talking about at the meeting. Didn't you understand that? Whenever we talk about film or tape video, that means television."

Looking decidedly more interested, Sean straightened in his chair. "But what if something happens? What if I can't fulfill my part of the contract?"

"What could happen? Listen to me, O'Mara, life's too short to worry about what if's. Why don't you let us worry for you? All you have to do right now is say yes, and we can get started."

Once more, Sean looked at her. She was tall and dark. Her hair was cropped close to her head, almost like a man's, yet on her it looked dramatic. Her dress was outrageously tight and so immodestly short it revealed her knees. Somehow, though, he couldn't picture her in a long dress from his time. This style was Danielle. But beyond the style and the smile, there was something else, something that was making her look at him with an almost imploring expression.

"This is important to you, isn't it?" he asked. "I think this means as much to you as it does to me."

For a brief moment, she turned away from him. Looking back, she said, "I'm very good at what I do, Sean. If that sounds like boasting, I'm sorry." She got up and paced in front of the huge windows overlooking Philadelphia's skyline. "However, I might never go any further in this company because I lack a diploma . . . that damned piece of paper." She held her hand up to stop any comment. "I made the decision not to continue my education and I have to think it was the right one. Look where I am," she said, waving an arm to indicate the luxurious office. "And I did it the hard way. Unfortunately, this might be as far as I'll rise at Brubakers unless I come up with something extraordinary."

She looked directly at him. "You, O'Mara, are my something extraordinary. You're the perfect man to represent Thoroughbred. I saw it at Kris's party in Virginia. The people who really matter saw it this morning." Taking a deep breath, she continued, "There's an offer to be a vice president, the seventh vice president, but still . . . a vice president. So, yes. You're right, Sean. This is very important to me."

He looked beyond her, beyond the tall buildings that seemed to blot out the sun, and said, "What if something . . . ah, unnatural . . . were to take place? Something that prevented me from executing this contract? I would hate to think—"

"What are you talking about? Unnatural? Do you mean a *force majeure?* An act of God, like an earthquake?"

How could he explain it to her? "Something like that."

She chuckled and sat back on the edge of her desk. "I believe there's a clause in every contract about those things. Is that why you're so concerned? Are you planning on moving to California, or something? Does Kris know this?"

He felt confused. "California? Why would I want to move there?"

Danni shrugged. Now she was confused. "I thought that's what you meant . . . Never mind. Look, O'Mara, this is a conflict of interest, I know, but if you get a decent agent—and I've already made up a list—then you might be able to swing a quarter of the money on signing the contract. When's this horse going up on the block?"

He grinned. "It seems indecent to me, getting this much to pose for a men's cologne advertisement, but I do need the money, Danielle. And I need it soon."

"And we need to start work soon. They'll push the contract through if you make that part of the deal. This project is already behind schedule. Believe me, they're as eager as you."

He stood up and held out his palm. "You'll make

a lovely vice president, Miss Rowe."

Taking his hand, she laughed and shook her head. "Where were you when women's liberation took place? I won't be a lovely vice president. I'll be an important vice president. And it's Ms., not Miss."

He didn't understand why she thought his compliment was amusing. "I beg your pardon? Miz?"

She decided not to question his seeming lack of awareness of modern protocol. She had only been jesting. Reaching into her briefcase, she pulled out a piece of paper. "Here's the list of agents in the city. I checked off the ones the agency seems to like. Maybe Kris can help you make a decision. I'm sure she could recommend a number from New York City that might even be— "

Taking the list from her, he held her hand in both of his. "You've been very kind, Danielle," he interrupted. "Thank you for everything you've done. I will always remember this."

Embarrassed, she shrugged and pulled her hand from his. "When are you going to tell Kris?" she asked as she walked him to the door of her office.

"Tonight. I wanted to wait until the meeting was over. And, of course, I didn't want to trouble her before her show this afternoon. It's the first, you know, under the new name."

Danni smiled and nodded. "Yes. I know. I'm going to tape it. I was thinking about coming over tonight with a bottle of wine to celebrate. What do you think?"

Turning around as he walked past the secretary, Sean beamed at Danni. "We would be honored to have you to dinner tonight. Seven-thirty?"

"Sounds great. I'll bring the wine."

He pushed open the door to the outer office and disappeared but not before Danni had caught the awestruck look on her secretary's face. It was the right decision. Sean O'Mara was going to knock 'em dead, as the saying went. He was totally male, yet somehow not threatening to other men. And the women were going to buy Thoroughbred because every one of them would want to turn her husband or lover into another Sean O'Mara. It was all fantasy . . . just what everyone wanted.

Including her.

So, where was he?

Kris instinctively knew the woman was trouble before she placed the microphone in front of her mouth. This was one of the gambles of live television, and Kris would have to sweat her way through it.

"First I wanna say that I watch your show every week, Lee, and I think it's the best. Then I wanna say that it's about time we had our own talk show here in Philly." She turned to Kris, amid the ensuing applause. "You remember the "Mike Douglas Show?" I used to go to that when I was younger."

Kris could sense that she was losing control, putting her hand on the woman's back, she politely interrupted. "That's terrific. Do you have a question for Lee?"

She could feel the tension in the woman's muscles. It should have been a warning.

"There's been a lot of rumors goin' on about you and your wife, Margi, and your business manager. That's what they're callin' him, anyway. How about that stuff? What'd it do to your career?"

Kris could feel beads of sweat popping out all over her. Three years ago, there was a vicious rumor that Lee Saunders was involved with his business manager—in more than business. Every rag had carried a shocking story from Saunders' wife. Though it was three years old, that kind of gossip could ruin a career.

Leaving the woman standing by herself, Kris walked toward her unhappy guest. Lee Saunders was steaming, and with good reason. Plastering a smile on her face, Kris said, "What about those newspapers that one finds at supermarket checkouts? Does anyone really take them seriously? You know . . . woman raped by alien delivers child that can see through steel."

The audience laughed and Lee Saunders joined in. With the pressure off him, he did three minutes of hilarious dialogue, raking the scandal sheets over the coals for their ridiculous headlines. As they went into a commercial, Saunders looked at Kris and gave her the thumbs-up signal.

Leaning closer, he whispered, "Thanks for that one. When I get back to the coast, I'll spread the word on you. You handled that better'n Phil."

As they came out of the commercial, Kris was almost looking forward to the next segment. Calmer now, she settled into the show, and from that time on, it went smoothly. She was composed and poised. It was okay. Even the crew looked relaxed. In her profession, instinct was as important as talent. And her every instinct told her that "Philly Live!" was going to be a success.

It was hard to keep her smile under control. She couldn't wait until she heard Sean's reaction to the show. Tonight, she thought. Tonight we will celebrate.

"You invited Danielle for dinner? Tonight?"

She had rushed out of the studio, still holding one of the many bouquets of flowers that had been sent to her. Irv had asked her to dinner, along with KLM's senior vice president, and she had turned them down so she could spend the night with Sean. And now Danielle? What the hell was going on with those two? Disappointed, Kris put the flowers into a vase and set it on the foyer table just as the doorbell rang.

She looked at Sean. All he could do was smile and motion for her to open the door.

"Danni. This is a surprise." She raised her head and kissed the taller woman's cheek.

Danni, dressed in a red outfit that leaned toward Japanese trends, hugged her best friend. "As soon

394

as I got home, I watched the tape. You were fantastic. I was so proud of you, Kris."

"Thanks. C'mon in." She waved Danni into the foyer. "I just heard we're all having dinner together."

Danni looked confused. "Didn't Sean check with you?" She turned and frowned at the man standing a few feet away. "Listen, Kris, if it's a problem, I can—"

Suddenly ashamed of her jealousy, Kris linked arms with the taller woman. "Don't be silly. I take it that's wine?"

Danni handed over the bottles. "We have a lot to celebrate, don't we?" She smiled at both Kris and Sean.

As it turned out the combined efforts of the three of them produced a fairly decent meal. Danni worked on the salad, Sean watched over the steak, and Kris produced string beans vinaigrette.

As she watched Danni and Sean from the corner of her eye, she hated herself for the thoughts that ran through her brain. Why were they looking at each other like that? It was as if they shared a secret, and she was excluded. There wasn't any doubt about it. As soon as dinner was over, she would have to make an excuse and get Danni alone. It was time for a talk.

When they were seated in the dining room, Sean raised his glass of wine in a toast. "To Kristine. You were wonderful today. May each show be as successful."

Danni held her glass up in agreement. "Here. Here."

Looking at him, Kris nearly moaned as a rush of desire suddenly surged up her. "Thank you," she murmured, and cleared her throat. "I don't know about tomorrow, though. My guest is the superintendent of Philadelphia's public schools. I expect the audience to be filled with parents, bristling with questions." She sipped her wine. "I'm afraid I have some homework to do tonight."

Kris watched the silent exchange taking place between Sean and Danni. Danni gave him a meaningful look, while Sean tried to convey something negative to her. It was as if her friend were asking Sean if he'd done something, and the answer was no. The steak felt like a brick in Kris's stomach when she thought of a possible reason for the silent conversation. Had Sean told her something yet? *What?*

Without further thought, she slammed her fork onto the table and said. "In the immortal words of Sister Marian Delores: 'Would you two care to share with the rest of the class what you find so interesting?' "

They both looked at her. Danni's expression shouted guilt. It was Sean who spoke. "I beg your pardon?"

Wiping her mouth, Kris very carefully placed the napkin back on her lap. "I'm tired. I'm not blind. The two of you look like mimes, for God's sake. I would like to know what's going on. I think, perhaps, one of you has something to tell me?" Oh God, she thought, my best friend and the man I love . . . please, don't let it be.

This time it was Sean who cleared his throat. "Well, as a matter of fact, I do have something to announce." He smiled. It wasn't successful. "Just today I have acquired a new position."

"What?"

It wasn't what she thought. An immense wash of relief ran through Kris.

"Yes. You see . . . ah, what I mean is . . . Danielle helped me to—"

Hearing the trouble he was having, Danni interrupted, "Sean is going to be the Thoroughbred man for Brubakers."

Kris leaned her elbows on the table and narrowed her eyes, as if studying them both. "Now I must beg your pardon," she said in a low, suspicious voice. "Would either of you care to run that by me again."

Danni and Sean exchanged another glance. Sean looked at Kris and said, "Danielle thought I might be the type of person her ad people and those who make the cologne were looking for. They are willing to pay me a ridiculous amount of money to have my picture taken."

"And there'd be commercials, maybe a couple of personal appearances." Danni shrugged. "Who knows?" She definitely did not like the angry glint in Kris's eyes.

"Maybe I know!" Kris interjected. "You did this!

How could you? I thought you were my friend—"

"Wait a minute!" Danni pushed her chair back from the table. "What has this got to do with you? I mean, really, why are you upset by Sean's good fortune? He's going to make a great deal of money. I'm sorry, Kris, probably more than you are. I didn't think that would bother you. I did think you'd be happy for him. You were the one who said he bred horses. Now he's going to have the money to do that."

Sean rose from the table. "Kristine. If I thought you'd be this—"

Kris held up her hand. *What was happening to her?* She was becoming suspicious, possessive. "I'm sorry," she said. "I don't know what's wrong with me." She couldn't prevent the tears from streaming down her cheeks. "Sit down, Sean. Of course, I'm happy for you."

She reached out across the linen tablecloth and clasped her friend's hand. "Danni, I'm so sorry for what I said. If you only knew what I was thinking. The two of you . . . together . . . meetings and secrets. I don't know . . . I guess it really got to me."

Both Danni and Sean looked shocked. Danni squeezed Kris's hand. "You thought . . . us? My God, Kris. This man doesn't even notice other women."

Kris looked up at Sean and sniffled. A smile broke out over her face. "Again, Mr. O'Mara, your life is going to change," she said in a soft voice. "A whole nation of women will want to take my place. I hope you can handle everything that's going to happen. And that I can."

His eyes locked with hers. "I think you're exaggerating, Kristine. The only thing I will allow to happen is that I will be earning more money than I ever thought possible. Though it is embarrassing to admit how it will be made." He finally grinned. "If you must know, that was the reason I insisted it be kept a secret. Even now, I feel ridiculous hearing that I will be called the Thoroughbred man. Why would anyone name a man's cologne after a breed of horses?"

"I know why," Kris admitted. "And I agree with their choice of a spokesperson."

"I'm glad this is settled," Danni proclaimed, though she didn't think the two of them were really listening to her. They were staring at each other with such searing intensity that she began to feel uncomfortable. Stabbing the romaine with her fork, she quietly announced, "Because this afternoon David Hendley offered me a vice president's seat on the board of Brubakers."

Amid shouts of congratulation, she winked at Sean. "You realize, O'Mara, this makes me your boss?"

Holding Kristine's hand, he grinned. "I suppose that means, Ms. Rowe, you're not going to help with the dishes?"

* * *

There was something so right about it that Kris's throat constricted with emotion. She was seated in the living room, studying the notes for the next day's show, when Sean walked up in back of her and began massaging the tense muscles at her shoulders. "If you continue, I'm going to fall asleep right here."

She heard his low voice, coming from behind her. "Go ahead. You've had a pretty exciting day."

She reached up, captured his hand, and brought him around the edge of the sofa. He sat down close to her.

Brushing the hair back from his forehead, she said, "I would say your day was pretty exciting, too. I was terrible tonight, Sean. I'm sorry. I behaved like a shrew. I know I don't have any . . . well, any claim on you."

His eyes widened. "You believe that?"

Her shoulders automatically lifted in a shrug. "I don't know. I'm not sure anymore. You seem to have so much on your mind. I know why. I'm not complaining. It's just that—"

He finished her sentence. "It's just that we haven't talked, Kristine. Not about some things. Important things."

She waited, knowing, sensing that he needed to think aloud.

"I'm very happy here, Kristine. Here in your home, with you. I think you know that," he began. "But there is a part of me that stayed in eighteen seventy-one. A part that says living here with you isn't right. I may have nothing to offer." He looked intensely into her eyes. "I don't even know if I'm still married. If I am, what have I made you? My God, what does that make me?"

She dropped the papers onto the floor. "Sean, you can't be serious about this! You're not married! Even if you had stayed in the past, you couldn't make that claim. What you had with Christina wasn't even close to a marriage. It wasn't real. It was entered into under false pretenses. It's invalid. It always was." She was near tears as she murmured, "Christina's gone. She's out of your life. And I'm . . ." She couldn't continue; she couldn't make herself that vulnerable again.

He traced her mouth with his finger and wiped away the tear that slid down her cheek. "And you're here, just as you've been since the moment you entered my life. You've been there for me. Even at Rivanna, my Rivanna, you were there for whoever needed you." He held her face between his hands with such gentleness that the gesture was one of adoration. "Well, I may not deserve you, but God help me, Kristine, I do love you."

Her eyes widened in surprise. "You love me?"

"You doubted it?"

"I didn't know."

"You should have known. Just as I know that you love me. For the first time in my life, I'm not afraid to believe that someone loves me, for me . . . not for any other reason. And I have nothing to offer you, except that. Just my love."

She was studying his face, wanting to memorize how he looked at this moment. "You amaze me, Sean O'Mara. What you offer is precious. And it's something I've never had before. I do love you, Sean. We're bonded, you and I . . . don't you know that?"

He smiled as he took her in his arms. "I do now. Come here to me." He covered her face with adoring kisses.

Closing her eyes, she wrapped her arms around his shoulders and enjoyed his attention. An astonishing hunger for him was building in her, and when she felt him slip her silk robe down her arms, she couldn't help smiling. "I guess the superintendent of schools will have to wait," she announced with a catch in her voice as Sean's cheek brushed the side of her breast.

He raised his head and gazed into her eyes. "I'm sorry, lass. I promise to help you . . . but later."

Never in her life had she expected to feel such intense love, to be filled with such astonishing emotion. Pulling him down to her, she breathed into his mouth, "Later . . . this is our time."

As the Amtrak train sped through the night, a lone woman sat in a seat by the window and looked out to the darkness of northern Virginia. To an observer, she looked like the type of woman that didn't wish company. A woman with a lot on her mind . . .

402

Christina couldn't suppress the gratified smirk that crossed her lips as she imagined Bobby Ray Evert's face when he discovered that he'd lost her — and thirty-eight thousand dollars. He deserves it, she thought with vicious satisfaction. He had treated her, Marie Delacroix, like a harlot, showing no regard for her sensibilities. Were it not for a small fortune she'd found in his attaché case, Bobby Ray Evert would have been a complete misadventure.

She patted the case that had not left her side since she'd discovered it. Now she had the means to travel in a style befitting her proper station in life. She was a lady. Why, once she'd taken a quick look at a current fashion periodical, she'd realized that Bobby Ray had dressed her completely wrong. His taste was as inferior as his recent frenzied lovemaking. Looking down at the skirt of her beige linen suit, Christina smiled with pride. Even if it had cost nearly three hundred dollars, it had been worth it. She'd seen the difference in the attitudes of those around her. Clothes did make a difference. Now she commanded respect. And it was given.

An excitement started to build in her belly and snake upward to her heart. She'd never been north of Washington in her life. And here she was, on a speeding train, on her way to Philadelphia.

On her way to her husband . . . and that whore.

Chapter Twenty-two

"But they're making me look like a woman, Danielle! I don't think I can go through with this!"

Danni tried not to look exasperated. "Look, Sean," she said while walking him away from the three makeup artists, "I know you're new to this. That's why Brubakers is sending me out on all shoots, so I can be here to answer any questions you might have . . . like this one." She looked back at the two men and the woman impatiently waiting for the lead-in in this commercial. She smiled, appealing for time. "It's just like when we were in the photography studio and they used makeup to even out your skin. Remember?"

Sean glanced around at the crew of workers trying to make midmorning in the country look like dawn. None of it made sense. "I don't wish to be difficult, Danielle, but I must disagree with you. Those were photographs; this is going to be real when it's on the television. I'll look ridiculous with this . . . these colors. Have you seen all the bottles and jars they have? It looks like a woman's toilette table."

"Carmine Del Playca is one of the best in the business. We flew him and his assistants out from California to do this. Between the sun and the bright lights, you'll look completely washed out without the makeup." She watched him stare at the ground, at his polished boots.

"Sean, in this business minutes are money. Every minute counts when we're shooting outside. Trust me on this. When you watch it on film, I promise you won't be able to see the makeup. Please? If you just do it this one time, then you'll understand. I'm promising you, you won't be humiliated. I wouldn't let that happen."

Taking a deep breath, Sean looked back toward the makeup people. "I won't let him make me look like a woman," he said in a gruff voice. "I draw the line at that."

She shook her head. "You won't look like a woman."

He started to walk back toward the makeup table, then stopped and turned around. "You understand why I was concerned," he stated, hoping he wouldn't have to be blunt.

After looking toward the Del Playca people, Danni let her gaze return to Sean. Grinning, she walked up to him and whispered, "Okay, so Carmine is not the most masculine of men. However, he knows what we want and he delivers. You won't look like him, Sean. I promise."

Once more seated in the high wooden chair, Sean posed stiffly and listened to the conversation taking place around him. Words were punctuated by waves of the long thin brushes and his eyes widened in horror as he listened.

"Carmine, what are you planning on going with for him? The Sea Teal or the Pink Parfait?"

"The teal, the teal, Chaz! Look at those eyes. My only dilemma is what to do with the cheeks. Look at those divine bones! I can't decide on nutmeg, the toasted cinnamon, or sage."

Sean stared down at the man with the dark Latin eyes. "What are you planning on doing?" he demanded. "Serving me up for lunch?"

Carmine gave him an outrageously flirty look. "Ohhh . . . how delicious!"

Sean's voice rose over those of the others. *"Danielle!"*

It was glorious to be on a horse again. He just wished that he could give the filly free rein and take off for the meadow. However, that was not what he had agreed to do. He patiently waited for the director to call him again. This would be the third time he brought the horse to a gallop and dismounted before the cameras. For some reason, the director, a man named Roy Fuller, insisted on perfection in all details, from the position of the horse to the degree of sunlight. It was tedious work and repetitious, and everything was . . . well, false.

He was supposed to look as though he'd just returned from a ride, at dawn, yet he was expected to travel no more than a few hundred feet. To counterfeit exertion, someone would squirt water on him from a bottle. And the dawn? Why, he couldn't believe they produced that with a machine which spurted out an imitation of early morning fog hovering over the grass and wild flowers. It was all incredible—and false. He was supposed to ride up to the huge country home, dismount, slowly run his hand over the neck of the horse, check the time in the pocket watch, and then look up at one of the windows . . . though no one was actually there.

It was acting, Danielle had said. He needed the money this job would produce; therefore, he had to become an actor. Maybe if he pretended that the large brick home in the distance was Rivanna. That he was back home and it was Kristine in the window, looking down at him . . .

"Action!"

Sean blinked several times, then dug his heels into the horses sides. He had to do this.

Danni stood next to Roy Fuller and watched Sean gallop in their direction. Her heart quickened as the horse and rider quickly reached them. She actually felt the raw sexuality of the moment as Sean slid off the horse, ran a gloved hand over the silky neck of the animal, and stared up at the house with such an intense longing that Danni actually looked up to the window, expecting to see a woman

. . . a lover.

"Cut! We've got it, people! We're out of here."

Roy Fuller walked up to Sean and shook his hand. "Congratulations. You did really well for your first time."

Completely embarrassed, Sean cleared his throat and patted the horse's cheek. "It's kind of you to say that."

"Listen, I'd like to get together with you and set up a schedule for the next shoot. Can you join me for dinner?"

Sean looked behind him to Danielle. She was making a horrible face. "I'm not sure," he stumbled. "My . . . that is . . . Danielle, Kristine and I . . ."

"What Sean is trying to say is that he has plans for dinner."

Roy Fuller looked over his shoulder at the tall woman and said, "They can't be adjusted? I'm on a flight back to California at six a.m."

Danielle stared at the man with the light brown hair that was in need of a barber's attention. From behind tortoise-shell glasses inquisitive hazel eyes looked back at her. Her first impression of Roy Fuller was that he closely resembled an absent-minded professor. Someone—a wife, a friend—ought to take the man in hand and dress him. She crossed her arms over her chest. "Can't we go over it now?"

Fuller shook his head and waved his hand toward the film crew. "I have to supervise this, then show your people the results of this morning." He looked directly into her eyes. "Unless you'd like to tell them why it's delayed?" he challenged.

She was about to tell him what she'd really like to do when Sean spoke up.

"Why don't you join us for dinner tonight?"

Danni glared at him. "Sean! Do you remember the last time you didn't consult Kristine about an additional guest?"

"That was different," he said easily. "Besides, we're going to a restaurant tonight. A Chinese one . . . What is it again, Danielle?"

"The Phoenix." Danni knew she was sulking, yet she couldn't help it. She absolutely hated the smirk on Fuller's face. Glaring at him, she muttered, "It's in Chinatown. I suppose you'll need a ride."

Fuller's grin widened. "Why thank you. I'm staying at the Adams Mark." He turned toward Sean. "What time shall we meet you?"

Looking at Danielle's annoyed expression, Sean said, "Ahh . . . we had planned to meet Danielle at eight o'clock."

Again, Fuller extended his hand. "Well then, we'll talk tonight." He glanced at Danielle. "Should I expect you around seven-thirty?"

"Seven forty-five."

Fuller continued to grin at her as he said, "Thanks for the invitation, Sean."

Sean nodded as the director walked away, then turned to Danni. She was blazing with indignation. "You said I should be congenial," said Sean. "I was doing what you had —"

"I said don't make trouble."

"I wasn't. I was trying to avoid it."

Danni blinked a few times and turned away from the sight of the annoying Fuller. God, his jacket had leather elbows . . . . "I'm sorry, Sean. It's not your fault. You're too nice; and Fuller's too . . . too assertive. What else would you expect from a Los Angeles director?"

"I didn't think he was assertive. I thought he seemed friendly."

Danni laughed sarcastically. "Friendly? Demanding, that's what he is." She'd sensed that Fuller was being overly patient with her, and knew it wasn't her imagination. He'd acted as if he couldn't find a good reason for Brubakers' head buyer to be on the set.

"Would you prefer that Kristine and I bring him to the restaurant?"

She groaned. "As the ninth vice president of Brubakers, I'd better do the grunt work. I'll pick him up." She looked at Sean's costume: a soft, white shirt, buttoned right up to his neck; black pants, tucked into gleaming leather boots; and a gold, antique pocket watch. He carried it off so well that he looked at though he'd stepped right out of another century.

Dismissing the silly notion, she said, "You'd better get changed. And congratulations on your first commercial. Have Carmine take that makeup off for you."

Sean swallowed. "Carmine? Can't I wash it off myself with soap and water?"

Glancing at the area where the Del Playca group waited, Danni couldn't help laughing. "C'mon. You've got two years to go on this contract. It's time to make friends."

As she led him toward the makeup people, Danni had cause to shake her head. Men! Sometimes Sean really confused her. Frequently, his lack of knowledge seemed downright childish. It was as if he'd been living in a sealed bubble, out of contact with the world. And then there was Roy Fuller, a character if she'd ever seen one. She was stuck playing chauffeur and dinner partner for him tonight!

My God, she'd rather have a root canal.

They were seated in the upstairs dining room when Kris spotted Danni leading a tall, studious-looking man toward their table. They are complete opposites, she thought. The man's tweed jacket looked worn, yet comfortable. His sandy-colored hair fell onto his collar, as though he'd run his fingers through it, instead of a comb. His glasses seemed to slide down his nose, and he used his forefinger to push them back. Danni, on the other hand, created a stir with her turquoise sheath and huge dangling, gold earrings. She looked like a tall, statuesque mandarin doll.

"That's him?" Kris asked Sean. "Roy Fuller?"

Sean nodded. "That's him," he whispered.

"From the looks on their faces, I'd say they aren't getting along any better tonight than they did this morning."

Kris smiled at Roy Fuller and accepted Danni's kiss.

"I'm sorry we're late," Fuller said as he held out a chair for Danielle. As soon as she was seated, he and Sean sat down.

"We only arrived a short time ago, ourselves." As he smiled at Kristine, Sean mentally pictured what had delayed them. He wondered if those around him could pick up the fragrance of her perfume. The bath they had shared was scented with something called Ivorie. He hadn't realized that until it was too late, and by then it didn't matter. They had more important matters to—

Danni broke Sean's thoughts. "What Mr. Fuller is trying to say is that we were delayed because I was late picking him up at his hotel."

Roy Fuller smiled, as if he were being patient with a child. "Actually, Danielle, I was going to say we had trouble finding a parking space."

Danni glared at him, and Kris, picking up her friend's anger, spoke up to fill in the void. "I've really enjoyed your work, Roy. That peanut commercial was wonderful. So innovative. It deserved the Cleo."

Fuller looked gratefully at her. "Thanks, Kristine. Actually the animators should get all the credit."

A young oriental man came up to them and took

412

their order. After much discussion and disagreement on the part of Danielle and her dinner partner, the four of them finally decided to share an eight-course meal that offered a wide variety of delicacies.

Kristine and Sean found it impossible to enjoy the food, for everything from the seasoning of a dish to the décor of the restaurant was hotly debated by Roy and Danielle. At one point, when Danni insinuated that Fuller was a tyrant, Kris kicked her friend under the table.

Seeing Danielle's blazing glance, Sean decided it was time to change the direction of the conversation. "Did either of you see Kristine's show today?"

Immediately, everyone became sober and sincere.

"That couldn't have been easy," Roy said in a low voice.

Danni forgot her food and leaned her elbows on the edge of the table. She shook her head with great sadness. "Can you imagine . . . thirteen, pregnant, and an addict? My God."

Kris was still haunted by that young girl—that child—who'd bravely told her story to the city of Philadelphia. "I talked to Irv today and we've decided that I'm not going to do any more appearances at women's groups or that sort of thing. We're going to put it out that I'm readily available to schools. I don't know how many kids saw the show today, but I'm going to make sure that as many as possible hear that story. We—adults—can talk all we want about drugs, but it's never going to really sink in. Tanya's real, she's one of their generation."

"Won't that take a lot of time? How will you ever work it all in?" Danni knew how compulsive Kris could get about a project.

"We're going to be putting together a presentation at the studio next week, mixing Tanya's interview with some cold, hard, facts. We're not going to be pulling any punches on this one. Irv even suggested we film an overdose down at the morgue. I don't know if I can do that, though."

"Oh my God . . ." Danni looked horrified.

Suddenly, Kris realized what she was doing. Her eyes took in the three people at her table. "I'm sorry. It certainly isn't great dinner conversation, is it?"

Sean reached out and held her hand in his. He didn't care who saw him or what anybody thought. "I'm sorry I brought the subject up. I just wanted everyone to know how proud I am of you."

Kris had to swallow several times to keep from crying. Taking a deep breath, she smiled and said to Roy Fuller, "So when do I get to see my future husband's commercial?"

Danni dropped her fork onto her plate. "What?"

Looking at Sean, Kris couldn't suppress a smile. She wondered how many women had received a proposal of marriage in the bathtub. "We're going to be married," she softly whispered, as if the thought were too new to be spoken aloud.

Beaming with pride, Sean brought her fingers to

his lips and lightly kissed them. It was an act of possession. "We're going to fly down and tell Kristine's brother this weekend. I think we owe him a visit."

Roy signaled for the waiter and ordered champagne, no easy task in a Chinese restaurant, and Danni jumped up and hugged both Sean and Kristine.

After she sat down again, she stared at the two of them as though they'd just walked off the pages of a fairy tale. "Roy," she asked, "can you drive an automobile yourself? Or do all you Hollywood people have drivers?"

Fuller looked amused. "I learned to drive in my father's Ford pickup. Does that qualify me?"

Danielle Rowe dragged her eyes away from the couple across from her, and she smiled at Roy Fuller for the very first time. "Good. You're driving tonight. I plan to drink myself under this table."

After the waiter had poured the champagne, she picked up her glass and said, "Congratulations . . . take good care of her, Sean."

He looked at Danielle and said solemnly. "I promise."

Thirtieth Street Station was busy for ten o'clock at night. A huge cavern of a building, it was filled with the noise of hurried conversations and announcements read in a low monotone by a nebu-

415

lous voice.

It was with great curiosity that Christina Mattson O'Mara stepped off the Amtrak train and followed the crowd up the moving steps to the main floor.

Philadelphia. Even the sound of it was exotic to her. She'd heard about it, read about it . . . and now she was here.

"Excuse me, but aren't you Kristine Gavin?"

Christina looked down at the matronly woman and frowned. "I beg your pardon?"

The woman appeared embarrassed. "I'm sorry. I just love your new show." She fumbled with her purse until she pulled out a note pad and pencil. "Nobody's going to believe that I met you. Would you mind . . . ?"

Looking at the offered paper, Christina asked impatiently, "Would I mind what? What do you want?"

"Well, I did want your autograph," the woman stated, while shoving the paper back into her purse. "Now you can keep it."

As she walked away in a huff, Christina heard the woman say, "And to think I thought you were a sweet girl. Another television lie!"

Christina watched the woman disappear into the crowd. Looking around her, she took notice of the sly glances cast in her direction. These people thought she was that whore on television! Throwing back her head, she laughed out loud, attracting more attention, then spotted a handsome man staring at her. Holding the attaché case close to her chest, she smiled flirtatiously.

She was going to enjoy ruining Kristine Gavin's reputation. It only seemed fair. She would repay the whore by doing exactly what had been done to her. She would exchange places with the impostor.

And then she would take back her husband.

Chapter Twenty-three

"Oh, Jack, I'm so sorry." Kris reached up to kiss her brother's cheek. "When did you find out that you'd lost the variance?"

Jack Gavin gave his younger sister a squeeze while leading her into the study. "Two weeks ago. They actually sent a committee up here to tell me."

"From the historical society?"

Jack nodded. "You're not going to believe this, but one of them professes to be related to us. A distant cousin, fourth or something. He claims his mother is ninety-three and living in Richmond."

They both watched as Sean and Elaine slowly entered the room. Sean looked preoccupied as he lovingly gazed about the study.

Coming to Kris's side, he slid an arm around her waist and said, "Thank you both for having us this weekend. I don't suppose there's any point in putting this off." He took a deep breath and then continued, "Jack, I'm here to ask your permission to marry your sister."

Elaine squealed her delight. Jack looked shocked. Finally, amid the others' laughter, he said, "You're asking for my permission?"

Sean first gazed down at Kris, then raised his head to look at her brother. "You are Kristine's only male relative. Your approval would be the same as your blessing."

Elaine moaned and sat on the edge of the sofa. "This is so romantic. Why didn't you ask my brother for his blessing?" she demanded of her husband.

"Because Richard doesn't like me," Jack stated.

Elaine shrugged. "That's right, he doesn't. Anyway, go ahead . . . give them your blessing."

Jack looked from his sister to the tall stranger. No one knew anything about the man, except that he'd shown up on Kris's birthday and the two of them had left before morning, with little explanation.

"Jack?" Kris's eyes narrowed.

"Look, I don't even know Sean. I suggest he and I leave you ladies and take a walk outside." He noticed that Sean hadn't taken offense, so far. "C'mon, Sean. I don't think you've seen Rivanna in the daytime. Might as well do it now. The place goes on the market on Monday."

"Oh, no." Kris looked at Sean and saw he was fighting to keep a smile on his face. "You're giving up?"

Walking toward the foyer, Jack said, "We went

to visit Elaine's family in San Francisco and found a great Victorian. With a variance, and few repairs . . . She'll tell you about it. We simply decided to cut our losses and start over."

As Sean joined him, he opened the front door and said, "According to our infamous historical society, Rivanna dates back before the Revolution. Let's walk down to the stables. They must have been something in their day."

Kris moved to the window and watched her brother and Sean make their way across the lawns. They seemed deep in conversation. Very softly, Elaine came up behind her and put an arm around her shoulder.

"I'm so happy for you. Don't worry about Jack. I think Sean floored him with that request for a blessing. It's so old-fashioned."

Kris grinned at her sister-in-law. "Sean is old-fashioned. That's one of the things I love about him."

They both gazed out the window toward their men.

"He loves you, Kris. You can see it in his eyes, in the way he touches you. Even though I don't know him, I think he must be very special for you to love him in return."

Smiling, Kris slid her arm around Elaine's waist. "Oh, Elaine, I could never explain it, but you're right. He is special."

They stood, two women, arm in arm, and watched as their men disappeared from view. Each was dying of curiosity and would have given almost anything to hear the conversation that was taking place.

"I feel a little foolish talking to you like this," Jack admitted. "You seem to be everything Kris wants. I guess it's that we know nothing about you."

Sean nodded. "I understand that. I was born in Pennsylvania. In Titusville."

"Whoa! That isn't what I mean." Jack smiled. "I was talking about other things: have you ever been married before, where do you intend to live, how will you support her?" He shook his head. "Thank God nobody in Elaine's family did this to me."

Sean smiled. "I expected it. In answer to your questions: Yes, I was married. She's no longer alive."

"I'm sorry," Jack interrupted. "Listen, we can have this talk some other time."

"No. That's all right, I'd rather we did it today. You see, I have a few questions I would like to ask you."

Jack laughed. "Okay. So how do you intend to support my sister?"

Sean walked into the stable, the one he had built in eighteen seventy-one, and looked around. He walked over to a wall and tested it's strength. Turning around to Jack, he said, "A few weeks ago I signed a contract to represent a men's cologne named Thoroughbred. Within the next two years I

421

will receive nine hundred and seventy-five thousand dollars." He smiled at Jack's shocked expression. "Kristine says I had a very good agent. And that's just the beginning."

He looked down the dusty corridor that separated the rows of stalls, stalls that had once held his many horses. It seemed like such a long time ago. Lightly slapping his future brother-in-law on the back, he added, "The rest depends on you, Jack."

"Me?" Jack almost choked.

"You. Did I understand you correctly? Are you planning on putting Rivanna up for sale on Monday?"

Jack nodded. "We have to unload it soon. We're anxious to start on the Victorian."

Turning back to the man that so closely resembled the woman he loved, Sean said, "Then sell it to me."

"What?" Jack was barely able to get the word out. This conversation was certainly not going the way he had expected.

"Sell it to me, Jack. I want it. I could slowly restore the house and stables. I've already purchased my first horse."

"Wait a minute! This is going a little bit too fast. I couldn't sell Rivanna to you."

Sean spun around. "Why not?"

"Because you're marrying my sister. You're going to be family. I certainly wouldn't make a profit off my sister's husband. I suppose I could deed

422

part of it to you both as a wedding present—"

"No. I need to own it. I don't want any part of it as a gift." Seeing the surprised expression on Jack's face, Sean apologized. "I'm sorry for being so blunt. You see, Rivanna is very special. I want to bring it back to the way it once was."

"But you've never been here before, except for Kris's birthday."

Sean looked out the stable door to the house. "Oh, but I have, Jack. A very long time ago."

Looking at the man next to him, Jack could actually see the love Sean had for this land. It was in the eyes. Confused, Jack surmised that Sean must have been on Rivanna before the Gavins bought it back. Sometime, when they both felt less emotional, he'd have to ask.

"A big wedding?"

Kris shook her head. "No. Sean and I want something small. Probably in July. Sean's free that month and I'm already scheduled to take some time off."

Sitting at the kitchen table, Kris sipped her coffee while watching Elaine's masterful preparation of dinner. How lucky Jack was, she thought, to find this remarkable woman. Elaine is the steady, calm force that brings tranquillity to this place, even though they are losing it. "How soon are you leaving?" she asked.

Elaine looked up from the wide butcher block

island that served as her work space, and gazed around the kitchen. "As soon as possible, Kris. I couldn't bear to put any more love into this house."

Suddenly, the hair on Kris's arms rose and a strange feeling crept up her back to settle in her scalp. This was Mae's kitchen. This was where she'd made that crazy Italian meal over a hundred years ago. Even though it now looked different, here in this room she had met Riva, Sada, and Grace. Slowly, she stood up and walked toward the back of the house. Elaine's modern pantry took the place of what once was a wash room—the room where she had found Tisha in early labor.

She heard Elaine's voice, as if from a distance, yet she couldn't answer as she looked toward the ceiling to the second floor. Up there, in a room that had yet to be remodeled, Naomi Mae had been born. And Beth . . . She had run through the halls with carefree abandon. What had turned that laughing, feminist tomboy into a proper matriarch? Beth . . . Kris's breath caught in the back of her throat and she swallowed down a sob.

My God, all those people, all that emotion . . . here, in this house. And now it was to go to strangers?

"Kris, are you okay?"

Blinking rapidly, she looked at her sister-in-law. They were standing in the hallway now. Elaine was holding a ladle, and tears were sliding down Kris's cheeks.

"Are you all right?" Elaine repeated. "We were talking and you just got up and walked back here."

As if waking from a dream, Kris ran her hands over her face. "Elaine, does Jack have the phone number of that man who says he's related to us?"

Elaine shrugged. "I suppose so. Are you going to contact him?"

Kris nodded and, together, they walked back into the kitchen. "Sean's researching something in Richmond, through the mail. Either the mail system is faulty, or his request is sitting on the desk of some overworked state employee. He hasn't heard a thing. Everything's closed on the weekend, but maybe this man or his mother could give him a feel for what he's looking for."

"And what's that?" Elaine asked, pulling out a large manila envelope and thumbing through a sheaf of papers.

"A heritage," Kris murmured. Her attention was drawn to the window. Approaching the back of the house, Jack was in deep conversation with the man she was about to marry. And his arm was thrown around Sean's shoulders, as if the two men had been friends for years.

She was immediately filled with love . . . for both of them.

He was so apprehensive that he wasn't able to enjoy the drive. And he thought it was a shame, since the car they had rented was much more to his

425

liking than Kristine's BMW. This one was black and was called a Trans Am. Running his fingers over the leather stitching of the steering wheel, Sean thought it was a fine automobile and wished they were driving back in the country instead of coming into Richmond. After all, neatly folded in his wallet was a driving permit from the state of Pennsylvania.

"You've adjusted so well," Kristine stated, as if reading his thoughts.

From the corner of his eye, he saw her smile. "I know why you're doing this, visiting these people. You can't really think they'll know anything about Rivanna and Beth." His breath left him in a frustrated rush. "I just wish we had come a day earlier, when everything was open."

"We really didn't plan this trip, Sean. Besides, aren't you even curious about this Dewayne Cornell and his mother?"

Stopping at a red light, Sean lovingly gazed to the woman at his side. "Kristine, I don't know what these people can tell you. Neither one of them were alive at the time. I still say the best thing to do is check with the city of Rich—"

She interrupted as the light turned green. "Yes, but since we can't do that, this doesn't seem like such a bad idea. Here." She pointed to a side street lined with old trees. "Turn here. It's number 708."

They both found the white brick house at the same time. Sean was thankful that the street was wide and very few cars were parked on it. Parking,

426

this type of parking, was the most difficult part of operating an automobile. Pulling in right by the curb, he shut the car off and waited until Kristine opened her door and looked down.

"Pretty good," she observed. "A little closer and it would have been perfect. Don't worry, you'll pass your test."

"All those questions," Sean remarked as they got out of the car. "I'm amazed that anyone passes."

She laughed. "They don't ask all of them, just enough so that you have to study the entire book. C'mon, I think Mr. Dewayne Cornell has been watching for our arrival."

They both smiled at the middle-aged man who stood in front of his house. He was short and balding, and appeared very eager for this meeting.

"Why, Miss Gavin, I can't tell you what a pleasure it is to meet you!" He held out his hand and Kris shook it.

After introducing Sean, she asked, "Have we ever met before?"

Dewayne motioned for them to enter his home. He followed right behind them. "Why no, not really. But we all saw you and Mr. O'Mara here on the television the other night. You were with Lee Saunders."

Knowing that the racetrack interview had gone national, Kris politely returned his smile. Oh God, she thought, does he think this is a prelude to an interview of him and his mother? For television? In part, the idea appealed to her. There was no

427

harm in letting him think that was what she had in mind. She wouldn't say anything, but she wouldn't deny it either. Sometimes, when people think they're going to be on television, they open up and reveal more about themselves than they ever intended.

"Please, call me Kristine," she said. "It was very kind of you to see us on such short notice. I hope we didn't interrupt your Sunday afternoon."

"Oh, not at all," Dewayne assured her. "Why Miss Barbara's been just animated, since we told her you're coming."

"Miss Barbara?" Sean asked, exchanging looks with Kristine.

Dewayne smiled. "My mother. Please . . . If you'll follow me . . . She's upstairs."

They entered a bedroom that was a cross between the coldness of a hospital and the warmth of a loving home. Everywhere were pictures of children and grandchildren. A wooden rocker was placed by the window, and potpourri burned on a small table, lessening the scent of medicine. In the hospital bed lay the most fragile-looking woman Kris had ever seen. Her gray hair still held a streak of dark brown, and her skin had a delicate sheen, like fine parchment. Her eyes had lost their true clear color, but none of the curiosity of younger days.

"You're a Mattson,"the woman whispered, and waved them closer.

Sean had to put his hand on Kris's back to make

her move. Finally, regaining her objectivity, Kris extended a hand to the old woman. "How do you do, Miss Barbara. I'm Kristine Gavin, and this is Sean O'Mara."

"Oh, I know who you are," she said in her gravelly voice. "My Eileen lets me watch the television after dinner. She only lets me have it at night . . . says it'll ruin my eyes . . . as if that matters anymore."

Kris and Sean smiled.

"Momma, Miss Gavin and Mr. O'Mara would like to talk to you about—"

"I know what they want, Dewayne," his mother said sharply. "Why don't you leave us for a bit?"

Embarrassed, Dewayne nodded and turned to Kris and Sean. "You'll have to talk up some for her." Without waiting for an answer, he walked from the room and closed the door behind him.

Miss Barbara looked over the couple, then whispered, "Dewayne's always been a good boy, but a mite too uppity for my taste. Why, I believe you made his day, Miss Gavin, by coming here." The woman stopped to catch her breath. "He's probably on the telephone right now to his cronies."

Kris smiled and moved closer to the hospital bed. "Miss Barbara, both you and your son are very kind to let us come over and pick your minds."

"Nobody wants to talk about the old days any more." She cleared her throat and reached for the paper towels she kept under her pillow. Wiping her mouth, she shuddered as she inhaled. "I can tell you got something you want to ask. What is it, child?"

Sean came up behind Kris and rested his hand on her shoulder. It was a silent offering of support.

"Your son, Dewayne, claims that we're related. Is that true?"

Miss Barbara smiled, for the first time since they'd met her. "Oh, it's true, girl. A bit confusing, but true. My daddy's people are the Gentrys. The Gentrys and the Mattsons married some time—"

"Harry Gentry?" Sean interrupted, his fingers tightening on Kris's shoulder.

Miss Barbara closed her eyes and nodded. "That's right. I can still see him and Miss Elizabeth when they came visiting my gran'daddy. I thought they were old then, but I guess they weren't more than sixty."

Sean's voice was almost as low and hoarse as that of the woman in the bed. "And what about Elizabeth's sister—Christina? What happened to her?"

Miss Barbara's eyes snapped open, shock clearly visible in them as she looked at Sean. "Who?"

"Christina," Sean repeated. "The older sister. What happened to her?"

Miss Barbara once more reached for her paper towel and began to wrap it around her index finger. "I never heard of her. You must be mistaken."

Sean raised his voice, thinking the woman's

hearing was at fault. "Christina. What happened to her?"

"There's no need for you to shout, boy! I heard you the first time. I'll repeat my answer, just so you hear it right. I never heard of a Christina."

Kris shook her head. "But you must have! Christina was Beth's older sister. At Rivanna—"

"How do you know this?" the woman demanded. "Somebody's been filling your head with stories. There was no Christina Mattson. Just Elizabeth.

Kris and Sean looked at each other, too confused to answer the woman.

"But . . ." Kris turned back and saw that Miss Barbara's eyes were closed. She was clearly agitated. If possible, she looked even older than when they'd entered the room.

"I believe I should rest now," the woman murmured. "I'm sure Dewayne is waiting for you downstairs. Thank you for coming."

They were dismissed. It was Sean who pulled Kris from the room. In the hallway, before they met with Dewayne, Sean whispered, "If you believe her, Christina didn't exist."

"I don't believe her."

Sean agreed. "Neither do I. She's definitely hiding something. It was as if we knew some terrible secret. But what? We know Christina lived. I married her!"

"I have proof."

"You do?" Sean asked as they approached the

stairs.

Kris smiled. "Jack gave me her portrait and the newspaper article that was behind it. It named her."

Sean stopped and looked at Kris. "That's right. Where is it?"

"At Rivanna. Jack has it. I left it there the night of my birthday party." She followed Sean down the stairs. "But I'm definitely going to see that it gets packed. This time I'm making sure it gets to Philadelphia."

Christina laid the scissors on the edge of the hotel sink and stared at her reflection. Propped up beside the mirror was the picture she'd cut out of the newspaper. Quickly her eyes traveled to the image of Kristine Gavin, and then returned to her own reflection.

It was remarkable. She and this Gavin woman could be twins, now that their hair was the same length.

She had been busy since she'd checked into the hotel, but fortunately the current issue of *Philadelphia Magazine* had been placed on a table in the suite she'd rented. In the magazine was a two-page article on Kristine Gavin and Christina had learned more about her from the daily newspapers. It appeared that Miss Gavin was very popular in this city. She even had her own television program. To Christina, that was exciting.

It would be the ultimate test. If she could walk into that place she'd read about—the television station here in the city—and pass for the Gavin woman, then she could set the rest of her plans in motion.

"Are you okay, Kristine? Looks like you turned your ankle."

She watched the uniformed man rush to her side and feigned the pain of an injury. "Please . . . if you could only help me to my—"

"Your office," the man supplied.

"Yes," Christina sighed. "My office."

She had to remind herself not to smile as the man led her to an elevator and pushed the number three button. When the doors opened, she saw a large room in which several people were busily working. As the guard helped her in to a smaller room, she finally let go of his arm and walked inside.

She was not impressed. It looked functional, with many boxes sitting on the floor.

"How's it feel to have your own office?" the uniformed man asked in a friendly voice.

She barely turned around to answer. "You may go now."

"What?"

She glared at him. "I said you may go. I don't need you any longer."

The man continued to stare at her.

433

"Are you that dense you can't understand an order." Christina waved an arm. "Go back to whatever your little job is."

The man was shaking his head disappointedly. "I wouldn't've believed it if I didn't hear it myself."

As he left, he closed the door and so was unable to see her wide grin.

It was a beginning.

Fifteen minutes later, after Christina had insulted at least seven other people, a man came out of the elevator just as she was about to step into it.

"Kris! What're you doing here on a Sunday?"

Christina turned her most haughty look on him. "And why would you want to know?"

The man looked confused. "We were having a meeting about the drug project. We're really making progress with some of the area schools. They've told us—"

She removed his hand from the door, as if it were a piece of odorous fish. "Go away. Do you honestly think I care about any project of yours?" Her voice was filled with scorn. As the elevator doors shut her eyes lit triumphantly. The man was completely shocked.

Irv Handleman continued to share at the elevator doors. She's under too much pressure, he told himself. She didn't even look right. Her eyes were frightening. He'd have Peg call her that night to see what was going on.

Too much was riding on Kristine for her to have anxiety problems now. If that was it, they'd have to find out right away. Friendship, or not, far too much was tied up in the new show to take any chances.

Chapter Twenty-four

On Monday morning Kris stood in front of her desk and stared at the scrawled writing on her yellow legal pad.

Your time is coming, Slut

Her eyes never leaving the ugly words, she grabbed the arms of her chair and slid down into it. My God, who could have written that? Who hated her this much? For that matter, who hated her?

Immediately, her brain registered the way Jerry, the guard at KLM's door had totally ignored her good morning only a few minutes ago. There had been no easy banter between them this morning as there usually was. She'd shrugged it off at the time, thinking that Jerry was entitled to a bad day, like anyone else.

She remembered the way several reporters, clerks, and technicians had stared at her as she'd walked through the newsroom toward her new office. She'd felt their animosity, seen a dislike that hadn't been there before.

But this wasn't jealousy over her rising from the ranks. This, she thought as she picked up the pad, was dangerous.

Making a decision, she dropped her purse into a desk drawer and stood up. Taking the pad with her, she left the office.

She knocked on Irv's door and poked her head inside. "Hi, are you busy?"

Irv Handleman leaned back in his chair and waved Kris inside. He watched as she closed the door and sat opposite him.

"Peg tried calling you last night, but all she could get was your machine."

Kris nodded. "Sean and I went down to Rivanna for the weekend. We didn't get back until after eleven—"

Irv straightened in his chair. "Wait a minute. I'm confused. You say you were gone this weekend?"

Kris smiled. "We wanted to tell Jack and Elaine about our plans."

She waited for Irv to ask about them. He didn't, and she was starting to feel uncomfortable. He was looking at her very strangely. Clearing her throat, she said, "Sean and I are getting married."

437

"You are?"

"Yes . . . and I'd like to know what's wrong with everyone around here. From the minute I walked into this building, I've been ostracized. The looks I'm receiving are enough to make you watch your back. And then this . . ."

She tossed the notepad onto his desk. "I found it in my office a few minutes ago. What the hell's going on, Irv?"

As he read the scrawled writing, Irv rubbed his forehead to ease the signs of a headache. "This was on your desk?"

Kris nodded. "If someone wants to frighten me, they're doing a good job—"

"Kristine, I saw you this weekend here at the station. You spoke to me—insulted me is more like it, at the elevator."

Kris's mouth opened in shock. *What? Irv, I was in Virginia yesterday. With Sean.*"

Irv looked worried. "Calm down, Kris. I'm only telling you what I saw. After you insulted me, I asked a few people who were here yesterday if they noticed anything wrong with you." He nervously played with his pencil. "They told me you spent some time in your office."

"You think I wrote this to myself?" She jumped up, clutching her stomach, anguish in her voice. "My God, Irv. You're my friend! I'd have to be crazy—"

She recognized the look in his eyes, and her hand came up to cover her mouth. *He didn't be-*

lieve her!

"Kristine, you called Marci Roberts a black upstart and questioned her morals."

"I did not!" Kris pictured the reporter she'd lunched with more times than any other co-worker. "I'd never say such a thing about anyone, least of all Marci. Irv, what's happening?"

He came around the desk and placed a fatherly arm around her shoulders. "Kristine . . . you've been under a lot of stress lately. I know what that can do. This business eats people alive. I don't want that to happen to you."

She pulled away from him. "Look, I don't know what you *think* you saw this weekend, but it wasn't me. I'm telling you I was in Virginia with Sean."

She backed up to the door. "I have to prepare for today's show. We'll . . . ah, we'll talk later. All right?"

She had to get away from that sorrowful look on Irv's face. He thought she was having a nervous breakdown!

"Sean, can you meet me for lunch today?"

"I suppose so. Sure. Are you all right? Your voice sounds strange."

Kris closed her eyes and swallowed down her panic. "I need to talk to you. I think someone's trying to destroy me. It's like a plot, or something." She stopped speaking, afraid that her phone might be bugged.

439

Realizing that thought had made her more paranoid, she said, "I'll meet you in the lobby of the station at twelve o'clock. Okay?"

"I'll be there."

Kris hung up the phone and looked around her new office. *My God, why are they saying these things about me?* I wasn't even here yesterday. . . .

She couldn't believe her good fortune in choosing a hotel that offered the most popular drinking salon in the city. As she sipped her glass of Madeira, Christina looked over the mix of attractive people who mingled with near desperation. When the tuxedoed man whispered in her ear, she smiled and withdrew the twenty dollar bill and pressed it in his waiting hand. Rising, she allowed those around her to admire her taupe silk outfit that was cut to reveal most of her back. It felt deliciously exciting not to wear any bindings and to allow her breasts freedom. Already they were erect, stimulated by the feel of the soft material and the expectation of possible risk.

Christina ignored the curious glances, the looks of recognition as she passed the men and women standing in clusters by the dance floor. She didn't acknowledge a single one of them, not until she walked up to the short, yet rather attractive, man who'd just entered the nightclub.

"I've been waiting for you," she said plainly, boldly.

He smiled and sipped his drink. "I couldn't believe it when you left that message." Indicating a table so they might sit down, he added, "Here I am."

Christina gave him her most flirtatious look. He wasn't as tall as he appeared on television. Nor, as she got closer, was he as attractive as she'd thought. But then, what did that matter? She'd picked Eric Wilson because he wasn't married, and she was told he was the bright new star at an opposing television station. He would serve her purpose.

"Eric, we seem to be attracting attention. I'm sorry I chose this place. I was hoping we would have a chance to talk."

Wilson's expression became sly, and Christina had to remind herself not to smile with satisfaction as he leaned closer and said, "I live less than two blocks from here. We could always talk at my place, if you'd like."

She leaned back and looked into his eyes. They were already filled with desire. After catching her bottom lip with her teeth, she whispered, "I think I would like that."

She let her fingers trace the slight cleft in his chin, then travel to the knot of his silk tie. He would serve her purpose well.

Together they walked out of Flair, and within seconds of their departure, gossip was spreading through Philadelphia's inner circle of the up and coming.

Wilson's apartment was completely decorated in black and white. A sure sign of his character, thought Christina. She had read in one of the periodicals she devoured that this style of furniture was called Ultra Modern. She didn't care for it, found it sparse, confusing, and cold. But then she wasn't here for warmth. She was here because tonight her plan for revenge truly began. Having paid well for information, Christina was certain that in the morning this man would be boasting about how he had bedded Kristine Gavin. She tried to hide her grin, for she'd also been told of the fierce competition between the two television stations. She was counting on tales of this evening's entertainment spreading to WKLM. Sipping her glass of sherry, she attempted to listen as Eric Wilson talked about the Gavin woman's afternoon show.

"You really took everybody by surprise with "Philly Live!" I think you've got us worried. Max Goodman is watching you closely to see if there really is an afternoon audience. I even watched you." He nodded. "I was impressed."

Christine smiled, not sure what answer she should give. Nervous, Wilson threw his jacket onto a chair and began to unbutton his striped shirt. She quickly realized that he wasn't expecting a response . . . at least not to his question.

Taking a leather box down from a shelf, Wilson

placed it on the small table before her. She leaned forward on the sofa and opened it. Somehow, the contents didn't surprise her. Maybe that was because of the sly expression on Wilson's face, the excited look in his eyes.

She'd seen them before.

"Consider it an appetizer to the rest of the evening," he said nervously, now waiting for her response.

She looked up at him. "You want me to do this?"

Wilson unconsciously wiped at his nose and shrugged. "If you want . . ."

Her gaze traveled down to the small mirror and the tiny packet lying beside it. Would she never escape it?

"I prefer sherry, but you go ahead." A shudder of distaste ran through her as she rose from the sofa and walked toward the curtained window. She knew she should stay close to Wilson, let him know that his indulgence didn't bother her, except the sight of the white powder reminded her of Bobby Ray Evert and the horrible things he'd made her do.

She heard the short man snorting the powder up his nose and looked at him over her shoulder. What if he was like Bobby Ray? Could she do those things again? Was her desire for vengeance strong enough to make her endure that kind of humiliation?

Eric Wilson looked up at her and grinned. Even

from across the room, she could see the difference in him. In the eyes . . . the stupid smile . . .

"Hey, you know, I never heard that trace of a Southern accent in your voice before. I always thought you grew up around here."

For a moment, she was frightened, fearing she'd made a mistake and would be found out. Then she relaxed and slowly walked back to him. "I don't know what you mean, Eric," she said in her practiced Northern voice. She then bent to pick up her glass of sherry, allowing the taupe silk to fall away from her throat and providing him with a tantalizing view.

It worked.

Everything else was forgotten. Wilson stood up and stared at her. Coming around the glass table, he reached for her wrist and pulled her to his chest.

"I don't know why you called me, Kristine." His breath fanned her cheeks. "Until tonight, I wouldn't have believed that you even liked me. But now I know we're two of a kind, you and me — made for each other."

Prepared to suffer his kisses, Christina found herself swept beyond anything she had ever experienced. His mouth went from a gentle caress to a hot, wet demand. He wanted a response, and surprisingly she gave it. His fingers were warm, yet challenging as they touch her bare back. Within seconds, he pulled the rest of her dress down around her waist.

She had never expected to feel this way with him. He was nothing that she admired in a man, yet his body, being short, fit exactly to hers. The heat of him seared into her through the material of her dress, and she struggled to rid herself of the restricting garment.

It was astonishing. As his hands cupped her breasts and he bent his head to give them more fervent attention, Christine reveled in the unexpected pleasure.

"Take me to bed," she whispered down to him as he knelt in front of her, caressing her until her legs quivered with desire.

He looked up at her and smiled. "No . . . here. Right here."

She didn't argue.

He kissed her shoulder as she sat up, and watched as she reached for her dress.

"I didn't expect tonight that we would have—"

"Yes you did." Christina smiled. "I think you expected this from the moment you received my message. But that's all right." She slowly let her breath out. "I enjoyed myself."

Eric Wilson ran a finger over the silky skin of her neck. "Will you come back?"

"Do you want me to?"

He stood up and walked across to the television set. After fooling with some buttons, he pressed another and Christina could hear the whir of a motor. Soon it stopped, and Wilson picked up what looked like a thin black box. He came back and handed it to her.

"Take it. You understand that I have to protect myself. I can't tell you how many times I've had to defend myself down at the station because of nights like these. Some women claim rape if they think it'll give them a foot in the doorway of television. It's a safeguard."

She continued to stare at him.

"Okay, so I watch them sometimes. But I want you to have this. I would never use it against you." He gazed down at her. "Tonight was special. I guess I just want you to know that."

Her voice was very low and precise. She wanted to understand. "Are you saying everything we've just done is . . . somehow is . . ."

"On the tape," he finished for her. "Yes."

"Show me."

She watched everything he did with the television and, within seconds, saw herself on the screen. Wilson came into view as he carried her drink.

"I'd just turned it on then," he said. "There. God, if anyone ever saw this . . ."

Christina stared at the screen as Wilson brought the cocaine to her. She was fascinated by her television image, and only when she saw them getting very intimate did she clear her voice and say, "That's enough. I don't need to see anymore."

Wilson walked back to the television and removed the tape. When Christina left the black and white apartment late that night, the tape was in her possession.

She couldn't believe her good fortune.

Chapter Twenty-five

At precisely three-thirty, Christina stepped out of the cab in front of the television station and briefly looked up toward the gray sky. If everything was going as planned, across town at this moment a messenger was delivering a copy of the tape to Eric Wilson's superior.

All she had to do, she thought as she stared up at the large WKLM letters, was walk into this building and ride the elevator to the fourth floor. She had been assured that there she would find the office of Harry Leech, vice president in charge of programming. Once she handed over the package to Leech's secretary, she would be home free . . . well, almost.

"Kristine," a woman exclaimed as she neared the elevator. "Shouldn't you be in studio six?" The woman glanced at her watch. "It's after three-thirty."

Nodding, Christina entered the elevator without saying a word. A smile curved her lips as she pushed the number four button. She'd had to pay that investigator the outrageous sum of three thousand dollars, but he had certainly come through for her. She could hardly wait for everything to unfold.

Today she would have her revenge on the Gavin woman.

And her husband.

Lou Camiere controlled studio six from a small room. In it were monitors feeding back to him what three cameras picked up down on the floor. Pressing a button, he activated the loudspeaker in the studio.

"Voice check, please."

Automatically, Mike Causson, the floor director, pointed to Kristine, and she looked positively mischievous as she recited:

"All the world's a stage,
And all the men and women merely players;
They have their exits and their entrances;
And one man in his time plays many parts,
His acts being seven ages . . . ."

Lou smiled. "Thank you. *Much Ado About*

Nothing?" he asked Kris. Ever since the first show, she had been quoting lines for her voice check, and he had been guessing the sources. Not too successfully. But the audience seemed to like his attempts.

Kris laughed and shook her head. *"As You Like It."*

Lou groaned and once more pressed the button. "Next time try something other than Shakespeare."

He watched the screens in front of him. On one was a shot of the audience as they took their seats. Another showed the set and the area where the guests would sit. The last one was devoted to Kris.

She nodded. "How about this then? 'Come close to the bar, boys. We'll drink all around. We'll drink to the pure, if any be found . . .' "

Lou laughed before interrupting. "Thank you very much, Miss Gavin. I think we'll stick to Shakespeare."

Kris walked out of camera range to shake hands with some elderly ladies who were still chuckling over the exchange on the loudspeaker. Grinning himself, Lou plugged into his lead camera.

"Roll tape, Pat. Tell me when we have speed." He studied the screens in front of him. "Pull back a little. I'm going to want full body shots.

That's it. You've got it."

Ready to instruct the second cameraman, Lou noticed the far screen. From the corner of his eye, the close-up shot drew his attention. "Why's Kris standing in the back of the studio? Who's she laughing at?" The hard, gloating expression in her eyes was almost frightening.

Within a split second, two cameras searched out Kris and Lou shook his head. "No . . . no, wait a minute. She was just in the back."

Don Averly came into the control room and sat down next to Lou. "Problem?"

Shrugging, Lou briefly glanced up at the producer, then his eyes quickly returned to the monitors. Two were showing Kristine mingling with the members of the audience in the front row. The lead camera was still focused on the stage. Shaking his head, he talked to his cameraman. "Tommy, give me a shot of the rear of the studio."

Don and Lou watched as the camera scanned the back of the room. Lou shook his head. Nothing. Only more elderly women coming to see one of the last of their generation of movie stars. "I could have sworn Kristine was back there a second ago."

He heard Tommy murmur, "I thought I saw her, too. What the hell . . ."

Seeing they were running short on time, Lou

again shrugged and muttered, "Yeah, what the hell. Okay, let's get on with it, people." He pressed the loudspeaker button. "Two minutes. Everyone, please take your seat. Mike, you want to get these people settled?"

Even in the control room, there was an aura of excitement. This was live television. And today it would be fun. There would be no painful tugging at the heart. Today was glitz . . . old-fashioned glitz. Lou and Don Averly discussed some minor details, made a few corrections and then it was time to pull it all together.

"All unessentials off the set, we're coming straight up."

Mike Causson stood ready as Kris took her seat on stage. Everyone listened to the "Philly Live!" theme music and then watched as the floor director did the countdown.

"Okay, here we go," Mike said, his right hand outstretched underneath camera two. "Four . . . three . . . two . . ." Then the fierce pointing of his finger toward Kris.

Kristine Gavin smiled, looked into the camera, and welcomed her television audience. She looked lovely, relaxed and confident.

Mike could actually feel the tension leaving his shoulders. It was going to be a good show. He could sense it.

Kris had made it a point to remain in the studio for at least ten to fifteen minutes after the show was completed. She wanted the people who'd come, who'd fought rush-hour traffic, to feel appreciated. She was talking with a lady from the Northeast section of town about the shopping malls there when Arlene, the assistant producer, told her that she was needed in Irv Handleman's office. Immediately.

Thanking the young woman, Kris excused herself and hurried out of the studio. It must be important if Irv wanted to talk to her during the five o'clock news. Usually, he was a nervous wreck until that was over. It took only a minute to reach his office, yet in that short span of time Kris imagined that Irv wanted to discuss that message on her notepad—maybe he had found out who'd really written that frightening message. Maybe he'd straightened out this whole incredible mess.

Maybe she could finally breathe a little more easily.

She knocked lightly and opened the office door. Poking her head inside, she said, "Reporting as ordered, sir. Didn't even stop to take the makeup off." She hated the strained feeling between them and tried to make a joke as she breezed into the office. "Thought I'd let you see

453

the other side of me."

"Sit down, Kris."

She stopped smiling. "Now what's wrong? I was only making a joke about the makeup. Remember our arguments?"

Irv reached for his Maalox. "Please sit down."

This time she did as she was asked. "Have you found out who wrote that note?" Suddenly she was frightened.

Almost ready to unscrew the lid of his antacid, Irv changed his mind. Instead he reached for two black video cases. As if they were tainted, he shoved them across the desk toward her. "One of them was delivered to Harry Leech right before you went on the air. The note attached said it was to be viewed immediately. Harry called me and Larry Goodman in for a meeting." Irv looked away from her, as if embarassed. "I'm not going to even discuss what we saw. I'm just going to tell you the results of the meeting."

Kris gripped the edge of his desk. "Irv, what the hell are you talking about?"

He put his hands up to fend off any questions. "Look, I stuck my neck out for you on this talk show. I didn't do it because you were my friend. I did it because I thought you were the right person for the job. But I was wrong. The pressure . . ." He shrugged. "I don't think I ever knew you."

Panic seized her at his words, and she stood up and leaned over the desk. "Tell me what you're talking about! Whose tapes are they?"

Irv stood, as if to put distance between them. "I told you. One was sent to Harry and the other was sent to Channel Five. Merve Maute had the decency to send it to us. They can't afford to have the slightest scandal associated with Eric Wilson. It seems you're expendable."

Her hands were shaking and she tried to control her voice. "Look, you'd better let me see one of those tapes. I have no idea what you're talking about! Eric Wilson! What does that pompous ass have to do with me?"

She had never seen Irv this upset. His face was alarmingly red as he shook his head.

"You're not seeing them here. I can't believe you're denying this. The tape's been checked and it's clean. I recommended you for 'Philly Live!' so everyone felt it would be best if I explained how KLM is going to handle this. As of right now, you're relieved of all your duties here at the station."

"What!" Kris's mouth opened in shock. She felt like the whole world was tilting and she was hanging on by her fingertips. "What have I done?"

Irv shook his head, refusing to discuss anything but what was on his mind. "Anne Jennings has already been called. Her morning sickness has lessened considerably and she's going to take over 'Philly Live!' until we can find a permanent replacement."

Kris frantically tried to come up with arguments, to think of something to stop this insane dismissal. "I have a contract. You can't fire—"

"Check your contract," Irv interrupted. "Clause eighteen. We can fire you. We're not going to say that you were fired. That would only add to the rumors that are already flying. Maute said they're trying to keep a lid on it over there at Channel Five, but you know how fast a scandal of this size spreads." He looked out the window and sighed. He seemed overcome by an intense sadness. "We're saying you're on a leave of absence."

"Irv, I have a right to see that tape and make a rebuttal. I swear to you that I've never even talked to Eric Wilson for more than twenty minutes."

He turned back to her and she could see that he was fighting for control. "Until this, I couldn't have been more proud of you if you were my own daughter. Now I thank God you're not. You need help, Kris. Ever since that man came into your life, you haven't been the same. What's happened to you?"

Kris picked up a tape and was about to insert it into his VCR when Irv pulled the plug out of the wall. He picked up the copy on his desk and pushed it at her. "I told you to take them out of here. My God, even here in this office you deny what I saw? And I thought I knew you." He ran a shaking hand through his thinning hair. "I've also been told to tell you that the station's attorney will contact your agent."

She couldn't believe this was happening to her! "What about . . . about the drug project? Irv—"

He gave her a look that stopped her cold. She'd never seen another human being look at her with such disgust.

Picking up the phone, he said in a strangled voice. "Jerry, Kristine Gavin'll be down in about five minutes. She's not feeling well. Make sure there's a cab waiting for her, will you?"

Irv thanked the guard at the front door and hung up the phone.

Kris was fighting to keep tears at bay. "I'm being thrown out? What the hell is on those tapes?"

"Get some help, Kris." Shaking his head, Irv Handleman turned back toward the window. "After you leave Jerry will be informed that you aren't to return to the station. You'd better hurry and clean out your office. It would only be embarrassing if you try to come back later."

His eyes closed when he heard the sound of the door opening. He didn't turn around, just reached out for the Maalox to stop the intense burning in his chest. He wished he had something that would wipe from his mind what he'd seen on that tape.

He was afraid it would haunt him forever.

She stood in the doorway, clutching a large box, and stared at him. She was drenched from the rain, and her hair hung in tight ringlets and dripped water onto the foyer tile.

"My God, Kris! What's wrong? Why didn't you use your umbrella?" Sean hurried to her side and took the box from her cold fingers. Seeing the yellow cab drive away, he shut the door and repeated, "What's wrong? You look like—"

"I've been fired." Her lips started to quiver and the tears she had been holding back freely mingled with the rain still on her face.

"Fired?" Shifting the box to his hip, he wrapped an arm around her and ushered her down the hall and into the kitchen. "I just saw you on the show. You were wonderful." He placed the box on the counter, then sat Kristine in a chair. "I'll make some tea and you can tell me about it."

"No!" She threw her purse onto the kitchen table and brought out the tape. "I'm going to see what's on this damned thing." She shook it in his face. "I told you someone was out to get me. This thing is the reason I was thrown out of KLM."

She rushed to the videocassette recorder and shoved in the tape. Her fingers, already shaking, fumbled with the buttons, and Sean came and knelt beside her.

"Here. I'll do it," he said as she rose and stood behind him.

Her arms were wrapped around her waist, as if to protect her from whatever she was about to see. The television screen was fuzzy for a few moments and then it cleared.

Frame by frame . . .

Her mind refused to accept what her brain was telling her. The image on the screen had to be false. For a split second, she truly believed that she was losing her mind. And then it happened—realization.

Her heart pounded against the wall of her chest. A faint buzzing started in her ears and increased with such speed that she immediately became dizzy and sick to her stomach.

Turning to her, Sean could only stare. His shocked expression said everything.

Her hands immediately came up to cover her mouth as she turned and ran for the kitchen sink. She barely made it before retching. She felt she was drowning in madness, clinging to sanity by a slim thread. Only when she sensed the coolness did she realize that Sean had come up behind her and was holding a wet towel to the back of her neck. Slowly, as if afraid to face him, Kris raised her head.

He looked as tortured as she felt.

"My God," he whispered, "how can it be? She's here!"

They watched the rest of the tape together. Many times, Kris wanted to shout out at Sean to stop the thing, that she couldn't take any more. But she had to know everything it contained. How else, Sean had asked, was she to fight back?

Fight back?

Kris felt defeated. She watched the image—it was so like her—condone Wilson's use of cocaine. No wonder Irv had given her that look of disgust when she'd asked about the drug project they'd been working on with the schools. And now she had to sit and watch Christina and Eric Wilson—together.

Christina . . .

The very name brought on chills, and once more Kris turned away from the television

460

screen. "Please, Sean. I can't watch anymore. I just don't care." She sat down on the sofa and buried her face in her hands.

"How can you say you don't care?" Sean demanded, taking her into his arms. "We have to fight her."

Kris lifted her head. She couldn't see him clearly, for tears distorted her vision. "You don't understand," she interrupted. "She's taken everything away from me. My job. Respect. I feel raped by her . . . and there's no way to fight back."

"There is."

"No there isn't. You saw that tape. For a second even I thought it was me." Clinging to him as outside the rain increased and thunder rumbled in the distance, she shook her head. "It's too big. The executives of the two largest television stations in the city have seen that tape. This business thrives on rumors, especially if they involve sex or drugs." Unconsciously, Kris shuddered and broke into fresh tears. "I feel like I'm swallowing down panic, just keeping it under the surface. There's no way to stop what's already happening, and she knows it."

"You must try," Sean insisted, his voice growing stronger. "You can't let her get away with destroying your reputation. Last night's date is on the tape. You were with me last night. I can

461

talk to them, tell them."

When she kept shaking her head, he cried, "What have I done to you, Kristine? This is all my fault. I've brought this shame on you. I have to try to reverse it. I'll tell them the truth."

"Never! I won't let her destroy you, too. Besides, no one would believe you." She felt his chin against her temple and smiled sadly. "I love you for trying, but it wouldn't work."

Suddenly, she looked up at him, terrified. "What are we going to do, Sean? She's actually here. My God, what does she want?"

He kissed her temple and left his mouth there, needing to feel Kristine's pulse, her lifeline. "I don't know, lass," he admitted. "I just don't know."

Chapter Twenty-six

When the phone rang, Sean gently put Kris aside and hurried to pick it up. The last thing they needed right now was any more confusion.

"Hello?"

"Ah . . . hello. This is Peg Handleman. May I please speak with Kris?"

Sean looked up at Kristine and said, "Just a moment, please."

Holding the receiver against his chest, he said, "It's Peg Handleman. Maybe you should talk to her."

Kris looked horrified and quickly shook her head. "I can't," she whispered. "Not now."

"Please, Kristine. You have nothing to be ashamed of."

Getting to her feet, she said, "You know it and I know it. But to the rest of this city, I'm that woman on the tape. I just can't talk to anyone right now, Sean. Especially Peg. Please, make an excuse." Without saying anything more, she almost ran out of the room.

Sean took a deep breath, then held the phone to his ear. "Mrs. Handleman? This is Sean O'Mara. Kristine isn't feeling too well at the moment."

"I'm sorry. I really wanted to talk to her. Could you ask her to call me back tonight . . . if she's feeling better?"

"Certainly. Could I have your number, please." Peg Handleman seemed surprised but gave it to him, and then Sean took another deep breath. Somehow, he had to help Kristine. After all, everything was his fault. Christina was his wife. "Mrs. Handleman, is your husband at home?"

"No. He did . . . call, though."

"Please, would you tell him it's imperative that I speak with him? There are some things he should know."

There was a long pause. Then, "I'll tell him as soon as he arrives."

Letting out his breath, Sean said, "Thank you very much. I'll wait to hear from him."

Hanging up, he took Kristine's tea with him and searched her out. He found her in the bathroom. Sitting on the edge of the tub, she was watching the force of hot water produce a tiny sea of fragrant bubbles.

"She asked if you would call her back."

Kris nodded.

464

He placed her tea on the vanity, then very gently brushed damp curls away from her face. "It's good that you're going to take a bath, Kristine."

Again, she nodded, too exhausted to answer. Sean left her but soon returned with her robe and slippers. He folded them neatly and looked at her, a pained expression on his face. "What else can I do for you, love?"

She shook her head and tried to smile as the phone rang again. "Maybe we should disconnect the damn thing," she murmured. "I can't talk to anyone, Sean."

Backing out of the bathroom, he nodded. "I'll take care of it," he promised, hoping Irv Handleman would listen to him.

He'd hurried so to pick up the telephone, there was a slight catch in his voice when he answered. "Hello?"

"Ahh . . . Sean. I'm glad it's you. Don't you find these telephones the strangest means of conversation? You can't see the other's face. And, I would dearly love to see the expression on your face right now."

He felt as if someone had punched him in the gut. His stomach muscles tightened, and he leaned his head against the wall. Closing his eyes, he whispered, *"Christina . . ."*

Her answer was a giggle, but that same childish response that had annoyed him in the past now brought on a shiver of fear. "How nice that you can recognize your wife's voice . . . considering the way you've been living."

Sean quickly looked toward the hallway, and although he knew Kristine couldn't hear him, he cupped the phone and whispered, "What do you want? Haven't you done enough?"

Again, the laughter. "Dear man, I've just begun. Actually, the reason for this communication is that I wish to see you. We have a lot to talk over, you and I."

"I can't. Not now."

Her voice became hard and demanding. "Right now. You don't have a choice, Sean. You see, I'm going to need money to live, and your mistress seems to have a great deal of it. Now, either I talk to you . . . or her."

Again, Sean looked toward the bathroom. He would do anything to stop the two women from meeting. "All right. Where?"

He could almost see her smile of satisfaction. "Very good, Sean. I'll meet you in twenty minutes in the lobby of the Four Seasons Hotel."

The phone went dead in his hand.

Replacing the receiver, he stared at it for a moment. What was he going to say to Kristine? How could he leave her right now? Running his fingers through his hair, he walked down the hallway to the bathroom door.

He leaned against the molding, his eyes studying the carpet at his feet as he tried to come up with a plausible excuse for leaving. Realizing nothing was going to sound legitimate, he stuck his head in the bathroom and forced himself to smile at the picture before him. Kristine's head was resting against the side of the tub; her body was completely obscured by white bubbles.

"I have to go out, love."

Her eyes opened and she blinked several times. "Out?" Her voice sounded weak to him. "Why?"

He continued to smile, even though he was frightened for both of them. "Food. I wasn't prepared for you to come home so early."

She closed her eyes. "I'm not hungry."

"Oh, but I am. Don't worry, I'll be—"

"Call and have something delivered." Again, she opened her eyes and looked at him. "Don't go out in this storm."

Grinning like fool, he shrugged. "That'd take too long." He blew her a kiss and backed into the hallway where she couldn't see him. "You relax. I'll be back soon."

As he walked down the hall toward the phone, he could hear her calling out to him.

He didn't answer. Instead, he picked up the receiver and dialed the number he had written on the pad. "Peg Handleman?" he asked when a woman's voice answered. He didn't care about formality now.

"Yes?"

"This is Sean O'Mara. Is your husband home?"

He could hear the surprise in the woman's voice. "Why, no. He's not."

"You must contact him immediately and tell

him to meet me in the lobby of the Four Seasons Hotel."

"I don't know—"

"Please, Peg," Sean interrupted in an urgent whisper. "This is important. I don't know how much you know about this, but there are two women involved. The woman on that tape isn't Kristine. I'm going to meet with that other woman now. At the Four Seasons. You must contact Irv and tell him to get there as soon as possible. He has to see this woman for himself."

There was no answer and Sean was desperate when he whispered, "Please. Kristine says you are her friend. Please, Peg. Do this one thing for her. She needs friends right now."

Silence. Then Peg said, "All right. I'll call him and tell him it's urgent. He's hurt, Sean. Kristine was like a daughter to him. What he had to do today was business. He had no choice, and it almost killed him. But this is personal. If he can make it, he'll be there."

Sean let out his breath. "Bless you."

Hanging up the phone, he raced out into the night.

As he hailed a cab and hurried to it, a flash of lightning revealed a shadowy silhouette not ten feet away.

It was not a night to venture out, without a purpose.

Kris could feel the bubbles evaporate, yet she didn't move. She listened and tried to clear her mind of everything. If she didn't, surely she would go crazy. Sudden thunder made her wonder if she should be taking a bath during the storm. Her ears caught a faint sound that reminded her of glass breaking, but she dismissed it as thunder vibrated through the floor of the townhouse. Maybe she would move away. Out into the country, away from the city. Away from the rumors . . . from everything.

How could she not think about it? Now this ugly mess was a part of her. She shuddered when she thought of all those who had already seen the tape—those who thought she was Christina . . . doing those things with Eric Wilson.

She brought her hand up from the steaming water and covered her eyes. My God, she would never overcome this. Even with proof, the rumors, the scandal would always follow her.

Don't think about it, she told herself. It's too much. If you really thought about all the terrible wrongs in the world, surely you would give in to panic and eventually give up. You can't think about them. You simply can't picture half the world starving or homeless and do nothing. You can't stop governments from building nuclear warheads and threatening the earth's very existence. Not alone. It's too much to comprehend. So you don't think about the big picture, or the futility of a single person trying to change the world. You just keep on going. Oh, God . . .

But she had begun to make a small difference. Now the drug project would be abandoned, and children like Tanya would repeat the same mistakes over and over.

Kris felt beaten, bruised; yet somewhere deep inside her the fighter in her started to surface. She knew she couldn't remain motionless forever. She had to move on, had to find a way to deal with this scandal and get on with her life. Her body felt weak, yet she forced her limbs to move. As she stood up and turned on the shower, she silently thanked God for Sean. It never occurred to her that without him none of this would have taken place.

Sean O'Mara was her lifeline. Thinking of him brought serenity, tranquillity. And as she let the shower wash the bubbles from her skin, she vowed that the two of them would make a life together . . . somewhere.

Christina watched the whore enter the bedroom and stand before a chest of drawers. Everything had worked so well that she was almost sorry that it was all at an end, for she derived great pleasure from manipulating them. She felt like a master puppeteer and was sorry that it was time to cut the lines and allow her victims to fall.

Pulling a small weapon from her pocket, she pointed it at the woman who so resembled her.

470

"No one's going to come to your rescue this time, whore. It's just the two of us now . . . and it's time to pay."

Sean paced the lobby of the Four Seasons Hotel. For the tenth time in the last five minutes, he checked his watch. Christina was ten minutes late. He glanced toward the huge doors that led outside and then turned back to the lobby. Again, his eyes scanned the large room. Men and women hurried past him. But she wasn't to be found.

"I'm here. I don't know why I'm here, but I am."

Sean spun around and let out his breath when he saw Irv Handleman. "Thank God, you've come."

Holding his dripping umbrella away from him, Irv brushed droplets of rain from the shoulder of his raincoat. "Peg reached me just as I was about to leave the station. What's this about another woman? Look, Sean, it sounds—"

Sean quickly viewed the lobby. "Irv. It's true. She's late, but she won't come near me if she sees me talking to you. Please, wait there." He nodded to a nearby wing chair. "That way you can see and hear her. When you do, you'll know Kristine was never that woman in the tape."

Shrugging, Irv muttered to himself as he sank into the chair and waited.

They both waited. . . .

471

Kris's heart actually stopped for a split second when she heard the Southern drawl, the hatred, and she couldn't help screaming as she spun around to face Christina.

Clutching her robe together, she stared at the woman sitting so casually in her bedroom chair. "My God," Kris whispered, "what are you doing here?"

Christina laughed. "I think you know. I think you've been expecting me. At least you should have been. I've come to extract my retribution."

"Why?" Kris demanded. "You've ruined me with that tape. What more do you want?"

Christina rose and began to unbutton her coat. "Why, your life," she stated, almost casually. "I thought you would have figured that out by now." She switched the gun from her right hand to her left several times as she divested herself of the coat and threw it onto the bed. As she pulled her taupe silk dress down her arms, she ordered, "Now get undressed. Throw that robe over here."

Kris could only stare as the woman removed her clothing. She knew she should be looking for a chance to grab the gun, to make an escape, but she was stunned by Christine's boldness. And it was like looking into a mirror, a distorted mirror, for surely Christina was insane. "My God, what are you doing?"

Christina threw the dress at her and extended the gun in her direction. "I said throw the robe over here, and then put that on. We can talk after you're dressed."

Kris's hands trembled as she untied the thick terry cloth belt. Sliding the robe down her arms, she quickly threw it at Christina, but it was too heavy to aim accurately. Nonetheless, standing in her slip, Christina caught the robe and put it on.

Smiling, she indicated the dress at Kris's feet, with the gun. "Pick it up. We have to hurry."

Kris could feel the woman's eyes taking in her every movement as she reached for the dress. Bringing it over her head, she smelled Christina's perfume still clinging to it.

"I don't know what he sees in you. Your breasts are too small. And you have no hips, at all. We're really nothing alike, without clothes."

This was no time to be embarrassed. Pulling the dress down over her head, Kris stared at Christina. Dear God, she thought, with her hair wet from the rain, she looks exactly like me in that robe. When Sean comes home, he's going to think she's me!

"What do you plan to do?" Keep her talking, Kris's brain screamed as she recognized the fanatical gleam in Christina's eyes. Kris was staring at madness. . . .

Christina giggled, like a naughty young girl. "Why, I'm going to kill you. Of course. What did you expect? You took my husband away from me."

"You never loved him," Kris whispered. "And we thought you were back in the past . . . back at

473

Rivanna . . . dead."

Christina's eyes widened. "But I will be, dear girl. Dead, that is. Only it'll be you they find. In my clothes. Don't you see how simple this is? The only way to clear your name is if one of us dies. Frankly, you have the better life. And I want it."

Kris shivered as she watched the woman smile. "You see, I intend to tell the police that I had to kill the intruder in self-defense. That's you." She again giggled. "And when dear Sean returns, I'll have to kill him—your accomplice."

Christina shrugged. "I'm running out of money here. I was actually shocked at what a decent set of drawers cost in this day and age. Now get on with you . . ." She jerked her head toward the hallway. "Let's wait for Sean in the front room. I wouldn't want him to surprise us."

As they walked into the living room, Kris heard the madwoman speaking behind her. The chill of dread that had settled in her bones now spread to her nerve endings, causing her to shake uncontrollably.

"He wanted to cheat me out of my home, take away everything from me. Now neither of us will get it. This time," Christina vowed, "this time I'll kill him myself, not like in the past where I waited for—"

Suddenly Kris heard the woman moan as they entered the living room. Turning around, she saw Christina staring at the portrait leaning against the wall.

As Kris moved toward her, Christina jerked the gun in her direction. "Don't move," she commanded in a crazed voice that turned Kris into ice. "I'll kill you right this second."

She slowly walked toward the portrait. "Where did you get it?" she demanded, her voice suddenly filled with emotion.

"It was at my brother's home. He thought it was . . ."

Christina wasn't listening. *"Judson . . ."* Her mouth quivered as she repeated his name over and over again. "Where are you, my love?"

"Judson painted that?" Kris asked, hoping to keep the other woman's mind preoccupied.

Christina ignored her. "No other man has loved me as much, or as well. My dear, dear Judson . . ." She picked up the painting with one hand, taking possession of it.

Kris shivered as another streak of lightning flashed through the living room curtains. Christina truly looked over the edge now, clutching the painting to her chest and trying to keep the gun steady in her other hand. Kris knew she had to keep the woman talking. "Why didn't you marry him, Christina? If you loved him that much?"

The woman issued a derisive laugh. "A lot you know of love. Sometimes love is sacrifice. I wasn't going to lose Rivanna to some damned Yankee and Judson understood that." She lovingly gazed at the painting. "He understood that," she repeated. "He was so patient. Not like Sean. Or

Bobby Ray. Why do you look like me? Who are you, really?"

Kris prayed for guidance as she came closer to the woman. "You're my aunt. Beth was my great-great grandmother."

Christina shook her head with confusion. "No. That can't be. . . ." The gun lowered slightly.

Together both women heard the sound of a car door slamming. And, together, they stared into the foyer.

"Damn him! Don't make a sound," Christina warned Kris. "He must not have waited." She straightened the gun and pointed it toward the foyer. "All right. I'll finish here what was started so long ago. He goes first."

Kris didn't think about safety or escape. All that entered her mind when she heard the click of the front door lock was that Sean was about to be killed.

As if in a movie, she lunged forward and grabbed hold of Christina's wrist. The gun fell to the floor at the same time Sean and Irv entered the room.

Christina was the first to see them and she called out, "Sean! Help me. Get her away from me."

Kris turned in time to see him race toward them. It happened so quickly, almost in a fraction of a second, and later she would find it hard to believe that it took place at all.

Incredibly, Sean grabbed Kris about the waist

and pushed Christina away from them, just as a bolt of lightning penetrated the room, making the air suddenly acrid. All Kris could remember was the silhouette of Sean's hand against pure white light as he pushed Christina away. The lightning was so brilliant, the energy so intense that Kris had to shield her eyes from it. Burying her face in Sean's shoulder, Kris knew — no, she could actually feel — the moment Christina was no longer in the room.

Christina was simply . . . gone.

Chapter Twenty-seven

"Jesus Christ! What the hell was that?"

Stumbling toward them, Irv clutched his umbrella tightly in his hand. He looked nothing like a hardened newsman.

Still clinging to each other, Kris and Sean turned as one. All three stared. It was Sean who finally spoke.

"You saw her, Irv? Didn't you?"

Irv Handleman looked around the room. "Where the hell did she go?"

Kris shook her head. "She's gone . . ."

"Then let's call the police. My God, Kris, when I think about what she tried to do—"

Kris broke free of Sean and grabbed Irv's sleeve. "Don't call the police," she said with surprising calmness. "They'll never find her."

Irv stared at her in amazement. "How do you

know that? Look, we could give them a perfect description. How many women look like you and are wearing a white bathrobe?"

Taking the phone out of his hands, Kris quietly hung it up and led him back into the living room. "Sit down, Irv. I think we all need a drink."

Slumping into a chair, he glanced at her sharply. "How the hell can you be so damn calm? That woman wanted to kill you!"

Kris noticed her hands were still shaking as she accepted a glass of bourbon from Sean. "Because," she stated with a sad smile, "I know it's over. She'll never come back."

Standing beside her, Sean brushed the hair back from her cheek. And when she looked at him, his face held such an expression of love that she immediately went back into his arms. She could feel devotion coming through his fingers, knew security in his embrace. "How did you know it was me?" she whispered against the cotton of his shirt. "She . . . she made me change clothes with her."

His arm tightened and he kissed the top of her head. "I knew you immediately. There was never any doubt."

She lifted her head. "How?"

Although still shaken by the experience, he managed to smile. "The moment you looked at me. I knew. Besides, you were the one who had no shoes."

Her eyes widened and she lowered her head to see her bare feet. "No shoes," she stated.

"Well, you both have lost me," Irv said in an irritated voice as he rose from the chair and picked up the gun. "What I'd like to know is what we're going to do about this. You realize, don't you, Kristine, that your career hangs in the balance? I still say we should call the police."

Kris shook her head. "Irv, it'll only draw more attention to the rumors. And let's be honest, nothing's going to stop them. I'm finished here in Philadelphia." Suddenly, her eyes narrowed and her mouth hung open. "Irv, what are you *doing* here? How did you—"

Sean tightened his arm around her. "I asked him to come with me. Christina called while you were in the tub and told me to meet her at a hotel. I telephoned Peg and asked her to contact Irv and tell him there was another woman, to come to that hotel. I wasn't sure whether he would or not."

The tears, the emotion that she had been holding in was finally released. Pulling Irv closer to her, Kris kissed his cheek. "He'd show . . ."

Uncomfortably, Irv cleared his throat and said, "We sat in that lobby for less than ten minutes before Sean grabbed my shoulder. He had this godawful look on his face and he scared the hell out of me when he realized that that woman must be here with you." Again, Irv looked around the living room as if not quite believing that a woman could vanish before his eyes. How did she get past him? Shaking his head, he said, "Listen, Kris . . . about what I said this afternoon in my office. I

480

feel like hell. I don't know how I'm going to make up for—"

She brought her finger to his lips. "Shh . . . I don't blame you. I really don't. Nothing's going to help me now, Irv. We both know this industry thrives on gossip. You said it yourself when we first talked about the new show. My biggest asset was that I was clean." She shook her head and smiled. "Nobody's going to believe that I am anymore."

"I'll work something out, Kris. I'm not going to let you take the heat for this. I'll talk to Larry tomorrow and try to explain . . . all this." Kris and Sean could see the confusion in his eyes.

"It's hopeless. Larry's not going to believe any of it. Would you, if you hadn't seen her?"

"Nothing's hopeless," Sean countered. "A few hours ago, only I believed in your innocence. Now, there are two of us."

Despite everything, Kris smiled at the men. "I couldn't ask for two better champions."

Grinning, Irv finished off his drink and placed the glass on the edge of a table. He turned to the couple. "You know," he said slowly, the grin back on his face as he pocketed the small revolver. "I haven't had this much excitement since I was working the police beat. Sorta gets the blood pumpin' again, doesn't it?"

Despite everything, Kris laughed. "I can do without this kind of excitement, thank you. Call Peg. I can't imagine what she's thinking after

Sean's phone call."

Irv nodded and picked up his umbrella. "I'll just go on home and try and explain it." They all walked into the foyer and stopped before the front door.

The right glass panel beside the door was shattered—evidence that Christina had existed. Irv spun around to them.

"Look, this is breaking and entering. And we have the gun. The police—"

"The police will never find her," Kris interrupted. "Trust me, she's never coming back."

Sean extended his hand. "Thank you for trusting me, Irv. And for your help. It couldn't have been easy."

Irv shook hands, then kissed Kristine's cheek. Looking at Sean, he said, "It's one hell of a way to get to know someone. But I'm glad I did."

When the door closed behind Irv Handleman, Kris quickly turned to Sean and buried her face against his chest. "Oh God, Sean. I was so frightened."

He felt her tears and picked her up in his arms. Carrying her into the bedroom, he whispered, "I know, lass. I wish I could have spared you that."

He set her on the bed and walked to his closet. Reaching inside, he pulled out his robe and held it up in front of her. "Why don't you take that dress off, and wear this?"

His eyes held hers with such tenderness that her throat felt thick with raw emotion.

"We want no reminders, love. This is our beginning."

Lou Camiere sat in his usual chair in the control room and stared off into space. He refused to believe the vicious rumors that were spreading about Kristine Gavin. He'd always prided himself on being a good judge of character. It was part of his business, being able to judge how people were going to react to a given circumstance. That was why he reigned supreme in the control room, knowing just when to pull back a camera to show body language, or to zoom in and capture the tear sliding down a cheek. And if there was one thing that bothered him, it was being wrong.

He just knew he wasn't wrong about Kristine.

As he started the voice check on Anne Jennings, Lou couldn't shake the feeling that he was missing something. Something important. It had been a hell of a two days since Kristine had been replaced. Nothing felt right. The audience was off. And everybody, from the assistant director to a little old lady from South Philly, was speculating on the validity of the current round of gossip. Depending on who you listened to Kristine Gavin had been busted for possession of cocaine, or she was being blackmailed because of incriminating pornographic pictures. Lou refused to believe any of it. All he'd been told, officially, was that she was on a leave of absence. And that Anne Jennings was a temporary replacement.

It wasn't working. The audience was uncomfortable with her precise language, her restrictive style of interviewing. In short, Anne didn't have Kristine's warmth, her ability to make her audience feel at home. She usually made it off the set before her guest did. She didn't greet her studio audience, or stay late to—

Suddenly, *finally,* it came back to him. Now he knew what had been bothering him for days. He did the unthinkable and rose from his chair, his position of power. Running his finger over the stack of tapes, he found Monday's show and inserted it into one of the many VCR's. Using fast forward, he was soon at the spot where he'd asked camera two to pick up Kris in the back of the studio.

There!

He froze the frame on the monitor. Now he remembered why it had bothered him. Besides the gloating look, a totally new expression for Kris, her clothes were different. It was his job to pick up jarring oddities on a set . . . but he hadn't spotted this one until now.

He set the tape at fast forward a few seconds more until a picture of Kris came up, in the green outfit she'd worn that day. He now remembered how a few stage hands had razzed her about it. She'd said since her guest was going to be a Hollywood legend, she'd thought she'd dress appropriately. Slowly, his finger touched the rewind button.

Then there she was. . . .

The woman in the back wasn't Kris. By God, there were two of them!

Leaving the image on the screen, he picked up the phone and called Irv Handleman. Everybody knew that Irv and Kris were close friends.

Maybe this was something important. It sure as hell was confusing.

"You didn't even talk to me about it. You just bought it?" Kris stared at Sean, not quite accepting what she had just heard. "I don't believe this! Jack sold you Rivanna? Why didn't anyone tell me"

"Kristine. Please try to understand what Rivanna means to me. It's my home."

"But this is my home. I can't just leave it." She walked back into the kitchen and poured herself another cup of coffee, the fourth in less than two hours. Then she sat down at the kitchen table and pulled her robe closed at her chest. Outside of taking a morning shower, she hadn't had the robe off since Sean had given it to her two days ago. She'd let her hair dry without benefit of a brush, and the curls had turned wild. She hadn't bothered with makeup. She wasn't eating. In short, she was a mess, and she knew it.

"Come with me to sign the papers, Kristine. You haven't been out of the house in days."

She glared at him. "What's that supposed to

mean?"

"Exactly what I said. A change of scenery will do you good."

"Oh God, spare me the clichés."

"I beg your pardon?" He was trying to be patient with her. She had suffered a terrible shock, and her reaction had been delayed. Fear had turned into anger and anger into downright surliness. Somehow, she must put all this behind her as he was trying to do.

And he would help her.

"I said spare me the clichés, Sean." She sipped her coffee and pushed a curl away from her eye. "A change of scenery . . . I don't have the energy to walk out that door."

"Jack and Elaine will be expecting you."

"You told them?" She stood up and glared at him. "Well, that's just great. Not only do you go behind my back and buy that place, but you discuss my private affairs with—"

"Your brother," he interrupted. "And I only told him that you were on a leave of absence, working on a special project."

She issued a sarcastic laugh. "And what's that? Trying to pull my life back together? That ought to keep me busy indefinitely."

"Kristine, I have to leave tonight for Virginia. I just assumed that you would go with me."

"Well, you assumed too much. I suppose you also assumed that I'd be thrilled with your surprise purchase?"

486

Sean slowly raised his chin. His eyes were filled with sadness. "I wanted it to be your wedding present. This time I wanted to give it to the woman I loved." He smiled sorrowfully. "You're right, of course. We should have discussed a decision of this magnitude."

She burst into tears, hating herself for doing so. Brushing past his outstretched hand, she rushed into the bedroom and closed the door.

She couldn't handle this.

Not now.

Oh God, not now.

She never expected to fall asleep. But then she felt she'd slept more in the last two days than in the last two weeks. It was an escape, and she knew it. Blinking, Kris listened to the soft knocking and watched as Sean opened the bedroom door.

"Do you feel better?" he asked, sitting on the edge of the bed.

Yawning, she pushed herself up toward the headboard and leaned against it. She shook her head and said, "I'm sorry for that scene. I . . . I . . . don't know why I said those things."

Sean smiled. "I do. You've had a hell of a week so far. And I'm afraid I have to add to it." He handed her an official-looking envelope. "I wanted you to be with me when I opened it."

Kris looked down and saw that it was from the State of Virginia. "Your reply . . ." She sounded frightened. "It finally came."

She handed the envelope back to him. "Open it."

He tore it open and they both watched as he withdrew two sheets of paper. One was a cover letter; the other, a copy of an obituary.

In bold black letters was the name CHRISTINA MATTSON O'MARA.

Bringing her fingers up to her mouth, Kris whispered, "Oh my God, read it."

Sean cleared his throat, yet his voice still held a note of dread.

" 'Christina Matson O'Mara, age 53, died yesterday at Willowbrook Rest Home where she had resided for the past twenty-four years. Mrs. O'Mara, known as Miss Christina, at one time had maintained a home at Rivanna plantation.

"'In a scandal that rocked the county, Mrs. O'Mara confessed to arranging her own drowning, but insisted she had nothing to do with her husband's mysterious disappearance. Her statement that her husband and his mistress had traveled to the future was treated with extreme skepticism; as was her claim of having done so herself.' "

Sean looked up at Kris. She hadn't moved, but her expression revealed how horrified she was.

He continued, too afraid now to stop. "'Although no formal charges were ever made, Mrs. O'Mara remained under suspicion for many years. The widow, after a period of lengthy illness, retired to Willowbrook Rest Home where she remained until her death.

" 'Surviving is her sister, Elizabeth Mattson Gentry.

" 'Services will be private.' "

Taking a deep steadying breath, Sean said, "Someone, the researcher I suppose, wrote underneath it: 'Christina O'Mara's immense estate was placed in trusteeship when she was committed to Willowbrook. Her sister, upon reaching her majority, inherited everything. From our records it appears that Elizabeth sold Rivanna immediately thereafter.' "

Looking up to Kristine, he muttered, "Well, I have my answer. Beth did inherit everything."

Kris's expression seemed carved out of stone. Her voice was tiny and afraid as she asked, "Sean, exactly what is Willowbrook?"

"The county insane asylum."

Her eyes widened and she backed away from him until she stood next to the bed. *"An insane asylum? She died in an insane asylum?"*

"Kristine! Stop it." He stood and walked in her direction. "She wasn't in her right mind before any of this took place. Before you came to Rivanna, she was disturbed. You had nothing to do with what took place."

"Nothing to do? My God, that woman was related to me, my . . . my aunt!" Fighting for control, she wrapped her arms about her waist and paced back and forth in front of the dresser. "All my life I've been fighting this . . . this rumor of

489

insanity in my family. Jack and I used to make jokes about it—about all the old ladies and their hysterics. God! No wonder my mother watched me . . . and her mother watched her. Beth was frightened that her sister's madness would be passed down, and she started it all with her own daughter."

She stopped and stared at him. "I'm part of all this!"

"Kristine . . ." He came up to her but she backed away. "You're distraught. You have good reason, but you must stop this. Christina died in an insane asylum. She *was* insane. You're not! No one else in your family became afflicted, did they?" He didn't wait for her answer. He was desperate, for he could see her closing down on him, like the petals of a flower at dusk. "Listen to me. you need to get away from here. I'm leaving for Virginia within the hour. I have a ticket for you. Come with me."

She shook her head. "You go. I . . . can't. I have too much to think about. I need to be alone."

"No, you don't." He held her arm so she couldn't pull away from him. "Don't do this, Kristine. Why are you deliberately pushing me away?"

She tried to break free. When his grip tightened, she panicked and shouted. "Because . . . because I can't be responsible for your happiness any longer! I don't even know how to make myself happy, let alone you. I can't take it anymore." She suddenly went limp, and he released her as she sank to the edge of the bed. She sat there, her chin resting on her chest, staring at the floor, a mere shell of her former self. "You want too much, Sean, when my whole life is falling apart."

"I never asked you to be responsible for my happiness. I realized early on when I came to this time that in the end I'd have to make the adjustment alone. That no matter what you did, I'd have to somehow find my own way." His voice almost cracked. "The only thing I ever asked of you was that you love me."

He packed and left, swiftly and without further discussion. Kris wanted to call him back, to ask him to wait, but she felt paralyzed. She kept silent, and so she spent the remainder of the afternoon listening to the terrible, echoing silence in that empty house.

"All right! If you won't pick up the damned phone, then listen to me. I'm coming over there in fifteen minutes. If you don't answer the door, I swear to God I'm calling the police." There was a pause on the tape. "Need I say more?"

Kris stared down at the answering machine. Danni. Was it too much to be asked to be left alone?

Precisely fifteen minutes later, Danielle Rowe banged on the front door of the townhouse and shouted, "Let me in, or I'll get Sister Marian Delores and she'll kick the damn thing down!"

Despite everything, Kris grinned wryly. Sister Delores was capable of doing it. She unlocked the door and walked back into the kitchen.

From behind her, she heard, "Well, about time! What the hell is going on in this house? Sean calls me from the airport and tells me to get right over here . . . that there is an emergency." Throwing her purse onto the Formica island that jutted out from the kitchen wall, she demanded, "So! What's going on? Why did you take a leave of absence?"

Kris spun around. "You heard?"

Danni's mouth hung open. "God, you look terrible. Are you sick?"

Kris smiled. "Heartsick. Now what did you hear?"

Danni averted her gaze and walked up to the range. Picking up the copper teakettle, she took it to the sink. "Just that you were working on a special project. I figured the drug project."

She turned around to her friend. "Why didn't you call me? I was waiting for you to tell me . . ." Danni broke off and shrugged. "I keep forgetting I've been replaced."

Kris's mouth started to tremble. "You could never be replaced, you know that. So . . . what are they saying? What's the word out on the street?"

Danni turned the heat up under the kettle. "Nothing but lies."

"Tell me. I want to hear it."

Danni took a deep breath. She stared at the silent kettle, wishing it would boil. "I've heard three versions of the same lie. You're either involved in a torrid love affair with Eric Wilson or blackmailing him with explicit pictures, or you're both drug dealers who snort cocaine and then indulge in wild orgies with the Mafia."

Kristine couldn't help it. She laughed. "Are you serious? The Mafia?"

"Okay, so I embellished a tad here and there. What the hell is going on? The media is tighter than a drum on this one."

Kris let out her breath as the kettle whistled. "Then I have something to be grateful for."

"Seriously, Kris, what's happening? Sean said he's buying Rivanna. I don't see you two for a week and it's like a hurricane came in and rearranged your lives."

Taking out mugs, Kris smiled. "Not a hurricane . . . just a storm. Anyway, it's over." She had to swallow several times, for she refused to cry. Again.

"Will you sit down and begin at the beginning?" Wrapping a dish towel around the hot handle of the kettle, Danni poured the boiling water into the mugs. When she was finished, she hung the towel over her shoulder and took the chair opposite her friend.

Kris had to smile at seeing the dish towel slung so carelessly over a beige, raw silk suit. That was Danni. Suddenly, Kris was glad that her best friend was sitting across the kitchen table from her. She hadn't realized just how much she'd

493

missed her.

"Do you really think Marian Delores would've been able to kick the door in?"

Danni laughed. "Are you kidding? Don't you remember gym? I bet she keeps Bruce Lee comics under her mattress." She watched Kris chuckle, then added, "Okay, now let's get serious. What happened?"

Taking a deep breath, Kris began. "Have you ever heard the saying that somewhere, at some-time, everyone has an exact double?"

Danni shrugged. "Sure. What's that got to—" She looked across the table. "Are you saying that someone, a woman who looks like you, did some-thing terrible and now you're being blamed?"

"That's pretty close. A video was delivered to KLM showing this woman and Eric Wilson doing a few lines of cocaine. No, Wilson was actually the one using the drug. And the tape kept running for the rest of the evening."

Danni's eyes widened. "You mean? . . ."

Kris nodded. "I mean everything."

"You saw Eric Wilson . . . in the act?"

Shaking her head, Kris couldn't help but laugh. "Danni! It was horrible!"

Ignoring her friend, Danni leaned into the table and whispered, *"So?* What was he like? From a video point of view, I mean."

Embarrassed, Kris tried to stop the giggle. "You're a sick person, Danielle, I have lost every-thing. *Everything.* My job . . . the respect of my peers . . . my show . . . probably even Sean. Why the hell am I laughing?"

Danni shrugged, her expression clearly stating that she was still waiting for an answer.

Finally, Kris stopped laughing long enough to mutter, "He seems to be a very hairy person."

Danni screamed with delight. "I knew it. What else?"

Kris looked bewildered. "Honestly, I wasn't studying the man! If you must know I walked away from it after a few minutes. Danni, this is serious. I really have lost everything. I could never recover from the sex and Mafia rumors."

"I made up that part about the Mafia."

Kris shrugged. "Doesn't matter. Give it a few days and that'll be the new rumor."

"KLM can't fire you. You just signed a new contract."

"There's a morals clause. Pretty standard and nothing to worry about unless you make a habit of getting arrested, or something like this—"

The phone rang and Kris looked to Danni. "As you know, I'm not answering," she whispered, even though both women realized that no one could hear them.

"Ah, but you are monitoring," Danni countered, right before they heard the beep and an excited, male voice.

"Kris, this is Irv. Get down here right away. We got our proof. Are you there? Kris? Kris?"

Without asking permission, Danni ran from the

kitchen and picked up the phone. "Irv? Are you still on the line? This is Danni. Danielle Rowe."

Kris watched with annoyance as Danni talked with Irv. She didn't care what anyone said, she could never walk back into that station.

"You're going," Danni pronounced two minutes later. "Irv said Lou somebody or other came across a tape of Monday's show. She was on it."

"What?" Kris stood up and stared at Danni. "She was in the studio?"

"That's what he said. He also mentioned that Larry Goodman wants to met with you and Irv. Who's he?"

"Station manager." Kris stared beyond Danni into the next room. "They believe me," she whispered.

Danni smiled. "Seems that way. Now . . . I'll go with you. When Sean called I was so frightened I took the rest of the afternoon off."

Kris felt ready to panic. Holding out her tangled curls, she moaned, "I can't go anywhere like this! I can't do it. Call him back."

Danni gave her an appraising stare. "You really do look like hell, Gavin. What did you do, sleep in that robe?"

Kris nodded.

"God! Do you realize how lucky you are that Irv called while I was here? Let's attack that closet of yours." She put an arm around the smaller woman and added, "Trust me, Kristine, I'll have you put together in less than forty-five minutes."

And she did.

She had her job back.

If she wanted it . . .

With Danni at her side, Kris had walked into KLM and met her agent, Mark Stone, who was waiting for them in the lobby. All three demanded attention. Each was striking, elegantly dressed . . . and determined.

No one, except Mark and Danni, knew that she was shaking as she walked past her co-workers, smiling and nodding hello in answer to their shocked stares. Once in Larry Goodman's office, she accepted a kiss from Irv Handleman but sat between Danni and Mark at the large conference table. She didn't want Goodman to think she was begging to return to work.

The tape of Monday's show was run, and almost everyone was shocked when Christina's image came on the screen.

Apologies were made, and Kris accepted them saying she understood that they'd had no choice.

She was offered her job back . . . but she could hear the hesitancy in Goodman's voice. He really didn't want her, not with the ugly rumors still spreading.

So she had a decision to make. Did she want to return to KLM and spend years fighting a negative image? Goodman had said the sales department was already getting calls from advertisers with questions, some not too discreet.

The question weighed heavily on her mind as she and Danni returned to the townhouse.

What was she going to do with her life? The choice was hers.

Kris felt lost as she sat down with Danni to a takeout Chinese dinner. How did one even begin to pick up the pieces? The first thing she had done was ask Mark to find tickets for the Shakespeare Festival opening next month to Philadelphia. She wanted the best seats available. It was a small gesture of thanks to Lou Camiere. Too small, considering the man had single-handedly proved she was telling the truth. But now what? she asked herself, while picking at the sweet and sour shrimp.

Sean was gone. He hadn't even called. He'd just walked out and got on that plane all by himself. A tiny glimmer of pride entered her heart when she thought about the courage that must have taken. My God, she loved him. But he had made it clear that his life was going to be at Rivanna.

Her life was here, in Philadelphia.

"I never thought I'd ever eat Chinese again," Danni muttered, interrupting Kris's thoughts. "I have a feeling that night at the Phoenix changed my life. And I don't think it's for the better."

Kris perked up. She could hear a familiar tone in her friend's voice.

"I thought we had a wonderful tine," she stated, while watching Danni from under her lashes. "Especially when you finally left poor Roy Fuller alone. You did get home all right, didn't you?" She pretended to be interested in the food before her. "We never really got a chance to talk. After the trip to Virginia, all hell broke loose." Concentrate on someone else, she told herself. For a moment—for as long as possible—concentrate on someone other than yourself.

Danni pushed her shrimp away from her, as if the sight of it brought up images of something unpleasant. "I don't want to be reminded. I haven't been that smashed since I was twenty."

Kris grinned. "But you got home all right. Roy drove your car."

Danni groaned. "Kris, he not only drove my car; he put me to bed."

Kristine's mouth hung open in shock. Blinking, she repeated, "He put you to bed? You hardly knew him!"

"He *put* me to bed," Danni interrupted. "Notice I did not say take, or join. The man kept me upright until we got inside the apartment, provided wet towels after I got sick, undressed me, and put me to bed"

"Ahhh . . ." Kris voiced her appreciation of the film director.

Danielle looked like she was about to cry. "The worst part was when I finally got up the next morning. He'd set my automatic coffeepot. And on the counter were a bottle of aspirins and a slip of paper with his telephone number in L.A."

"What did you do?" Kris asked, intently interested. The man sounded too good to be true.

Danni pushed back her already short hair and said, "Well, I had to call and apologize, didn't I?" She looked sheepish. "He's asked me to come out to California and . . . visit, I guess."

Kris smiled. "Are you going?"

"He's not my type."

"What do you mean, not your type? I watched the two of you at the Phoenix. Neither one of you could keep your eyes off the other, when you weren't arguing."

Danni again seemed embarrassed. "He's . . . nerdy."

"He isn't!" Kris protested.

"C'mon, he's the absentminded professor type, if I ever saw one." Once more her lower lip trembled. "The trouble is, he's also one of the sweetest men I've ever met." Wiping away an unexpected tear, she muttered, "What's really crazy is that I find him incredibly sexy."

Kris didn't say anything. She merely smiled at her dearest friend.

"Pretty kinky, isn't it?" Danni asked. "How can I be so affected by a man that's everything I'm not, and one who's seen me at my very worst?"

"And still wants to see you again," Kris added while shaking her head. "You don't think he actually likes you, do you? I mean the Danielle Rowe without the designer clothes and witty repartee? Why are you so afraid that someone might want you without those masks?"

Danni sat up straighter, marshalling her defenses. "Wait a minute. What about you, Miss Perfect Communications Major? You just let Sean O'Mara walk out of your life. Sounds like you're having a few problems with masks yourself."

"That's unfair! My whole life has been—"

"Your whole life has been pretty good," Danni interrupted. "With the exception of the past week. I've never known you to lie down and not fight back. What are you going to do?"

Damn. It all came back to that question.

"He wants to live at Rivanna," she whispered. "How can I do that? I have a job."

"Great job," Danni mocked. "One minor affair with hairy Wilson and the Mafia, and you're out on the street."

Kris laughed. It felt good to laugh. But still, the dilemma . . .

"Are you suggesting I give up my career and follow him to Virginia?"

Danni shrugged her elegant shoulders. "I'm suggesting you think about what you really want. Do you love him?"

"Yes." The answer was immediate.

"Will he come back? And if he does, will he be happy in Philadelphia?"

"No, and no." She knew Sean's heart was in Rivanna.

"Could you be happy in Virginia?"

Blinking rapidly, Kris seemed to mull over the question. "This could set back women's liberation ten years: Give it all up and follow your man."

"You're not getting it," Danni insisted. "If we're truly liberated, doesn't that mean freedom of choice? And without guilt as long as we're happy?"

Kris gazed at her fondly. They had shared so much together, growing up. Had they finally done it? Grown up?

Sniffling back her tears, she held out her hand and whispered, "We'd have to promise. Once a month . . . more if we can. Alternating homes . . . frequent flyer programs . . . a Watts line . . . That's the only way I could stand—"

"Are you saying you're going to Virginia?"

Kris let the tear roll down her cheek. "I'm saying I love you, and I'm going to miss you terribly."

Danni squeezed her hand.

He kept telling himself that it was for the best. They hadn't been apart since they'd come to this century. They each needed this time to think things through. That was what he told himself. It wasn't what he believed. He missed her and wanted her at his side.

Walking past a row of boxes in the foyer, Sean sat down on one. Elaine had marked each for the moving company. She and Jack had left for San

Francisco immediately after they had completed the sale of Rivanna. That was yesterday. Last night had been interminable. He'd never realized the house could be that lonely, and at least ten times he had reached for the telephone, intending to call Kristine.

But he hadn't. Perhaps she was right. Maybe he had expected too much of her. Maybe he was wrong to think that she wanted Rivanna as much as he.

The only thing he was certain of was that he would give it up if she asked. Without her, it meant nothing. Just a big lonely house. The only certainty was that he wanted her.

Anywhere.

She stepped out of the cab and looked up at the house. Rivanna . . . She wasn't sure what she'd expected. Perhaps to feel the presence of another woman, another's claim to the plantation. What she felt was history, and love. For centuries members of her family had been born here. And now, from Jack and Elaine, Sean had claimed that heritage. There was no other presence.

Only love.

He opened the massive front door, and Kris knew in that instant she had made the right decision. Sean O'Mara was everything right about Rivanna. He belonged in this home.

"You came," he said, as the cab disappeared

503

down the stone drive. He kept staring at her as he moved closer.

She smiled, suddenly shy. "I thought I'd come and check out my wedding present." When he took her in his arms, she whispered, "How's the plumbing?"

He grinned down at her. "I never asked."

She looked at his face: the slight cleft in his chin, the black shining hair, the desire in his eyes. "See, you do still need me."

His lips brushed hers in an astonishingly sweet caress.

"Always, lass. Welcome home. . . ."

Epilogue

Virginia 1871

It was madness! Beth's mind refused to accept what her eyes were seeing. It couldn't be! She was being punished for eavesdropping, yet she clung to the study door, unable to drag her eyes away from the incredible sight.

There were two of them! *Two sisters!* They were arguing . . . the lightning . . . Sean and Judson . . .

Then, only Judson remained.

Oh God, please help me, she prayed as Judson Taylor yelled out in fright, then ran past her and out into the storm.

Where have they gone? Terrified, Beth covered her face for protection from whatever it was that took them away.

When next the lightning came, she instinctively dropped her hands and raised her face. It was then she saw it.

The two women, one her sister, the other? . . . Both of them had reappeared for an instant, still struggling, yet this time they were dressed differently. This time one was in a white robe, clutching a portrait in one hand and fighting the other who was dressed in a scandalously short gown.

Immediately, Beth remembered the crazy talk that she'd had with Christina, the one she'd thought was Christina. The woman had said something about the future, about a great-great grandchild. Beth knew one of these women belonged to her. One of them was her own future.

Terrified that one would destroy the other, and her along with them, she called out, *"Christina!"*

Never had she seen such brightness, never would she be able to describe what took place next. In an instant, too short a span of time to measure, there was only one woman left, one sister.

Clutching the portrait to her chest, the vision in the white robe threw back her head and screamed out her rage.

Never would Beth forget the sound of it, nor the fear that raced through her young body. In that moment, she vowed to protect her own, to be watchful of her children so this curse would never be revealed. She would safeguard all future generations, and keep this horror a secret forever.

And in that moment, Beth sorrowfully left her childhood behind and became the new mistress of Rivanna.

"Aren't you the Thoroughbred man?" The young nurse blushed as she handed Sean the green uniform that would admit him into the delivery room.

Sean nodded, quickly reaching for the paper clothes and putting them on. "Where's my wife?" he asked, more nervous than he dared to admit. What if something went wrong? Hadn't he seen hundreds of mares with difficult deliveries? What if —

"Your wife is in Delivery Room Three, Mr. Gavin."

Sean covered his hair with the ridiculous cap. "Mr. O'Mara," he corrected as he held the door open for her.

The young girl looked embarassed as she led him down a long corridor. "I'm sorry. I thought . . . you know, because of the talk show and everything."

Sean couldn't help smiling. "My wife uses her maiden name in her profession."

"Well, you ought to hear the buzzing on this floor," the girl said. "Even the newspaper called after your wife was admitted. Imagine, the host of "Richmond Mornings" here!"

Sean wished the girl would walk faster. As an incentive he increased his own steps. "My wife will be very happy to know you watch," he muttered as they approached a huge door.

"Watch? I have to tape it when I work days, but I never miss it."

"That's wonderful. Now, where do we go from here?" Why was she so calm? His wife was having a baby! What kind of nurse was she?

Pushing a button on the wall that made the huge doors open, the nurse ushered Sean into the inner sanctum of the maternity floor.

"This way . . . Delivery room three."

He burst into the room, as if nature had been waiting for him to appear before the birth process could move on. Rushing to Kristine's side, he pulled the mask down and said, "Are you all right?"

Straining with the pain of a contraction, Kris glared at him. When it was over, she gasped for breath and muttered, "Where were you? You're supposed to be my coach?"

"The nurse was talking about your show and I—"

"Did she like it?" Kris interrupted in a hoarse voice, letting out a moan as another contraction started to build.

The doctor took over as instructor and told Sean to support her back as she pushed. He tried to

508

remember everything from the classes they had attended, but nothing had prepared him for this . . . seeing Kristine in such agony. His entire body began to perspire. Soon, he was as drenched as his wife.

When the contraction eased, Kris panted. "Did she like it?" she demanded a second time.

"Yes! yes!" Sean insisted, wondering why he was more nervous now than Kristine.

"I showed them, didn't I?" she challenged, blinking away the sweat from her eyes and gasping for breath. "Just because we're below the Mason-Dixon Line, doesn't mean we don't have opinions. You can produce a successful show . . . even if you don't originate from the Midwest, or the East Coast. . . . Oh, God, Sean . . . I don't think I can do this!"

She grabbed hold of his hand and pushed. Closing her eyes, she heard him say in a heavy Irish accent, "You can do it, lass. You can."

Several times Sean was about to offer suggestions to the physician, but he held himself in check. Kristine had made him promise not to interfere. Instead, he watched in fascination as his child slowly, then very quickly, came into this world.

"Kristine! Look, you were right! A son. It's a boy!" Sean exclaimed to anyone within earshot.

The doctor turned the slippery infant around and said, "That's the umbilical cord, Mr. O'Mara. You have a healthy daughter."

509

The nurses laughed and Sean became ecstatic. "It's a girl! Kristine! We have a daughter!" He kissed his wife's cheek, hugging her as she tried to see over his shoulder.

A daughter! Kris blinked several times. She'd been so sure. The nursery was even blue and white. Shocked, she watched as they separated this tiny human who'd been growing inside her for almost a year.

"Look at the hair on her!" a nurse exclaimed as they cleaned her up.

Kris kept watching, too stunned to answer. When they placed her daughter in her arms, she looked down at the tiny bundle.

The infant's face was a crimson color that suddenly turned white at the slightest provocation. She had a mass of miniature dark brown curls. She was tiny and wrinkled, but when she opened her eyes, she was the most beautiful creature Kris had ever seen.

There was something so familiar about her. It wasn't just that they had shared the same body for nine months. This was different. It was an immediate bonding, as if it had actually taken place a long time ago.

Sean touched her tiny hand and kissed Kristine's cheek. "Thank you, lass. Thank you for our daughter."

When they were asked for a name, Kris and Sean looked at each other.

"What do we do?" Sean asked softly. "We never

settled on a girl's name."

Kris could feel the tightening of her throat, the acrid burning of unshed tears as she gazed down at her daughter. Now she knew. It was all there for the careful eye to see.

"We'll call her Elizabeth," she said in a hushed voice. "Beth . . ."

Afterword

"Dost thou love life? Then do not squander time,
for that's the stuff life is made of."
— *Benjamin Franklin*
       Poor Richard's Almanack